THE JEWEL OF ST. PETERSBURG

"Furnivall skillfully intertwines historical fact with a heartfelt love story . . . a delight for [her] fans, and equally a joy for those new to her work."
—*Publishers Weekly*

"Gripping, elegant, and fierce, this is a classic war-torn love story, and Furnivall's best yet."
—*Library Journal*

"Furnivall portrays a country in dreadful conflict, with the grinding poverty of the masses fueling rebellion against the privileged classes. A must for readers of *The Russian Concubine* and Furnivall's *The Red Scarf*."
—*Booklist*

"Furnivall sweeps readers full circle, taking them to turn-of-the-twentieth-century Russia and right into a glittering whirl of tsarist St. Petersburg. Her vivid descriptions and the shimmering beauty and treachery of the era combine with a memorable love story that will speak to readers' hearts and minds."
—*Romantic Times*

THE GIRL FROM JUNCHOW

"An engrossing adventure that sweeps readers in lush waves of drama and romance."
—*Library Journal*

"Furnivall deftly evokes the details of a bygone era." —*Publishers Weekly*

D00064015

continued . . .

THE RED SCARF

"This romantic confection can make a reader shiver with dread for the horrors visited on the two heroines imprisoned in a labor camp and quiver with anticipation for their happy endings. Furnivall shows she has the narrative skills to deliver a sweeping historical epic."

—Library Journal

"Furnivall again pinpoints a little-known historical setting and brings it vividly to life through the emotions and insights of her characters. Beautifully detailed descriptions of the land and the compelling characters who move through a surprisingly upbeat plot make this one of the year's best reads." *—Booklist*

THE RUSSIAN CONCUBINE

"I read it in one sitting! Not only a gripping love story, but a novel which captures the sights, smells, hopes, and desires of Russia at the dawn of the twentieth century, and pre-Revolutionary China, so skillfully that readers will feel they are there." *—Kate Mosse*

"The kaleidoscopic intensity of British writer Kate Furnivall's debut novel, *The Russian Concubine*, compellingly transports us back to 1928 and across the globe to the city of Junchow in northern China . . . Lydia is an endearing character, a young woman with pluck and determination . . . With artistry, Furnivall weaves a main plot that hinges on Lydia's love affair with Chang An Lo, a Chinese youth who is a dedicated Communist at a time when Chiang Kai-shek's Nationalists are gaining ground . . . Furnivall's novel is an admirable work of historical fiction."

—Minneapolis Star Tribune

"Furnivall vividly evokes Lydia's character and personal struggles against a backdrop of depravity and corruption." *—Publishers Weekly*

"The wonderfully drawn and all-too-human characters struggle to survive in a world of danger and bewildering change . . . caught between cultures, ideologies—and the growing realization that only the frail reed of love is strong enough to withstand the destroying winds of time."

—Diana Gabaldon

"This stunning debut brings the atmosphere of 1920s China vividly to life. . . . Furnivall draws an excellent portrait of this distant time and place."

—*Historical Novels Review*

THE

WHITE
PEARL

Kate Furnivall

B

BERKLEY BOOKS, NEW YORK

THE BERKLEY PUBLISHING GROUP
Published by the Penguin Group
Penguin Group (USA) Inc.
375 Hudson Street, New York, New York 10014, USA
Penguin Group (Canada), 90 Eglinton Avenue East, Suite 700, Toronto, Ontario M4P 2Y3, Canada
(a division of Pearson Penguin Canada Inc.)
Penguin Books Ltd., 80 Strand, London WC2R 0RL, England
Penguin Group Ireland, 25 St. Stephen's Green, Dublin 2, Ireland (a division of Penguin Books Ltd.)
Penguin Group (Australia), 250 Camberwell Road, Camberwell, Victoria 3124, Australia
(a division of Pearson Australia Group Pty. Ltd.)
Penguin Books India Pvt. Ltd., 11 Community Centre, Panchsheel Park, New Delhi—110 017, India
Penguin Group (NZ), 67 Apollo Drive, Rosedale, Auckland 0632, New Zealand
(a division of Pearson New Zealand Ltd.)
Penguin Books (South Africa) (Pty.) Ltd., 24 Sturdee Avenue, Rosebank, Johannesburg 2196,
South Africa

Penguin Books Ltd., Registered Offices: 80 Strand, London WC2R 0RL, England

This book is an original publication of the Berkley Publishing Group.

This is a work of fiction. Names, characters, places, and incidents either are the product of the author's imagination or are used fictitiously, and any resemblance to actual persons, living or dead, business establishments, events, or locales is entirely coincidental. The publisher does not have any control over and does not assume any responsibility for author or third-party websites or their content.

Copyright © 2012 by Kate Furnivall
Cover design by Erika Fusari
Cover photos: Moorea, Tahiti © Purestock / Shutterstock; Woman © Ricardo Demurez / Trevillion
Book design by Kristin del Rosario

PUBLISHING HISTORY
Berkely trade paperback edition / March 2012

Library of Congress Cataloging-in-Publication Data

Furnivall, Kate.
The White Pearl / by Kate Furnivall. — Berkley trade paperback ed.
    p. cm.
  ISBN 978-0-425-24100-4
  1. British—Malaysia—Malaya—Fiction. 2. Japanese—Malaysia—Malaya—Fiction.
3. World War, 1939–1945—Fiction. 4. Pirates—Malay Archipelago—Fiction.
5. Malaya—Fiction. I. Title.
  PR6116.U76W55 2012
  823'.92—dc22   2011026808

PRINTED IN THE UNITED STATES OF AMERICA

10   9   8   7   6   5   4   3   2   1

To Sam and Duncan with love

ACKNOWLEDGMENTS

I would like to say a huge thank-you to Jackie Cantor, my editor at Berkley, for her wise and insightful comments, which improved the manuscript immeasurably. I am grateful yet again to Pam Barricklow and all at Berkley for their superb dedication and commitment. Thanks also to Amy Schneider who is a rare gem.

Special thanks to my agent, Teresa Chris, for believing so fervently in the book and to Patty Moosbrugger. They make my job easier.

Also I owe thanks to Marie Bedford for her sharp eye and expertise concerning all sailing matters, to Anne Goring for her intimate knowledge of Malaya, and to Marian Churchward for her mastery of my keyboard.

And as always, many thanks to Norman for living through each page with me.

CHAPTER ONE

Malaya 1941

It was not the first time Connie had killed someone. But today there were witnesses.

A car's bumper should be a mute object, but in November 1941 the chrome bumper on Constance Hadley's 1938 Chrysler Royal found its voice. It screeched, an ear-ripping noise of metal against metal. It cracked, snapping one of the wooden supports on the covered walkway that ran along Alexandra Parade. It thudded, a warm, muffled grunt as it smacked into human flesh. Those sounds were to play over and over in Connie's head. A screech. A crack. A thud. Over and over, like one of the merry-go-rounds where the tinny music knows no end.

The sun is a source of life. Whoever said that had never lived in Malaya. Connie squinted through the windscreen as she drove through the crowded streets of Palur and felt the sun battering her brain with its fist. She had considered, on more than one occasion, taking her husband's best hunting rifle, the one he'd had specially shipped over from London last year, aiming it at that massive yellow orb hanging in the sky and pulling the trigger. Popping it like a balloon. She'd once mentioned this desire to Nigel, and he'd looked at her oddly.

Today she'd broken her sunglasses, damn it. That was what was making her bad-tempered. Without those, she always developed a vicious headache in the sunshine. *Sunshine.* She grimaced as she peeled her back off the seat, feeling her damp blouse stick to the upholstery. *Sunshine* was far too gentle a word. Sunshine was what existed in England. It warmed your toes in the grass and peeked at you under the brim of your straw hat. She loved sunshine. The brutal heat and humidity here in the heart of Malaya were killing her.

There had been a mud slip that had delayed her drive into town, and she was hurrying now to make it to the Victoria Club in time for a swim with Harriet Court. She squeezed her big American car past one of the bicycle rickshaws that darted up and down the high street, as irritating as the fat black flies, and spotted a gap in the traffic. Instantly she accelerated into it. She swung the wheel to take the corner into Alexandra Parade, an elegant boulevard of imposing buildings where the British Empire had placed its colonial stamp on this docile patch of the Malay Peninsula.

At exactly that moment, another car did the same, as sleek and ruthless as a black-finned shark.

"Damn you, look out!" Connie shouted, and slammed on her brakes.

It was too late. She fought the steering wheel, but the back end of the Chrysler cut loose. With a sickening lurch of her stomach, she felt it start to swing in a wide, uncontrollable arc. Her wing raked the black car, but instead of slowing, it seemed to gather momentum from the impact. It was the screech of her bumper that alerted people. Faces turned to stare at her, wide-eyed with shock as the two-ton metal missile hurtled toward them on the sidewalk. The car jerked when its wheel caught in one of the deep storm drains, but still it didn't stop, and figures scattered in all directions.

The moment seemed to elongate. Appalled, Connie watched it happen. She saw a woman yank her child off its feet and open her mouth in a huge melon-sized scream. An old man in a straw boater stood paralyzed with fear directly in front of her, and a dark moist patch blossomed on the front of his pale flannel trousers. Connie dragged at the steering wheel, her heart slamming against her ribs. The car's hood shifted a fraction to the right and took down one of the timber uprights of the covered walkway that gave shoppers respite from the scorching sun. The crack of the wood was like a gunshot. The old man ducked, so that the bumper missed him by the width of the brim of his hat, and instead selected a different victim: a stocky native woman wearing a bright green sarong, a woven basket perched on her shoulder.

Connie screamed at her through the windscreen as she stamped on the brake pedal. "Run! Run!"

Please, please, run faster!

But the woman knew that her time had come. That the spirits had chosen her, and there was no escape. She swung round at the last moment and faced the oncoming car. She stared straight into Connie's eyes and her lips moved, but the words were swallowed by Connie's own scream as the bumper uttered its muffled grunt. It had found flesh. The woman's eyes became huge black pools of pain for one brief moment before she disappeared from Connie's sight and the car shuddered to a halt.

No!

Connie was shaking, teeth chattering. With an effort of will she unclamped each finger from around the steering wheel and seized the chrome door handle. She tumbled out of the car and raced to the front of the hood. She caught sight of a pair of bare feet, their soles covered in red dust, then caramel-colored legs and the edge of a green sarong. On the ground, the rest of the woman's body was hidden from sight behind the crowd that had gathered around her, but they drew back at Connie's approach, opening a path for her. As if she were unclean.

"Call an ambulance! *Pangil ambulans!*" she shouted to a man in a striped butcher's apron, and he said something in reply, but the connection between her ears and her mind seemed to have broken because the sounds meant nothing to her.

The Malay woman lay on her back, not crumpled, not in a tangle of blood and fractured bones, but straight and unharmed as though she had dozed off by mistake in the heat. With a rush of relief Connie dropped to her knees on the sidewalk beside her and lifted the limp hand. It felt warm and dry against her own damp palms, with short stubby fingers that curled around hers in a stubborn grip. *She isn't dead, thank God, she isn't dead.* But the woman's eyes remained firmly closed.

"An ambulance is coming, a doctor will be here very soon. Don't try to move," Connie told her, her throat so tight the words sounded as if they'd come from someone else's mouth. She leaned over the motionless figure, shielding her from the glare of the sun, and asked softly, "Are you in much pain?"

No response.

"I'm so sorry," Connie said. "I didn't mean to . . ." Her voice trickled away. She wanted to wrap the woman in her arms and rock her gently. "Please," she murmured, "open your eyes if you can hear me."

Still no response.

Thick black lashes lay on the plump dusky cheeks, and fine veins traced a network back into her temple where the beginnings of a bruise were starting to form. She looked a similar age to Connie herself, about thirty-four, but the woman's dense black hair that she wore pulled back into a knot behind her head was showing the first few streaks of gray. Maybe she was older. Her nose was broad, and the skin of her arms a patchy, uneven brown as if she worked with chemicals of some sort. *What world have I wrenched her out of?*

There was no blood. Not a mark on the sarong or on the woman herself, except for the slight bruise, and Connie allowed herself to hope it was just a concussion. Softly she started to talk to her, to entice the woman's stunned brain back into action. She asked her name, her address, who should be told about the accident, what was in the crushed basket at her side. She stroked her hand, tapped her arm, touched her cheek.

"I'm so sorry," she said again.

The eyes opened suddenly. There was no flicker of warning, just closed one moment, open the next, in a narrow slit of life that sent Connie's heart clawing up into her throat.

"*Selamat pagi,*" she said to the woman. "Hello."

The eyes weren't black any more; they were drenched in blood.

"An ambulance is coming," Connie said quickly.

The woman's lips moved, but no sound emerged. The stubby fingers gripped harder, pulling at her, and Connie leaned forward, so close she could feel the moist breath on her ear as she tried to catch the faint words. For the first time since she'd knelt down, she became aware of the circle of people gathered around her in the street. White faces. Sun hats. A ginger mustache. A dark uniform with brass buttons. Voices aimed at her but jumbled together in a blur. With a jolt she realized that there was a young native girl of about sixteen crouched on the other side of the woman, a curtain of silky black hair half obscuring her face, but her eyes were fixed on Connie and her expression was accusing. Behind her stood a tall native youth, his face set hard. He was wearing a waist sarong and a sleeveless shirt from which his fingers were unconsciously tearing a button.

"Do you know her?" Connie asked.

The girl stared at her coldly. "She is our mother."

"I'm sorry," Connie said yet again. Empty, useless words. "It was an accident."

"White lady." The English words came in a guttural gasp from the lips of the woman lying on the sidewalk, a flutter of sound that barely reached her.

"I'm here," Connie squeezed her hand. "And your children are here."

"Listen, white lady."

"I'm listening." Her ear was almost brushing against the struggling lips and there was a long pause, during which the heat of the day seemed to gather itself and launch an attack like a blow on the back of Connie's neck. "I'm listening."

"I curse you. You family. You children. And you. I curse you all."

Words sharp as a cobra's bite, but Connie did not release her grip on the small hand. The blood-filled eyes opened wider, flashed at her full of malice, and then abruptly closed. Her fingers grew limp.

"No!" Connie cried. "No, don't go. Curse me again, curse me as much as you wish, call your evil spirits down on my head, but don't go."

A policeman stepped into her field of vision. "Mrs. Hadley, the ambulance is here. They'll take over."

Men in white uniforms gently moved Connie aside. She rose to her feet, tremors grinding up through her body and jamming her mind. Soft voices spoke to her, careful hands guided her, treating her as if she were glass and might shatter. When she realized she was being ushered off the street into the shade of a nearby building, she broke free and searched the crowd for the woman's son and daughter, but they had vanished.

"Sit down, Mrs. Hadley."

"Drink this, Mrs. Hadley."

"You've had a nasty shock."

"It wasn't your fault. We have witnesses."

Policemen, with questions and notebooks, brandished their sympathetic smiles in her face and told her she could go home, they would drive her home, but she shook her head. It was almost one o'clock.

"No, thank you. I have to pick up my son from school."

The building that had given her refuge was a British bank with thick stone walls to keep out the heat, and a vast, cooling fan that stirred the leaden air with brisk efficiency in the small office where she was seated. The bank manager had a sunburned bald head and a kind smile.

"Take your time, my dear," he said. "Take all the time you need."

She sat there alone, listening to the sounds in her head. The screech. The crack. The thud.

ᗅ·ᗡ

How do you tell your seven-year-old son that you have killed a woman in the street?

Connie's fingers gripped the steering wheel, her knuckles chalk white. She didn't say anything at all in case the wrong words spilled out of her dry mouth. Heavy insects blundered against the windscreen as she drove out of town with her son, Teddy, on the front passenger seat, swinging his legs and chattering about the different colors of a python's skin.

Did children in England talk of such things? How many told their mother, as Teddy did, that a king cobra could move as fast as a galloping horse? Was this normal?

In Malaya, nothing was normal.

They were heading back home along the eight miles to the Hadley Estate. It was a vast tract of land that had been in the Hadley family for three generations, hacked by hand out of the raw jungle at the end of the nineteenth century, and was now the largest rubber plantation in the region, just to the northeast of Kuala Lumpur. It stretched in shimmering layers of dense green for over five thousand acres toward mountains that reared up blue and hazy in the distance, and employed nearly seven hundred laborers, a mongrel mix of Malays, Tamils, and Chinese.

Nine years ago when Connie, full of youthful excitement, first stepped off the boat into the sweltering heat of Malaya, she had been astounded not only by the size and lush extravagance of the beauty of the estate, but also by the power of an estate owner—the *Tuan Besar*—over his workforce. It seemed to her that Nigel was like a god, a father, a judge, a bank manager, a doctor, and King Solomon all rolled into one. If he put a black mark against a laborer's name, then that native would find work nowhere else in the district, but if a man was a skilled rubber tapper or a diligent finisher of the rubber sheets in the packing sheds who buckled down to the tough discipline of plantation life, he was highly valued and treated well.

Nigel knew nearly all his workmen by name. That fact alone had stuck in Connie's mind and impressed her enormously when he had mentioned it as she danced in his arms to a slow foxtrot at the Dorchester Hotel in London. Out here in the tropics, swamped by a never-ending tide of brown and yellow faces, she had found it even more incredible.

"Why are you driving so slowly, Mummy?" Her son's voice was impatient.

"I'm being careful, sweetheart."

"But it will take ages to get home."

"There's no rush."

Teddy swiveled to face her on the front seat of the Chrysler. "Yes, there is, Mummy. I have to build my airplane again."

She risked taking her eyes off the dirt road for a split second. It was full of potholes and gullies where monsoon rains had scoured channels in the red earth that could crack a car's crankcase if you weren't alert. Teddy's young face was so earnest, his eyes as round and bright as chestnuts. She noticed that his school uniform of white shirt and gray shorts was streaked with grass stains, the collar torn, and there was a telltale scratch on the tip of his chin.

"What is it, Teddy?" she asked. "Have you been fighting with Jack?"

Her son shook his head adamantly, the waves of his thick brown hair ruffling in the breeze from the open window. As fast as he had his hair cut it seemed to grow again overnight, framing his small face and sticking out over his ears.

"No," he said. But he was no good at lying.

"Jack is your best friend," she said gently.

"No, he's not."

"Oh, Teddy, what was the fight about this time?"

His slight seven-year-old body slumped back in the seat, and he picked in silence at a scab on his leg. Connie gave him time, as immaculate straight lines of plantation trees slid past the window. It was Field 16, a fine stand of hundreds of young rubber saplings planted in rows thirty feet apart, the trees ten feet from each other. The Rubber Research Institute of Malaya recommended an initial planting of 240 trees to the acre, reducing to 100 trees an acre once they were grown and ready for tapping for their white flow of latex. But Nigel insisted he kept the land so well fed with fertilizer and rock phosphate that he could get away with 120 trees per acre and still produce a top-class yield.

The sun hung directly overhead, so that shadows formed in dark balls at the base of the trunks. School started for Teddy at eight o'clock in the morning and finished at one o'clock, to avoid the worst of the exhausting heat of the afternoon. In the car the air was as oppressive as Connie's thoughts.

Listen, white lady. The words hissed through her brain.

"Nothing lasts here."

She hadn't meant to say it out loud. She felt Teddy's gaze turn to her, and he tucked his hand between the seat and her damp back, something he did only when he was worried.

"Won't we last?" he asked.

"Of course we will, sweetheart. So will your friendship with Jack. I only meant . . ." *Oh Christ, what did she mean?* "I only meant that the tires wear out quickly on these rough roads. Cars break down easily."

"Is that why you had the crash today? Did the car break?"

"No, darling. It was an accident caused by another nasty car, but don't worry about it. We'll get the dents mended and we'll be fine. Now tell me what happened with Jack."

"His Brewster Buffalo shot down my Fairey Battle."

Connie's heart sank. Her young son had spent all of last weekend building the airplane out of balsa wood with painstaking care, the tip of his tongue clamped between his small white teeth. His dogged patience amazed her. The results were sometimes a little rough and ragged at the edges, but they were all his own work and Connie was immensely proud of his sticky little fingers. Since the war in Europe started two years ago in 1939, her son had become obsessed with airplanes, his bedroom walls covered in recognition charts. He could name every aircraft in the sky the way other people named birds.

"Don't worry, Teddy, I'll help you build a new one."

She pulled over to the side of the road and dropped ten cents into her son's hand. This was one of their rituals. Each day on the journey home from school Teddy bought a slice of fruit from the roadside stall. It stood next to a small shrine that was constructed out of brightly painted stones and adorned with frangipani flowers, a small blue statue of a Hindu goddess, and a bowl of colored rice. A rat, fat and bold, sat on its haunches beside the shrine, munching on stolen rice grains.

Teddy skipped over the ruts to the fruit stall and pointed at two large slices of watermelon. She watched him chatter away to the man serving on the stall—Teddy's command of the Malay language was far superior to her own. He seemed to absorb the strange words as readily as her pillow absorbed her strange dreams at night. He had lived here all his short life, and had no fear of this alien and exotic country. He wasn't afraid of snakes the way she was, nor did he shiver at the thought of one of the Communist agitators in the workforce slitting Nigel's throat in bed at night.

This year, there had been numerous labor strikes in the tin mines up at Gambang and in the gold mines at Raub, and now the unrest was spreading to the rubber plantations up and down the length of the Malay Peninsula. The demand for rubber for tires and waterproofing had increased in a steady climb ever since the war had started in Europe, and rubber had been designated priority cargo for the war effort. America and Britain were clamoring for it. Inevitably the price had skyrocketed. From five pence a pound to twelve pence a pound, and now the labor force that helped to produce it was demanding a hefty raise in their meager wages. She could see their point. It was the Chinese workers who were the troublemakers, stirring up the easygoing Malays, but Nigel assured her it would blow over eventually. It was the Japanese, not the Chinese, they should be worrying about, he said.

Connie and Teddy sat in the car together eating the red flesh of the melon, spitting the black pips out of the open windows with expert aim, a brief moment of normality in a day that was anything but normal. When she'd finished she tossed the green rind out onto the roadside and within half a minute it was covered in a shiny black coating of ants, their huge jaws capable of reducing it to nothing in the blink of an eye. This was a country in which the jungle and its voracious insects smothered and devoured everything. Especially tender-skinned white people.

She wiped her hands on her handkerchief and dabbed at Teddy's face with it. She smiled at him. "Come on, Pilot Officer Hadley, let's go and build you a new Fairey Battle plane."

"I think a Blenheim will be better. It carries more bombs."

She tweaked his chin toward her and inspected the scratch. She must remember to put antiseptic on it. If not, in a day or two she could be picking tiny white maggots out of it with tweezers.

"Very well, a Blenheim it shall be."

She eased the car forward.

"Mummy, why are you crying?"

"I'm not crying."

"Yes you are."

"No, sweetheart, it's just that my eyes are watering because I broke my sunglasses."

"Will Daddy mind that you broke the car?"

"Don't worry, Teddy, it can be easily mended."

Unlike the dusty feet. Or the pair of bloodshot eyes.

CHAPTER TWO

Connie sat in the bungalow in silence. All white men's houses were called bungalows, however many floors they possessed. Darkness squeezed like oil between the wooden slats of the shutters and flowed into the room, filling the slender gap of time that lay between day and night in the tropics. The air scarcely grew cooler, but it stopped growing hotter, which gave some sort of relief. Outside in the garden and in the lush jungle that skirted it, the night creatures started their endless cries and squeaks, booms and chirrups, so loud that they drilled into her mind and splintered her thoughts.

"Just block the noises out, old thing," Nigel always told her cheerfully back in the early days when she used to complain.

Block the noises out. Like she could block out breathing. She closed her eyes and thought about the woman who wouldn't hear the cicadas any more, about her daughter kneeling on the sidewalk, about her son with the black, angry eyes and the long lashes. Voices in her head echoed the ones in Palur that had assured her, "You are not to blame," and "It was the other car's fault. A reckless driver."

How on earth could it not be your fault when you run a woman down on the sidewalk? Were they blind?

I curse you.

The words pinned her to the guilt.

I . . . the woman's hot breath smelled of cardamom.

Curse . . . her broad nostrils had flared, scenting death.

You . . . the blood in her eyes was drowning the fury in the dark pupils.

Connie didn't even know her name. She shivered, her hands shaking on her lap. Was this what Malaya had done to her? Turned her into a person who went around killing others, who took lives as carelessly as the houseboys stamped on cockroaches? Another memory surged forward into her mind, one that she had sought to bury under a daily avalanche of committee meetings and tennis matches. Anything to drown out the sound of a human head bumping down wooden steps. *Thump, thump, thump.* A soft, insidious noise that woke her up night after night, thumping through her dreams when her sheets were drenched with sweat and the song of mosquitoes was whining on the other side of the mosquito net.

"What on earth are you doing, sitting here in the dark?"

The overhead light flashed on, blinding Connie, and she blinked. She hadn't heard Nigel arrive home.

"Didn't the good-for-nothing houseboy switch the lamps on for you?" he demanded in a disgruntled tone.

"Yes, he came, but I sent him away."

"Whatever for, old thing?"

She smiled up at her husband. It never failed to amaze her that even after a long, hot day that started in the dark at five thirty in the morning when he set out for the daily muster of field coolies, Nigel could still look crisp and fresh in his white shirt with rolled-up sleeves and khaki shorts. How did he do it? Others wilted and their clothes looked like wet rags hanging on them. She experienced a ripple of pride in him. He wasn't exactly good looking, with cropped brown hair and rather long features, but he possessed a certain presence. It was the self-assurance of an Englishman who believed he had a right to own and civilize other countries, without questioning whether they wanted to be civilized.

"I felt like enjoying some peace and quiet," she said.

"Bad day?"

"Yes."

"Mine too. Absolutely bloody." He walked over to the cocktail cabinet, a stylish piece of modern furniture made from sycamore and shipped over from Maple & Co. of London. He opened its curved front to reveal shelves of pale green glass and a row of bottles. "Let's have a drink," he suggested. "Gin sling?"

"Why not?"

Why not? Why not drown in gin slings? Why not pour them down her throat until the noises in her head blurred into a dull, unrecognizable murmur that had no meaning? Why not? Well, for one thing she didn't have much of a taste for alcohol, and for another she had a son to watch over. She had to make certain Malaya didn't get the chance to choke him the way it was choking her.

"Thank you, Nigel," she said as she accepted her glass. "So tell me, why was your day so bad?"

"It's the damned Restriction Committee."

"Oh? What are they up to now?"

The Restriction Committee was an international organization set up to restrict the supply of rubber onto the market to prevent the price dropping through overproduction. The scheme allotted each country— Malaya, Dutch East Indies, Indochina—a specific tonnage, declaring that they could export that much and no more. Their dictates were a constant thorn in the flesh of plantation owners, who preferred to work in cartels that set their own agreed limits.

"I received a cable today. They are refusing to raise the allocation," he grumbled, and sank into a battered old rattan chair that was his favorite.

"But that's absurd. Don't they know there's a war on?" She meant it as a joke to lighten his mood, but he set his jaw and took it seriously.

"It doesn't look like it, damn fools. But a young officer from the American attaché's office flew up from Singapore to see me today, and admitted that America and Britain are stockpiling the stuff like mad in case the supplies get cut off by Jap warships and . . ." He stopped. "What's the matter, old thing? You're shaking. Not going down with fever, are you?"

"No, of course not. It's just that the word gives me the shivers."

"Warship? Can't say I blame you."

No, not warship. Jap. She experienced a flash of memory, of long, narrow eyes staring intently into hers, lean male shoulders and an exquisite neatness in the incline of a shapely Japanese head in greeting.

Nigel lifted his glass to his lips and studied her over its rim. "What's up? You look a bit peaky, old thing."

She was more than *a thing*, and not *old*. Not yet.

"I'm fine." She sipped her gin and let it slide down to her stomach before she added, "I had an accident in the car today."

"What?"

"Another car scraped my wing and I lost control of the steering."

"Oh, Christ! Much damage?"

"I killed a woman."

Four small words. Like a bomb going off in the room, deafening them both. Nigel put down his glass and rose to his feet, his cheeks flushed, his lips tight. He ran a hand over his short hair and came to stand directly in front of her. He leaned over her. "Constance, my dear, are you all right?"

"Yes."

"Good. Don't worry, I'll ring Tommy immediately."

Tommy Macintire was their lawyer, a big man prone to a stammer unless oiled by Scotch whisky. Nigel moved quickly to the telephone, lifted the earpiece, and dialed a number. He was staring back over his shoulder at Connie, and the expression on his face startled her. It was one of such sorrow, of loss, as if he could already see her behind bars. She looked away and finished her drink in a long swallow, feeling its heat scorch her stomach. After a moment of brief conversation, Nigel hung up.

"He's over in KL tonight," he said.

Kuala Lumpur was the capital of Malaya, originally a small and scruffy tin-mining town set up by Chinese miners in the middle of the nineteenth century, but now it had grown into a bustling city since the British set up business there and put in a Colonial Office Resident to work with the local sultans. Nigel started to pace the room in swift, uneasy steps.

"I'm sorry, Nigel," she said quietly.

"This is a bad show, Constance. Tell me exactly what happened."

"I told you, a black car scraped my wing and the Chrysler was catapulted up onto the pavement where it hit a woman." *I hit a woman.* That was what she meant, not *it hit a woman*. "She died."

"In the street?"

"Yes. Her son and daughter were there."

"Dear God, that's even worse."

"I know. A thousand times worse. Watching their mother—no older than I am—die in front of them like that. It was horrible."

"What did the police say?"

"They let me come home."

"I'll ring Duffy at once. He'll know what's going on and when they are going to charge you."

Duffy was Chief Inspector George Duffery, a cricketing companion of her husband's. He dialed again and spoke in low tones with his back to her. When he replaced the earpiece on the hook, he took a moment to turn to face her. When he did so, it was obvious he was annoyed.

"Constance, what a scare you gave me!"

"What do you mean?"

He picked up his glass, strolled over to the open cabinet, and topped up his drink, throwing in a handful of ice. "You didn't tell me the damn woman was a native."

"Does it make any difference?"

But she knew it did. She could see it in his face.

"The police are bringing no charges," he told her. "So we can breathe again."

"The Malay woman can't."

"What?"

"She can't breathe again." Connie stood up and put her glass down on the side table. "I think I'll take a cold shower."

"Constance."

He crossed the room till he was standing close to her, inspecting her face with worried eyes. Brown teddy-bear eyes, she always thought. It was one of the things that had attracted her to him when they first met at a party in Kensington in London. Within a month they were engaged. He had proposed to her in the tropical hothouse in Kew Gardens. It was a long time since she had thought of that.

"It's all right, Nigel." She rested a hand lightly on his tanned bare arm and felt the muscles instantly grow tense under her palm. "You can forget about it now, and concentrate on your American attaché." She made an effort to smile at him one more time, and resisted the urge to throw herself against his crisp white chest, to beg for some kind of comfort. Instead she removed her hand and watched the tiny muscles around his mouth flicker with relief. He never showed it in his eyes, but he always forgot to control his mouth.

"Do remember to pop in on Teddy," she said brightly. "He's been building a new airplane."

Just the mention of his son's name softened her husband's long features. "As soon as I've finished my drink, I'll go and say good night to the little blighter." He lifted his glass to his lips, but before he took a sip he said in clipped tones, "By the way, old thing, next time make sure you take the *syce* into town with you. That's what chauffeurs are for, you know. If you'd done as I asked and let our *syce* drive you into town, maybe this accident would never have happened and that woman wouldn't be dead."

Connie left the room.

∂·Ɛ

After her shower, Connie headed along the landing toward the master bedroom. Hadley House was a large, rambling building dating back to 1875, built by Nigel's grandfather, not as grand and imposing as some of the more elaborate estate mansions, but Connie was fond of it. She especially appreciated the verandas that surrounded it on all sides, where she could sit with a book in the evening to catch the faintest breeze from whichever direction it was blowing.

Her only criticism was that the house was overly masculine, with an excess of somber teak paneling and a heavily carved central staircase that swept down into the wide entrance hall. It set the mood of masculine dominance that she had come to learn epitomized life in colonial Malaya. She had tried to lighten the tone with bright curtains and had replaced the gloomy overbearing furniture with paler modern pieces, but there was nothing she could do about the blasted staircase.

As she passed her son's bedroom she heard the murmur of Nigel's voice, reading a bedtime story to Teddy. He had a good voice that was unfailingly gentle with his son. He never raised it, not even with his field coolies when he was angry about something, and its calm control inspired confidence. Just occasionally she found herself wishing that the calmness would slip, that the control would crack and lay bare whatever was hidden underneath.

The door to the bedroom stood half open, and she paused. Nigel and Teddy were sitting on the edge of the bed alongside each other, with her son's bristle-haired terrier, Pippin, curled up on his knee. The sight of them gave her a sense of touching her feet on solid ground after the shipwreck that had been her day. She loved their closeness, the way Teddy's slight frame in his striped pajamas leaned against his father, unconscious of how he nodded his head whenever his father did, and drew his eyebrows down in imitation of Nigel when the words grew serious. On a chair beside the bed sat Teddy's *amah*, Chala, his nurse. She was a tiny little Malay woman, dressed in a patterned tunic over a long straight skirt, her hands clasped under her chin as she listened, entranced by Rudyard Kipling's story of Rikki-tikki-tavi, a mongoose in India. Connie lingered in the corridor outside till the end.

"He kept that garden as a mongoose should keep it, with tooth and jump and spring and bite, till never a cobra dared show its head inside the walls," Nigel finished with a flourish.

On silent feet, she made her way to the heavy door of Burmese teak at the end of the corridor.

ට·ୡ

Hold my hand.

Connie's unspoken words fell into the gap that cut a chasm along the center of the white sheet of finest Egyptian cotton, between her side of the bed and her husband's side.

Hold my hand. I'm here and I need you. Can't you hear me?

The night was sultry, the weight of air pressing down on her skin, her scalp tight and aching as she lay stretched out naked under the muslin tent of the mosquito net. She couldn't make out its milky shape above her in the darkness, but she knew it was there, hanging like a shroud around her marriage. Beside her, Nigel was lying on his back, snoring gently, a polite and controlled sound, as though even in his sleep he made a point of not disturbing her.

Connie's hand crept closer to his on the sheet. She held her breath until the space between them was less than the width of her little finger, and she could feel the springy hairs on the back of his wrist tickling her skin. It was a faint, feathery touch that she allowed herself once each night while he slept, stealing it in the darkness. Like a thief. Outside, beyond the extensive lawns and the scented hibiscus, the jungle was stamping its feet, making itself heard as it took possession of the night. The endless chirruping and croaking, the humming and the cackling, the echoing sobs and booming barks, all seeped into the room, soaking into her sweat and into the clammy folds of the sheet that twined around her legs.

As she lay there, she retraced those moments in Palur when her car and her life slid out of control.

If she had not taken the corner so fast . . .

If the black car had not been so greedy . . .

If she had fought harder, braked quicker . . .

If she hadn't broken her sunglasses or arranged to meet Harriet for a swim before picking up Teddy . . .

Was this a punishment? Was that it?

She shook her head on the damp pillow, strands of her restless blond hair grasping at her throat like tentacles. Her mind replayed each image relentlessly again and again: the slippery feel of the steering wheel under her palms, the roadside stall on the corner selling hot roasted corn husks, the stallholder open mouthed and toothless as she skidded past him, the tires fighting for grip. A tan-colored dog scampering out of her path, its tail rigid between its legs. All things she didn't even know she had seen. But worse, far worse, was the look on the faces of the daughter and the son while their mother's eyes drowned in blood.

Hold my hand.

Connie rolled onto her side, so that she was facing the black shape that was her husband and let her arm brush his as she did so. He snatched it away as though she had burned him and murmured something in his sleep. Her chest hurt, ached with a sharp physical pain, and she realized she had not breathed. So she drew in air and with it came a rush of vivid memories of another masculine arm, cool and smooth, hairless as a mirror. A strong arm that belonged to Sho Takehashi.

For one startling moment she could hear Sho's breath, alive in the room. She lay still, listening hard. Frightened he would touch her face.

CHAPTER THREE

Connie had never set foot inside a police station before. The one in Palur was situated on Swettenham Road at the back of the public library, with a clock tower that chimed every quarter of an hour. Connie removed her new sunglasses and walked up the front steps.

Inside, it was much smarter than she had expected. This morning as she'd sat stiffly in the back of the car behind Ho Bah, their Chinese *syce*, she had conjured up an image in her head of a cramped waiting room with stained linoleum and a wooden hatch through which she would have to speak to a burly uniform. She was prepared for a hard and skeptical gaze. But the room was large and airy with cream-painted walls and windows that looked out toward the tall areca palm trees in the park opposite. A ceiling fan stirred the sluggish air. The moment Connie approached the counter, the duty officer shifted his attention from the notepad in front of him and focused on her.

"Mrs. Hadley, good morning to you."

That took her by surprise. He knew her.

"I'm Constable Forester. I took down your statement yesterday," he explained. "In the bank."

"I'm sorry, I wasn't thinking clearly."

"Of course not. It's understandable, you'd had a nasty shock. How can I help you?" he asked courteously.

"Constable Forester, I've come because I need to know the name of the woman I . . ." *I killed. Say it, go on, say it, say it out loud for everyone to hear. The woman I killed.* ". . . the woman who died in the accident yesterday."

He frowned. With a sudden change of manner he was ushering her into a small office at the back of the room, and she was shaking hands with a heavily built older man in uniform whose gaze was much more what she had expected: keen and questioning. He had a small mustache that straggled over his upper lip. The handshake left her in no doubt of his authority, and it was reinforced by the silver braid on his uniform.

"Mrs. Hadley, I am Inspector Stoner."

He gestured to a chair, but she remained standing. She wasn't staying here a moment longer than she had to.

"Good morning, Inspector. I don't mean to disturb you. I've only come to ask for the name of the woman who died in the car accident yesterday."

He nodded. Not in a good way. "I offer my condolences, Mrs. Hadley. I'm glad you were not hurt. But I do not think the deceased woman's name need concern you."

Connie said nothing. She wasn't the one who deserved condolences.

"Unfortunately," he added, "the black sports car that caused the incident vanished from the scene, so we have not been able to detain the driver responsible. Is there anything you would like to add to your earlier statement?"

"No."

He studied her carefully, eyes razor sharp.

She asked again, "The name of the woman, please?"

There was a pause, long enough to be awkward, while she kept her eyes firmly on his and he worked out how far he could upset a member of the powerful Hadley family.

"Sai-Ru Jumat," he said reluctantly.

"Do you know how old she was?"

"Thirty-five, I believe."

"With two children?"

He looked away, determined to hide his irritation.

"What was her address?" Connie persisted.

"I think it best," he said, "if we leave it there, Mrs. Hadley."

"Come now, Inspector, I only want to make certain that her poor children are all right. It must have been a terrible experience for them to witness their mother . . ." The final words stuck like pebbles in her throat.

"You mustn't concern yourself. Your husband's solicitor, Mr. Macintire, is dealing with it." He reached toward her and for one sickening moment Connie believed he was going to seize her, take her wrist in his broad fist, and clamp handcuffs on her. But he patted her arm consolingly. "Don't fret over it, my dear. These things are best left to us professionals, you know. My advice to you is to forget about it."

She removed her arm. "Inspector Stoner, I would appreciate it if you would take my request seriously. Just because they are Malays it doesn't mean . . ."

"Mrs. Hadley, we have to deal with situations like this with delicacy."

"I realize that."

"Have you spoken to your husband about this?"

"Of course. He was the one who suggested I come to you for her address."

The lie was blatant. Not for one second did he believe her. Stiffly he opened the door and summoned the duty officer. "Forester, give what assistance you can to Mrs. Hadley."

"Thank you," she said in a polite voice, and left the room.

๑·๕

Palur was a town built by Englishmen for Englishmen. It made them feel that they were walking down Piccadilly in London. In this strange country of Malaya that was so alien in every way to European sensibilities, the early colonials had brought their buildings with them to demonstrate to the natives how civilized people lived. Not in flimsy *attap* houses with fronds for roofs that blew off in the monsoon, or built up on bamboo stilts looking for all the world like a child's treehouse. These were solid and permanent, with elegant porticos and Corinthian columns. Good, respectable, English homes. It meant that if Connie blocked out all her other senses except sight, she could imagine she was at home in England.

She could look up at the brick-built trading hall where the prices of rubber, copra, and spices were argued over, at the British banks with their brass plaques, or at the church steeple, and be transported to England. Only the window boxes spoiled the illusion. Too vivid, too ebullient, altogether too promiscuous. Too damn full of the life force of Malaya. It produced ferns that drilled through paving stones and creeper that dismantled buildings if you turned your back on it for even a moment.

Nine years ago when Nigel had dropped on one knee, his face as red as one of his favorite hibiscus flowers, clasped her hands in his, and invited her to be his wife and join him in Malaya, Connie's heart had leaped. A streak of pure joy had ripped through her. She couldn't say yes fast enough. She closed her eyes now and tried to recapture that urgent desire, but it was as elusive as the mist that slunk out of the jungle at dawn and crept across the lawns of Hadley House. She had scoured maps and atlases to learn more about this wild and wonderful place that was to become her home, and relished the exotic sounds of it in her mouth—Malacca, Kuala Lumpur, and Penang.

Oh yes, she'd learned the facts and the names of the towns. She'd discovered that Malaya consisted of a long shapely finger of land that stretched for more than four hundred miles from Siam in the north right down to the steamy island of Singapore in the south. It was one of the principal rubber and tin exporters in the world, crowded by dense jungle with a backbone of mountains running down the center.

She had found out that its population of Malays, Chinese, and Indians possessed hereditary rulers called sultans who elected from their number a *Yang di-Pertuan Agong*, the glorious title—it made her laugh—of the king of Malaya. On the map she explored with excitement regions with exotic names like Selangor, Terengganu, and Johore, and in the history books she discovered that the Dutch had colonized the country before surrendering it to the British under the Anglo-Dutch Treaty of 1824. Sir Thomas Stamford Raffles had run up the flag for England and turned Singapore into the greatest trading port in the Far East.

"It's almost on the equator," Nigel warned her. "That means it's hot."

She'd laughed. She recalled that careless, girlish, ignorant laugh when she had said, "How exotic! I shall love it. There will be parrots."

There were parrots, she'd been right about that. Gaudy clouds of them. Parrots and weird hornbills and the screeching *pekaka*, all flashing their strident colors in her face. Worst was the brainfever bird, the *burong mati anak*, which uttered its tuneless dirge hour after hour. Teddy told her that *burong mati anak* meant "dead child bird," which made her want to cry each time she heard its call.

But no one had warned her that it was a country of sweltering nights and fierce smells—of the stink of bad drains and of fish frying in coconut oil in the streets, of sandalwood and hair oil. A country of ferocious insects that would devour you alive, and of jungle sounds that marched through your dreams. A country where towns boasted wide avenues and monolithic government buildings set back to back with tawdry dance halls and wretched slums.

When Connie emerged from the police station, she squinted at the sun and turned left, adjusting the wide brim of her sun hat to shield her eyes. She set off in the direction of the town's busy harbor. It was not somewhere she normally cared to venture. As the familiar streets with their shops and restaurants slid away behind her, she felt her certainty slide away with them.

Was she making a mistake? Inspector Stoner was convinced she was. But she couldn't leave it there.

She couldn't.

৯·৫

Underfoot was unpleasant, slippery, and slimy. Connie picked her way carefully over the remains of rotting fruit and vegetables, and God knows what else. The air down here by the quays tasted of fish and clung to her hair and her skirts, as hawkers shouted to her, pushing slabs of meaty-looking raw fish, lobster claws, and live octopus under her nose.

"*Tidak.* No, thank you."

On her left rose the rows of godowns, the huge warehouses where trade goods were stored before being loaded onto ships bound first for

Singapore and then on to Europe. Her eyes automatically sought out her husband's godowns with the name *Hadley* emblazoned above their doors in huge black letters. Inside, she knew, lay the large rectangular sheets of finished rubber that the Hadley Estate produced. Rubber was the lifeblood of Malaya but oddly not native to the country. Nigel had told Connie in detail about how rubber-tree seeds from Brazil in South America had been germinated in London's Kew Gardens at the end of the nineteenth century and sent out as fourteen-foot saplings with Frank Swettenham to Malaya, where a patch of jungle was cleared for them. It was a match made in heaven, Malaya and rubber, in the same way that the British had brought poppy seeds to China and started the opium trade. Europeans had a lot to answer for, it seemed to her.

She ventured into the shabby shantytown, a collection of shacks that ran alongside the rail track, built from scraps of corrugated tin and rough lengths of bamboo. She ducked through layers of washing that hung limp in the humid air, stretching across the street on drunken wooden poles. She was acutely aware that she was conspicuous and unwelcome. And the smell of the place made her stomach heave. White women didn't come here, didn't step gingerly in clean white shoes over the central gully that ran along the alleyway, holding her breath so that she wouldn't have to inhale the stench of excrement and cooking waste that clogged its path.

But still she searched until she found the house where Sai-Ru Jumat lived. It was a tumbledown hut, leaning against its neighbor, and Connie tapped the half-open door that only just clung on by one hinge. There was no sound from within, and she felt a treacherous ripple of relief. She could leave. But as her eyes adjusted to the gloom she made out the figure of a young man sitting cross-legged, alone on the floor in the center of the room. With a jolt she recognized him. Neat limbs elegantly folded, dense black hair and smooth skin that glowed like amber. His eyes were fixed on her, unblinking, and the expression in them, even in the dim light inside the shack, shocked her. *Hate* was too weak a word for what she saw in them. He was Sai-Ru Jumat's son.

"*Selamat pagi.* Good morning," she said. "My name is Constance Hadley."

He did not reply. But neither did he remove his gaze.

"Excuse me, *maaf*," she contined awkwardly. "I know this must be a bad time for you, but may I come in?"

Still no response. No flicker of movement. She stepped into the room, and stifling heat hit her like a hammer to the chest. Her lungs struggled for air. She became aware of the strong smell of glue and wood cuttings. He was seated on a woven mat surrounded by small flat wooden cases of various sizes and in different stages of finish. Some had glass fronts and had been polished; others were still raw and awaiting attention. He must have seen her eyes flick to them, but he made no comment.

"I've come to apologize," she said softly, "for what I did to your mother, and to offer you help." She waited.

For the first time, those intense black eyes released her and turned away. She removed her hat and crouched down on her knees on the sawdust that speckled the floor, so that her eyes were on a level with his.

"I know you hate me," she said evenly, "and you have good reason to. But don't let it stop you accepting some recompense from me because . . ."

She noticed he was looking at his hand. On its palm lay a butterfly. Not just one of the small, garish creatures that flitted through the riot of bougainvillea and frangipani in her garden, but one of the gigantic jungle ones, its wingspan wider than his whole hand and trailing two long black tails like bootlaces waiting to be tied. It was exquisite. The colors of its wings filled her eyes with iridescent blues and lilacs and a vivid splash of gold. It must have been dead, because it didn't move, and it dawned on her that that was what the cases were for. Already, she realized, two of them were lined with white satin and inside was pinned an assortment of butterflies. They were like miniature coffins.

Sai-Ru's son did not take his eyes off the butterfly on his hand, as if its beauty created a refuge from the ugliness he saw in Connie. She wanted to snatch it from him, to hold it to her heart. To steal its beauty.

"Do you sell them?" she asked.

Without looking at her he murmured, "White people buy. Dead things. They like."

Connie thought about the antelope's head on the wall of her husband's study, of the magnificent tiger-skin rug on the floor of her friend Harriet's drawing room. Of the elephant's foot that was a useful stool at the club.

She blushed. "Yes," she admitted. "They do."

A silence filled the tiny room. Connie looked around her. In one corner lay two bedrolls bundled out of the way, but she noted no sign of mosquito nets. On a shelf were a few pots and pans, while under it a primitive stove had been built out of bricks. Surely it was dangerous to light a fire here? She glanced up at the roof where a spider the size of Nigel's SS Jaguar was hanging by a thread from a rafter above her head. *Don't scream.*

"What is your name?" she asked.

"Razak." He licked his strong white teeth as he said it, his attention still on the butterfly. If he was aware of the spider, he was indifferent to it.

"Well, Razak, as I said, I would like to help you and your sister."

"Don't want. No help. Not you."

"Let me. *Tolong.* Please."

"*Tidak.* No."

Nevertheless, she took a manila envelope from her handbag and pushed it toward him, the paper rustling like lizard's skin over the matting. "This will pay for your mother's funeral. And a bit more."

A lot more.

This time he looked at her. A cold, direct stare from black eyes. "Go away."

He was young, she reminded herself, no more than fifteen or sixteen. His hatred had made him arrogant; his rage had hardened the soft line of his mouth. She had done that to him.

"I would also like to offer you a job," she continued as if he hadn't spoken. "Either on my husband's rubber plantation, the Hadley Estate, learning skills with the trees, or if you would prefer, in the smoke sheds or the godowns here in Palur."

She watched his face. He half closed his eyes, dipping his thick long lashes to hide himself from her. But his hand must have tightened because the butterfly suddenly fluttered its great wings, and Connie cried out, startled.

"It's alive!" she exclaimed, and saw that the lower half of its body was trapped between two of his fingers.

He lifted his other hand and stroked its furry back.

"It's beautiful," she murmured.

"White people want to kill everything."

Her cheeks were burning, and sweat zigzagged down her neck. "If you prefer, you could work in my garden."

Again the black stare, and then, with the butterfly still between his fingers, he reached behind him and drew the tiny stub of a candle in front of him and a cardboard book of matches that bore the name of a nightclub: The Purple Parrot. He struck a match, lit the candle, and stood it on the mat before picking up the envelope and opening it. He extracted a twenty-dollar note and held it over the flame. It caught quickly, flared between his fingers, and curled into black flakes as he dropped it on the mat. He took another note and another. Each one burned.

Connie said nothing. In silence, he burned ten notes in the hot little room before she leaned forward and snatched the envelope from the mat.

"Enough!" she said. "You've made your point."

She rose quickly to her feet, ducking to one side to avoid the spider. "I can't bring her back," Connie said quietly to the sleek head bent over the butterfly. "But I can give you what your mother would have wished for you—a better house, a job, even an education. Isn't that what you want?"

"*Tidak biak,*" he said. "No good. You no good. You go. She curse you." He spat on the mat.

Connie said no more. She tucked the envelope of money at the back of the shelf, forcing herself to ignore the centipede that was slithering around inside one of the cooking pots, and walked out of the door. Her throat was tight, her hands shaking. Sweat ran between her breasts. As she set off up the alleyway, bombarded by the sun's onslaught, she realized that she had forgotten her hat. She cursed under her breath and glanced back inside the gloomy interior but she chose not to return there. Razak was still sitting, his hands in his lap. He had torn both wings off the butterfly.

CHAPTER FOUR

The sky ached today, as though it still mourned her mother's death. Maya Jumat could feel its white pain like cuts in her dark skin. The air tasted of salt on her tongue and she licked her lips, feeling them tighten with anticipation. Today would be a good day. She tucked a vivid scarlet flower behind her ear, gripped the stems of the other blooms in her arms, and dodged between the cars, nimble as a cat.

"You want buy, lady?"

She thrust her hand clutching a few blossoms through the open window of the purring black car that had stopped at the crossroads in front of the station and flashed a wide smile. She wasn't stupid. The flowers were for the white lady, a weasel creature with aimless eyes, but the smile was for the red-faced man behind the wheel.

"No," the woman said flatly. "No."

"*Plees.* Pretty. For you." She dropped the bunch in the woman's over-ripe lap. The man revved the engine. Maya stood on the running board and widened her smile at him, showing him the tip of her pink tongue. "A dollar?"

"For God's sake, Eunice, give the bloody girl a dollar, will you?"

The lady switched her attention to her man, saw the spark in his eyes as he followed the soft folds of Maya's sarong draped over the curve of her young breasts. With undue haste she pushed a dollar into Maya's hand, but as the car drove off she tossed the flowers out of the window. Maya scrambled and scooped them up before the car behind had a chance to drive over them, and she received a loud blare on the horn in return. She ran between the rickshaws and motorcars, searching again for a good one to target, watching out for her bare feet. More than once some bastard had rolled a tire over her toes. She spotted a Rolls slowing down.

"Flowers? Pretty. You buy."

"Get in."

The rear door of the chauffeur-driven car swung open, and a white man with doughy skin and a ginger mustache as big as a fox under his nose reached for her wrist. She backed off fast. The Sikh in a turban in the driving seat didn't even glance over his shoulder, as though he were used to such moments.

"I no for sale," Maya declared. "Just flowers. Two dollar."

"Don't be silly, girl, come for a ride. How much?"

"Ten dollars. I virgin."

"Like hell you are."

"Show money."

The car behind sounded its Klaxon.

"I'm no fool," he smiled sourly. "I know girls like you."

"I not like other girls."

She darted her head forward as if to kiss him and he preened himself on the leather seat, but instead she snatched the gold tiepin from his cravat and vanished. Melted into the crowd of brown faces as easily as a fish makes itself invisible as it slides and shimmers within its shoal.

"Why man so stupid?" Maya shrugged, and for the next two hours she touted her flowers, hopping from car to car. Yes, today was a good day; she had been right. She sealed the precious dollars safely in the pouch tied at her waist and kept a sharp, hostile lookout for others encroaching on her patch. When the sun was at its highest in the sky and the tarmac burned the soles of her feet, the traffic at last grew thin, so she took a break in the shade at the back of the station's ticket office.

She squatted on the ground in the red dust and sucked on the discarded skin of an orange. She closed her eyes and took her time deciding which dream to unfold in her head today. The one where she married an old man who died suddenly—with a little help from herself—and left her the richest woman in the whole of Malaya, to do whatever she chose. Or the one where she was paddling in the river, the water as cool as ice cream on her hot shins, and she found a giant pearl as big as a kingfisher's egg, and when she showed it to Razak, like a bright eye in the center of the palm of her hand . . .

"Get up!" A kick landed firmly on her thigh, jarring the bone.

In less than a heartbeat she was on her feet, ready to run. "Piss off, Hakim."

"What the hell are you doing? I don't pay you good money to sleep all day, you lazy slut."

"You don't pay me anything, you liar," she retorted.

But she was careful not to push him too far. Hakim was the boss. He was the one who allocated the various roads to his street sellers. He was short and plump and owned a network of businesses throughout Palur that always required a never-ending stream of cheap labor. It was in his hands to give her a bad patch for the day or a good one, if he felt friendly. Today he had given her a decent patch near the station because she'd allowed him to kiss her this morning. Just her lips, she'd insisted, nothing more. She was strict about that. No one touched her body. Not ever. No one.

That, she had to admit, was the trouble with the rich-old-man dream. He'd want to put parts of himself inside her, and rub his ancient lizard skin against hers. She shuddered.

Hakim clipped her around the ear and laughed, flashing a row of gold teeth as though he would take a bite out of her.

"Don't you get smart with me, Maya. Let's see what you've got."

He reached for her pouch. She knew better than to resist. She stood immobile, scowling at him while he emptied its contents into his hand, counted it twice, and pocketed the coins.

"What about me?" she demanded.

He dropped a meager few cents back into the pouch.

"That's not enough!"

He laughed. Behind him, four gangly youths laughed with him, his pet wolf pack.

"That's all you get," he sneered. "You've been lazy today."

She clamped her teeth on the inside of her cheek to shut herself up.

With no comment she turned to scamper away, but Hakim seized her hair and wound its long strands around his fist, dragging her head back, stretching her neck painfully. She squealed. He leaned his face so close that the dark skin of his oily cheeks touched hers, but there was no pleasure in it this time. His eyes were black and cold as a shark's. His other hand shot down the front of her sarong, his fingers groping her small breasts as he yanked out the silk fold of material fastened there. She moaned.

"Thieving whore!" he shouted.

He slapped a hand carelessly across her face. Not hard; she'd felt worse. But enough to knock her off balance, so that she stumbled into one of the wolf pack. It was the one with a milky eye and knife scar across his throat. He was probably younger than she was but already heavily muscled, and he twisted her arm almost out of its socket just for the fun of it. She whimpered pitifully, but Hakim took no notice.

He removed the dollar bills from inside the silk. "Listen to me, you slut. Try to cheat me again and I will mark you so bad that no one will want to look at your smile ever again." His gold teeth loomed over her. "Understand?"

She nodded and tried to squirm out of the wolf cub's grip. Her bare feet scrabbled in the dirt.

"Shut up and listen. I want you at The Purple Parrot tonight. Leena is sick."

"No. Please, Hakim. I don't like . . ."

He hit her, harder this time. She felt blood ripple down her chin.

"Just be there." He raised his hand again.

She didn't wait for it to land. She sank her teeth into the wolf cub's cheek, sprang free when he screamed, and was off racing round the corner of the building when she heard Hakim's final shout.

"Be there or be dead, whore!"

She didn't stop running. People looked at her. No one except little children ran in the tropics. It was too hot, and sweat glistened on her limbs. *Damn Hakim. Damn the gold-fanged snake spawn to a thousand hells.* But as Maya wove her way through the crowded streets and lingered for a moment to catch her breath in the dusty shade of a Buddhist temple, listening to the insistent wind chimes hanging from its swooping eaves, her hand clutched at the gold tiepin fixed to the inside of the knot that held her sarong and she laughed, a wild, angry sound.

ᕲᐧᑕ

Maya bit into the warm chapati she'd bought from a street stall with her morning's pittance and headed home. She found the harbor busier than usual. She scoured the river, its surface as brown as a turtle's back, and spotted the newly arrived ships. Military ones, gray as river eels. So more British uniforms in town, more guns, more drunks. Would the white man never tire of his game of war? It was like opium to their weak minds, exciting and addictive. But Malaya didn't want their gunboats any more than it wanted their chicken pox or their net curtains.

She shrugged her narrow shoulders and trotted along her street, eager to reach home now that she could be certain her mother would not be there to shout at her or take a stick to her. Maya would have vanished from Palur years ago if it hadn't been for her brother, Razak. She glanced up at the sky. Good, she nodded, rain was coming. It meant she could wash her hair before . . .

Her eyes registered the blond head in the street. In this narrow, crowded world of jet-black hair, of skins darker than tea, of broad cheekbones and wide nostrils, the woman with the golden hair and pale, delicate features stood out in sharp contrast. Instead of the bright sarongs and *kebayas* that surrounded her, she wore a crisp cream linen dress and picked her way in white leather shoes. She looked like a fragile egret in a world of crows.

Maya knew her at once, like she knew the lines on her own hand. It was the white woman who had driven the car that had killed her mother. She had just walked out of her mother's house and hurried past Maya, close enough to touch her arm, but the woman saw only another dark anonymous face in a forest of dark anonymous faces.

"Razak!" Maya called, alarmed, and sprang quickly through the open door.

The room had been dipped in darkness. A black mood hung in the air and brushed against her face, as sticky as cobwebs.

"Razak!"

Her twin brother was seated on the mat, surrounded by his butterfly cases, his hands clenched together. He stared at her the way he'd stare at a stranger.

"Razak, what did the white woman want?"

"Forgiveness."

"Did she beg for it?"

He shook his head in an angry gesture. "No. She tried to buy it."

Maya crouched down beside him, her voice eager. "How much?"

Razak scowled at her and turned away, but she seized his shoulder and shook him. "How much did you accept?"

"Nothing."

"You fool!"

"That white woman killed our family. We owe respect to our mother's spirit."

He glared blindly out at the street, seeing things that Maya could only guess at. She sighed softly. Razak had no idea how beautiful he was, far more beautiful than she would ever be. The gods must have been drunk when they spotted the new-formed twins in her mother's womb, and decided to have some sport at the humans' expense. They stirred their fingers in the mix and gave all the beauty to the male twin and all the brains to the female one. Maya could still hear them laughing some nights, harsh, rattling roars in the heavens, but she didn't curse them. She loved her brother too much for that.

Each morning she enjoyed the sight of his deep golden skin, his impressive black eyes that were incapable of hiding any of the emotions that poured through him, and his thick black hair and straight, strong limbs. Only his mouth let him down. It was red and full, much softer than her own, more vulnerable. It upset her sometimes to look at it because it revealed how easily he could be hurt. That frightened her. It was why she had stayed in Palur.

"Respect?" She demanded. "For our mother? For the woman who sold my body to the highest bidder when I was ten years old, and who beat your legs with a stick till they were black and blue and you couldn't stand? Respect for her?"

"Shut up! Take back your words." He swung around to face her, his eyes wide with anger, but Maya knew it was not at her. It was at their mother, for dying. For living. "She was not well," he insisted. "Not herself."

"How could she be well," Maya asked, running a soothing hand down his arm, "when every cent you or I could earn or beg or steal she spent on the happy pipe?"

He sank his chin on his chest. "Don't, Maya. Show her spirit the respect it deserves as our mother."

Maya fell silent. She didn't want to upset him. That was when she noticed the straw hat on the floor, winking at her in the dim light as if calling her name. Maya picked it up, felt the quality of its brim and popped it on her own head, grinning at him.

"Look, Razak, do I look like the white lady?"

"Take it off. It's bad luck."

She took it off quickly. "What did she offer?"

"Money. I burned it. And she offered a job."

"A job?"

"On the Hadley Estate."

"Did you accept?"

"No. I would not dishonor our mother's peace of soul."

"Did she offer anything for me?"

"No."

"So. She's forgotten me and remembered only you." She undid the knot on her sarong and extracted the gold pin. "Look."

He stared at it without asking where it came from. "It will pay for our mother's funeral," he said.

"No." It came out of her as a wail of dismay.

"Yes." He reached over and took it from her. "Thank you, Maya. *Terimah kasih.* It will help the journey our mother's soul must make."

It will line the priests' pockets, Maya thought, but kept it miserably to herself. For a long time the two of them sat in silence, indifferent to the heat and the insects, their thoughts entwining together. Gradually Maya sensed the blackness lift in the dingy little room.

"So you didn't accept a job from her either?"

"No. I will not work for this Constance Hadley, nor help her in any way."

Maya shifted closer to him on the mat, pushing aside his pieces of wood, and wrapped her arms around his neck. "We will not help her, my brother." She leaned forward and whispered in his ear, "But if you do as I say, we will destroy her."

ꤶ·ꤢ

"Don't you want it?"

A drunk hung onto the edge of his chair, his head wobbling unsteadily, and wafted a dollar bill in the air as if the smell of it would entice Maya over. She balanced her tray of drinks on one hand and gyrated her tiny hips in his direction until he added another dollar to the offering.

The stink of cigarette smoke and the musky odor of cheap sex stifled the air in The Purple Parrot nightclub. It was a trashy place, its lights kept low to hide the seediness of its interior, and its prices kept high to line Hakim's pockets. Its beer was watered. Maya hated it here. The stench, the sweat, the stares, the hungry hands that reached out for her whenever she placed a drink on a table. She was only a waitress, not one of the strippers on stage, but the difference between the two seemed to blur in the beer-soaked heads of the customers. Her costume didn't help. It was a skimpy froth of purple silk and feathers that left too much flesh on view, inviting hot sweaty palms to linger on her naked midriff or slide up her bare thigh as she wove between tables.

"Come and get it." The drunk held out a ten-dollar note. "Come over here, little birdie."

It wasn't just Malays who came to The Purple Parrot; at least half the patrons were white. The two men at the front table were obviously military types, though out of uniform, and the quiet one who invariably sat at a table in the far corner, his back to the wall, had a married look about him. He never drank more than two whiskies and never applauded, just watched the stage with sad eyes.

The Purple Parrot prided itself on providing something for all tastes. There were strippers of all skin colors: black, brown, yellow, and even white—a skinny Russian girl who had traveled down from China. There were ladyboys more beautiful than the girls, and an assortment of acts of young men, oiled and acrobatic, who threw each other across the stage. One tall Ethiopian strutted the stage brandishing a whip over a submissive band of naked slaves, male and female, who whimpered and moaned.

Applause and shouts rattled the walls now, and the drunk banged his fists on the table as a Malay girl on stage slowly unwound the feathery boa that covered her breasts. Maya darted forward, snatched the ten dollars from between the drunk's fingers, and skipped out of reach before he realized what had happened. It was the end of her shift and, with luck, Hakim would be too drunk on cheap whisky to bother her.

She scurried to the communal changing room backstage. Everyone was crammed into it, donning or removing clothes; men, boys, and girls all fought for the mirrors. No one took any notice of nudity. The odor of sweating bodies was intense.

Maya rescued her sarong from the floor. She wanted to make her escape with the ten dollars before Hakim caught her, but as she started to push her way to the door she saw the Russian girl crying in front of a broken scrap of mirror propped on a shelf. She was coating her cheek with a heavy layer of face paint, covering a dirty bruise that looked fresh.

"Hakim?" Maya said.

The girl nodded. No need to ask why. Hakim could always find an excuse if he was in the mood to use his fists.

"Are you all right?" Maya asked.

The girl shrugged. There was something so broken about her that Maya could imagine Hakim being tempted to finish the job. Like putting a wounded bird out of its pain.

Maya hesitated. "You ought to give this up," she said. "Before he ends up killing you."

The girl turned and gave a sweet smile, resigned to her misery. "*Tak.* No."

"There are other clubs."

"I've tried them," she said in accented Malay. "They're no different. Anyway, none of us will be here much longer."

"What do you mean?"

"They'll be marching in here soon."

"Who?" Maya tucked her money into her sarong knot.

"The Japanese, of course."

"What?" Maya held her breath.

"Haven't you heard?"

"No."

"They've been stomping over China for years. Now they're getting ready for Malaya."

Maya laughed, relieved. "No, you've heard wrong. That tiger will never dare to put its claws in the British." She started to move away. She didn't like what this girl was saying.

"I'm warning you, I've seen them," the Russian continued in her soft tones. "I've seen what they did to people in China. You don't want to be here when they march in."

Maya could hear the catch of tears in the girl's throat and seized her thin wrist. "You are wrong, you hear me? The British are dog shit, the way they have stolen our country from us, but they have a giant army. They have guns and hundreds of planes. I see them in the sky. No one can ever beat the British." She released her grip on the girl. "Malaya is safe, I promise you."

CHAPTER FIVE

Fifty miles south of Palur, in a ramshackle wooden building that clung to the banks of the muddy Sungai Lereh river, Morgan Madoc threw a naked man out of an upstairs bedroom window. It was dark outside, the jungle's nightly chorus vibrating the sultry air, but the splash was audible as he hit the water.

"Can he swim?" a native girl on the bed asked, horrified.

"Who cares?"

Madoc seized the man's clothes from the floor, removed a fistful of Malay dollars from the wallet he found in the jacket and a cheap pocket watch from beside the bed, and then tossed the rest out of the window after their owner. The shirt flapped its arms briefly, then fluttered in defeat down to the waves and, in the smear of yellow light that floated on the surface of the river, Madoc took pleasure in watching both shoes sink at once.

"Don't let me catch you here again!" he yelled.

There was no answer from the darkness. He couldn't hear splashing. But maybe the man was a strong, silent swimmer. Or maybe not. Madoc shrugged his broad shoulders, closed the window and turned to the girl.

"What happened?"

She was naked. Her slender, caramel-colored legs were still sprawled across the clean white sheet, her hands rubbing at her throat. A vicious red mark stretched from one ear to the other like a noose and she was coughing with a soft little bleat. It reminded Madoc of the newborn lambs on his father's farm in the Brecon Beacons when he was a child. A lifetime ago.

"You all right?" he asked.

"Me OK. He like it rough."

He ran an expert eye over her limp figure and nodded to himself. Except for her neck, no harm done. For a twenty-eight-year-old she still looked good, small and neat with not a ripple of fat on her. Not to his liking. He preferred something with a bit of solid flesh on it that you could really grab hold of, but his customers liked the girls to look like twigs. Breakable. With luck, he could still pass her off as eighteen for another year or two, as long as she kept those blasted black eyes of hers tucked away behind her long lashes. Her eyes carried her whole life in them.

"I'll send up your next johnny, then," he told her.

She twitched her shoulders. "Something for me first, *tuan*, boss?"

He didn't like wasting his good stuff on the girls, but her eyes were jumping like crickets and she looked as if she might not last the night without it. He reached into his shirt pocket and pulled out a couple of hand-rolled ganja-weed cigarettes—kept there for special clients—tossed them on the bedsheet, and watched her scramble for them. Immediately she lit one from the oil lamp on the dresser and closed her eyes with secret pleasure as she inhaled, drawing the drug deep into her lungs, swilling it round her bloodstream like sugar in tea. Madoc snorted in disgust. For much of his forty-four years he had been smuggling opium in rickety boats up and down the west coast of Malaya, but not once did he touch the poison itself. He'd seen what it could do. Destroy a man's life. Rot his mind. Only fools and losers fell into that pit.

"You've got five minutes," he said, not unkindly, and went downstairs.

ϑ·Ϭ

The bar was busy tonight because it was payday at the logging camp upriver. Madoc stood at the top of the stairs for a moment, lit himself a Craven A and let his eyes roam over the smoky barroom below. OK, so it wasn't the Raffles Hotel in Singapore, but it was his. He grinned to himself; the place felt wild and lawless, packed with men with money in their back pockets and one thing on their mind—how fast they could spend it.

Morgan's Bar was more than ready to relieve them of their hard-earned cash. The girls in the upstairs rooms were doing fierce business, and in the bar the drinks couldn't flow fast enough. He shouldered a path across the wide room, slapping backs and exchanging greetings with his customers in fluent Malay and Cantonese, before he slid behind the bar where a middle-aged white woman was mixing a lime juice and lemonade for a wiry Tamil with severe pockmarks on his face. She was a big woman, full-breasted and a behind like a hippo's, but she stood no nonsense from the other side of the counter. She filled the small space, and as Madoc edged past her, he couldn't resist a quick squeeze of her buttocks, her flesh heavy as a sun-warmed melon in his palm. He could feel her skin moist with sweat under her cotton skirt before she reached behind and swatted his paw away. She didn't even jog the bottle in her other hand.

"Madoc," the Tamil logger moaned, "keep your greedy hands off Kitty while I'm talking to her."

"Take no notice of the Welshman," Kitty chuckled. "I don't."

Madoc scooped up a good bottle of sake from beneath the counter, brushing the back of his wrist over one of her sturdy calves as he did so, and headed out the other end, raising the flap of the counter to emerge among the drinkers. The woman swiveled her eyes across to where he was heading toward a table at the far end of the bar where three men in clean white shirts were seated, and then back to Madoc. For a moment their gaze snagged on each other, and she blinked a silent warning to him. *Be careful.* He tipped her a nod, then sauntered over to the table where the three men were sitting. They were Japanese.

"More sake, gentlemen?" he suggested in English, and placed the bottle in the center of the table. He ousted a nearby drinker from a chair and hitched it up to join the quiet group of white shirts. "Enjoying your evening?"

"*Arigato*, thank you, Madoc-san. It is good business here tonight."

The one who spoke was the youngest of the three, and as Madoc knew from experience, the politest. He was the only one who seemed capable of a smile. All three were lean and narrow-shouldered but looked fit, with smooth, unlined faces and hair cropped short. The oldest, a man a little more than Madoc's own age judging by the shadowy gray stubble on his head, possessed cold, implacable eyes that rarely blinked. He spoke little. Madoc wasn't sure whether it was because his English was poor or because he chose not to communicate his thoughts. He suspected it was the latter. He offered them his cigarettes, but they all declined with a precise shake of the head, a small gesture of distaste before taking out their own cigarettes and lighting up. It was a little routine they went through each time, so he should be used to it by now. But still it irked him.

"You've heard, I'd guess?" he said.

"*Hai.* Yes." The polite one again.

The third one, a man who had the look of someone eager to get the moment over and done with, said, "That's why we're here, Madoc-san." He nudged his glass nearer the bottle.

Madoc picked up the sake and poured each of them a drink. For the first time they showed a flicker of interest.

"Down the hatch!" he said, though he didn't drink himself.

They knocked back the rice wine, replaced the glasses on the table and regarded him with the faintest shadow of impatience. He leaned forward, elbows on the table, and the young one did the same.

"So," Madoc began, "you've heard that our boys in the north are on the move."

"It has come to our notice, *hai*, yes. What would be advantageous to our Command Planning is to know how many battalions and . . ."

At that point, two sailors pushed open the door to the bar. As Madoc gave them a quick appraisal, he felt his table companions grow tense.

"Junior ratings," he muttered under his breath. "Relax."

The pair had probably come upriver by sampan to taste what the jungle had to offer, in search of wilder women and rougher whisky. Word of Morgan's Bar was whispered in the towns on the coast. *You want good girls? Good ganja? Good gambling? I take you.*

These sailors were still wet behind the ears, fresh reinforcements shipped in as nerves curled tighter in this part of the world. He knew that the battle cruiser *Repulse* and the battleship *Prince of Wales* were patrolling the seas. The sailors inspected the bar with interest but stopped in their tracks when they caught sight of the Japs.

"Gentlemen," Madoc said softly to his companions, "shall we step outside for some air?"

He opened the door, took a deep breath of the night air, as moist and heavy as the sake, and walked out into the darkness. The jungle and the Sungai Lereh river muttered to him like old friends, the booming call of the frogs, as insistent as toothache.

Madoc had created the muddy patch for Morgan's Bar out of densely packed jungle, with no reference to anyone else. He'd chugged up by boat one humid afternoon, avoiding the mangrove swamps that stretched their gray roots like dead arms reaching out of the jungle, and dynamited himself a space about fifty yards square. He'd slept that night in a stifling tent in the middle of his crater, and next morning set about taming it. That was twelve years ago.

As he lit himself another cigarette from the old butt and watched one draw life from the other, the three Japanese joined him. They moved as soundlessly as snakes.

"Madoc-san," the polite spokesman said in low tones. "We are waiting."

Madoc drew them out of the splash of yellow light thrown from the bar's windows and into the deep shadow of the building on his right. It loomed up with a jagged profile against the starless night sky, only half constructed, a black shapeless shell. But at the sight of its unfinished walls, Madoc's blood kicked hard in a vein at his temple, almost as sharp as a mosquito bite. Month by month the walls were clawing their way up, but he needed more bricks, more sand, more cement, more lead piping, more wiring, more . . . More money. He swallowed a sigh in the guise of drawing on his cigarette, flicked its ash on a passing moth, and told them what they wanted to know.

"General Brooke-Popham is holed up in Singapore at the moment, in conference with General Heath. They're putting out propaganda that we Brits are confident that our defenses are strong and our weapons efficient. He scoffs at the Jap army."

There was a hiss in the darkness. It came from the oldest of the three.

"Brooke-Popham is convinced you will not have the nerve to touch Malaya. Maybe Sumatra or Siam, but not the peninsula itself. He claims you haven't the guts to march against the British army and that anyway you could never get your tanks through the jungle. He claims our RAF is second to none. You wouldn't stand a chance." Madoc smiled in the secrecy of the black shadows. Part of him was enjoying this. "After all, he reminds us that your forces have been battling that rabble of a Chinese army for years in China, and still can't teach them who's boss."

"Facts, Madoc. I want facts. Not a gin-soaked old general's lies."

So. The gray-stubbled Jap did speak English after all. Interesting.

"Facts you shall have," Madoc replied coolly. "The governor has said he believes any attack will be launched from landings at Singora and Patani in Siam. Defenses are in place."

"Where?"

"At the Ledge."

"*Hai.* Yes," one of them murmured softly.

Solid defense would be essential on the road from Patani. It led across the mountains to the rich and vulnerable west coast. The rice-growing areas of Perlis and Kedah would need protection, of course, but far more important was the aerodrome at Alor Star. If that fell, so would Penang and even Butterworth, God forbid.

"Alor Star?" the oldest one asked, as if he could pick out Madoc's thoughts with a pin.

"Defended."

"Where?"

"North of the aerodrome. At Jitra."

There was a long silence. They all knew that if the Japanese succeeded in coming down the difficult Patani mountain road, they would hit the Brits on their soft underbelly *behind* the Jitra defenses.

"How did you learn this?"

"One of my girls is mistress to an army lieutenant-colonel in Intelligence."

"Can we rely on it?"

"Of course. As always."

"How many soldiers defending the Ledge?"

"That, I'm afraid, I don't know."

He did know. General Heath was holding two battalions in reserve for that purpose. But he kept that information to himself. You can make a cat sick if you give it too much cream. The oldest one stepped so close that Madoc could smell the spices on his breath. The move was meant to be intimidating, but Madoc exhaled cigarette smoke directly in the man's face. The gray head turned away with a curse in Japanese. It was the polite one who placed a packet in his hand.

"British pounds?" Madoc asked.

"Of course. As you requested."

Madoc wasn't going to touch any Mexican dollars, the flimsy currency of much of Malaya. He only trusted notes with the king's head on them. He flicked open the packet, checked its contents, then nodded at the three men, who were watching him in silence. His heart skittered inside his chest.

"*Sayonara*, gentlemen," he said cheerfully. "Good-bye. You know where to find me."

"Yes," the oldest one said in a flat voice. "We know exactly where to find you."

As Madoc stepped away, lightning flickered across the canopy of the jungle like a flash fire in the treetops. The storm was rumbling somewhere close and the first raindrops began to fall, as flat as pennies on the dark banana palms. The men hurried onto the jetty where their boat was tied up, and Madoc stood watching in the rain as they jostled each other to climb inside it. Its engine finally rattled off downriver.

We know exactly where to find you.

That didn't sound good.

CHAPTER SIX

"Oh, Constance, why on earth are you reading that?" Nigel failed to keep his annoyance out of his voice.

Connie smiled sheepishly at him. The book was dog-eared from years of handling, and she read its title aloud.

"The English Country Garden."

She ruffled its pages, and pictures of lupins and delphiniums flicked past, along with instructions on the best mulch to use for peonies in an English garden. She heard her husband sigh.

"One extra for Sunday lunch today," he said.

"Who is it?"

"Johnnie Blake."

"Johnnie? I didn't know he was back."

She was already smiling broadly. It was impossible not to. Flight Lieutenant John Blake was always bursting with vitality, but he tempered it with such charm and good humor that he was much in demand at dinner tables. He and Nigel had been school friends at Eton, lost touch for a while, and had bumped into each other a number of years back at a grand dinner at Government House in Singapore.

"Like two long-lost penguins," Connie had laughed when she saw them clasp each other in their dress suits, both the same height, both the same age, only Nigel's brown hair lay neatly oiled into submission, whereas Johnnie's golden-colored mop was tossing about, as flyaway as his smile.

"Watch out for this blighter," Nigel had warned with affection as he brought the pilot over to her and introduced him. "He's left a string of broken hearts in his wake."

But Johnnie had never overstepped the mark with her, not once. Sometimes she found herself half wishing that he would.

"How wonderful," she exclaimed. "Teddy will be thrilled."

Her son hero-worshipped Flight Lieutenant Blake. That worried her a little. When you gave your heart so completely, it was bound to get crushed one of these days.

ᘖ·ᘕ

Connie checked that the table was well laid with the best china and the finest crystal glasses that had once belonged to Nigel's mother. His parents had both been killed in a midair collision on a local airfield just outside Palur when Nigel was eighteen. He'd watched it happen. She often wondered what it did to you to watch your parents die so violently. Did it build an anger in you like she'd seen in Razak, so high that avalanches of it came careening down to suffocate you when you least expected it?

She didn't know.

Maybe even the sight of his mother's crystal wineglasses was enough to set one off. With a sudden instruction to Masur, she bundled them on a tray.

"Put these away. Bring out the other glasses instead. Be quick. *Lekas!* Hurry."

Masur, who had worked for the Hadleys for nearly six years, looked at her with gently bemused eyes but he did as she asked.

"*Terimah kasih.* Thank you, Masur."

"*Tuan* Blake come today?"

"That's right, he'll be here for lunch."

"He jolly busy in sky now."

"Yes, he certainly is. The RAF is keeping a sharp eye out for intruders, don't you worry, Masur." She didn't say who the intruders were. They left it unspoken.

�·Ꮗ

"You look wonderful, Connie. How do you keep growing younger every time I see you, while old Nigel here is getting as cranky as his father?"

"Flight Lieutenant Blake, you are an outrageous flirt," she smiled.

Johnnie Blake kissed both her cheeks in the French fashion, holding on to her hands so that she couldn't escape his admiring gaze. She had changed her frock for a pale blue one that she knew sat well on her slight hips and had twined her long blond hair up in a loose pleat with a pearl clip for a more sophisticated look. Somehow Palur and its fusty colonial ways felt very provincial whenever Johnnie was around.

Stylish was the word for him. None other fitted him so well. As he swung Teddy up in the air in greeting, Connie felt the atmosphere in the house brighten, and even the dark staircase lost its gloomy mood. He was tall and elegant in his RAF blue-gray uniform and careless in the manner with which he tossed his jacket aside for Teddy to seize upon.

"Constance, let me introduce Mr. Fitzpayne."

Nigel turned to a figure standing behind him, still in the doorway. Connie had an impression of strength as the man stepped forward. He was shorter than her husband and bulkier, the muscles of his forearms clearly visible in the dark short-sleeved shirt he wore, and his gray eyes did not smile at her. Something in the cold slate of his gaze made her want to move back, away from him. Instead, she held out her hand.

"Welcome to Hadley House, Mr. Fitzpayne."

"I'm sorry to intrude on your Sunday, Mrs. Hadley. But your husband was kind enough to invite me to lunch."

"Couldn't let the chap starve, now could I?" Nigel laughed.

"It's my fault," Johnnie said with an apologetic smile. "Fitz and I traveled up together on the train from KL and took a bit of a shine to each other. He's a real sea dog, aren't you, Fitz? Knows a hell of a lot about boats, and I was sure Nigel would want to talk to him about *The White Pearl*."

The White Pearl was the love of Nigel's life: his sixty-five-foot sailing yacht that rode the waves like the thoroughbred she was.

"You're very welcome to join us for lunch, Mr. Fitzpayne," Connie said. "We will be delighted to learn about life as a sea dog."

"Not very interesting, I'm afraid," he said blandly.

"Oh, come now," Connie smiled, "I'm sure you have some secrets to tell."

Fitzpayne's heavy brows pulled together. "We all have our secrets, Mrs. Hadley."

Connie felt her throat tighten. "Indeed we do." She forced a laugh.

"Some bigger than others," Johnnie cut in, and waved a hand vaguely in the direction of Singapore. "For instance, they say that General Gordon Bennett . . ." He raised a querying eyebrow at Teddy.

"The commander of the Australian Imperial Force in Malaya," the boy responded at once.

"Spot on! Well done, Teddy. You certainly know your stuff." He ruffled the boy's hair.

"I don't want to hear about the general's skeletons, thank you," Nigel stated. "Not in front of the nipper, anyway."

"Save it for the brandies, Blake," the newcomer commented.

He glanced around the room, taking in its elegant proportions, its silk hangings, its mahogany glass-fronted cabinet displaying shelves of antique silver. Connie did not warm to this man who was inspecting her room with such a critical eye.

"Let's have drinks on the north veranda," she said brightly. "It's shady there."

"Good idea," Nigel agreed.

"Come on, Pilot Officer," Johnnie said to Teddy. "Let's see what might be hiding in this bag, shall we?" He swung a leather satchel from his shoulder and Teddy's face lit up. He trotted after him like a miniature shadow. Nigel followed, interested.

"Shall we join them?" Connie said to Fitzpayne.

His attention flicked from the room to her. He seemed about to say something, his gray eyes quick to register her unease, but instead something like a satisfied smile tipped one corner of his mouth. Slats of light and dark lay on the parquet floor where the sunlight had sidled in between the shutters, and he walked across them without a word, picking his feet up as if he were treading on glass.

꘏·꘎

The lunch was unusually animated. Maybe it was all the talk of how the British forces were planning under Sir Robert Brooke-Popham to strengthen Malaya's defenses. Or maybe it was just that Connie's own unsettled mood made her drink too many glasses of wine. She talked too much. She was aware of it, but her tongue wouldn't stop, as though frightened to lie still. She asked Johnnie about Singapore, where he had been at a dinner with the governor, Sir Shenton Thomas.

"What else?" she asked. "What else did you do there?"

"I went to the pictures. Watched Orson Welles in *Citizen Kane* at the Cathay Cinema. You should see it if it comes to Palur," he urged. "It's a great film."

"Were there airplanes in it?" Teddy asked hopefully. He had never been to the cinema.

"No, but the film for you is *Dumbo*. He's an elephant that flies." He laughed at Teddy's expression. "And I came across a shop on Tanglin Road selling this." With a flourish, Johnnie drew out a package from the satchel and handed it across the table to the boy.

Teddy unwrapped it eagerly and drew out a cardboard box containing a flying model of an airplane. "It's a Frog Interceptor!" he squealed.

He opened the box and inspected its contents with awe. His small fingers caressed the foil fuselage of the aircraft, only ten inches long and driven by a rubber band. He touched its wings tucked neatly at its side. When out of the box, they would slot onto pegs attached to the body of the plane.

"Thank you, Uncle Johnnie, thank you." Beaming from ear to ear, he turned to his father at the head of the table. "It'll fly for three hundred feet when you wind it up. That's what my friend Jack says, but he's not getting one till Christmas."

Nigel smiled. "You spoil the boy."

"Can I fly it, Papa?"

"Of course, but don't be in such an almighty rush. Wait until we finish tiffin."

Teddy's impatient eyes flitted around their plates. He started pushing forkfuls of roast lamb into his mouth, trying by example to encourage the others to speed up. On Connie's left Mr. Fitzpayne was observing her son in moody silence. The stranger had said so little during the meal that she wondered why on earth he bothered to come at all. His broad face with its heavy features and thick dark eyebrows studied his four luncheon companions, and even the dog who was sniffing at his boots, in a way that made her faintly uncomfortable. She wished Johnnie hadn't brought him along.

"Mr. Fitzpayne." She made a polite attempt to include him in the conversation. "Have you also been down to Singapore recently?"

He laid down his fork and regarded her solemnly. "I have."

"What is the mood down there? I read in the *Straits Times* that there is talk of war."

"There is."

"Surely not in Malaya itself."

"Very probably."

"It's preposterous," Nigel burst out. "The Japs wouldn't risk it. They may have a go at Siam or Java but not here, I promise you. We have fifteen-inch guns facing the seas around Singapore. We'd blast the yellow bastards out of the water."

"There's always the jungle," Fitzpayne pointed out flatly. "They could come down from the north, you are forgetting that."

It was the way he said it. Something cold crept up Connie's spine.

"That's absurd, Fitz," Johnnie responded. "No army could hack its way through the jungle and the mountains of Malaya. They are impenetrable." He raised his wineglass good-naturedly. "Come on now, no scaremongering, my friend. Especially not with ladies and children present."

But the damage was done.

"Is a war really coming?" Teddy asked. His young voice was as excited as if he had asked if Christmas was coming.

"Of course not," his father insisted.

Fitzpayne laughed. "I'll take a wager with you, Hadley."

"Blast your damn cheek!" Nigel muttered, and signaled to a servant to refill his glass. "The Japs won't be sticking their nose in here. General Percival will see to that. You and your RAF boys will give any Jap warships a hammering, eh, Johnnie?" He smiled at his son. "So no need to worry, young man."

Teddy prodded a piece of carrot across his plate. He looked disappointed.

Connie abandoned her meal.

"Are you connected with the military, Mr. Fitzpayne?" she inquired.

He looked at her a beat too long for politeness before he answered, "No. I'm in pleasure boats."

"Really. My husband loves to sail, don't you, Nigel?"

Nigel grunted into his wine. There was an awkward lull at the table, and this time Connie let it lie there like a sick dog. Johnnie Blake was the one to give it a shake.

"I heard in the club in Palur yesterday that they are contemplating rounding up any Japanese still hanging around and putting them to work in camps."

Connie looked up sharply. "In camps?"

"Yes, in case they're spying for Japan."

Why did she feel it, like a blow beneath her ribs even now?

"There aren't many Japanese in Palur," she pointed out. She was breathing too fast. Suddenly she longed for a thin black cheroot with a tiny gold band around the filter. To have one lit for her. To feel its gossamer brown tip placed between her lips.

"That's true," Nigel agreed. "They've mostly vanished into the woodwork."

"What happened to the one who used to hang around here a while back?" Johnnie asked. "Ever hear from him these days?"

It was like a black fog. It descended in front of Connie's eyes so quickly she had to hold on to the edge of the tablecloth.

"Remember him, Connie?" Johnnie asked. "What was that blighter's name?"

From a long way away, rising from the bottom of a dirty disused well, the words climbed up to her, hand over hand, clinging to the bricks, fighting to get at her.

Remember him, Connie? What was that blighter's name?

୨·୧

She remembered him. His name was Shohei Takehashi. Sho for short.

"Will you dance?"

Those were the first words he spoke to her. He had been observing her all evening from behind a cloud of cigarette smoke at the next table at the Mayfair nightclub in Palur, and she had pretended to be totally unaware of his black eyes fixed on her as the band played Cole Porter's *Don't Fence Me In*. The band was called Siroc, and the music was as hot as the wind from the desert. She could feel her pulse at her wrists.

"Will you dance?"

She opened her mouth to refuse. But someone else at her table—was it Harriet's husband?—rose to his feet and greeted the elegant Japanese stranger like a long-lost cousin, the way businessmen tend to do until they no longer need each other. Images burned in her mind, even now. The way his neck bent forward to bow a courteous acknowledgment, the skin as rich and smooth as butter. The grace of his movements, the delicacy of his bones. The fullness of his lips.

He had stood there, patient as one of his Shinto monks, listening, talking, waiting. He didn't move from the edge of their round table. There were ten people in their party, four of them already on the dance floor, the others drinking and laughing. And when Nigel was deep in conversation about the replanting tax with William Barratt from Jardine's, the largest trading house in the Pacific, Sho leaned forward once more and asked again.

"Will you dance?"

This time she said yes. The dance floor was crowded and he drew her body close. He was taller than she was but not by much, and she could feel the tension in his muscles under the silk of his jacket where her hand lay lightly on his shoulder. He smelled of a musky spice that set the fragile skin in her nostrils on fire. They barely spoke. Just her hand in his, her eyes drawn to his neatly manicured nails and the pearly color of them, their half-moons white and silken. Clearly he did not work with his hands.

Their feet moved in time together, his fingers firm on the small of her back, their tips moving over the curve of her spine. How long was it since a man had touched her like this? As if his skin drew something from hers. A thirst, a need, a hunger, the rumbling of an undercurrent when the tide goes out? She could sense it, the way she could sense his gaze on her lips, on her hair, and on the bones of her cheeks even when her eyes were turned away from him. When the music stopped, the movement around them ceased and she looked him full in the face.

"Thank you," she said.

"For what?"

"For waiting."

"Waiting for something worthwhile is not hard."

"It depends, doesn't it?" she said softly. "Something that is worthwhile to one person may be worthless to another."

"We all make our own choices." His long almond eyes smiled at her but didn't hide the desire behind the polite words.

"And we all have to live with the consequences of our choices," she pointed out.

But this was not a man who would ever call her *old thing*. They danced one more dance, a slow waltz, and that was all. He walked her courteously back to her table, bowed, and left. But they met the following day. And the next.

ꝯ·Ꝗ

"Good God, Constance, who the hell is that?" Nigel demanded, pointing with his fork at the French windows behind her.

She blinked. The lunch party was still in progress. An untouched pudding of papaya and vanilla custard stood before her. She had no recollection of its being placed there. Everyone had turned to look at what Nigel was indicating and sweat, as sticky as honey, broke out on Connie's palms. She was sure it was Sho. So sure, she lifted the cheese knife that lay next to her plate and wrapped her fingers tightly around its handle. Slowly she turned.

At first she saw nothing, blinded by the dazzle of the sun. The French doors stood wide open, framing a rectangle of peaceful green lawn sloping gently up to the house. She could hear Nigel breathing hard through his nose at the other end of the table. Three wide, semicircular steps ran down to the lawn and at the bottom of them stood a figure. It was male. She squinted against the light and made out a patterned waist sarong and a black sleeveless shirt. She frowned. Sho would die rather than wear a sarong. The figure moved and relief crushed her throat. She couldn't swallow.

"Masur," Nigel shouted out. "Get rid of this person."

Connie leaped to her feet, knocking over her chair in her haste. "It's all right, Nigel, I know him. It's Razak. Sai-Ru Jumat's son, the woman in the accident."

Razak was staring straight at her. For a moment the intensity of his dark gaze made her skin crawl, but then he dipped his head shyly and smiled. *How beautiful he is*, she thought.

"Come in, Razak," she called.

As lithe as a gazelle, he leaped up the steps.

CHAPTER SEVEN

Connie showed Razak around the garden. He had requested work at Hadley House and clearly wanted nothing to do with the rubber estate. She explained carefully that he would earn more if he became a skilled tapper than he could as a gardener, but he was adamant. He had shaken his head and kept his eyes firmly on his feet, on his dusty sandals, the kind with a thong between the toes.

"How old are you, Razak?"

"Sixteen."

"And your sister?"

"Sixteen."

"So you're twins. How lovely."

"Yes."

"What's her name?"

"Maya."

"Does she have a job?"

A faint frown. "She works."

He looked embarrassed, so she dropped the subject. She couldn't blame him for not wanting her prying into his life. Instead she continued with the garden. He didn't seem to know much about plants, but as they walked past the shrubs, she liked the way he touched the petals of the bird of paradise blooms, as though they were something to be valued, and brushed the back of his hand over the shiny green leaves of the *jejarum*. The rest he'd learn.

"Come," she said.

She drew the young Malay along a path that ran round to the rear of Hadley House, where a tall cypress hedge formed the edge of the separate part of the garden.

"This is the veg patch," she told him, and led him through an archway cut into the hedge. "This is probably where Malik, our head gardener, will keep you working first of all."

It was just a vegetable garden. That was all. Nothing special. She liked to grow vegetables even more than flowers and performed much of the planting and picking herself. It was just something that was always there, a part of her life she took for granted. Until she saw Razak's reaction. His eyes were huge and his mouth hung open in astonishment.

"Very, very big," he murmured.

Was it? It seemed a normal size to her. "We manage to eat everything," she commented.

He held up three fingers. "You, *Tuan* Hadley, and boy."

"And the servants, of course. They eat the produce as well. It's only fair, as they are the ones who have to chase off the monkeys and parrots. I swear there is one particular monkey with a bald tail who believes I grow all the melon and squash just for his personal use."

He laughed. For the first time something relaxed in this young man's stance, and he no longer seemed ready to run off like one of the small deer that ventured into the garden occasionally. They would flee if you so much as blinked at them. She didn't want Razak to flee.

"Would you like to take some vegetables home with you?" she offered.

"I not a monkey. Not parrot."

Connie blushed. "I know."

He knelt on the red earth, plucked a yellow pepper from its stem and took a bite out of it. She could imagine it warm and sunny on his tongue. He looked up and he smiled at her, and in that moment she knew he would stay.

"Welcome to Hadley House," she said.

"Thank you. *Terimah kasih.*"

"Where did you learn to speak English?"

"I was houseboy. In Palur."

"Really? Well, if you prefer, you could be a houseboy here, and . . ."

But she could feel him withdraw. As if she'd suggested he step into a snake pit. He shook his head and sank his teeth into the yellow flesh of the pepper once more.

"I like veg patch."

She laughed. "So do I."

ꝑ·ꝑ

"Where have you been all this time?" Maya demanded.

Razak's arms were piled high with vegetables, with melons and adzuki beans and other greenery stacked all the way up to his chin.

"I went to Hadley House," he said. "Like you told me."

He moved over to the corner, opened his arms, and dropped the heap of produce on the floor. Dust rose in the air.

"Give it all to Salid for his pigs," Razak muttered. "I will eat nothing that *she* has grown."

Maya sat him down on the mat, poured him a cup of *chaya*, and waited cross-legged on the floor for her brother to come back to her. *The white lady has stolen him.*

"I asked," he said at last, "to work in the garden. Like you told me."

"Good."

"She took me over it." He paused, and Maya saw something of pleasure in his eyes. "It is a beautiful garden. So much space for just three people."

They both looked at their own tiny room and said nothing.

"Then?" she prompted.

"The vegetable garden is huge. She calls it her *veg patch*. It is five times the size of old Grenya's plot, remember him? He used to feed his family of ten off it, and still have plenty left over to sell in the market."

"I remember."

"She said it was grown for her family and her servants. But the servants must be selling it in the market and she doesn't realize." He shook his head in bemusement. "How could she be so stupid?"

"All whites are stupid about understanding anyone but themselves. What happened after that?"

"She left me with the head gardener. He comes from Penang and talks as if the garden is his own. I think he may be turning into a plant himself because he has strange growths on his feet that look like roots and his tongue is as loose as an aging leaf."

Eagerness sharpened Maya's voice. "What did this old leaf say?"

"He told me that she takes the boy to school in Palur each morning and collects him when the sun is high. She no longer drives. Their *syce* drives her instead."

"What else?"

"She rides her horse early when the morning is still cool. The *Tuan Besar* leaves when it is still dark and doesn't come back until the sun has set. Sometimes they drive out to friends in the evening. The gardener says the *syce* takes them. That is because the *Tuan* likes to drink and the roads are rough."

He stopped talking and studied his sister closely from under his long dark lashes. "You are satisfied?"

She smiled at him. "I love this gardener as if he were my own father."

"More than our own father, you mean."

They both laughed, but it was a fragile ripple of sound in the hot room. Their father was a tin-mine worker. He used to beat them and his wife whenever the mood took him, but one day he vanished. *Gone to live with his brother snakes*, their mother used to say.

Maya gestured toward the pile of vegetables in the corner. "Let me sell them."

Razak shook his head. "They are fit only for pigs."

Maya sighed but didn't argue. Instead she laid out before him a meal of lamb curry with rice, and a Tiger beer to wash it down.

"I had a good day with the flower selling," she lied.

She didn't tell him about the envelope she'd found behind the pots on the shelf.

ꁰꁰ

Connie was restless. It rained that night, a fierce, shuddering downpour that seemed to shake the house and rattle the roof. She checked on Teddy, but he hadn't stirred.

When she reached her own bedroom, Nigel was sitting on the bed removing his socks. He had nice feet, smooth and elegantly shaped. Which was just as well because his lower legs and lower arms were about all she got to see of his person, these days. For a moment she wondered what he would do if she walked over to him and started undoing his shirt buttons. Flap her away probably, the way he flapped at moths that sneaked in through the shutters.

"I didn't think much of that Fitzpayne fellow," Nigel commented. "Don't like his ideas."

Connie sighed and stretched out on her side of the bed, arms above her head. The murmur of the fan on the ceiling was as incessant as the rain.

"No," she agreed. "I didn't take to him. But he's a friend of Johnnie's, so we couldn't exactly throw him out on his ear, could we?"

Nigel grunted and departed into his dressing room. She raised both legs straight in the air. Her skirt tumbled around her hips and she enjoyed the pleasure of having naked thighs, the breeze from the fan brushing against them, warm as someone's breath. She closed her eyes.

"Constance, I don't think you should employ that native boy."

"Why ever not?"

"No good will come of it."

She could hear him puffing, his breath strained. He performed fifty push-ups every night in his dressing room.

"Nigel, I just want to help them. After what I did, it's the least I can offer."

"It wasn't your fault, Macintire said so. You don't owe them anything."

She said nothing. Her hand stroked the curve of her calf and the soft underside of her knee.

"Better not to get involved, old thing."

Old thing. She swung her legs over the edge of the bed and jumped to her feet. She walked over to his dressing room and leaned against the door frame. He was forcing himself through his push-ups, elbows shaking now, his cheeks vermilion. A vein clicked in and out at his temple.

"Nigel, what if he's right?"

"Who?"

"That Fitzpayne fellow. What if the Japanese do come down through the jungle from the north? We'll be right in their path."

"There's no chance"—he struggled to straighten his arms—"of that."

"But shouldn't we be prepared? Just in case. I mean . . ."

"No need."

"But it seems to me that . . ."

"Don't fret so."

She bit her tongue and waited against the door frame while he finished his exercises. God, she needed a cigarette. She always did when she was annoyed. Nigel eventually stood up and headed straight into the bathroom, splashing water around like a hippo. It was the same every night. When he emerged, wrapped in his silk robe, she was still waiting. He looked at her and frowned.

"Let it go, Constance. The Japs have no backbone and no aircraft worth a damn against our Brewster Buffaloes. They don't stand a chance and they know it, so don't get yourself upset about it. People like Johnnie know what they're talking about. Take no notice of Fitzpayne and his like. They're spineless." He patted her shoulder and climbed into bed, lowering the mosquito net around himself like a bridal veil.

Connie perched on the edge of the bed. "But we should still be prepared."

"For heaven's sake, Constance, even if by the remotest chance they did somehow get through the mountains and the jungle, they'd have more sense than to harm people like us. They need our rubber. They need me to make it for them. So," he smiled at her reassuringly, "come to bed and stop worrying."

She walked into her own dressing room and dropped her clothes on the floor, inspecting her naked body in the cheval glass with a critical eye.

"But they don't need me," she murmured. "Or Teddy."

ว·ร

"I want to make love to you, Connie."

The words made the lines blur on the page of the book she was reading. Even now, she recalled it. It was *The Big Sleep* by Raymond Chandler. Sho had brought her high up into the hills, miles away from anyone or any place she knew. The clarity and the coolness of the air made her giddy with relief. They were seated on a patch of grass in the shade, back to back, reading their books, propping each other up like bookends.

"I want to make love to you, Connie."

She'd put down her book and kissed Sho's mouth. Slowly she unbuttoned his white shirt and kissed his heart. Her hands caressed his chest, fingering each muscle, each rib, each rise and fall as his breath came fast. His skin tasted as warm and spicy as cinnamon toast.

They made love in the open air, something she had never done before, with only a gibbon monkey booming somewhere in the distance and the sound of crickets all around them. It felt extraordinary. The beat of her own heart thundered in her ears and her body stretched its limbs and abandoned itself like a cat in the sun. She knew she had jumped off a cliff but instead of falling to earth, she was flying.

ϑ·ϛ

It was still dark when she woke, but at least the rain had stopped. She could hear it dripping from the trees outside like tears. She lay flat on her back, remembering. Once when she and Sho were naked on the bed in a hotel room in KL popping tiny wild strawberries into each other's mouths and laughing as he painted one of her nipples with the pink juice, he had asked, "When were you last held by your husband like this?" He wrapped his arms around her, trailing sticky fingers down her shoulder blades and over her hip bones.

"Years ago."

He dipped his head and licked her nipple, and she moaned.

"And when did you last make love with your husband?"

"Years and years ago."

Four years and three months ago, to be exact. Her eyes struggled now to find her husband's shape in the darkness. In the first months of their marriage everything had been normal, or as normal as she imagined other newlyweds to be, which meant a kiss good night before Nigel turned out the light every weekday and sex on Saturdays and Sundays. He worked damn hard on the estate, she told herself. He was too tired during the week. It was normal.

But the way Harriet Court went on about her demure and running-to-fat husband, Henry, pestering her in bed several times a night—*voracious* was her word for him—Connie did wonder, how normal was *normal?* After Teddy was born Nigel didn't touch her for a year and then only because she instigated it. It was when she suggested another baby that his interest in her was rekindled, but the sex became perfunctory. No lingering. No licking of nipples. No mouth-to-mouth kissing. Outwardly she smiled and kissed his cheek; inwardly she screamed.

For whatever reason the second baby didn't happen, and Nigel looked at her as if he'd been stabbed in the stomach each month when the first treacherous spots of her period started.

"I'm sorry," she used to say. Because she *was* sorry. Sorry for both of them.

"That's all right, old thing. Next time, I expect."

But his brown eyes looked muddy and his mouth was tight. Eventually he'd stopped hoping. Stopped trying. He left her alone on her side of the bed and lay alone on his, politely rebuffing any advances from her. That was when the chasm spread down the center of the sheet and Connie had watched it widen. Night by night, year by year. Bed became a place that she dreaded because it was a place of . . . Of failure. Of frustration. Of loneliness. Take your pick. Some nights she would sit outside on the veranda braving the mosquitoes, reading her book until the early hours of the morning. Nigel never mentioned that she was missing from his bed. Sometimes she wondered if he noticed.

She rolled onto her side, facing her husband's back, listening to his steady breathing and the murmur of the wind ruffling the leaves of the coral tree outside. For a long time she lay like that, eyes wide open. Then she moved forward and gently wrapped herself around his body, molding her curves to his, her arm draped across his waist. He didn't move. Didn't break the rhythm of his breath. But she was certain he was awake and, what was worse, that he was aware that she knew he was awake.

She remained like that, unmoving for what must have been half an hour, breathing quietly against the back of his neck, inhaling the scent of him again. When she finally rolled away onto her own side of the bed, he made no sound. The silence in the room belonged to a grave.

CHAPTER EIGHT

Connie loved Harriet Court because of her laugh. It was a raucous, witchlike cackle that had a tendency to silence a room, but it always gave Connie the giggles. Harriet wore her dark hair in a sharp bob at jaw level and possessed strong, almost masculine features, in total contrast to her dreamy blue eyes and soft little chin, which she often propped in her hand, as if her head and all it contained were too heavy for the narrow stem of her neck.

"Tell all, dearest Connie," Harriet declared when Connie joined her in the shade on the veranda at the club. A tall glass of iced lime juice awaited her, but Connie waved a hand at one of the boys to bring two coffees as well. "A little bird with a handlebar mustache," Harriet continued, "informed me that the gorgeous Flight Lieutenant John Blake blew into town and headed straight for the Hadley Estate without so much as a nod to anyone else." She grinned at Connie. "Now I wonder why that was."

"You've got it all wrong. Johnnie arrived here with a friend from KL and Nigel invited them over."

"Honest truth?"

"Cross my heart."

"Very well, I'll believe you." Harriet leaned forward, eyes curious. "Is he still as handsome as ever?"

"Handsomer!"

They both laughed and fell into a discussion of arrangements for the next charity event they were organizing, a dance to raise more money for the Buy a Bomber for Britain fund. All the colonial wives were engaged in similar activities. It made them feel they were doing their bit for the war effort back home, while their husbands beavered away shipping out rubber, tin, and rice for the troops. Patriotism was worn like a badge, despite being so many thousands of miles away from their homeland.

"Harriet, what does Henry say about the war?" Henry Court, Harriet's husband, was a top-level accountant, constantly closeted in smoky offices with the colonial ruling echelon. "He must have some inside knowledge, surely."

"The war in Europe, you mean?"

"No. Here in Malaya. Does he believe it will happen?"

"Good heavens, no." Harriet's broad nose flared, reminding Connie of her horse when it balked at a fence. "That's an absurd idea."

"Is it?"

"Why? Did Johnnie Blake say anything?"

"No. Quite the opposite. He says we have a force of three hundred and thirty-five first-class aircraft defending Malaya. He thinks the Japanese won't attempt it."

"Well, he should know. He's the one who sits in on the High Command powwows. Henry says it would be impossible. Singapore is too well guarded, and the rest of the peninsula's coast is constantly patrolled by the RAF."

"So they say."

"Oh, come on, Connie. General Brooke-Popham and General Percival know what they're doing. Don't look so gloomy. The Japanese will never get through that jungle.

"Johnnie brought a friend with him who seemed to think it was possible."

"Well, tell him he's bloody wrong," Harriet snorted.

Connie wanted to believe her. Their coffee arrived and she sipped it thoughtfully in silence, eyes focused on the Malay figure at the other end of the veranda. The figure was small and female, polishing the brass fittings on a sea chest that was used to hoard costumes for masquerade parties. It was all too easy for the eye not even to notice the army of native workers who kept the club running smoothly.

"Harriet, everyone here claims that the Japanese have no discipline and no backbone. But I don't think that's true."

"What on earth makes you think that?"

"Their army has already taken Korea, Manchuria, and most of China. Of course it must be disciplined and well equipped to do that."

Harriet stared at her, open mouthed. "Are you out of your mind? The Japanese will turn and run with their tails between their legs at the first shot, I assure you."

"Harriet, they have a huge air force."

"Who says so?"

"Someone told me."

"Well, your *someone* has got his facts wrong. Anyway, everyone knows the Japs make terrible pilots. They have no sense of balance because they're carried about on their mothers' backs as children. Dreadful habit."

Despite being seated in the shade, Connie picked up her sunglasses lying on the table beside her and put them on. She didn't want Harriet to see her eyes. Because she was remembering Sho jumping from rock to rock as he crossed a river at the bottom of a wooded valley. In the green moist air his bare limbs looked golden, flashing in and out of the dappled sunlight, his leaps as free and effortless as a flying fish. There was nothing wrong with his balance. Nothing at all. When he reached the far side he plucked a durian fruit from high up in the tree and came bounding back with it for her. He presented the thorny husk to her on his knees and bowed his head to her feet as if the foul-smelling fruit were the keys to his kingdom. She recalled now the feel of his breath on her toes and the warmth of his hair as she crouched and ran her fingers through it.

In some strange way, he was a man who belonged to the ground, not in the air. She wasn't quite sure why. Maybe it had something to do with the way he would pull her down onto the red earth or the hard tiled floor or the tatami mat in the shack in the forest. The skin of her back became a mosaic of scrapes and scratches and insect bites. Not that it mattered; Nigel never saw them.

"I think," she said to Harriet, "we are the ones who are in for a shock."

Connie rose to her feet and crossed the veranda to where the servant

THE WHITE PEARL · 67

girl was on her knees polishing a brass table. Her dark limbs glistened with sweat with the effort she was putting into it. Her back was toward the two women.

"Maya? It is you, isn't it?"

The girl looked up. Black fringed eyes, alert and guarded. No surprise in them. So she'd known it was Connie sitting there.

"Yes, *mem*," the girl said. She looked older than she had before, less of a child in her bland white uniform and with her hair pinned up in a knot with a flower at the back of her head. The tone was polite, no hint of the fury Connie had feared.

"You got the job then?"

"Yes, *mem*. Thank you." The girl remained on her knees.

Connie had pulled strings to arrange for Maya to be offered a position working two half days a week at the club. A silence as thick as river slime slid between them, and the girl lowered her eyes submissively to the table once more. A fat glossy fly settled on the flower in her hair, and Connie flicked it away. This was the first time she had seen or spoken to the girl since the day of the accident.

"Maya, I'm so sorry. *Maaf.*"

The girl murmured something inaudible in Malay but didn't look up. Her hand curled tight round the polishing cloth she was holding. They remained there like that, neither moving. Connie was aware of Harriet watching them, mystified, and of the rattle of the overhead fan like dead bones in a can.

"Maya, I could do with your help this afternoon, if you're free."

At last. The black eyes flicked up to her face. Cautious.

"I'll pay you for your time," Connie added.

The small mouth curved up at its corners, but there was no trace of a smile in the eyes. "Yes. I help you."

"Thank you." Connie rested a hand on the girl's shoulder and felt the heat of her skin under the thin white cotton.

৯·৫

Maya was on edge. She skulked two steps behind Constance Hadley as they walked into the dry-goods store on Marlborough Street. *Walked?*

No, this white lady with the pale hair and the ivory skin didn't walk. Maya watched every step, the way she took possession of each scrap of ground her foot touched, as though it had been put there just for her. The air seemed to part for her like a pair of damp curtains and close behind her again, shutting others out. So private. Maya narrowed her eyes. So secretive.

"Wait here."

Maya obeyed. She tucked herself against some shelves and tugged the pins from her hair, shaking it into a black veil around her face. The last time she was in this store, she'd been thrown out into the muddy gutter for pocketing a handful of rice. She ducked behind a tower of canned fruit and stared at the illustration on the labels: peaches. What white-skinned fool would eat pretend peaches when they could be had fresh in the market every day?

She watched the white lady. Studied her gestures. The way she held her back straight and her neck long. Her smile at the whiskery man behind the counter who was in a brown overall with buttons like black eyes down his front. The lady's easy confidence. It came to her as naturally as a fish to water. She was pointing to a sack of flour and a sack of rice.

"Shall I arrange to have them delivered, Mrs. Hadley?"

"No, thank you, Mr. Endicott. I'll take them with me in the car. And these." She handed him a list.

The man's cheeks swelled with pleasure as if he'd stuffed his peaches into them. "Certainly, Mrs. Hadley. Would you care to take a seat for a moment? A cup of tea, Mrs. Hadley, while you wait? My boy could easily drive everything over in the van if . . ."

But she dismissed it with a shake of her head. With a pleasant but firm smile she sent him scuttling to his shelves. He glanced at Maya as he passed but barely saw her, his head was so full of dollar signs. He hustled together packets and cartons, stacked up on the counter, puffing when he had to climb a ladder to reach for boxes of candles.

Maya couldn't read words, but she could read pictures. Pictures of cows on the square cans, of pigs on the round ones. They were tins of meat. Pictures of tea leaves, coffee beans, and spoonfuls of sugar on the packets, and biscuits inside big colorful boxes. She watched bottles and matches being added to the pile, as well as a bag of dried beans and a large block of salt. The white lady nodded, satisfied, whenever something more arrived.

What was she doing? Was this like the *veg patch*? Far more than she needed because she was too stupid to know better?

"Maya, come here."

Maya moved closer.

"Choose one for yourself."

Maya looked at her blankly. What did she mean?

"I'm picking a green one for Teddy. They are his favorite," the lady continued with a light laugh.

She was holding a fat glass jar tucked under her arm and it was packed full of brightly colored sticks. Maya stood motionless, uncertain what to do.

The lady put her hand into the mouth of the jar and pulled out a green one, wrapped in a sort of shiny paper. "See?" she said. "This one is peppermint. The others are different flavors. Which one would you like?"

She was smiling encouragement, waiting for a response. And suddenly Maya understood. This lady was expecting to exchange her mother's death for a colored stick. It pained Maya's heart not to spit on her pretty white feet in her pretty white shoes.

She thrust her fingers into the jar and yanked out a stick. It was a red one. "*Terimah kasih*. Thank you, *mem*," she muttered.

"That's a black currant one."

Maya peered at the stick. What was she meant to do with it? Push it down the lady's throat?

"It's a stick of rock."

Rock?

"A kind of sweet." The *mem*'s words were gentle. "I think you'll like it." She rattled the jar, startling Maya. "The yellow ones are banana, the orange ones are peach, the striped one is watermelon, and . . ." She stopped, her eyes fixed on Maya's face. "It's nothing, Maya. Just a sweet."

Maya nodded. Then she hid behind her hair and slid her hand into the jar's jaws once more, snatching out a striped one. "For Razak."

"Of course."

The man in the overall and the buttons planted himself in front of them and preened his whiskers like a brown mouse. "Is that all, Mrs. Hadley?"

"Yes, thank you. Put it on my account, please."

"Is your car outside?"

"Yes."

"Boy!" he shouted.

A native youth appeared from a back room holding a broom. He ignored Maya but smiled shyly at the *mem.*

"Load up, boy," the whiskers ordered.

"I carry rock, *mem,*" Maya volunteered.

With the jar gripped like a baby under her arm, she followed the white lady out of the store.

Ꙅ·Ϛ

Maya sat up front next to the *syce* in the car. He was Chinese, Ho Bah, a thin bony face with gray hair like a bird's nest under his chauffeur's cap. His dark green uniform hung loose on him, as if he hoped one day to grow fatter. He didn't speak to her. Didn't look at her. The car was American. Big and gaudy, like all Americans. Shiny chrome handles and a long purposeful nose.

She'd ridden in a car before, in the days when her mother used to sell her again and again. Sometimes white men's cars, sometimes black men's cars. It made no difference to her. With their clothes off in the dark, all men are the same. All men want the same. Some even did it to her in the car, some with their *syce* watching in the mirror. In a moment of panic she stared now at this silent Chinese driver, but no, she didn't recognize him. She was good with faces.

The car swung through the streets of Palur, and she enjoyed seeing people turn to stare at the sleek black motorcar as it purred past. But instead of taking the road north, up toward the Hadley plantation, Maya was surprised when it left the broad avenues of brick buildings and threaded its way through narrow lanes toward the wharves. Why were they heading down there? To the quays and the shantytown where she and Razak lived?

Then it dawned on her. It was obvious that this *mem*, this white lady, this killer of her mother, was going to help her. By giving her all this. She pictured the mountains of canned meat in the boot, the sacks of flour and rice in the back, the candles and the biscuits on the seat. She grinned, she couldn't help it. She and Razak would be set up for months. But she would have to get one of the local urchins to guard it while they were out. She'd pay him with sweet sticks.

A bicycle rickshaw swerved in front of their path and wharf coolies carrying rattan baskets on their backs blocked the narrow route that led to the railway track and the shantytown. She wanted to yell at them. To tell bony-face to blast his horn at them. The wharf was seething with activity and she could see a lumbering merchant ship with red funnels, busy unloading its cargo on hoists. Sweat and heat shimmered in the air, heavy with the stink of the river. She grew impatient and leaned forward as if she could force the car to move faster. Just then, a gap appeared on the left and she was about to urge the *syce* through it, but he slipped neatly down a side road to the right.

"No! *Tak!*" she breathed. "No!"

The *syce* looked at her for the first time, his eyes dark slits of dislike. "Quiet, gutter trash," he muttered.

She swiveled around on the seat. "*Mem,*" she cried out, "where we go?"

The white lady lifted her eyes from the list of items in her hand and gazed at Maya as though she'd forgotten she was there. "To our boat, of course. To *The White Pearl.*"

·CHAPTER NINE·

"Fuck!"

The teeth of the saw had slipped.

"Fuck!" Madoc swore again when he saw the blood flowing from his knuckles. It stained the timber and dripped onto the ground.

Instantly a shiny bootlace of black flies swarmed all over it. Out here in the jungle, cuts didn't heal; infection set in no matter how fast you threw iodine over them. Madoc was making window frames for the new casino that he was building alongside Morgan's Bar, sawing lengths of timber on the open square of beaten earth that lay between the bar and the jetty. The smell of sawdust spiced the air, and beside him Kitty was wielding a strip of sandpaper, smoothing the edges of the wood when he had finished with them. As she straightened up to look at the damage, a pool of sweat sat like a creamy saucer of milk in the hollow of her ample breasts.

"Oh, Christ!" she moaned. "Come here." She seized his wrist and pressed down hard with her fist on the jagged edges of his flesh. "Inside."

Kitty frog-marched him into their kitchen, leaving him dripping into the sink while she dug out antiseptic and bandage. By the time she'd finished with him, his hand was clad in white gauze and his empty stomach burned from the quantity of brandy she'd chucked down him.

"Better?" she asked, inspecting him, her hands perched on her broad hips.

"Much."

"No more sawing today."

"I have to finish those windows before—"

"No more sawing." She wasn't smiling.

"Fuck!" he swore again.

She stepped close, so close he could smell the tang of her sweat. She patted his cheek and grinned. "Not now, tiger."

He laughed and kissed her full on the lips. "Cook me some breakfast and then I'll go into town instead."

She pulled away and frowned at him. "What for?"

"Business."

She didn't ask further, though her eyebrows lifted and he could feel her disapproval. She turned to the stove. "Eggs?"

"Sounds good."

She was one of the few women he had come across who knew how to keep her mouth shut.

"I'll finish the sawing while you're in town," she said cracking eggs into a bowl.

"No need. I'll be OK to carry on with it tomorrow."

She shrugged one fleshy shoulder inside her loose tunic and he knew she'd do the sawing, whatever he said. As she threw a frying pan on the stove, he watched her. Her skin was the skin of a woman who has spent too long in the tropics but he loved to feel it, soft and pliant under his fingers. Even after nearly twenty-five years of marriage to this woman, he still wanted to touch her.

"Anything you want in town?" he asked.

"Yes. Salt."

Salt in the tropics was as essential as air. "I'll bring some back."

She turned to face him, a furrow creasing her brow. "Watch yourself, Madoc. In town."

He nodded. That was enough.

Kitty would be fifty in December, six years older than he was. She might have pigeon-gray hair and wrinkles like lace around her eyes; she might have lost two back teeth and have a wonky knee sometimes. But she had a will of iron. She'd patched up his wounds and dragged him out of jail more than once. She'd drunk champagne from a golden goblet with him, and she'd eaten bitter tree bark when there was nothing else. Either way, she'd stuck with him.

He'd watch himself all right. He still had a casino to build for her.

ఎ·౬

His boat chugged upriver, and the water moved like a brown shadow beneath him. Gray morning mist had swallowed it and was twining fingers up into the trees, stealing every landmark that would tell him where he was. It was just a shallow native boat, long and thin, with an ancient outboard engine hitched on the back, but it always got him where he wanted to go and was good when he needed to duck unseen into narrow outlets or hide out in the mangrove swamps.

He had business in town. In Tampang, seven miles by river. Something kicked into life in his gut at the prospect. *Christ, no. Behave, Madoc. Just get the job done and get your hide back home.* The trouble was that he was never satisfied, not with his life, not with Morgan's Bar. He craved more. Always more. He shook his head, hunching lower in the boat, and his eye was caught by a movement in the water. A snake as thick as his wrist was swimming past. Madoc was tempted to lean down and snatch it from the murky waters, to take it home as a meal for tonight, but at the last second he came to his senses. He withdrew his hand and set the boat leaping forward, the old engine complaining at the sudden burst of speed. Kitty knew him too well. *Watch yourself, Madoc.* She knew all about the lure of danger. How it bewitched him.

ఎ·౬

Tampang was less a town than a gob of spit in the mud of the jungle. This used to be tin country. Not any more, though. The tin was exhausted long ago, and the miners had moved on. Most had been shipped in from China, and a handful of them stayed behind. Chinese labor is made of stern stuff. It didn't take them long to knock the raw huddle of metal shacks into a proper community, to build solid houses. Some worked smallholdings of rubber trees; others traded in rice and coffee beans or spices, papayas, and pineapples. Men flocked in to find work, and it quickly expanded into what some called a town. Madoc still called it a gob of spit in the jungle.

Most of the houses were wooden, but a pretty little Buddhist temple with gold latticework and a set of bronze bells sat right in the middle of town. Its monks in their saffron robes gave a splash of color to the main street. A mosque, side by side with a stiff-necked Methodist chapel, added to the mix. A noisy market of native stalls offered him everything from a mynah bird in a cage and a hat of lizard skin to a scratched gramophone record of Noel Coward's "Mad about the Boy." He brushed aside the shouts of the hawkers and crossed the street to the only hotel in town: the Ritz. He laughed at the name every time he pushed open its shabby doors.

"A bath," he requested.

The slender Malay girl who showed him to one of the private bathrooms slid her eyes sideways at him as she placed a towel in his hand and asked, "Will that be all?"

"That's all," he said firmly, shooing her out with a smack on the bottom and locking the door after her.

The tiny bathroom was filling up with steam, and when he'd stripped off his clothes he stared at his blurred image in the mirror on the wall. Not something he liked to do as he grew older because it was too much like looking at his father. Average height, passable-looking, but always on the wiry side. He regarded himself as a greyhound, fast and nimble, but also as Mr. Average, easily forgotten in a crowd. That suited him just fine.

With a sigh of pleasure he sank down into the bubbles, lit himself a cigar, and, with his bandaged hand balanced safely on the edge of the bath, he contemplated the options open to him.

꒦꒷

The sun had beaten back the mist by the time Madoc emerged, and the street had the look of a sleepy child, soft and lazy. He headed for the barber shop and settled into a chair.

"*Selamat datang.*" The Malayan barber greeted him with a bow. "Welcome."

Madoc knew that the man was a chatterbox, but he didn't mind that. It was surprising what you could pick up in these places. The young Indian male assistant wrapped a warm, damp towel around his jaw, and when their eyes met for an instant, the Indian raised an eyebrow. Madoc responded with the faintest of nods.

"Aiyee, trouble everywhere," the barber moaned as he set to work with a cutthroat razor and a flourish of his wrist. "Wild elephant trample my wife's maize field last night. And last week, her brother's boat seized by pirates from Sumatra." He spat on his nice clean floor. "They're the curse of the sea."

Madoc chuckled. "I don't think it's the elephants and the pirates you need to be worrying about right now. Even they will retreat if the Japs come."

"Japs no come," the man said with a wide smile. "We British."

"Let's hope you're right."

"I right. You see."

The chatter droned on until the job was done and the barber vanished behind a bamboo curtain to fetch a prized photograph of his new grandson in Penang. As soon as the curtain swung shut, the Indian assistant whipped up his apron and pulled a gun from his waistband. Madoc tabbed it at once: a Tokarev TT-33, a Russian service pistol. Good condition.

He didn't ask where it had come from, just slid it into the deep pocket of his jacket and slapped five dollars into the Indian's waiting palm. The transaction was conducted in silence and took less than a minute, so that when the barber bustled back, his customer was sitting up, bracing himself to admire the photograph and be patted with the obligatory aftershave. Christ, it stank.

❧

"Madoc, you stink like a brothel!"

Madoc laughed. He was seated at a table in a bar in Tampang, drinking with its Scottish owner, Andrew Tarrow. He was a tight-fisted bastard but knew where to find the right kind of girls and sold a good brandy. He was one of the white men who had gone native, adopting a waist sarong and living with a succession of Malayan girls, all with sleek black hair and narrow hips. "Interchangeable," Kitty claimed. "He doesn't even notice when one leaves and another arrives." But Madoc knew that wasn't true. Each time he saw this craggy Scot fall in love all over again with one of the black-eyed lovelies, he warned him. But it was always the same. They took him for all they could get and moved on. It was why Tarrow still labored day and night behind his bar to make a living when he should have had enough tucked away under his mattress to retire by now. He wasn't the only one. Malaya was littered with men like him.

The bar was dim, the shutters closed to keep out the heat. Flies droned, heavy-winged, too soporific to evade Tarrow's jabs with the flyswatter that never left his hand.

"Have you found me the two I ordered?" Madoc asked, getting down to business.

"Yes. I've got four for you to choose from. Arriving next week."

"How much?"

Tarrow gave him a slow, patient smile. "Wait till you see them. Then we'll negotiate."

"Good ones?"

"Mmm."

Madoc slapped twenty dollars on the table. "A down payment."

They vanished into Tarrow's pocket before a fly could even think of landing on them. Madoc was investing in two more girls for upstairs in Morgan's Bar. Trade was good with all the military personnel moving around the country. He finished his brandy, but before he could leave, Tarrow cleared his throat. Madoc eyed the nervous set of his mouth.

"What is it, Andrew?"

"It's Bull Chan."

"What about him?"

"He's in town."

"So?"

"He's looking for you."

Madoc felt a shiver in his bowels. He rose to his feet. "Thanks for the warning."

"What are we going to do, Madoc, you and I?"

"About Bull Chan?"

"No." Tarrow shook his head, and the gesture was a sad one. "If the bloody Japanese come. They'll massacre us all, every last one of us."

"Not," Madoc said quietly, "if you've taken out insurance."

"What the hell does that mean?"

"It means that I'm not willing to lose everything I've put together for Kitty and me."

"How do you plan on stopping the bastards from burning your place to the ground?"

Madoc kicked his chair back from the table. "I'm protecting it. The only way I know how."

꤮꤮

No hanging around this time; out of Tampang fast. Madoc bought a block of salt for Kitty but skirted the main street, sticking to the back alleyways heading down toward the riverbank. He moved quickly down the wooden steps to the jetty, where he'd left his boat tucked under one of the piers. His hand was throbbing and he knew it was the nerve endings dancing to the pulse of fear in his throat. Four more steps. The sun kicked up off the sluggish surface of the river in a warning flash and somewhere a tock-tock bird was calling its alarm.

The blow, when it came, lifted him off his feet and carried him down the last steps. The ground smacked him in the face, but he'd learned over the years to keep moving, so he rolled with the momentum, springing onto one knee, only to get a mouthful of boot. Something snapped. He tasted blood. Fought to focus.

"Madoc!"

The voice was harsh. Rough as a death rattle. Madoc knew it at once. Its owner was the man he'd been avoiding: Bull Chan. He was short and squat with a thick neck and a massive chest and was headman of the local Chinese triad. Madoc had crossed him before and only just lived to tell the tale. Chan was standing on the bottom step, a gun in his hand. The stupid part of Madoc's brain noticed it was a German Mauser HSc, a semiautomatic, but the other part, the smart part, saw that it was pointing straight at his chest.

He forced himself to his feet. On each side of him stood a Chinese thug.

"Well, Bull Chan, what a pleasure. I heard that you'd moved down to KL. That you'd taken over Han Tu's patch." He picked up his pack of salt lying on the grass and turned to leave. "Don't mind me, I'm just off."

"Madoc!"

A metal bar slapped down on his shoulder. Christ! One side of his face went numb.

"Get your bloody thugs off me, Chan!"

"This is *my* river, Madoc."

"Sure it is."

"So stay off it."

"What do you mean, Bull? I'm clean. Just a few opium runs up the coast now and then. Just to keep my hand in. Nothing much. Never on your territory, Bull."

"You have shit for brains, Madoc. A sewer rat that eats its own tail."

"You've got me wrong, Bull."

"I know you been gun-running."

"Not me."

"German Karabiner rifles. Upriver."

"No."

"Your mouth is a dog's arse, full of shit."

"Listen, Bull, you've been fed wrong . . ." He reached for the Tokarev pistol in his waistband.

Bull Chan's boot lashed out. It slammed into Madoc's groin. Pain raced up through his body and exploded in his brain.

"Madoc, you dead meat."

The metal bars fell. *Kitty, I didn't watch myself.*

CHAPTER TEN

*N*ever.

　　Maya stared down at the narrow gangplank in front of her feet, and at the oily water of Palur harbor swirling beneath it, licking up at the jetty posts with long tongues of spume.

Never in this lifetime.

The white lady bounded off the gangplank and onto the yacht with a carton of canned meat under one arm and four bags of sugar under the other. As if it were easy. Once on deck, she disappeared. Maya backed off two paces, still clutching the jar of sweet sticks to her chest. Some distance behind her on the quayside, the Hadleys' car was parked and the chauffeur was unloading the goods from the boot.

"Maya!" The white lady's voice called from inside the yacht. "I want you to help put away the . . ."

Maya stopped listening. She could vanish back into the crowds on the wharf, away from these swaying, shifting water-homes that the sea could devour in one mouthful. She tightened her grip on the sweet sticks.

"Going on board?"

Maya spun around. The broad figure of a white man was standing right behind her, too close for comfort. Instead of the usual European uniform of shirt and shorts, he was dressed in loose black trousers like the Chinese wore, an open-necked tunic over them. Her eyes were level with his chest, and she could see dark wiry hairs twisting up from beneath the tunic. It was extraordinary the way white men had hairs springing from their bodies in strange places, but when she lifted her eyes to this white man's face, she forgot about his hair and knew she had to be careful. This man had a cool gray gaze that would sneak into her mind if she didn't keep the shutters down tight.

"Going on board?" he asked again, and she sensed he was laughing at her.

"Yes."

"Don't let me stop you."

He had blocked off her escape route.

Her cheeks were rigid as she turned to face the gangplank. It swayed alarmingly. Abruptly, a pair of strong hands lifted her under her armpits from behind, marched her out onto the plank, and deposited her in the middle of it. She stood where he'd put her, too frightened to scream.

"It won't bite you," the man laughed. "Get aboard."

He gave her a prod in the small of her back and she scampered forward, clambering on deck in a rush, almost dropping her jar. Her heart hammered in her throat as the boat rocked beneath her feet.

"So is this your first time on a boat?" He laughed easily, still standing in the middle of the wretched plank, scarcely aware of the way it bucked beneath him.

She glared at him. "What you want?"

"Would you please inform Mrs. Hadley that I'm here?"

"What name?"

But at that moment *Mem* Hadley emerged from deep inside the boat's belly and saw the man standing on her gangplank. Maya noticed a flash of annoyance cross her face before she adjusted it to a bright smile.

"Good day, Mr. Fitzpayne. What brings you down here?"

"I was looking at a boat for someone"—he gestured along the quay—"and saw you unloading your car. I came across to offer a hand."

"How kind of you."

But her words were stiff and her smile was uninviting. She advanced toward the gangplank to return to the car, forcing the intruder to retreat.

"Maya," she said as she stepped off the boat, "take the sweet jar down into the galley and put it in one of the lockers, please."

Galley? Lockers? What new language was this? Maya felt the boat lurch under her and her stomach churned, but she hurried down the steps in front of her, anything rather than risk the gangplank again. She dropped down into the bowels of the boat. Immediately varnished wood and brass wrapped themselves around her, glossy and gleaming, and she stared open mouthed. She had expected something rough. Slatted benches to sit on and a few tea chests to contain things. That was what she'd seen on fishing boats and sampans, and that was what she had expected here. Not this luxury.

I could live here. Me and Razak.

She was about to push the jar into one of the many cupboards that covered the walls, when the boat gave a subdued hiccup, knocking her off balance. She righted herself and glared out of one of the small round windows.

The river was tossing up waves. Playing with her.

ꑚ·ꑔ

"That's a fine yacht you have, Mrs. Hadley."

"Thank you." Connie continued walking briskly along the jetty toward the car on the quayside.

"Have you owned her long?"

"A few years."

Nine years, to be precise. Nigel had bought the sleek bermuda-rigged schooner for Connie as a wedding present, and named her *The White Pearl* in her honor.

"Do you sail her often?" Fitzpayne persisted.

"Often enough to suit us."

In the early years they used to take her out every weekend, but now it had dwindled to an occasional jaunt down the straits and around the islands with friends. Like everything else in their marriage, it was for show only.

"Ho Bah," she said to her driver as they reached the car, "I'll take these." She scooped up a box of biscuits, a pack of bandages, and a small sack of coffee beans. "If you can bring the flour and . . ."

Ho Bah made a grunting noise in his nose. It indicated disapproval. He had folded his arms across his chest. She sighed. The trouble was that Ho Bah was a good age now—he had been *syce* to Nigel's father for many years—and believed he was above many of the tasks that a chauffeur normally undertook. But Nigel refused to pension him off.

"Let me," Fitzpayne interrupted, and swung a sack onto each shoulder without waiting for a reply from her, striding off back toward the boat.

Something about this whole encounter made Connie uneasy. It felt as though Fitzpayne had sought it out and deliberately maneuvered her into it, yet she couldn't imagine why. With her arms laden she caught up with him and in silence they walked the length of the jetty, past the other yachts rocking at their moorings. Out on the muddy river, sampans and narrow fishing boats scurried about their business, while a westerly wind blew the odor of the sea from the stinking fishing nets draped like oversized cobwebs over the quay. Natives in wide coolie hats sat lazily mending them hour after hour in the scorching sun.

When they reached the gangplank of *The White Pearl*, Fitzpayne paused, his face half hidden from her by the sacks.

"Mrs. Hadley, are you thinking of sailing away from Palur?"

"Mr. Fitzpayne, you ask a lot of questions."

"That's because boats are my business."

"What exactly is it you do with boats?"

"I sell them."

"Well, I'm afraid this one is not for sale."

For the first time he fixed his eyes on hers directly in a sharp, assessing stare. He was probably in his late thirties, with strong features, not handsome because his jaw was too heavy and his brow too prominent, emphasized by the way he wore his thick brown hair swept back from it. It was a stern and uncompromising statement of who he was. She was just about to turn from him and continue along the plank when a gust of wind snatched at the butter-yellow hem of her dress and lifted its skirt. It flew up around her, and she saw his gaze linger on her bare legs.

She flicked down her skirt with impatience and went on board to the saloon, where she found Maya perched in a corner like a small brown owl, eyes wide and head swiveling back and forth at every creak of the boat. The sweet jar was still clamped to her chest.

"Are you all right, Maya?" Connie dumped everything on the table.

"Yes, *mem*."

"You don't look too good."

"Yes, *mem*."

Connie approached and touched her forehead. Her skin was cold and clammy.

"Is it the boat, Maya? Does its movement make you feel ill?"

"No, *mem*. I like boat."

"Would you prefer to wait back at the car?"

"No, *mem*." Her eyes sank deep into her head, and she swallowed hard as though about to be sick.

"I'll make us some tea."

A moment later, Fitzpayne appeared with the sacks.

"Could you stow them in the forward locker, please, Mr. Fitzpayne? Would you care for a cup of tea?" She was confident he'd say no.

"Thank you, I would. I'll just fetch the rest of the boxes."

"There's no need, I can—"

"No trouble. Back before the kettle boils."

He vanished. *Damn the man!*

৯·৫

Maya felt sick. A sea monster was blundering around inside her stomach. The white lady had killed her mother and now she had turned the curse onto Maya herself, somehow making her ill with just a touch of her hand.

Maya had seen it happen before, out in the jungle. A native spirit-man. He could heal with the breath from his nose or he could kill with the touch of a finger. Her stomach heaved, and she felt the sea monster's tentacles slither up to her throat. She moaned. The white lady immediately abandoned her teapot and stalked her again, touching her head this time. Soft, dangerous strokes.

She couldn't run, as she did from Hakim. She was trapped by the gangplank and by the man with the big shoulders. He was standing near the steps, drinking his tea, smiling at her. Waiting for her to die.

ఎ·ဌ

"She doesn't look well," Connie said.

"Never been on the water before, I suspect," Fitzpayne commented. He was still standing by the door, watching her.

"Why are you here, Mr. Fitzpayne?" she asked quietly.

"I told you. Looking at boats."

"For what purpose?"

"I like to keep my eyes open." He glanced around the saloon. "It's obvious to a blind man that you're planning to flee on *The White Pearl*."

Connie's cheeks flushed. Sweat trickled into her shoes. "Do you really think my husband is wrong when he says that the Japanese cannot bring an army into the Malayan jungle?"

"With the greatest respect, he is talking like a colonial. Oblivious to everything but the glory of the British Empire, ignoring what is under his nose."

"What do you mean?"

"The Japanese economy is in ruins. Its silk trade to America and Europe made up forty percent of its total exports, and now their market has collapsed. It needs to find its raw materials elsewhere."

"But not here, surely."

"Why not here? And Siam, and Burma, and Sumatra, and the Philippines, and—"

"Enough! The League of Nations will prevent them."

He stepped forward and placed his cup down on the table with a scornful laugh. "Like they prevented the war in Europe? The League is a toothless old dog. It has no power. The Japanese know that. Their prime minister, General Tojo, will not stand by and let the oil embargo imposed on Japan by America continue with impunity."

She could hear his breath harsh in the sudden silence. "Tell me, Mrs. Hadley, what would you do in their situation? Sit in your empty kitchen and starve?" His gray eyes were hard. "Or arm yourself and fight to survive?"

Connie rose to her feet. "Not all of us are ready to steal what is not ours. My husband is an honorable man who has brought a good living to thousands of Malay natives. So I'll thank you not to speak ill of someone who . . ."

He bowed to her crisply. The way Sho used to. Then he stood upright and with a cold smile said, "My mistake. I apologize."

For a moment they stared at each other before Connie nodded briefly. "Come, Maya. Time to leave."

The girl shook her head. "I stay."

"What?"

"It's the gangplank," Fitzpayne said.

With an unexpected boisterous laugh he swept the girl onto his shoulder as easily as one of the sacks, then leaped up the steps and off the boat with Maya mewing like a kitten. The moment she was deposited on the jetty, she scampered off into the milling crowd. Connie stood on the deck and watched her go.

"She's taken my sweet jar," she muttered.

Fitzpayne raised a hand in farewell and set off up the quay. Connie didn't like the way he walked—as if he could march through anything. But she was certain that they would both be back.

ᔪ·ᕮ

"What are you running from, little whore?"

No, no, no. Not Hakim. Maya's heart jerked in her chest. She swerved to avoid his fist and dodged behind a fish stall, but one of the wolf cubs seized her from behind and hauled her over to Hakim.

"Where have you been hiding, little whore?"

"Nowhere, Hakim. I've been working."

The slap, backhanded, landed on her jaw and she heard something crunch in the back of her neck. Pinpoints of light wavered across her vision.

"You work for me, whore!"

"No." She spat at him, but it had no force and fell in an aimless arc between them.

"The Purple Parrot. Every night this week," he hissed. "The stupid Russian bitch has knifed herself."

Maya's eyes widened.

"So you'd better be there. Or I'll send my boys to fetch you and they won't be as friendly as me. To you. Or to your brother."

His black eyes were sucking the life out of her, turning her into a dead thing. She spat again and this time it hit.

He snatched the jar of sweet sticks from her arms, ignoring her whimpers of dismay, and swaggered away. If only the Russian bitch had sunk her knife between Hakim's greasy shoulder blades.

CHAPTER ELEVEN

Connie would fight to survive; she knew she would.

Sit in your empty kitchen and starve?

She pulled open the top drawer of the chest of drawers in her dressing room and lifted out a pile of neatly folded scarves made from finest Chinese silk.

Or arm yourself and fight to survive?

"Yes, Mr. Fitzpayne," she admitted in the privacy of her own room, "you are right. Whether it's a country or an individual, it doesn't matter; we fight to exist. For Teddy, I intend to survive."

She slid her hand to the bottom of the drawer and her fingers brushed against something hard. She curled them around it and drew out an object that glinted in the shaft of sunlight, sending a rainbow shimmering up the wall. It was a silver cigarette case. She clicked it open and regarded the cigarettes inside it with distaste. A year ago, when she first hid it under her scarves, it had contained ten cigarettes and now only three remained. She removed one and snapped the case shut. The small metallic sound made her heart flip and her hand tremble. Her eye could not resist the pull of the elegant engraving in pride of place in the center of the lid—the initials *S.T.*, initials branded on her brain. Shohei Takehashi.

Why could she not hurl it in the bin even now?

"Caught you."

Flight Lieutenant John Blake laughed and threw himself down in the rattan chair beside Connie's. She was seated on the veranda finishing her cigarette, inhaling the smoke in long cool threads, exhaling it abruptly to dispel the clouds of insects that hummed around her head. All the time she was watching the quiet figure of Razak as he raked the azalea bed on the other side of the lawn.

"I thought you'd given up smoking, Connie."

"I did." She laughed, the tension trickling from her as she stretched her limbs on the bamboo chaise longue. Why did Johnnie always have that effect on her? "So don't tell Nigel."

Johnnie put a finger to his lips in a pact of silence. He had good fingers, long and capable. Trustworthy hands. She could imagine them on the control column of an aircraft, holding the lives of others in their grip. He smiled at her, blue eyes bright with amusement, and drew out a pack of Dunhill cigarettes from his top pocket. He was in uniform again, and it suddenly struck her as ominous.

"Not leaving are you, Johnnie?"

"'Fraid so. My Brewster Buffalo calls."

She sat up, swinging her feet to the floor. "Why? What's happened?"

"Oh, you know, a bit of a flap on. Rumors flying around."

"What rumors?"

"Nothing to take a blind bit of notice of, I promise you." But he rubbed a knuckle over his chin.

So it was a lie. She sensed that his mind and soul were already up in the sky, strapped into his Brewster Buffalo. But still he had come to Hadley House.

She stood up and pulled him to his feet. "Come on, let's take a stroll."

"Where's Teddy?"

"He's at his friend Jack's birthday party, eating mounds of jelly and showing off his Interceptor, no doubt. It was very generous of you. He will be so disappointed to have missed your departure."

"He's a fine boy."

She smiled and slipped an arm through his as they walked along the path, past the tulip trees with their fleshy orange flowers. Everything was damp and clammy after an earlier downpour, which had encouraged the cicadas to give vent with frenzied energy. She let her footsteps fall into rhythm with Johnnie's, his polished shoes crunching the gravel, his blue-gray trousers hanging crisp and freshly pressed on his long limbs, lean as sticks. He always had the knack of making her feel he would prefer to be here than anywhere else on earth. She enjoyed the warmth of his arm against hers as they strolled, her body starved of such contact, but she never betrayed it by even a fraction of pressure beyond what was correct between friends.

"Take care," she said. "You know I'll worry. Nigel too, of course."

He stopped suddenly, pulling her up short. They had wandered through the archway in the hedge and entered the vegetable garden, but she had a feeling that he was looking inward rather than outward. When he raised his hands and wiped them over his cropped blond hair, it was with a lurch of misery that she realized what was happening. He was wiping away the fear that lay on him like sweat.

"Oh, Johnnie," she murmured, and circled her arms around him.

She could feel him shaking, small vibrations rippling through him as he stood, ashen and silent. For less than a minute he buried his face in her hair and she could hear him inhale deeply, and then he stepped back and turned his head away.

"My apologies, Connie," he muttered.

"Will it be bad?" she asked quietly.

"No, far from it." He straightened up. "Can't think what's up with me. Damned embarrassing." He shook himself and swung back to her with a smile on his face, which she pretended not to notice wasn't quite straight. "Nothing to get into a tizz over," he added. "Just that a convoy of Japanese troopships has been spotted out in the Pacific with battleship protection."

"Is it coming here?"

"Highly unlikely. Cloud cover is so extensive and so low that the sighting was only brief. Don't look alarmed." He tucked an arm around her waist, and they continued their progress past the melon bed. "They're probably heading for Saigon on a routine exercise. General Percival is being cautious, that's all."

"But you have to go out looking for them?"

He nodded. "That's the idea. Like finding a pin in a haystack, but my squadron boys have eyes like hawks."

"I wish you luck, Johnnie."

"Thanks." He paused awkwardly, and she wondered what was coming next. "I heard in the club that you had a bit of an accident yourself the other day."

She blinked hard. The yellow melons seemed to swell into suns. "Yes."

"Sorry about that."

She didn't want to discuss it. "Nigel is over in the smoke sheds," she told him.

"Right."

"Will you say good-bye to him?"

"Of course."

He removed his arm from her waist and his shadow separated from hers. "I don't have to ship out till late tonight, so I was thinking of going to the cinema."

"Oh, what a shame, Nigel has a white-tie gathering of the planters' council to attend this evening."

He leaned over and inspected a row of onions with exaggerated concentration. "I know." Without shifting his attention from the onions, he added casually, "It's Katharine Hepburn and Cary Grant in *The Philadelphia Story*. Supposed to be a stunner. I wondered whether you would like to come with me."

She hadn't expected that, and as she glanced up she found the figure of Razak in the archway, watching them. Slowly Connie let the breath out of her lungs.

༄·༄

"Are you sure you don't mind?"

Nigel asked the question as Connie was in the middle of tying his bow tie. She liked to do this small task for him. It was one of the rare times he invited her to touch him.

They were standing in his dressing room where the tall mirror reflected an elegant couple, one in his new white dinner jacket, the other in a cool eau-de-nil linen frock that left her arms bare and made her throat look soft and delicate. If she had caught sight of the two of them in a mirror, the woman attending to her husband's tie in such an intimate and familiar manner, the man looking down at her with concern creasing his brow, she would have thought, *What a happy couple.*

"Are you sure you don't mind?" he asked again.

"Of course not. I'll enjoy it."

"Thanks, old thing. I just can't get out of this blasted dinner, and I hate to think of Johnnie spending his last night alone. You'd be doing me a favor."

"I told you." She maneuvered the fingers of silk back over on themselves with precision. "I will enjoy the film. It's ages since I've been to the pictures."

"So you won't be bored?"

"No."

"Johnnie is good company," Nigel pointed out.

"Yes, he is."

"So have fun."

She put the finishing touches to the tie, straightened it, and patted the front of his dress shirt with the palms of both hands. "You are a good-looking man, Nigel Hadley."

"Don't be daft." But he was pleased, she could tell.

The wireless was playing, Jack Hilton's dance band, but there had been no mention of a convoy of troopships.

"Nigel, don't you think we should build some kind of underground shelter, like they have in London? An Anderson shelter, I think they call them."

He had moved over to a small teak cabinet from which he had taken a silver hip flask, but he looked round at her with a frown, making his long face even longer, the flask poised halfway to his lips.

"Whatever for?" he asked.

"In case we need . . . well . . . protection."

He took a quick swig from the flask. Brandy, probably. "No," he said sternly, "don't talk like that, Constance. It's defeatist."

She let it go. Instead, she walked over and kissed his cheek before he could escape. His skin smelled of a musky cologne that she wanted to linger over, but she stepped back, patted his chest once more, and smiled.

"I wish you were coming to see the film with us," she said.

"Don't worry. You'll be in good hands with Johnnie."

Oh, Nigel. Don't you see? It's not Johnnie's hands I'm worried about. It's my own.

ᘐ·ᘓ

Nigel was not good at seeing things. Or was it that she was too good at hiding them? Sho had once told Connie that no one would ever guess what turmoil churned within her and that even he caught glimpses of it only when they were entwined in bed together, making love. Only then did she let her guard slip. Then she would go for him with her fingers as if she would tear him apart.

That had upset her. And afterward Sho had, perversely, taken to making a friend of Nigel, seeking him out in town and accepting his invitations to dine at Hadley House. She had been forced to sit at the table with her lover, as if he were a stranger.

"What is your interest in aircraft, Mr. Takehashi?" she had inquired politely on one of these occasions.

Sho had turned his attention from the outline of a Bristol Beaufighter that Johnnie Blake was sketching with a fork on his linen napkin, and fixed his gaze on her. His eyes held amusement and she was acutely aware how much he was enjoying himself. There were eight guests seated in the Hadleys' dining room, six of them British, one from Egypt and one from Japan. Just businessmen enjoying shop-talk over a coffee and a brandy, while the four wives present sipped gin and talked of the black-out in London causing so many accidents.

"We should all be interested in them, Mrs. Hadley. Airplanes are a beautiful invention," Sho declared. "I do believe they will change the future of our world."

"Quite so," Johnnie agreed.

"And do you want your future changed, Mr. Takehashi?" Connie asked lightly.

She saw Sho hesitate as he lifted his glass to his lips, then lean back in his chair considering the question.

"I believe I do," he answered, and his smooth face remained expressionless as he asked, "And what about you, Mrs. Hadley? Do you want your future changed?"

"Life would get very boring if it always stayed the same."

"Don't worry." Johnnie smiled and gestured around the crowd at the table. "How could she ever be bored here?"

Sho's eyes sparked, but it was Connie who leaned forward and raised her glass.

"To change," she laughed.

"And to excitement," Sho added.

Others raised their glasses and the moment passed effortlessly, forgotten in the general chatter of conversation. But Nigel at the far end of the table frowned and shook his head at Connie. She looked away. Into the black eyes of Shohei Takehashi. They were shining with expectation.

༁·༃

Dead meat.

The words thudded dully inside Madoc's aching skull. His mind was all over the place, his thoughts fractured into a thousand parts that wouldn't join up. He opened one eye a crack. He was in his own bed. Twilight outside. Morning or night? He had no idea. He could smell the river. He could smell his own body. He attempted to move, but everything hurt. He tried to open his other eye, but it was swollen shut.

"Awake at last! About bloody time. I've never known anyone so determined to stay asleep."

Kitty was standing next to his bed, a cup of something in one hand, a washcloth in the other. He made his one eye focus on her face. It was plump and lined and angry, but right now it was the most beautiful face in the whole damn world.

"Kitty, what happened?"

"How the hell do I know?"

"I don't remember coming home."

"I daresay."

Slowly images were trickling back into his mind.

"Fuck the bastard!" He licked his teeth, and his tongue caught on a broken tooth.

"Who was it?" she asked.

"Bull Chan."

"You stupid, imbecilic oaf! I told you to watch yourself." She leaned over him and peered closely into his eye. "Is it bad?"

He made the mistake of shaking his head, and strange colored sparks burst into life inside it, explosions numbing his ears.

"No. How did I get home?"

"When you weren't back here by nightfall, I took the canoe and went looking for you."

"You paddled all that way in the dark?"

She shrugged. "You were just lazing around on the riverbank. I brought you home." She frowned sternly. "Next time I promise I'll leave you there for the rats to chew on."

"There won't be a next time."

"There had better not be." She started to wash his face. She wasn't gentle. "When will you learn not to tread on Bull Chan's toes?"

Madoc closed his good eye and submitted to her vigorous ministrations. When she'd finished he forced his aching body to sit up, feeling the jagged ends of his ribs grating on each other.

Kitty shook her head at him slowly. "How would I ever finish building our casino without you?"

Madoc spat out part of a tooth. "Is that all I am to you? A fucking bricklayer?"

"Yes."

But she wrapped her arms around him, breathing hard against his skin, and held him close.

꒐꒤

The Purple Parrot's doors opened onto a backstreet of the town, the kind of street where bets were laid on cockfights and men with the whites of their eyes smeared yellow by opium led their lives in a fog of lies and fantasies, eyes rolling like marbles in their head. It was a street of pimps and prostitutes, of short tempers and long hatreds. Fights flared and knives flashed. Sometimes men cried out in that street; sometimes they died.

Maya hurried on silent feet through the darkness, alert for one of Hakim's stray wolf cubs. They had a tendency to hang around outside, wanting to finger the merchandise before it went inside, but tonight she reached the entrance unscathed. In the cramped and crowded dressing room she dropped her *kebaya* and sarong on the floor and started to oil her limbs so that they would gleam under the lights. An extraordinarily tall Malay boy with eyes outlined in kohl like a woman's and wearing a dress of seven veils was biting his long, painted nails nervously. He was next on stage.

"Don't worry, Tunku," she told him. "Once you're waving your little ass in their faces, no one will even notice the spots on your chin."

"I look a wreck."

She paused in the process of oiling her skin. "Tunku, you look good enough to eat. They'll gobble you up."

He giggled, blew her a kiss, and scuttled out the door. She pulled on her skimpy costume and made her way to the bar. The air in the club was as gray and thick as rabbit's fur, cigarette smoke hanging like a shroud above the tables. The mood was rowdy tonight. Most of the bawdy shouts at the boy with veils were coming from a table of British soldiers right at the front. She would have to watch out when she served them. They might try to touch. At the side against the wall, on his own as usual, sat the man with the sad eyes, hunched over his whisky, and right in the middle of the club sprawled two fat men at a table with a bottle of gin on it, almost empty. In the dim light she could see the sweat in the folds of their skin and the hunger rippling in their eyes. She knew she was in for a tough night.

This was the last time. She swore it under her breath. Never again. She cursed The Purple Parrot and she cursed Hakim. She had to get away. Had to get Razak away. Somewhere safe.

Ꝺ·Ɛ

Johnnie Blake and Connie walked out of the Empire cinema smiling. It was impossible not to smile after a film like that, impossible not to laugh when a tipsy Katharine Hepburn was carried up to the house in the arms of the glamorous James Stewart, and Johnnie had leaned close to whisper, "It must be like carrying a scrawny giraffe, all legs and teeth."

Afterward Johnnie walked Connie to the Sequin Club, where a band called The Silver Stars blasted out syncopated rhythms on trumpets and saxophones, and the strummer of the double bass rolled his eyes at Connie each time Johnnie swept her past on the dance floor. He danced well. He talked well. He listened well. He held her lightly in his arms as they performed a foxtrot, and neither of them breathed a word about what had taken place in the vegetable garden earlier that day. Instead, they talked of jazz and Fred Astaire's films and whether King George VI would ever let his brother, Edward, take over a useful role in England now that he had abdicated for the American divorcée, Mrs. Simpson. They talked of many things, but they didn't mention Nigel. Not once.

They drank a bottle of champagne between them, and Connie tried hard not to enjoy herself so much, but she noticed the way they leaned nearer to each other across the small round table till their heads were almost touching. The way their fingers skimmed the other's sleeve or bare arm, feeling the imprint on their skin, and the way gaps started to open up in their conversation. Small, dangerous holes.

She made herself stand up. "I should be getting home."

"Must you? It's only eleven o'clock. Those planters' dinners of Nigel's go on into the early hours, and I don't have to make a move until . . ."

"No, Johnnie. I'm tired."

He knew she was lying, but he jumped to his feet with an unexpected burst of energy, a wide smile in place.

"Of course, I'm being selfish. You must be dead on your feet after . . ."

Words drifted from nowhere into her head. *Dead on your feet. Dead in the air. Shot out of the sky in a ball of flames.* "Johnnie," she said quietly, "don't take any risks, will you?" She took his hand in hers and held it.

"Don't you know, Connie, that the whole of life is a risk?"

For a moment in the middle of the crowded, smoky nightclub with lights glittering on diamonds and music blaring out a seductive beat, they stood totally alone. Their eyes locked together. Finally, with an effort, she dropped his hand and moved aside, denying herself something that would fill the empty place in her chest.

"Connie."

She made herself smile.

"Let's drink," he said, scooping up their champagne glasses from the table, each with a mouthful at the bottom. It was flat but it didn't matter. "To our future." He pressed the stem of the glass into her hand.

She raised the rim to her lips. "To *your* future," she corrected in a gentle tone, "a safe and happy future."

They stared at each other, then drank.

Outside, the world was dark and damp. A fine drizzle was falling from a bank of low clouds, but the day's heat still radiated off the buildings and wafted along the sidewalks like something alive and venomous. They walked with a discreet distance between them, heading toward the Victoria Club where her Chrysler was parked in the care of Ho Bah, their footsteps echoing on the deserted sidewalks. Streetlamps cast yellow triangles like stepping-stones across the road, and the storm drains gurgled contentedly. They hurried, heads ducked against the raindrops, but suddenly Connie felt Johnnie's hand under her elbow and he was steering her down a side street away from the reach of the occasional car headlights that slid down the main road.

"Johnnie, what is it?"

He drew her into a doorway to shelter from the rain. "I have a bad feeling, Connie, about this mission that I'll be flying. I have a nagging sense that something is going to go wrong."

"Oh, Johnnie, I'm sure you'll come back to us safe and sound."

"I want to say good-bye to you properly, not in front of all the others hanging around the club car park."

"It's been a wonderful evening. Thank you, I . . ."

He leaned forward and kissed her lips. She shot backward as if she'd been burned. "No, Johnnie, I'm married. And my husband is your good friend." She stepped out into the rain, hurrying blindly toward the lights, but Johnnie caught up with her just before the main road. He swung her round to face him.

"Connie," he breathed, "don't."

This time when he kissed her she couldn't make herself pull away, and without reference to her wishes her limbs entwined around him, relishing the texture of his hair, the softness of the skin below his ear, the muscular strength of his arms gripping her, and the crippling need that fused her together with him. She was shamed by her body. By its refusal to let him go. By its blatant desire, by the pulsing heat between her legs and the eagerness of her mouth to open to his.

Neither of them heard the footsteps approaching out of the darkness.

"Good evening, Johnnie."

Connie and Johnnie leaped apart.

"Good evening, Nigel," Johnnie said.

೨· G

"It meant nothing, you know, Nigel," Connie insisted.

"Did it?"

"We were saying good-bye, that's all."

They were in Nigel's SS Jaguar, bumping over the rough road out to the estate after saying good night to Johnnie at the club. Somewhere in the distance lightning flashed, splitting the night sky in half, and the rain fell harder.

"If it was nothing, Constance, just a good-bye, why did you both hide in a backstreet to say it?" He didn't look at her. Eyes straight ahead on the road.

"We weren't hiding."

"Weren't you?"

"No. It was more private there than in the club's car park, that's why. Johnnie is nervous about tomorrow."

"Is he?"

"Yes. He needed someone to hold on to for a moment, to steady him. Nothing more."

"I see."

She swiveled in her seat, so that she was facing him. His profile was picked out by the lights of her Chrysler behind, and she could see that something wasn't right in the set of his jaw.

"Do you see, Nigel? That sometimes a person needs physical contact with another, to remind them that life is more than—"

"I know," he interrupted curtly. "Is that why he had a hand in your hair? His mouth on yours? Is that why you looked as though you were trying to climb inside him? Just to say good-bye?"

"Yes."

She heard his teeth click together sharply in the darkness. She slumped back against the passenger door and for a long time neither of them spoke. They listened to the croak of the frogs and the song of the cicadas because it was preferable to listening to each other's quietly controlled breathing.

"Why were *you* in that backstreet, Nigel?" Connie asked at last, when they could make out the lights of Hadley House up on the black hillside ahead.

"I'd had enough. Of the speeches and the cigars, and the never-ending arguments. I needed some air, so I went down to the river."

Connie had never realized it before. That Nigel felt suffocated, too. Slowly, Hadley House—with all its responsibilities and inherent duties—drew closer.

"What was the name again of that Jap who used to hang around here?" Nigel asked abruptly.

Her heart jumped to her throat. "Shohei Takehashi."

"That's the one. Do you know what he told me?"

"No." It came out as a whisper.

"He told me that we Brits couldn't keep Malaya forever. He claimed that we'd milked the country dry, had made ourselves rich and now it was someone else's turn. He boasted that the *someone else* would be the Japanese."

Her tongue licked her dry lips. "Did he?"

The conversation seemed to stop as abruptly as if it had run out of petrol, and she heard Nigel release a long sigh. "Constance," he said dully, "if the war comes to Malaya, it will wreck everything."

· CHAPTER TWELVE ·

It was two days later, after the cinema incident, that Maya turned up at Hadley House. Connie watched the young girl trudging up the long white gravel drive at ten o'clock in the morning, her limbs dusty, her turquoise *kebaya* top and sarong skirt as bright as a peacock's tail. It was obvious that she had walked the eight miles from Palur. Connie surprised herself with the strength of her pleasure at seeing the small, lonely figure. The strange thing was that the girl was carrying a dead chicken in her hand, gripped by its scrawny neck and swinging at her side as she walked. Connie rose from her desk and went down the front steps to meet her.

"Hello, Maya!"

The girl approached warily. The chicken advanced first, held out in front of her, humming with flies. Above them the sky was a sheet of blue, as vivid as Maya's sarong but with scraps of ragged white clouds, as though it had been torn in places.

"For you, *mem*," Maya said, and pushed the dead creature at Connie. "I lost sweet sticks."

"Thank you, *terimah kasih*, Maya." Connie bowed her thanks with her hands pressed together in front of her, then took hold of the chicken by the neck.

꒹·꒒

Connie knew she had made a mistake. As soon as she sat the twins down in her study, she realized that she'd gotten it wrong. It was too formal, too intimidating an environment. They were perched like a pair of nervous black-eyed finches on the edges of their chairs in front of her maple desk. Oil paintings of Nigel's parents in evening dress stared down at them, as well as one of herself as a young girl on a swing. It was a world that must look like an alien planet to them. She should have sat them on the veranda outside; at least there they could run if they wanted.

Nevertheless, she pressed ahead. She sat at her desk. "I want to discuss with you what I can do to help you, now that your mother is"—before she could say the word, she heard Razak's fierce intake of breath through flared nostrils—"is . . . gone," she continued lamely. "I was thinking that you might like to attend school."

In unison the twins shook their heads.

"I think it's what your mother would have wanted for you," Connie urged.

To her astonishment, Razak curled forward until his forehead was touching his knees, and he uttered a high-pitched keening note. It went on and on, filling the room, scraping against the ceiling and banging into the windows.

"Razak," Connie whispered, "I'm sorry."

As suddenly as it started, it ceased and the air stood still in the room.

"Whatever I can do to make up for what I did to your mother, I will do."

"*Tidak*. No," Razak insisted, sitting upright again. "Only job. Nothing more. Not from you."

The girl hissed something at her brother in Malay, too fast for Connie to catch. He shuddered and clutched his chest as though wounded, but then rose, and on silent feet he moved to the door. "We work," he said, and left.

The girl sat immobile in the chair, her young face creased with fury.

"Maya," Connie said with care, "Razak has made his decision. It needn't be yours."

Maya glared at her. "We twins," she said.

"It's your choice, Maya. You can work here and live in one of the houses we have for employees, if that's what you want. It would save you the journey from Palur every day."

The creases vanished from the girl's skin and she grew calmer. "I talk to Razak." But her head was nodding agreement already, and Connie felt a sense of minor achievement. She was making progress in helping them.

"Good, I'll take you to the kitchen now to—"

The soft knock at the study door interrupted her. She opened it and found Teddy on the other side, his brown hair tousled and windblown, his cheeks gleaming like polished apples, and she knew he had been running.

"Mummy, look what I caught."

He held out his hand. On its palm sat a bright orange lizard. Connie laughed and took it from him, cupped gently between her hands. Only then did Teddy notice Maya standing behind her, and he gave the girl his sweet shy smile.

"Maya is coming to work for us," Connie said. "Maya, this is my son, Teddy."

Maya's eyes were huge. Black pools of envy.

ℑ·Ɛ

Connie and Teddy sat on the veranda doing their jigsaw. It was the Victory one of the farmyard with wooden pieces and beautiful soft English colors. No bright kingfisher blues or garish sun-bird yellows. Even the peacock—why on earth was there a peacock in a farmyard?—was painted in muted tints. It was their favorite. For Connie, the sight of the old shire horse always brought with it a rush of smells and sounds from home— no, not home, Hadley House was home now—from England, she meant, but it bemused her why Teddy should like this jigsaw so much.

Maya watched, fascinated. She was perched cross-legged on a stool, making indecipherable mutterings, attention firmly fixed on the strange wooden shapes. When Teddy gave a squeal of pleasure each time he fitted in a new piece, her gaze would leap to his face before swiveling to Connie's and back to the jigsaw. In the corner, Chala, Teddy's *amah*, sat humming dissonant sounds to herself and sewing, her fingers nimble, and all the time she ignored Maya the way she would ignore a stray dog.

A door banged in the house, and a moment later Nigel strolled onto the veranda. He brought with him an aroma of the outside world, and immediately Connie looked up to see if he had news of Johnnie but knew by his face that he did not.

"You're home early," she said, surprised. It was only midday.

"Bit of an emergency with the export permissions. I had to come home to fetch some forms from my desk." His white shirt lay open at the neck, revealing the triangle of skin there that was weathered by the sun.

"Look, Daddy, look what I caught." Teddy flicked open the lid of the precious cigar box next to him on the table and revealed the lizard. It darted its eyes at Nigel but otherwise didn't move.

"Well done, young man. That's a fine catch you have there. You should try pushing a stick through it and roasting it over a fire to learn what lizard meat tastes like. That's what I did at your age."

Teddy regarded his father with rebuke. "No, Daddy, I have to look after it. To feed it."

"With what?"

"Crickets."

Nigel chuckled and said, "Over to you, Constance."

She groaned with mock dismay while he bent over, still chuckling, and dropped a kiss on his son's head. She wished he'd do the same to her. Only then did he take note of the native girl perched on the stool, and at once his smile fell away, his limbs stiff and angular as he straightened up.

"Who's this?" he asked.

"This is Maya Jumat."

"Jumat? Isn't that the name of the woman you . . . ?"

"Yes. Maya is her daughter."

"Get her out of here."

"What? Nigel, don't—"

"Get her out of here, Constance," he said adamantly. He turned his back on the girl. "I do not want her in my house."

Connie rose to her feet, bemused by what could have prompted this sudden wave of dislike. "I've taken her on to work in the house," she explained.

"No, I forbid it." The veins in his cheeks had darkened.

"What on earth is the matter?"

He swung around and faced the girl, who was gazing impassively at her sandaled feet. On her face there was no reaction to his outburst.

"Get out, girl." Nigel did not raise his voice, but hostility sharpened each word.

"Why, Nigel?" Connie demanded. "I want her to stay."

But it was too late. The girl slid off her stool, walked down the veranda steps, and disappeared round the corner of the house, her shadow stretching behind her as though eager to remain. There was a long, unmanageable silence. Connie was aware of Teddy staring at his parents, his cheeks blotchy and flushed.

"Chala," Connie said, "take Teddy out for a ride on his bicycle, will you, please?"

"Yes, *mem*."

Chala wrapped Teddy's small fist in hers and led him toward the garage block where his bicycle was kept. Normally he would jump at the offer, but today he hung back, dragging his feet in the dust and looking over his shoulder at the veranda in a way that pulled at Connie's heart. His lizard crouched forgotten in its box on the table.

Connie sat down heavily in her chair. "What was that about, Nigel?"

"I don't want the girl here."

"Why not?"

"You know nothing at all about her." He was striding up and down the length of the veranda. "For heaven's sake, Constance, you kill a woman and then invite her daughter into our home, where you have a vulnerable young child. It's too much of a risk. Isn't it enough that you already have her brother working in the garden?"

"I'm trying to help them."

His footsteps ceased as he came to stand opposite her. He was breathing hard. She could hear it stirring the air, and in an odd sort of way she felt the confrontation stirring their relationship, drawing up some emotions that were buried deep. It was a long time since she and Nigel had had a row. But why over this slip of a girl? Why now? She wiped her hand across her damp forehead. The shade of the veranda provided only slight protection from the heat, and an ink trail of red ants was beginning to explore the wooden pieces of the farmyard. Nothing in this country was safe from them.

"Nigel," she said in a calm voice, "I mean to help this girl."

"Just give her some money, for Christ's sake."

"I tried. Her brother refuses to accept our money. It would offend his mother's spirit, it seems."

I curse you, white lady. The words whispered through her mind, and there was the taste of ash in her mouth. She desperately needed a cigarette. She pushed back her chair and headed toward the veranda steps.

"Where are you going?"

"To find Maya."

"I won't have her here, Constance. Not on my estate."

Connie froze. Her foot hung suspended above the step down to the gravel path that ran like a white ribbon around the house, and her heart missed a beat as it tumbled to the bottom of her chest. In four words Nigel had robbed her of everything. Everything that she had put into the last nine years of being a rubber planter's wife. All the suffocating heat she had endured in silence, all the servants she had organized, the dinner parties she had given, all the tennis bashes she had attended, all the smiles she had pasted on her face. Even the son she had borne him. In four simple, effortless words he had destroyed it all.

Not on *my* estate.

He didn't say on *the Hadley* Estate.

Or on *this* estate.

Or on *our* estate.

No. It was *his* estate. *His* alone. Not *theirs*. She didn't count for anything out here in Malaya. With a jerky movement of her hand, she brushed aside the air in front of her as if she couldn't bear to inhale it a moment more, and then she turned and walked past Nigel, entered the house, and ran upstairs, taking them two at a time. She reached the bedroom and slammed the door behind her. The room was dim, the shutters closed, so that blue shadows drifted across the floor. An exhausted bee, heavy with laden pollen sacs, was buzzing frantically against the glass. The sound of its wings seemed to batter at her ears.

She hurried into her dressing room and yanked open the drawer. The cigarette case was still there. Each time she expected it to have vanished. She took out a cigarette, leaving only one remaining in the silver case, then sat down on the bed and lit it. With slow, ragged breaths she inhaled, drawing the scent of Shohei Takehashi into her lungs, into the dark recesses of her mind.

᎔·Ꮢ

"You are beautiful, Connie."

"Don't change the subject."

"You have no idea how perfectly exquisite you are."

"Sho, stop it! Listen to me."

He kissed her throat, raising a ripple of delight along her skin; he nibbled her earlobe and caressed her breast. It was always like this. He knew how to distract her, to detach her mind from her body so that her thoughts floated loose and unfocused.

Don't, Sho. Don't dismantle me. Don't unpick the person I have so carefully sewn together.

"Listen to me," she insisted again. "You must stop coming for visits to Hadley House. I know you think that in a social group no one will be suspicious of us because you're a respectable trader in town and speak English better than most Englishmen because you went to Cambridge University, but . . ."

He laughed and kissed her naked stomach.

"But that doesn't mean," she finished, "that you can pass unnoticed."

"Why?" he asked. "Nigel likes my visits."

"Because it's too dangerous."

"No, my sweet Connie. There's no danger."

"He will suspect."

"Hah! You overestimate his awareness. I talk to him by the hour about the rubber business."

"What on earth do you find to discuss?"

"He tells me about the new varieties that will produce twice as much latex per tree, and about how much the Americans are shipping out of here. He moans about the excess profits tax that the British government has imposed and worries about his rubber stocks in the godowns. He is only too pleased to have an ear into which he can pour his passion." He brushed his lips along the top of each of her breasts, and she could not stop her hand from stroking his sleek black hair. "Because rubber is your husband's passion, my love."

A flush rose from her neck to her cheeks. "I know. It's true. Rubber is his passion, not me."

She sat up in bed and drew herself away from him. The bedroom was stuffy and hot, a tiny room in a scruffy little hut built of *attap* that Sho had discovered abandoned in the jungle. It was only a few miles from the Hadley Estate, down an overgrown track where no one ventured. She could just about squeeze her car between the dense foliage most of the way there and she walked the rest, to the perfect hideaway, guarded on one side by a brown, turbulent river that murmured to them while they made love. Sho had brought clean sheets and a teapot to it, and she had laughed at him. She had filled the room with flowers, large, luscious blooms that made the air languorous with their scent.

"Anyway," he said edging closer, trailing a finger over her thigh, "I like seeing you at home. You are different there."

"Different? How?"

"You are the perfect English hostess at home, elegant and charming." He lifted her foot in his hand and started to massage the underside of its big toe. It felt as though his fingers were caressing a nerve that connected in a direct line straight up to her heart. "So untouchable," he continued. "So serene. So . . . in control." He squeezed the tip of her toe till she gave a high-pitched yip of pain and snatched her foot away.

"Sho, we can always meet here. Don't come to my house anymore. I mean it."

The moment hung between them. They both heard the jungle exhale its dank breath over the crumpled confines of their bed and, despite the heat, Connie shivered.

"I mean it, Sho." She drew her knees close to her chest and wrapped her arms around her shins, reclaiming her feet.

He leaned forward, his chin sharp, his eyes black and impenetrable. "Do you know what is happening inside Japan right now? Do you?"

"I know your armies are marching all over Korea and China, and that . . ."

"No, I said *inside* Japan."

She stared at him. "No. Tell me."

"We are creating a new nationalist breed of men. From their earliest days in school their minds and bodies have been prepared for war. They train rigorously day after day from the age of five; they wear military clothes and chant military songs. They are being indoctrinated with the code of the samurai warrior. To die in battle is to fall in the moment of perfection, just like the cherry blossom when it falls from the tree. They are convinced that Emperor Hirohito is divine, that Japan is invincible and that the Japanese are the chosen race, which means they cannot wait to hurl themselves into war."

Connie put her hand to her mouth. "Is that what you believe too, Shohei Takehashi-san?"

His hand shot out and seized hers from her mouth. He dragged her close. "I want you to know what is coming," he said in an urgent whisper. "The old textile and trading firms of Japan like Mitsubishi and Yasuda have moved into munitions and armaments, as well as new firms like Mori and Nissan. Each day the workforces of these factories bow down three times in the direction of the palace in Tokyo. They are ready to die for their emperor." Sho's eyes glittered in the gloom. "I want you to know this, because you have to understand that all you British and your empire will be wiped off the face of Asia. You will fall to the samurai sword in thousands upon thousands. The weak will always kneel to the strong, and my people are the strongest here in Asia."

She tried to twist her wrist from his grip, but it was the grip of the warrior, not the silk merchant. The sun had leaked through the mesh that she had pinned over the window to keep out insects and it painted a grid of dusky lines over his face, as if it were a samurai face mask.

"But I will protect you, my Connie. I will stand by you when the time comes."

She stared at him. "Why would you do that?"

"Because you are mine." His rigid features softened, and he bowed his head to kiss the back of her hand.

"Sho, don't be foolish. You are teasing me."

He laughed easily. "Of course I am."

So why did she shudder? Why did she feel a sliver of something in her stomach, something cold and wretched?

After the unpleasant scene with her husband on the veranda, Connie stubbed out her cigarette in an angry gesture as if she could stub out the memory of it. It was a whole year ago, twelve long months since the hut in the jungle, yet the pictures were still so pin-sharp. Wasn't it time they started to blur round the edges, like old photographs?

She pushed back the shutters of the bedroom, letting in a tidal wave of heat, and looked out over the lawns and garden. There were the beginnings of the jungle on one side, as thick and solid as a wall, and the Hadley Estate on the other, stretching for miles across the distant hills and valleys. Shimmering shades of dense green, great lakes of it in which you could drown. Connie's throat was dry, and an ache was making itself felt somewhere deep within her head. She turned, tempted by the final cigarette in the silver case, but at that moment a quiet tap sounded on her door.

"Come in."

It was Chala, the *amah*, who opened the door and poked her chubby face tentatively around it. "You need me?" she asked.

Chala had been with the family for the last six years, a cheerful woman of forty who liked her chapatis somewhat more than was wise. Her dark eyes looked at Connie with concern. Her wrist jangled with bracelets as she shook them and asked again, "You need me?"

"Not now, Chala, no."

"*Mem* sure?"

"Yes, I'm sure. Thank you."

But the bracelets remained at the door, Chala shuffling her feet until Connie sighed and walked over to her.

"What is it, Chala? Tell me what's the matter?"

"She say *mem* not happy. She say you need me. Need my help."

"For heaven's sake, Chala, I'm perfectly happy, and am just taking a breather up here away from . . ." She stopped as Chala's words sank into her head. "What do you mean, Chala? Who is this *she*? Who told you that I need you?"

"The alley cat."

For a moment Connie didn't understand. "Alley cat? Oh, you mean Maya."

"Yes, *mem*."

"She said I'd asked for you to come to me?"

"No, *mem*." Chala proffered a small smile to bridge the misunderstanding. "She say you need me. I ask what for, and she say you unhappy." Her feet started shuffling once more. "You unhappy, *mem*?"

"Thank you for your concern, Chala. I appreciate it, but no, I'm fine." Connie frowned. "Chala, where is Teddy?"

"On the cycle." The woman's amiable face broke into a grin and she started to chuckle. "He learn to turn in rings," she twirled her fingers to demonstrate, "but the black pest"—she always labeled Pippin *the black pest*—"he—"

"Chala!"

The *amah* stopped. Checked the laughter rising in her throat. "What, *mem*?"

"Where is Maya?"

"She watch Teddy."

A cold sensation spread from Connie's feet up through her limbs. She rushed from the room, flew down the stairs, and burst out through the front door into the blinding sunlight.

"Teddy!" she screamed. "Teddy!"

ᘒ·ᘓ

She couldn't find him. She couldn't find her son. Or his dog. His scarlet Raleigh bicycle lay abandoned on its side on the concrete behind the garage, its chrome handlebars glinting like a thousand eyes in the rays of the sun.

Maya, don't hurt him. I beg you, don't do this. Don't do to my child what I did to your mother. He's only a little boy, he's not to blame.

She pinned her hopes on Pippin. If the dog was with him, then maybe he was just playing somewhere—in the bushes and under the long fingers of the casuarina tree, or in the stables, tumbling around in the hay, or crawling under the shed in search of one of his beloved frogs.

"Ajib," she shouted to one of the gardeners, "have you seen *Tuan* Teddy?"

He shook his head. "He play," he smiled, and started to say something about the state of the lawn, but she cut him off.

"Find him, Ajib. Find him quickly."

She ran from one end of the garden to the other, calling her son's name, searching the vegetable patch, the orchard, the henhouses behind the stables. Her breath grew ragged.

"Keep searching!" she shouted to Ajib. "Get all the gardeners to search thoroughly."

In the garage she found that Nigel's Jaguar had gone. He had driven back to town, but Ho Bah, their chauffeur, was there.

"Did *Tuan* take his son?" she demanded.

The wiry little figure was polishing the glass of her Chrysler. "No, *mem*. He go alone."

"Ho Bah, my son has gone missing."

His old eyes popped wide, and the lines of his face drooped in sympathy. "Bad boy," he said. "I find him."

"I want you to take my car and search the road."

She could picture her son, his legs thin and dusty under his shorts, trudging down the eight miles to town, his small hand in Maya's. What had the girl promised him? What would tempt him to break the strict rule about never leaving the garden? Ho Bah jumped into the driving seat and backed the car out of the garage, but as he vanished down the drive, a thought hit her: *Razak. Where is Razak?* An image fluttered into Connie's head of the butterfly caught between Razak's fingers in his house, its wings crushed, its beauty destroyed. Darkness settled in her mind.

"Razak!" she shouted at the top of her voice, startling the parrots, but no answer came.

She raced back to the house, hurrying from room to room, Chala behind her now, close on her heels. All the time she called his name.

"Teddy!"

Chala's high-pitched "Teddy!" followed like an echo.

Connie ordered the houseboys to hunt through every cupboard, under every bed, in every wardrobe. She stripped Teddy's bed, as if he might be hiding under a pillow. She tore down the wigwam in the playroom and the igloo made of white sheets under the billiard table. She marched into the kitchen, where she dragged the heavy rice sacks from the back of the larder, in case he had squeezed in behind them.

What kind of mother loses her son?

A car's engine sounded in her ears, wheels on the gravel. Ho Bah? Nigel? She hurried from the house and found a yellow Ford taxi parked on the drive. Out of it stepped the broad figure of Fitzpayne in khaki shirt and twill trousers.

"Mr. Fitzpayne, now is not a good moment to come visiting."

"I've come on business. To speak with your husband. I was told he was here."

"No. He has gone."

He stood stiffly for a moment, inspecting her. She knew she must look a mess, but she didn't care. She felt a gust of annoyance at his reluctance to leave.

"Mr. Fitzpayne, I am busy," she said curtly. "Too busy for chatter about boats. Good day to you."

She turned away. Where next, where next? Where hadn't she searched? Why wasn't Pippin barking? Why had Maya . . . ?

"Mrs. Hadley? What is wrong, Mrs. Hadley?"

Go away. Go away.

She speeded up her steps. The orchard, she'd search it again. She hurried past the vegetable garden with its high, protective hedge and ran into the orchard, all the time her eyes shredding the trees and shrubs for a glimpse of white shirt or tangled brown curls. To her surprise, she found Fitzpayne right behind her.

"What is the problem, Mrs. Hadley?"

"I've lost my son." The enormity of the words nearly choked her.

"Have you searched everywhere in the house and garden?"

"Yes, of course I've searched everywhere."

"Then he must be elsewhere."

"Teddy knows he is never allowed to leave the garden."

He snorted dismissively. "He's a boy—and boys are built to break rules."

"My chauffeur is searching the road," she told him.

"I didn't spot a child anywhere along the route coming here."

A small sliver of hope died.

"So," he said, glancing beyond the garden confines, "he is either in the rubber plantation or in the jungle." He spoke about it as casually as he might about a mislaid shoe. "My money's on the jungle."

"No." *Please, no.*

"Is there an easy way through the fence?"

She didn't reply but led him behind the rhododendron bushes to a narrow gate in the perimeter fence. It was used by the servants to gather wood for fuel, or to hunt monkeys for their supper.

"Shall we?" Fitzpayne stepped back and waited for her to make the decision.

She seized the latch and threw it open.

꿍·ꭱ

The jungle air was suffocating, as though someone had clamped a damp cloth over her nose. It smelled of rotting vegetation and musky animals. Huge rattan trees closed in on her, green tendrils looping down from their branches as if eager to throttle her, and the whoops of gibbons in the canopy sounded eerie down on the ground. The intense heat hit her the moment she stepped onto the tiny trail that wriggled through the foliage. Somewhere far above her she knew there was a sky, but she couldn't see it, just a lid of green, as solid as a croquet lawn.

She tried to move fast, but it was hopeless. Giant ferns barricaded her route. She had to scramble around them, her feet sucked into sodden earth, the scent of her skin attracting a thousand winged insects. Within two minutes her blouse was sticking to her back; within six, the green barrier all around her deadened her senses. It absorbed all sound. Eighty feet up in the tree canopy she could hear hornbills calling, but here on the ground every rustle and murmur was immediately swallowed by the dripping ranks of leaves. It felt like being wrapped up in a wet carpet.

The curse of Sai-Ru Jumat was real. And it was destroying her life.

ꝺ·ꞇ

"Listen!"

Connie listened. Nothing. She shook her head.

"I hear a dog."

Fitzpayne had sharp ears. She couldn't hear a dog. Her heart pricked in her chest.

"Where?" she asked quickly.

He veered off the narrow path and barged aside the curtain of foliage. Instantly Connie heard a bark.

"Teddy! Teddy!" she shouted, but the sound died the moment it left her mouth. Dark green leaves shimmered, wrapping themselves around her words.

She pushed on, striking out at the forest, breaking her way through it, resenting its power to seize her son. To her astonishment, the figure of Teddy swung abruptly into view. *Swung into view.* Literally. He was up in the air, suspended ten feet above a narrow gully, sitting astride a length of wood. It dangled on the end of a rope that ran up to a hefty branch twenty feet above him. He was swinging back and forth like a pendulum. His hands clutched tightly to the rope, but he was leaning back, a look of intense happiness on his young face. His lips were moving, sound bubbling out of them, and it took Connie a moment to recognize it as the noise of an engine. Teddy was flying, swooping his imaginary aircraft through the skies.

On the edge of the gully, Pippin saw her and barked with delight.

"Mummy!" Teddy called; he released one hand and waved, grinning wildly. "Mummy, look, I'm"—he swung so close she reached out to seize him, but the rope snatched him away at the last second and swept him back to the other side—"I'm flying."

Sweat froze on Connie's cheeks as she stared across the gully straight into the eyes of Maya and Razak Jumat. Their brown hands were holding on to Teddy's white shirt, preventing him from swinging back to her.

I curse you, white lady. The words lay unspoken between them, crawling in the gully, rustling in the dead undergrowth.

"Give me my son," Connie ordered.

Beside her, she was aware of sudden movement. She caught sight of Fitzpayne's khaki shirt disappearing down into the gully. Previously he had struck her as bullish in his movements, solid and heavy, but now he streaked forward with the smooth speed of a leopard. The twins' hands instantly released their grip on Teddy's shirt. As her son swung toward her, she snatched him off the rope and landed him firmly at her side. His face was dirty, his shirt was covered in green smears, his feet were thick with mud almost up to his knees, but his eyes were shining and out of his mouth tumbled a torrent of excitement. He pointed to the spot where the rope was tied to the tree high above.

"Razak climbed all the way up there."

Connie didn't hear any of his words. Her eyes fed on him, drank him in, imprinted again into her head the soft texture of his skin, the curl of his eyelashes, the tilt of his chin. Her hand clasped his small fingers tightly against her side as if she could sew him to her, the way Chala sewed bright strips of beads around her ankles. Dimly she became aware of other things. That the ache had stopped. That Razak and Maya were standing right in front of her, Fitzpayne behind them. That Teddy wanted his hand back.

"Right," she said firmly, "back to the house."

Teddy opened his mouth to moan, but before he could begin to object Fitzpayne swept him up under his arm like a roll of old tarpaulin and strode back the way they had come. Teddy kicked and squealed with delight, his muddy legs flailing against leaves and branches. It occurred to Connie that Nigel would never treat him so roughly—but then, neither would she.

Maybe that was the problem.

ͻ·Ϛ

She sent the Jumat twins home.

"Teddy is not allowed to leave the garden," she told them. She frowned sternly at her son. "He knows that's the rule."

"But I was with Maya and Razak, I wasn't on my own," he grumbled. His brown eyes were darker now, cross with her.

"You know the rule," she insisted. "Whose idea was it?"

"It my idea," Razak admitted. "Good play for boy."

"Yes," Teddy added. "Good play."

"Not without asking me first. You should have asked my permission."

"You gone," Maya said softly.

"I cannot employ you if I can't trust you. Come back tomorrow morning and I will let you know my decision about your jobs. Go now."

They didn't argue but turned and walked away down the drive. She was conscious of Fitzpayne on the front step, smoking a cigarette and watching her with close attention. It irritated her. She whisked Teddy's hand into hers and marched him into the house. As she passed Fitzpayne she said a final, "Thank you for your help."

In the hall, Chala fussed over Teddy, kissing his dirty cheeks and scolding him for worrying his mother.

"Bath time," Connie said.

"One moment, please." It was Fitzpayne, still at the open front door. "I would like a word with you, Mrs. Hadley."

"Not now, I'm sorry, Mr. Fitzpayne. I'm grateful for the help you've given me, but . . ." She stopped. He had walked across the hall and entered the drawing room, as though she had suggested it. She strode after him quickly. "Excuse me, I don't recall inviting you into my house."

"Just sit a minute."

"No, thank you. I have a son to bathe."

"Just sit."

He came over to her, placed his hands on her shoulders, and sat her down on one of the sofas. Her knees just buckled under her. No resistance, nothing in them. It shocked her. Then her whole body started to shake.

"Mrs. Hadley, you look pale. You've had an unpleasant shock. Just sit for a moment."

He moved over to the cocktail cabinet, opened it, poured out a stiff brandy and brought it to her. She shook her head. He crouched down in front of her, regarding her carefully.

"You need it," he said.

"No. Thank you."

He didn't insist, but shrugged and drank it down himself. "Shall I call a servant for you?"

"No." Her teeth chattered. She closed her eyes.

He remained there in front of her, not patting her knee or holding her hand. He just left her to deal with whatever she had to deal with alone. But he didn't leave. Minutes ticked past and the nausea in her stomach began to lessen; the beat of her heart, which had slowed to a sluggish murmur, picked up and a pulse tapped impatiently at her temple. When she opened her eyes, Fitzpayne was gazing out through the window. She saw that his wide jaw was tense and his large nostrils flared with annoyance. She sat up straight and immediately he returned his attention to her, offering her a cigarette. She accepted. He lit hers and one for himself, inhaled deeply, then stood up and walked to the door.

"Better?" he asked.

"Yes."

"Your cheeks have more color, your lips are no longer blue."

His words embarrassed her. "Thank you."

"Do you want to tell me what that was all about?"

"No."

He nodded. "I said last time I was in this house that we all have our secrets." With a tip of his head to her, Fitzpayne was gone.

ꝉ·ꝉ

"I mean it, Teddy. You must never leave our garden without permission from me or Daddy. Even if someone you know invites you to. This is important."

"Why?" He made the bow of his boat bump against the white

porcelain of the bath, and the corner of his mouth drooped down. "It's boring in the garden."

"Because something bad might happen. You might have an accident or . . ."

"Like you had in the car?"

She swallowed. "Yes, exactly like that. Or you might fall over. And we wouldn't know where you were to help you. We would be worried, like I was worried today." She caught hold of a strand of his wet hair. "Do you understand?"

He ducked his head away, sulkily. "Yes, Mummy."

"Good. Because I have an idea."

Instantly his eyes flashed to hers. "What kind of idea?"

"I've decided," she continued, "that we all need a bit of adventure—you, Daddy, and me."

"Yes." He abandoned his boat.

"I think we need to live rough for a day. Out in the plantation."

He beamed at her. "Can we light a fire?"

"Yes."

"And cook food?"

"Yes. And we'll build a hut."

He splashed his hand down on the water with excitement, spraying bubbles over them both and laughing, but after a moment he looked back at her cautiously.

"Us?" he said. "Just us? No servants?"

"No servants," she promised him. "We'll do everything ourselves. Unless we want someone to come along to show us how to light a fire without matches, and how to make a waterproof roof. It's up to you."

Her son thought for a moment, his young face solemn as he considered the options. "Yes," he said at last. "We must take Razak with us."

Her heart sank. "Not necessarily Razak, sweetheart. We could take one of our gardeners instead—how about Ajib? He knows about—"

"Please let's take Razak!" His voice was full of yearning.

"I'll have to discuss it with Daddy."

"You won't sack them, will you, Mummy? Because I got them into trouble."

She heard the guilt. She recognized it in his voice instantly, that dull, dragging sensation that tightens the throat.

"Teddy, what they did was wrong."

He placed his small hand over hers on the edge of the bath. "I'm sorry I broke the rules, Mummy. I won't leave the garden again, I promise."

She kissed his wet skin and accepted his peace offering.

э·ᢏ

Razak was blank-eyed and far away, though his shoulder pressed against Maya's as they sat in the back of the ancient truck that had stopped to give them a lift. The sun directly overhead beat down on the top of her head but the wind had risen, moaning through the rubber trees. She knew a storm was on its way. She could see the clouds marching over the hills in the distance, and she wanted to get home quickly.

"Razak," she said crossly, "you have the heart of a bleating goat."

He blinked, his long black lashes moving slowly as he came back from wherever he had gone. "The woman must suffer," he said solemnly. "Not the child. We did steal the boy, Maya. She did suffer." He turned to her, and she glimpsed the satisfaction in his eyes. "You saw her face."

Maya could not resist a smile. "Yes, I saw her face."

"The agony."

"And the fury."

He made a soft, contented noise in his chest. "She will die before she forgets that day."

"You made us waste time with your stupid game with the boy." She slapped her brother's thigh, and he caught her wrist and pinned it down.

"The boy is a pup, Maya. He needs to play. Not in a bed of goose down. He needs—"

"Razak, I don't care what the boy needs. He is a tool for us, nothing more."

He sighed beside her, his breath mingling with the hot wind and the dust. "Sometimes, Maya, it weighs on my heart, the fear that you have no soul."

His words hurt her, but she kept it hidden. She trod carefully.

"Tomorrow," she said, "you must go back to the white lady alone. She will keep you working there, but not me. It's up to you now to squeeze the blood from her veins." She watched the black clouds. "But my time will come with her, I know."

"Why? We must go to Hadley House together in the morning."

"He will never allow it."

"Who?"

"Her husband."

"Why not?"

"Because I know him."

He swiveled round to face her, curious. "You know him?"

"Yes. He is the man with the sad eyes and the whisky who comes and sits against the wall in The Purple Parrot."

ᘔ·Ϛ

Nigel was late home that evening. He arrived out of the rain just when Connie was in the middle of dancing a snappy quickstep on her own across the drawing room floor. She had pushed back the furniture, kicked away the rug, turned down the lights, and put one of her dance band records on the gramophone, a Glenn Miller. She let her eyes fall almost closed as she danced, her steps complicated and fast, her blood pounding in rhythm to the beat. She stopped as soon as she saw Nigel in the doorway, but she had no idea how long he had been there, watching her with astonished eyes. She came to a halt in front of him and on impulse held out her arms to him.

"Dance with me," she whispered, swaying her hips.

To her surprise he slipped off his jacket, took her in his arms, and twirled her around the room in a series of quick turns. She tilted her head backward, stretching her neck and letting her hair swing free, feeling the pleasure of being held for once by her husband, his palm warm on her back, his grip light on her fingers. He rarely took to the floor even on social occasions, which was a shame because he was a damn good dancer.

When the music ended he immediately released his hold on her, walked over to the gramophone, and lifted the needle from the record.

She remained where she was, standing with her arms loose at her sides, tendrils of hair clinging to the moist skin of her neck. In the dim light with the rain lashing down outside, the room felt intimate despite the expanse of polished floor between them. It struck Connie that Nigel's face looked tired, the set of it older than his thirty-eight years, especially along the jawline where shadows gathered.

She gave him an affectionate smile. "Would you like a drink? A *stengah*?"

But neither of them moved.

"Do you often dance?" he asked.

"Sometimes. When I'm lonely. Or restless."

"Are you restless now?"

She shrugged. "Colonial wives are restless most of the time. There's not much for us to do."

He made no comment but walked over to her till he was so close that for one stupid moment she thought he intended to kiss her.

"Don't ever kiss Johnnie again. Promise me."

His words were the last she had expected. He spoke in such a low voice she barely heard them. Hesitantly she raised her hand, cupping his cheek in it, but for once he didn't back away.

"I promise," she said.

"Thank you."

"Have you heard from him?"

"No, not yet."

He was lying, she could tell, but she let it sit there between them as if it were the truth. "You'll tell me when you do?"

"Of course."

She removed her hand, but he remained where he was and she could smell whisky on his breath.

"What is it, Nigel?"

"Constance, I insist that you don't employ that girl who was here this afternoon. Find someone else. Please. I think she's dangerous."

She nodded. "If it makes you happy."

That's the trouble with guilt. It makes you say yes when what you mean is no.

CHAPTER FOURTEEN

Madoc worked harder and faster on the casino than ever before. He had a sense of time running out. Kitty had strapped up his ribs and bathed his wounds, and he dosed himself each morning with a glass of cheap brandy to numb the pain.

"You're drinking too much," Kitty commented.

"I'm drinking enough," he countered.

"Eat something."

To oblige her, he sat down at the table and watched her move around the cramped kitchen as she served him a plate of fried belly pork and eggs. It smelled good, but he wasn't hungry. He was never hungry these days, not since his run-in with Bull Chan. Something was churning inside him, eating him up. He stuck a fork in the eggs, pushing them round his plate.

"Sit down, Kitty. There's something I want to tell you."

Quietly she abandoned the pan and sat opposite him at the battered old table where she had once cut a bullet from his thigh. She folded her hands in front of her and narrowed her eyes at him.

"If anything happens to me—I mean anything bad—I want you to—"

"Nothing bad will happen to you," she retorted. "Not if you don't do anything stupid or go begging to get your thick skull knocked in." She didn't raise her voice, but he could hear that she wanted to.

He tried again. "If anything bad happens to me, I want you to know that there is a box buried behind the banyan tree. It's an old Huntley and Palmers biscuit tin with a picture of King George on the front. It's buried a good way down and there is enough money in it to get you back home."

He'd expected surprise from her. Probably annoyance. Maybe even a veiled relief. But what he got was a soft melting of something at the core of her; he could see it like liquid honey in her hazel eyes.

Her hand slid forward and took hold of one of his. "Don't you know, I *am* home?" She said it with the kind of smile that meant she could think of a better use for the table than scoffing belly pork and eggs.

ᗡ·ᘜ

Madoc was up a ladder, hammering the roof beams in place.

He whistled cheerfully, despite the fact that everything was wet from a recent downpour, so that he and the timbers were drenched and the ground squelched beneath his ladder. Later, when he thought back on it, he realized his mistake was the whistling. It masked other sounds. So he didn't hear the boat glide up to the jetty, or the footsteps that approached. If he had, maybe it would have turned out differently.

"Madoc-san."

Madoc's hammer paused midstrike. He glanced down onto a neat male head, raindrops glistening in the cropped gray hair, and an upturned face that looked pleased with itself. It was one of his Japanese contacts, the oldest one, the one in authority who liked to pretend he spoke little English.

"Good morning," Madoc said, and shinned down the ladder. He kept the hammer in his hand. "To what do I owe this pleasure?"

He watched the pale face of the man in front of him, the way it made no attempt to hide its arrogance and its dislike of him.

"I have a task for you," the Japanese said with the utmost politeness.

"Does it pay well?"

"Of course."

"You want more information?"

"No." The man was sweating in the heat. Or was there something more? He wore a raincoat over dark, spotless trousers, but his shoes were spattered with Morgan's Bar's mud. "Not this time. What I want is this: one hundred bicycles."

Madoc burst out laughing, it was so absurd. "What? Is the great Imperial Japanese Army going to invade Malaya by bike?"

He was still chuckling at the idea when his companion said coldly, "That is exactly what we intend to do."

Madoc's laughter instantly dried up. In the silence he heard the palm trees chafing against each other in the same way that this man's manner chafed on Madoc's nerves.

"That's insane," he said. Perhaps unwisely.

The small man pulled back his shoulders and pushed out his narrow chest. "The Imperial Japanese Army does nothing that is *insane*. It is a supreme fighting force."

"On bicycles!"

"You are a fool! You and your British army know nothing. You think that the Malayan jungle will stop us!" Spittle gathered in one corner of his mouth, and he clenched a fist to his chest as though to stop his heart from launching itself at Madoc. "We have tanks that will blast your defenses, and we have bicycles that will carry our infantry so fast along the jungle tracks that our forces will outflank yours before you can finish drinking your English cup of tea."

"Christ!" Suddenly Madoc could see the sense of it. The natives of Malaya criss-crossed the jungle on bicycles every day. Why not an army? "A hundred bicycles? You'll need a thousand."

The man stiffened. "Don't think we won't convey our own."

"So why do you need me to find any more?"

"Many will be damaged. We need replacements ready along our route."

"Christ!" Madoc said again. The chill finger of reality touched the base of his spine, and for the first time he believed the bloody Japanese army might actually manage it.

"One hundred bicycles," the man repeated.

"That's a tall order. How soon do you want them?"

"Immediately."

Madoc laughed in the man's face and started back toward his ladder.

"Madoc-san, don't you dare walk away from me!"

Madoc swung round. "I do not care for your manners," he snapped.

The Japanese pulled out two manila envelopes from his raincoat pocket and held them out. "One to pay the cost of the bicycles," his mouth tipped into a sneer, "the other to pay the cost of you."

The envelopes were fat. Madoc knew he could buy a native's bicycle for little more than a beer and a couple of dollars. He snatched the envelopes without looking at the man and ripped open the one for himself. It took an effort to keep his face straight. Inside lay real temptation, more than enough money to fit out the new casino to a standard that would draw punters from far and wide. He could employ the best girls, get in a stock of good Scotch whisky, buy Kitty a wedding ring at last, he could . . .

Fuck! He spat on the ground and pocketed the money.

The Jap's eyes glittered, cold and unforgiving. "Two days. I want them in two days."

"Four."

"Three."

"It's a deal."

Abruptly the Jap turned his head, conscious of someone staring at him. It was Kitty. She was standing with the iron pan swinging loosely from her hand. She wore a bright green blouse with sweat stains and a yellow sarong around her ample waist, her hair bundled up in an unruly knot. She didn't look dangerous.

She ambled over, swaying her hips. "Any problems, Madoc?" she asked casually.

"No. Our friend is just leaving."

"Good."

The man bristled like a fighting dog and drew himself up to his full height, but still he was several inches shorter than Kitty. "Your husband and I are doing business," he said. His tone was dismissive.

"If you ask me, you do too much fucking business with my husband. Now get your yellow hide off our land."

Madoc fought hard not to laugh at the expression on the Jap's face, but his laughter changed to dismay when he saw his wife sidle up to the ladder and give it a nudge with her shoulder. It came crashing down. Madoc jumped clear, but it twisted and gave a glancing blow to the Japanese, sending him sprawling in the mud. With a scrabble of limbs he leaped immediately back to his feet, but his trousers and raincoat were caked in mud. A flash of something like hatred passed through his dark eyes as he bowed stiffly to Kitty, then strutted off back to the jetty without a word.

Madoc wanted to scold his wife. She had made the Jap lose face in a big way, and you didn't do that to a Japanese if you wanted to keep your fingernails. But instead he seized hold of her, pressing the large fleshy mound of her breasts against his chest to keep her safe.

ꙅ·Ꙅ

White gold.

That was the name for rubber. The milky-white fluid that spilled like liquid gold dust into the white man's pocket. As Connie rode her horse along the plantation trail, she gazed around her. Here was order. Here was control. Here was certainty. They soothed Connie's thoughts. Regular rows of rubber trees—*Hevea brasiliensis*—that stretched for mile after mile, tall mottled trunks as straight and fundamental as marble columns in a church, while a smattering of foliage sprouted underfoot like a carpet of bright green feathers. Here there was room to breathe.

Nothing like the chaos of the jungle.

They'd chosen a Sunday. Early morning, when the air was at its coolest and a thin green mist rose up like the earth's breath. She wore a broad-brimmed hat and a light muslin blouse with jodhpurs and a pair of sturdy walking shoes. She and Nigel had saddled their horses and Teddy's small Turkish pony. Razak opted to walk. When Connie offered him a horse to ride, he looked at her as if she'd suggested putting a firecracker between his legs. She'd been amazed at how readily Nigel had agreed to this Jumat twin accompanying them on their trek, and it touched her that he should want to please her and Teddy like this. They rode in single file along the trails through the plantation, passing from groves of younger trees to the old-timers that towered above them, creaking their heavy branches like old men with sore joints.

"Here we are," Nigel announced suddenly. "The perfect spot."

Connie gazed around her. At first glance it looked no different from every other spot they had ridden through, but then she realized that just ahead of them sprawled a patch of jungle forest. She regarded it warily.

"Yes! We can make camp," Teddy crowed, and slid off his horse with an energy she envied after two hours in the saddle.

"We'll collect material for the hut from over there," Nigel waved a hand toward the forest, "and build our camp right here, I think." He surveyed his chosen territory with satisfaction. "There's a river just beyond those trees."

Connie dismounted. She had to admit that this spot did indeed look perfect: a narrow strip of open grassland tucked between the rubber trees and the dark ribbon of the jungle's edge. She left the others to make a start as she took care of the horses. She removed their saddles, rubbed down their hot sweating backs, and led them to drink and cool their feet in the river, then tethered them in the shade and returned to the camp area. Already a pile of areca palm fronds lay in a heap, and Teddy was dragging more across the grass, his face red with effort. Behind him, Razak was carrying five long straight poles and Nigel held an armful of sticks. He grinned as he approached, waving his parang at her. They had agreed with Teddy what to bring: one parang, an evil-looking native machete, and a long-bladed knife for skinning anything they caught, as well as a billycan for heating water. In her back pocket Connie had secreted a box of matches and a hip flask of antiseptic. Just in case.

It took some time to build a hut, an A-shaped shelter with fronds for the roof.

There was a lot of shouting and laughing, but the hut slowly emerged, a bit shaky but definitely a respectable hut, and Connie noticed that even Razak seemed to be enjoying the experience. His black eyes shone, glancing at her shyly as he worked. Only Nigel was allowed to wield the parang because they wanted no accidents, but Razak was as quick as lightning with the knife when they all descended on the river to try for fish. He poised himself, still as a statue, up to his waist in the current, waiting for long moments, then struck hard and fast. He lifted the fish from the water, skewered on the point of the knife.

"Good show," Nigel called, and Teddy clapped.

Razak bowed, holding his catch aloft, a wide smile on his handsome face.

ᗭ·ᘿ

They made a fire—using her matches—and cooked the fish. Teddy caught a pair of speckled lizards with bright yellow eyes but refused all his father's urging to roast them over the fire. The rain sheeted down for an hour in the afternoon as it did most days, and the four of them huddled inside the hut, which, to Connie's amazement, kept them dry with only a few drips sneaking down her neck. At least it was cooler for a brief time, but as they emerged from their cramped confinement into a green world that was steaming around them like a hot bath, Connie noticed a restlessness surfacing in Nigel. As though he'd had his fill of this game. She recalled Sho's comment about her husband's passion.

"Nigel," she said, "why don't you take the opportunity to teach Teddy about rubber trees?"

Nigel looked across at his son. "Good idea. Would you like that?"

Teddy didn't exactly jump at the offer.

"It'll be your job one of these days," Nigel pointed out.

"I like." It was Razak who spoke. He pointed to the rows of rubber trees. "I like learn."

Nigel beamed at the native boy. "Come along then, chaps."

He led them all on foot deeper into the plantation, occasionally touching the mottled bark of a tree as he passed, in the same way that Connie would ruffle her son's hair.

"So, who can tell me their name?" Nigel boomed as if talking to a class of fifty.

"They have names?" Teddy asked.

"*Pokok getah,*" Razak offered.

"Correct. That's their native Malay name."

"*Hevea brasiliensis,*" Connie smiled.

"Well done. That's the scientific name. *Hevea brasiliensis.*" He drew them close to a tree to inspect the long diagonal cut that ran around half the outer circumference like a massive appendix scar. "This," he said, "takes great skill. If a tapper cuts too deep, he will destroy the productive life of a tree. He has a special knife to excise only a thin sliver of bark, less than a quarter of an inch, and he makes an incision through the latex vessels. He mustn't damage the cambium—that's a paperlike skin between the bark and the wood—or the tree is ruined. And he has to work fast. I expect a tapper to do between five hundred and six hundred trees in a day, if he's any good."

Connie looked at the huge wound on each tree and felt sorry for them. Sliced open day after day, never allowed to heal. Around every trunk was a metal wire that held a glazed porcelain cup to the base of the scar where the milky substance had gathered. Teddy stuck his finger in it.

"Latex," Nigel announced. "I make it into rubber down in the smoke sheds." He pointed to a smear of white latex that had gathered all down the length of the scar. "This is called tree lace." He peeled it off. "Already coagulated." He rolled it into a sticky ball and tossed it to Teddy. "A rubber tree," he said, "has enormous tenacity, though they look slender. Their timber is as hard as teak."

Razak moved closer and tentatively ran his hand over the tree, touching its wound, stroking its bark. "How old?"

"We start tapping seven years after planting, on alternate days throughout the whole year. Yields increase as the tree matures. Each tree has a production life of about thirty years."

"The latex is solid now," Connie pointed out to Teddy, "but it's liquid when it starts to flow."

"Tree blood," Razak whispered.

"That's right," Nigel agreed. "It flows better before the heat of the day. That's why tappers have to start before dawn. They trek along their grove making the six hundred or so cuts, and then return a few hours later to collect it once the latex has stopped flowing for that day." He reached into the cup and scraped out a fistful. "This is called *cup lump*." He tossed it to Razak.

Teddy ran to the next tree, his hand hovering over the cup as he looked across at his father for permission.

"Go ahead," Nigel laughed.

Teddy drew out the viscous substance and started molding it into a ball. He held it to his nose and sniffed it. In the shifting light that drifted between the trees, Connie saw something in his young face change, as if he had just smelled his future.

ᏭᎶ

Nigel sat with Connie on a thick branch that was lying on the ground, and together they watched the boys laughing and throwing the rubber balls at each other. Nigel slapped his thigh with satisfaction each time Teddy scored a direct hit.

"It's been a good day," Connie said, "for all of us."

He nodded, his attention on the boys.

She waited. "What is it, Nigel?"

"Johnnie Blake is in hospital. His plane crashed on landing. Apparently the undercarriage collapsed."

Her heart thudded. "Oh, poor Johnnie. How badly is he hurt?"

"It seems his shoulder is in pieces."

She put a hand over her mouth. "But it could have been worse."

"He's leaving hospital but has refused to be sent back to England to recuperate, so he's coming to Palur. I've invited him to stay at Hadley House. I don't want him stuck at the Victoria Club on his own."

"Of course not. When is he arriving?"

"Tomorrow."

Connie could feel sweat gathering in the hollow of her collarbones, and a beetle, the size of a Ping-Pong ball, started to crawl up onto her shoe. She kicked it off.

"We'll take good care of him," she said, and rose to her feet. "I'm going to check on the horses."

As she started to move away, Nigel said behind her, "I'll hold you to your promise, Constance. Don't forget it."

Without comment, she walked down toward the river.

ᏭᎶ

She had watered the horses and was crouched at the river's edge watching a pair of bright yellow butterflies chase each other around the rocks like children. "Poor Johnnie," she murmured. She dipped her hat in the tepid water of the river, but as she placed it on her head once more, she heard a rough noise nearby that made her turn. A noise like a smoker's gravelly cough.

Oh, Christ!

Six feet away from her crouched a giant monitor lizard. Connie didn't move a muscle. The monster creature looked like the cousin of a crocodile, longer than a man, its huge scaly body built of solid muscle. Its narrow head darted forward, flicking out a gray tongue, tasting the air, smelling her sweat. Its massive tail started to whip back and forth, shuffling the stones by the river, frightening the horses.

Slowly, Connie uncurled from her position at the water's edge and rose to her feet. Not often did monitor lizards attack humans, that's what people said, unless the humans were small or wounded. Or dead. Its fleshy mouth opened and hissed at her. She started to back up the slope from the river, and that was when a scream started somewhere behind her. A high-pitched scream that went on and on and froze the blood in her veins. It was Teddy.

She forgot the lizard. She flew up the bank, and at the top she saw that Teddy was running toward her, his mouth wide open, showing all his small white teeth, his screams solidifying into one desperate word: "Mummeeee!"

He was covered in blood. There was blood on his hands. On his shirt. On the V of his throat. Running down his small tanned leg into his shoe.

No, no, no!

He flew into her arms, stinking of blood and fear. She swept him up, racing back toward their camp hut. She saw Razak, standing and looking down at something on the ground.

"Mummy," Teddy screamed in her ear. "Daddy's hurt. Not me."

ꙮ·ꙮ

"Nigel!"

Her husband was on the ground, lying flat on his back, both arms wrapped around his face as though holding everything in. "Constance." The word came out through clenched teeth. "For God's sake, help me."

His trouser leg was soaked in blood from the ankle all the way up to the thigh. Quickly Connie knelt on the damp grass beside her husband. Already the ground was thick with blood under her knee.

"It's all right, Nigel," she said calmly. "Let me take a look at it." Without raising her head she said, "Razak, move Teddy away, please." Her eyes skimmed the immediate area and spotted the parang lying nearby. There was blood on the blade.

"What happened?"

She started to lift the torn material off his leg. It was drenched in scarlet and stuck to his skin, but she eased it away as gently as she could. She heard Nigel's sharp intake of breath, his faint sob. What she saw made bile shoot up to her throat. The flesh of one whole side of his calf was severed from his leg, hanging on by a flimsy flap of skin, blood pouring into the cavity. Bone showed red and glistening, tendons drowning in the mess.

"From parang," Razak whispered over her shoulder.

"Who did it?"

"*Tuan*, of course. He do it."

"Nigel." She bent over her husband's face and peeled his arms away. The pallor of his skin shocked her. His lips were blue. "It's OK, Nigel. Not too bad. I don't think the bone is broken, but you're losing blood." As she spoke she tore off her blouse, leaving her half-decent in a damp silk chemise, and yanked out the leather cord that held her hat on. "I'll do everything I can." His brown eyes were so dark they were almost purple. "It will hurt, I'm afraid, but . . ." She touched his cheek.

He nodded and closed his eyes, sweat beading on his skin. Immediately she bound the hat cord around his leg just above the knee and fastened it as tightly as she could. She seized a thin stick from the ground, pushed it under the cord, and twisted until the tourniquet bit into his skin.

"Nigel," she said in a firm voice, "don't worry. It's just a flap of flesh that is lying open. I'll close it, bandage it up, and get you home. Dr. Rossiter will give you stitches. You're going to be fine."

I'll get you home. How? How, in this godforsaken country?

Quickly she took out the hip flask of antiseptic, poured a few drops over her fingers, then began picking out the snippets of bark and leaf that the parang had deposited in the wound. The tourniquet must be hurting Nigel, but it was doing its job of stemming the flow, and only once did he let out a brief shout when she pulled a flake of bark and a length of muscle lifted up with it.

She murmured to him nonstop, a gentle flow of words but she had no idea what they were. Sweat was stinging her eyes. When she looked up she was grateful to see Razak kneeling on one side of Nigel holding his hand and muttering to him in Malay, while Teddy knelt on his other side, gripping his hand as if he were drowning, never taking his stricken eyes from his father's face.

Connie wiped the sweat from her eyes with the back of her hand and set about closing the wound. She lifted the loose chunk of his calf and pressed it back on his leg, holding it down hard and trying to ignore the mute shivers that shook her husband's body. With care she smoothed the ridges from the skin and bandaged her blouse around his leg. She cut strips off the sleeves to use as ties to keep it tight.

"There," she said, and from somewhere the muscles of her face found the strength to smile. "All done. I've fixed it up as best I can until a doctor can take a look at it. But the leg will be fine, I'm sure."

"Thank you."

He said it so politely, she had to fight back tears. *I'm your wife, Nigel, your wife.*

She wiped her hands on the grass while Teddy rounded up the horses and led them over. She gave him a hug. Razak was silent, still on his knees beside Nigel, but his large black eyes were on Connie. He gave no sign of what was going on in his head, and it took all her self-control not to shout at him the things that were going on in hers.

"You'll have to ride," she said quietly to Nigel.

"I know."

"I could leave you here and ride home to fetch a doctor, but it would mean a much longer delay."

"No." He pushed himself up on his elbows. "I can ride."

"You've lost a lot of blood. You'll be weak."

He gave her a lopsided grimace. "I can ride in my sleep."

"So you're the last of the wild cavalrymen," she smiled.

He nodded awkwardly and held out a hand for her to help him up. It was a struggle, but with the aid of Teddy and Razak they hoisted Nigel up onto one leg and then onto his horse. Connie saw the scarlet flower on the muslin bandage swell in size the moment he was vertical.

"Lead the way, son," Nigel said to Teddy.

The boy cast an anxious glance at his father and kicked his pony into a slow trot. Connie walked beside Nigel, leading her horse, while Razak walked on the other side of him. Together they held him steady.

"No need," Nigel muttered.

"I don't want you falling off," she said.

He scowled. "I don't intend to fall off."

But after a while the effort of sitting upright was too much, and he slumped over his horse's neck. The journey home was agonizingly slow. The heat grew worse, the humidity under the trees suffocating, while around their heads swirled clouds of hungry black flies drawn by the blood. But all Connie was aware of was the darkening of the muslin and what looked like scarlet coins that started to tumble from her husband's leg to lay a trail along the moist ground.

And all the time she hated the way the beautiful dark-skinned boy talked quietly to Nigel in a language she couldn't understand, and she couldn't believe the way he'd said so eagerly, *Tuan, of course. He do it.* In her mind there was no *of course* about it.

CHAPTER FIFTEEN

Nigel, how did it happen?"

"Just an accident."

Connie was seated beside the bed. Nigel was sitting up in his pajamas and there was a bamboo cage over his leg to keep the sheet off the bandages. A tray lay on his lap and she was encouraging him to eat some egg and toast, but he had little appetite. His cheeks were flushed. He had a slight fever.

Dr. Rossiter had been wonderful, the skill in his gentle hands spilling into the room and calming fears. The wound was thoroughly cleaned, tendons and ligaments stitched together, the skin sutured, the leg bandaged. Nigel was as weak as a kitten from loss of blood but was given something that looked like a horse tablet to make him sleep. At four o'clock in the morning he had woken in the dark to find Connie in a chair at his bedside.

"Hungry?" she'd asked hopefully. He needed to eat, the doctor said, because he'd lost so much blood.

"No."

"How's the pain?"

She didn't wait for an answer but shook out two tablets from the bottle on the bedside table and handed them to him with a cup of milky tea. He grimaced but swallowed them. So the pain must be bad. He dozed in and out of a troubled sleep for the next hour. While it was still dark, Teddy crept in and sat quietly on her lap for some time but eventually slid away on tiptoes to feed Pippin. When Nigel woke again, the sun was starting to sneak its fingers through the gaps of the shutters, and there was the sound of activity on the gravel outside. Nigel narrowed his eyes at the window and frowned.

"Don't worry," Connie told him. "Davenport is taking care of everything."

Davenport was the plantation manager, a man with a big voice and an insatiable capacity for hard work.

"Thank you, Constance."

"For what?"

"For bringing me home yesterday."

"Nigel, how did it happen?"

"Just an accident." He flicked his fingers to dismiss the question, but they had no strength.

"You've chopped branches before, and always been so careful."

"I was careful this time."

She let her gaze linger on his face. There was something lost about it, a muddy uncertainty in his eyes and an unaccustomed looseness about his mouth. As if he had frightened himself. She rested her hand on his arm and stroked it, not on his skin but on the sheet that covered it.

"Not careful enough," she said gently. "Did something happen to make your hand slip?"

"No."

Too fast. Much too fast. She could feel the heat under her fingers.

"Try to eat a little more."

But he'd closed his eyes. Shut her out.

Ð·Ɛ

"Teddy."

Her son was bent over his farmyard jigsaw, clutching the cockerel in his hand, the tip of his tongue tucked into the corner of his mouth. He looked up at her quickly, as though fearing bad news. It was Monday morning and she should be taking him to school, but she didn't have the heart. He needed to be near his father today.

"Daddy is asleep now, but he's on the mend. He asked me to tell you that you were a big help to him yesterday. Riding just ahead of him, leading the way home."

"I remembered the paths well, didn't I?"

"You certainly did. Better than I could. I was proud of you."

She saw tears spring into his eyes, and he looked down at his jigsaw, abandoned the cockerel, and picked up a patch of blue sky.

"Daddy will get better soon," she said with conviction.

He nodded and pretended to concentrate on finding a matching piece of sky, his nose two inches from the jigsaw.

"Teddy"—Connie sat down at the table beside her son—"tell me what happened. Just before the accident."

His eyes skipped to hers. "Nothing."

"What were you and Razak doing?"

"Playing."

"With the rubber balls?"

"Yes."

"While Daddy was chopping the branch."

"Yes."

A small gap of silence opened up between them. She lifted a piece of tree, an old English oak, and slotted it into place, aware of Teddy's gaze still locked on her face.

"Were you throwing the balls at each other?" she asked without looking at him.

"No. We were throwing them up in the air, as high as we could. Taking turns. To see who throws highest."

"That was fun."

"Yes." He sounded cautious. Waiting to hear what he'd done wrong.

"Did Razak throw the ball at Daddy?"

"No!" Teddy looked at her, aghast.

૭·૯

Connie found Razak at the far end of the vegetable garden. He was laboring in the shade of the hedge, digging a hole with a spade in a bed of freshly turned earth, his sandals too flimsy for such work.

"Razak."

He lifted his head and waited for her to approach. His expression was guarded, as if he knew what was coming. His skin shone darker in the shadows.

"Razak."

"How *Tuan*?"

"He's getting better."

"I glad."

"Are you?"

He nodded vigorously. "*Ya*, yes."

"I've come to tell you that I no longer need you to work here."

"In veg patch?"

He had deliberately misunderstood.

"No, Razak, I mean anywhere at Hadley House."

They stood in silence, except for the call of a mynah bird somewhere nearby. She felt stiff and awkward, angry with him but unwilling to show it. He regarded her for a long moment, his black eyebrows drawing low over his eyes.

"I not bad," he said.

"I want you to leave. But have this."

She held out a leather wallet stuffed with banknotes. When he didn't take it or even drop his gaze from her face to see what she was offering, she took hold of his hand and pressed the wallet between his fingers. He let it fall from his grip into the hole in the earth and kicked soil over it.

"Good-bye, Razak," she said curtly, and started to move away.

But suddenly he was in front of her on the path, his beautiful features taut with rage. "I not bad, *mem*. You bad. Evil spirits all round you head. Chatter in ear." He made his hands into talking mouths, opening and shutting fast, pushing them in her face. "I see them," he hissed. "They lie to you."

He swung round and raced away out of the vegetable garden. Connie stood absolutely still, stunned. Was he right? Could she hear them? The whisperings of evil spirits that haunted this wretched country? Was that what the soft whooshing sound in her head was? She'd thought it was from tension and lack of sleep, but maybe she was wrong.

As she walked back to the house, her early-morning shadow darting ahead of her like a black demon, it took all her self-control not to flap her hands around her head to knock the bad spirits out of the air.

꘎·꘎

Flight Lieutenant Johnnie Blake arrived just after eight o'clock in the morning. His left arm was in a sling across his chest and he was out of uniform in an open-necked shirt and gray flannels. Connie greeted him at the door with a hug and led him into the drawing room, but when she held him at arm's length and studied his face, she was saddened by what she saw. His handsome face looked exhausted, with dark smudges under his eyes and a shiny burn mark like a puddle of ice just in front of his left ear.

"What a silly idiot you are!" she laughed. "You and Nigel both make a fine pair of wounded soldiers."

"Nigel? What's wrong with him?"

"It's all right, don't look like that. He's upstairs, banished to bed for a few days."

"What happened? Connie, is he hurt?"

"He tried to chop his leg off with a parang."

"Christ! They are lethal." He closed his eyes for a second, then opened them and matched her smile. "So how is the foolish fellow?"

"Recovering. Dr. Rossiter patched him up. What about you? How's your poor shoulder?"

"A scratch only." He rolled his blue eyes at her. "I'm just damned furious at being invalided out for a month, especially now."

"Well, I shall keep you here as long as I can to act as official enter-tainer to Nigel—to make him stay off that leg of his until it's properly healed. Agreed?"

"Agreed," he laughed. "I'll wear a court jester's hat if it will help."

"Excellent! Run upstairs and say hello to him. He's dying of boredom up there. Please remind him that I say that he's not to smoke in bed! I'll bring you a couple of coffees . . ."

"*Pajits* would be better."

"At this hour? Johnnie, it's far too early for alcohol."

"Not today. Bring one for yourself, too. You're going to need it."

For a moment he didn't move, just looked at her with an expression she couldn't fathom. Then he was gone, his long limbs and rumpled blond hair speeding through the hall and racing up the stairs. Quickly she mixed three glasses of gin and bitters and hurried up the stairs with them. When she walked into the bedroom Nigel was sitting on the edge of the bed, his feet on the floor. She opened her mouth to scold him, but when she saw his face she shut it again. His expression was one of horror. His skin was the color of old wax as he stared, appalled, at Johnnie who was leaning against the windowsill.

"No!" Nigel bellowed.

"What is it?" she asked quickly.

"It's the bloody murdering Japs. They've bombed Pearl Harbor."

"Pearl Harbor?"

"In Hawaii. The American naval base. Oh God, this means disaster for us and the whole of East Asia. They've destroyed the American fleet." Nigel dragged a wrist across his mouth as if he could wipe away the words.

Quietly Johnnie added, "Seventeen of their G3M bombers attacked Singapore, too. Raffles Place was hit, sixty people killed and more than seven hundred injured. They went for the airfields at Tengah and Seletar, and the poor Gurkha Rifles took a terrible pounding."

Connie put her hand to her throat to hold in the cries that rose like wraiths from her lungs. The evil spirits were laughing in her ears.

"It's war, Constance," Nigel said. "We're at war."

ᗡ·G

They are addicted. The thought darted into Connie's mind as she looked around her at the men and women in the smoke-filled bar of the Victoria Club. *They are addicted to mastery. If ownership of this country with its tin and its rubber and its timber is wrenched from their grip, they will lose their sense of who they are and what their purpose in life is.* Nigel was at home in bed, but in spirit he was here with them, one of the addicts, one of the owners of the rich earth of Malaya.

"The attack on Pearl Harbor signals that the balance of power in the Pacific has fundamentally changed," Henry Court announced as he knocked back an early Bloody Mary. "But at least the Japs have forced the blasted Yanks into this war at last, with a kick up the backside."

"About bloody time," someone shouted.

The bar was bristling with people eager to make their voices heard. They had gathered in tight clusters, around the radio and in the smoking room, herded into close-knit groups like nervous livestock who know a wolf is prowling the fences.

"Prime Minister Churchill has appointed Duff Cooper as Resident Cabinet Minister for Far Eastern Affairs in Singapore to oversee matters. He's a damn good man," Henry Court reminded everyone.

Connie sat in silence at a low table with Harriet Court sipping coffee, listening to the men raising their voices.

"We've all heard the rumors," a retired major with a tobacco-stained mustache chipped in, "that the Japs are trying for an amphibious assault up in the north, around Kota Bharu."

"General Arthur Percival and our Fifty-Third Infantry will put a stop to that."

"And he has the Indian and Australian divisions as backup. The Japs will run like sheep."

"They have the RAF to reckon with too."

"Our boys will blast them from the skies."

All wanted to have their say.

Connie rolled her eyes at Harriet, who was eating with grim determination, demolishing a plate of choux pastries. Food was always her first haven when nervous.

"That's not what Johnnie Blake tells us," Connie told her in a low voice. "He says we don't have nearly enough planes in Malaya, and that the Brewster Buffaloes are poorly built and ill equipped."

"Oh, Christ!"

They had listened to President Franklin D. Roosevelt's address to Congress, declaring 7 December 1941 to be a date that would live in infamy, and they had read in the *Straits Times* about Prime Minister Churchill's missive to the imperial Japanese government announcing that "a state of war exists between our two countries."

A state of war.

The four words were so huge. Massive great boulders that could crush them all.

The sudden drone of an airplane made all eyes turn toward the ceiling, hearts racing. But a lone figure standing just inside the French doors and smoking a cheroot called out with dry reassurance, "You can relax. It's one of ours, a Blenheim bomber. Our boys will protect us. Like they protected Penang."

It was Fitzpayne, mockery in the twist of his mouth. Everyone knew that the island of Penang was being hammered day after day by Jap fighters and bombers. Hundreds of civilians were dead or wounded.

"Who's he?" Harriet paused to ask, a cake fork hovering in front of her mouth.

"No one. A boat buyer."

Harriet nodded but didn't take her eyes off him.

One of the plantation owners was on his feet. "Sir," he addressed Fitzpayne, "I can't say I like your tone."

"Are you aware," Fitzpayne said flatly, "that there is not one single tank in Malaya? How can you expect to fight against modern warfare methods without tanks?"

"That just shows how little you know about the terrain of this country. No tanks could penetrate the jungle. No army will ever attack that way, and we have guns pointing out to sea at Singapore."

There was a general murmur of agreement.

Fitzpayne smiled, a tightening of his mouth into a straight scornful line. "Gentlemen, that just shows how little you know about the Japanese." He shrugged and drifted out of the French windows into the garden outside.

"Christ!" Harriet stuffed an eclair pastry wrapped in a napkin into her handbag for later. "Who knows anything about the Japs? They are a law unto themselves."

Connie leaned forward and said in an undertone, "Harriet, we have our boat ready to go. If you and Henry want to join us, you're welcome to come."

Harriet squeezed Connie's hand. "Thank you." Her gaze strayed across the room to her husband. "I'll talk to Henry. But what about Nigel? Surely he would never abandon the Hadley Estate. It's his life."

"I'll persuade him."

"How?"

"I know the one thing he loves even more than he loves the estate."

Harriet smiled enviously. "You?"

Connie flushed. "No. It's Teddy."

�94

"The Japanese are a determined and disciplined nation."

They were Sho's words. She thought of them now as she queued to buy cans of kerosene oil. The people of Palur were just starting to panic, stockpiling basic necessities so that some shops were already rationing the amount allowed per customer for staple goods such as tea and sugar, rice and flour. She recalled that Sho had been sipping warm sake, eating thin slivers of raw fish as he sat cross-legged on the floor in their jungle hut. He was wearing a black and purple kimono wreathed in the coils of a dragon, its colors as vivid as the flowers of Malaya itself. He looked fragrant, his skin cool despite the sultry heat and the intermittent thunderstorms that shook the fragile building.

"I believe you," she had replied.

"That we are determined and disciplined."

"Yes. If you are a typical example of the Japanese mentality."

That pleased him. His black eyes shone in the dim light, and his lips parted in the way they did when he wanted something from her. Usually it was a kiss or a caress somewhere new, but today he had been acting strangely, his manner more formal from the moment she'd made her way up the front steps. He had brought silk kimonos for both of them, when usually they spent every moment naked, and he'd laid a square of white silk no bigger than a headscarf on the floor as their table. As she sat opposite Sho on her side of the white square, she badly wanted a cigarette instead of a thimbleful of sake. She had grown to dislike the hut. She would prefer to meet anywhere but here. Sho had hung a scroll of Japanese writing on the wall and strung carved wooden charms of peculiar mean-faced animals from the roof beams. It had begun to feel like a cage, a rough, ill-kempt bamboo one, but still a cage, just as much as the elegant mansion of Hadley House with its dark brooding staircase was a cage.

"Sho, why don't we go up to one of the hill stations next week? It's so much cooler there. I can arrange for Teddy to be picked up from school by his friend's mother, and we . . ."

"I like it here."

"It's time for a change."

His gaze fixed on her. "You are right. That is why today I want to start to prepare you for coming to Japan."

"Sho, don't be foolish. I can't leave Malaya." She smiled at him to soften her words and reached forward to touch the smooth pale skin of his chest where the kimono hung loose, but he swayed backward out of reach.

"A person can do whatever he or she wants," he said.

"Sho, I have a son."

"A fine boy."

"I would never leave him."

"You must bring him to Japan too."

"No. I respect your country, but I have no wish to live there."

Silence swirled into the hut, rippled around her ankles, cold and clingy as if the nearby river had overflowed its banks. The silence had the same dank smell, the stink of something rotten inside it. Sho rose to his feet, walked once around the tiny room, and knelt down again immediately behind her. He placed his hands on either side of her head, cupping her ears, so that she couldn't turn to look at him.

"Connie," he said in an odd, soft voice, "you are my life."

She lifted her fingers to his hands to prize them away, but they held firm, making the rush of blood in her ears echo through the bones of her head.

"Sho, let go of me."

His breath brushed the side of her neck. "I won't ever let you go. You are my life, you are my love, you are my reason for being on this earth."

Connie felt a flutter of fear touch her throat. She stroked his hands. "This isn't one of those affairs," she told him. "Not a life-and-death *grand amour*. It's . . ."

"What? What is it, then?"

She tried to shake her head and laugh, but still he insisted on holding it in a firm grip. "It's a wonderful moment of pleasure, an interlude of delight which we both longed for in our lives and for which I am grateful. But you don't love me, Sho. You just love the excitement and the secrecy. You are a man born to crave excitement." She tapped his fingers, keeping her voice as light as possible. "Now let's forget the sake and go to bed." She slipped the kimono from her shoulders and immediately his hands released her head, unable to resist the allure of her skin.

He kissed her shoulder blade. "I don't want your gratitude," he whispered. "I want your love. You are part of me now, and you belong to me. You and I are meant to be together . . ."

She turned and put her hands in his hair, her lips on his mouth. "Hush." She removed his dragon kimono and inhaled the warm musk of his body. She had told him from the start that she would never leave Nigel or Teddy. She hadn't lied, hadn't deceived him. She had been straight with Shohei Takehashi. But all the time he had been lying to her, pretending their romance was a lighthearted affair, when in his heart he was hoarding little pieces of her. How could she not have noticed? He was trying to steal her and whisk her back to Japan. She didn't want to hurt him, but she knew now that she couldn't avoid it. She rose to her feet and led him to the bed, her fingers entwined with his.

This would be their last time.

꒦·꒷

Sho's arm lay wrapped around her throat, the weight of it heavy on her windpipe. But Connie didn't move. She waited, still and silent in the bed. She breathed with a shallow rhythm, matching it to Sho's in case he was deceiving her in this as well. Eyes tight shut, aware of the whine of flies and the spidery touch of a thread of sunlight on her bare leg. It reminded her of lying in bed beside Nigel, the same rigid wakefulness, and it made her skin quiver at the irony of it.

She didn't trust Sho. Not any more.

When she was absolutely certain he was fast asleep, exhausted by their earlier passionate exertions, she slid out from under the possessive grip of his arm and padded over to her clothes. They had been neatly folded by Sho and placed on a clean sheet he had laid in one corner for the purpose. He was a precise man with precise habits. She had become one of them, without realizing the full impact of what that meant to a man like Sho. She experienced a wave of sorrow for him, and for the loss of what they'd had together. *Why is it that men feel the urge to control women in the same way they feel the urge to control a country? Can't they let things be?*

She needed a cigarette. Ridges of anger seemed to have formed on her tongue—neither anger at Sho, nor anger at Nigel, but a sharp rage at herself. She stepped into her underwear and reached into Sho's attaché case that he always brought with him, from which he produced sugary sweetmeats for her with a flourish. She couldn't see his cigarettes, so she lifted out the manila folder of papers in the case and spotted the pack of Dunhills at the bottom. She removed one, lit it with his lighter, and drew the smoke deep into her lungs. She must leave now. No good-byes. But a sheet of typed paper slid from the folder that was still in her hand and drifted in a spiral to the floor.

Connie picked it up and saw that it was in English. She started to read.

CHAPTER SIXTEEN

Madoc lay wide awake in bed, listening to the wind and the river trying to outroar each other, the sound deep and resonant, vibrating the roof of his house above him. He hadn't slept well, but then he never did. Kitty always blamed it on the sharp cries from the jungle and its incessant heavy breathing, but he knew it wasn't that. There was too much in his head. Too much of the past stomping around in his brain, keeping him awake with its heavy boots.

He had told Kitty about the bicycles, and she hadn't liked it. He wasn't sure he liked it himself, but the Jap had handed over payment in advance, and he had taken it. The deal was done, and he had more sense than to back out of an agreement with the Japanese army. He'd paid for the new gaming tables now. That was a weight off his shoulders.

Madoc slid his hand down the silky pillow of Kitty's thigh. Though her face and hands displayed the skin of the tropics, tanned and leathery, the secret places of her body still had the soft, smooth skin of a young girl. Since meeting Kitty, he'd never lusted after other women. She had been tall and statuesque as a girl. He smiled when he remembered the wild hair and restless eyes that caught his attention when he had gone into a draper's shop in Putney in London to buy a reel of white thread. He needed to sew buttons back onto his shirt—they had been torn off in a fight. In those days he was always getting into fights. Afterward, he waited for her outside the shop at the end of the day and walked her home in the rain.

They'd had fun together in those early years. She never asked where his money came from when he had pockets bulging with the stuff, or where it had gone when he had none. He took her dancing at the Ritz and punting on Oxford's river Isis, but when he had no money for food for a month Kitty fed him her lunchtime sandwiches under the trees in Hyde Park. He lived on his wits. Never had a proper job. He dealt in anything he could get his hands on—cars, cigarettes, greyhounds, girls, and when he couldn't lay hold of something legit, he knew where to find it in the back alleyways of London's docklands.

The day he came to Kitty with blood on his hands and his shoulders shaking, she didn't hesitate. She bound his wounds and hid him in a shed on her father's allotment while she arranged for a wedding license and passports. There was no ring, no church bells, and not even a posy of flowers, but the day after the brief marriage ceremony they were on a ship to Australia. Where the money came from for the tickets he didn't ask, but she never mentioned her parents again, and certainly they hadn't come to the wedding.

Madoc didn't take to Australia. Too full of dust and dingoes. So after knocking around there for a year or two, they'd shipped out first to the Philippines and then to Singapore. After a spot of bother over a forged signature, they shifted upcountry to Kuala Lumpur and eventually to Tampang, and for the first time they put down roots. Long, stringy ones that bound him to this patch of earth and to Morgan's Bar. He loved Malaya, adored the smell of it, the hot and greasy sweat of it. He was fond of the natives, a warm and easygoing people, but hated the English dandies who had stolen the country for themselves from a handful of sultans and carved it up between them. Stamford Raffles had one hell of a lot to answer for when he rammed the Union Jack into the rich and fertile soil of Malaya.

A sound stopped his thoughts. With a start he realized that the pitch darkness of the jungle night had given way to the first murmurs of daylight, just a smattering of golden shimmers sliding along the wall like shooting stars. The sound was faint at first, but coming closer fast, the deep growl of an engine in the sky.

"Kitty!" Madoc shook his wife's shoulder. "Kitty, wake up. Listen!"

With a muffled groan of protest, she raised her head and listened.

"An airplane," Madoc hissed in her ear.

"One of ours."

"Maybe not."

The drone of the engine was clearly audible now.

He leaped out from under the mosquito net and into his clothes, thrown over a chair last night. He shook his shoes for spiders. "Get up! No lights. Be quick!"

"For God's sake, Madoc, leave me alone." She burrowed into her pillow once more.

He yanked the sheet off her. "Up! Now!" He picked up her clothes from the floor and threw them on top of her.

She sat up and yawned. "You know you're overreacting, don't you?"

"Get dressed," he said urgently. "We need to get out of here."

She chucked a shoe at him and he vanished into the kitchen. Less than two minutes later when she walked in, stretching her limbs like a sleepy cat, Madoc had tossed a carving knife, matches, candles, a torch, and a hunk of cheese into a bag. The Russian pistol was tucked under his belt.

"Christ, Madoc! I tell you it will be the bloody RAF."

He didn't stop to argue. He seized her arm, propelled her out of the front door, and raced for the line of darkness that was the jungle. Not for one minute did he think the aircraft would bear RAF roundels. The moment they reached the trees, they halted, Madoc's pulse pounding in his ears, and he could feel the sweat snaking down Kitty's arm. They didn't move, hidden in the fringe of the jungle, looking up at the sky that was fast turning gold in the east, staring at the black silhouette of a twin-engine bomber that was clearly visible.

"Madoc, tell me I'm right and you're wrong," Kitty whispered.

But as she spoke, a sprinkling of what looked like black eggs dropped out of the bottom of the aircraft and plummeted toward the clearing where Morgan's Bar stood. Madoc couldn't bear to look. He drew his wife deeper into the dark heart of the jungle, indifferent to the spiderwebs that clung to their cheeks and the leeches that buried blunt little heads into their flesh as they passed.

೨·೮

When daylight came, they returned, in no hurry now. Not that Madoc doubted what they would find. Rage burned his lungs, cramping them badly as he hacked out a trail with the knife. Neither talked. Neither mentioned the explosions they had heard or the roar, like a volcano blasting off, which Madoc knew was the fuel tank for his generator blowing up.

The sight that met their eyes tore something from Madoc that he knew he would never regain. Everything was gone. The bar, the casino, the outhouses, the jetty, and the boat had all vanished, as though a giant hand had reached down and snatched them up. Scorched earth and blackened rubble were all that remained. He had started up afresh and created a new life for himself time after time in his past, a new place, a new name, but this was different: This was a home, the only real one he and Kitty had ever owned. At forty-four he was too old for this.

After one brief glance at it, he walked down to the river and stood on its bank. Even the water smelled of smoke. He turned his back on the clearing and remained stubbornly like that, his chin on his chest and his eyes closed, though he could hear Kitty rummaging among the burned ruins behind him. Yet again he had failed her, and yet again she wouldn't blame him for it. If he had steered clear of the Japs, if he hadn't been so bloody greedy, this would never have happened.

He turned his head and saw her broad bottom bend over as she tugged at something in the blackened mess on the ground. At her feet she had piled a few oddments from her search: the steel blade of a parang but with no haft to hold it by, a scorched tin of corned beef, a shard of cracked mirror, a zinc bowl, and, miraculously, an undamaged toothbrush.

She lifted her head and saw him watching. The look on her face told him more than he needed to know about what was going on in her head. He walked quickly over to her, but she backed away.

"I'm sorry," she whispered.

"It wasn't you."

"Yes, it was. I knocked the ladder down on him."

"No, they did this to stop me from telling the authorities about the bicycles I supplied to them."

"Bicycles! Don't treat me like I'm stupid, Madoc," she snapped. "They know you'd end up in prison if you told the authorities anything at all about your business with them."

"No, if it wasn't the bicycles, it was the other stuff I've done with the Japs." He wanted her to believe the lie. "I'm so sorry, Kitty. I should have known it would end badly."

She wiped her filthy palms on her skirt and looked at him with a wonky attempt at a smile. "It always ends like this," she said.

He nodded slowly. "So much the better. Just you and me against the rest of the bastards."

꩜

Connie held Teddy's hand tight. She had picked him up from school after depositing the kerosene on the boat and was now heading for the library.

Teddy loved the library. It was an imposing building with thick stone walls and a small clock tower above its studded front doors. Teddy loved it for the abundance of books to choose from, but Connie loved it because it was the coolest building in the whole of Palur and it reminded her of England. They took their time choosing, their heads bent over the pages as they assessed a book's attraction. Their final selection after half an hour was Jack London's *White Fang* for Teddy, while for herself Connie took out the latest Agatha Christie and a biography of Ernest Shackleton. Just the thought of all that ice and snow made her feel better.

"Good afternoon, Mrs. Hadley. You're looking well. Hello, Teddy."

"Mr. Fitzpayne. We meet again."

His handshake was firm but brief. He had emerged from the library's reading room, but Connie couldn't rid herself of the feeling that he wasn't here by accident, that this was no coincidence. He was wearing a canvas cap and loose trousers that made him look as if he'd been working on one of the fishing boats.

"I thought you might have left Palur," he said, "with all this excitement going on."

"Excitement? Is that what you call it?"

"I noticed you at *The White Pearl* today."

Is there anything I do that you don't notice?

They stepped out into the street and she donned her sunglasses. After the soft gray silence of the library, the noise of the town struck Connie as harsh and brittle, busy with traffic and people gathered in huddles on the sidewalk, eager to share every scrap of news.

"No more adventures in the jungle to report?" Fitzpayne asked her son.

Teddy grinned. "No, sir."

"So what are you reading?"

Teddy held out the book. "It's about a sled dog."

"Good choice. I read it when I was a boy."

There was a pause as they stood on the sidewalk, and Fitzpayne lifted his gaze from the boy to Connie. "I'm sorry to hear your husband is unwell."

"Is there anything about my family you don't hear?" It came out sharper than she intended.

He looked at her keenly as he raised his cap to her. "I hope he recovers quickly." But he didn't stride off, just stood in front of her as if there were unfinished business between them.

What was it he wanted from her?

"Thank you, Mr. Fitzpayne," she said. "Good afternoon to you."

She walked away, Teddy at her side.

৯·৫

Connie headed quickly in the direction of her car, which was parked in the shade with the *syce* at the wheel. The encounter with Fitzpayne had unsettled her. He was constantly intruding, but she had no idea what it was he wanted. Were there business dealings with Nigel that he thought she could help with? Was it *The White Pearl*? Was that what he was after?

A familiar noise caught her attention and she heard a voice shout, "Go get 'em, boys! Give the bastards hell!" It was the drone of an aircraft overhead. She glanced up and saw five planes silhouetted against the fierce blue sky, their fuselages glinting in the sun, a fighter and four heavy bombers. Someone waved to them and cheered the RAF. The drone grew louder.

"Mummy!" Teddy shouted, his mouth wide open in alarm. "Mummy, they're not ours! They have twin tails. They're Japanese."

Connie seized his hand and started to run. The first bomb hit the market square, a great wall of sound that blasted Teddy right off his feet, slamming him into the curb, tearing at their eardrums and scrambling their minds. Connie picked him up in her arms and hurried forward. More bombs hurtled down, their impact shaking the earth beneath her feet.

Screams ripped through the street as explosions roared from the direction of the harbor and the bang and crump of falling bombs seemed neverending. The air shuddered, turned gray. Filled Connie's lungs with dust and dirt and smoke as buildings collapsed and fires started to rage from one shop to another.

The library, I have to get us back to the library. The library had a basement that would be safe. She held Teddy tight, his arms entwined around her neck, his legs locked around her waist, his eyes dazed and disbelieving. Bodies lay torn to pieces on the road in front of him. A man screamed at them, his beard on fire. Connie slapped out the flames with her bare hands and ran on. A telegraph pole crashed down inches ahead of her, its wires writhing across her path. She dodged them, her heart thumping.

"Mummy!" Teddy screamed a warning in her ear. "A Japanese fighter. A Zero!"

Over the roar she heard the new sound, the spit and crack of machine-gun fire. She swung around, clasping her son. At the far end of the street a single-engine fighter was flying very low, coming toward her as though it had smelled her blood. Its guns were strafing the injured and shattering the windows, kicking up chunks of rubble from the buildings, killing a horse, ripping open the plump cheeks of a native woman who was shaking her fist at the monster in the sky. The library lay just ahead. Connie urged her legs to move faster, but as she raced for its front steps a man in a safari jacket, his trousers blasted into rags, stumbled across the street. He collapsed onto his knees in front of her.

"Help me!" he gasped. Where his left ear should be lay a dark bubbling hole. Blood dribbled down his neck and pumped from his legs.

Not now, she wanted to scream at him. *Not now.*

Instead, she released her hold on her son. She stood him on the ground, seized the man's arm, and tried to yank him to his feet, but his legs were broken. The roar of the aircraft engine bombarded her senses, vibrating the air in her lungs as it grew closer. The guns rattled, deadening all other sounds. Teddy's mouth was opening and shutting, shouting something as he struggled to help raise the injured man by pushing his shoulder under the limp arm. But she couldn't hear his voice.

"Run, Teddy!" she screamed at him. "Into the library!"

She hauled the man up, but he slid to his knees once more, his face full of anguish and his hands clawing at her. She pushed Teddy away.

"Run!"

The Zero was almost upon them. Teddy wrenched her sleeve, breaking her grip on the man. He yelled something at her. In desperation she bent double, lifted the man onto her back, and started to stagger as fast as she could toward the library. Teddy's young face crumpled in horror, but he made an effort to help her, slowing his scampering steps to hers and trying to take some of the weight.

"No, Teddy. Run!"

The blow of someone crashing into her back should have knocked her off her feet. The only reason it didn't was that a strong hand held her upright. Someone had charged into her, yanking the man off her back so that he slumped to the ground where bullets were already hissing and spitting and chips of paving stone were dancing in the sunlight. Connie and Teddy were propelled at speed into the stone wall of the library, jammed hard against it, and held there. The cry of the wounded man fluttered in the air somewhere behind her.

The plane ripped past overhead. Connie twisted her head and saw people fleeing in panic and falling in the street. More bodies lay on the shimmering tarmac. Connie's ears throbbed, and her hand was twisted firmly into Teddy's hair.

"Now, move!"

The person crushing them against the wall stood back, releasing them, and at once she spun round to see who had saved them. She was met by Fitzpayne's grim eyes.

"Inside. Quick," he ordered. "The plane will make a return run."

"Now, Teddy!"

Connie ran, hauling her son along with her, but she paused to stare at the man on the ground who had asked for their help. He was lying in a pool of blood, and bullet holes were dotted over the front of his safari jacket like scarlet buttons. His glazed eyes were opened to the sun, and a fly had landed at the corner of one of them.

"I'm sorry," she whispered.

"You are a fool," Fitzpayne said savagely behind her. "You and your son would have died."

She shook her head at him in anger. "But how many people have to die here in Palur before this country is satisfied and spits me out?"

ﬄ·ﬄ

Blood and books: The smells mingled in the basement room of the library. It was stiflingly hot and airless, so that sweat soaked Connie's clothes. But at least she still had a body and limbs for them to cling to. The image of the safari jacket with its crimson holes haunted her, and rage burned the back of her throat. She wanted to tear that Jap plane out of the skies and shake it to pieces.

Other people came. Some brought the injured and wounded with them; some tumbled down the steps into the basement, sobbing. A few crawled, leaving a trail of scarlet slime in their wake. She bandaged them using petticoats and shirts cut into strips; she murmured soft words of comfort to soothe their fears and rocked in her arms the ones who needed to cry and hold on to someone. When a bomb landed close by and made them flinch, she covered their ears. She wiped their tears. And all the time she swore under her breath.

"Talking to yourself?"

It was Fitzpayne again. She had not seen him for the couple of hours she had spent inside the basement.

"No," Connie muttered, straightening her back, "just telling the Japs what I would do to people who wage war on innocent civilians." She pushed away her hair, and it felt slick against her skin. "What's it like outside?"

"Not good. The planes keep coming, waves of them."

"What have you been doing out there?"

"Not much. Digging out survivors from the rubble of buildings."

She looked at him properly. He was covered in dirt, his hair almost white with dust; his shirt was torn, and blood on his arm had dried in a crust. Was it his own blood, or someone else's? His face looked utterly exhausted.

"Mr. Fitzpayne, I—"

"Call me Fitz."

"Fitz, I think you need a rest."

He shrugged and gave her a crooked smile. "So do you, Mrs. Hadley." He looked around and frowned. "Where's the boy?"

"Teddy?" She pointed to the far corner of the room, where her son was sitting on the floor surrounded by a group of young children. He was reading to them. "He's been helping me. Very brave."

"Like his mother."

Her eyes flicked up to his face, but he wasn't laughing at her. He took her elbow and steered her away from the woman whose head she had just bandaged, to a quiet patch where he leaned against a wall and for a moment closed his eyes.

"Do you have a cigarette?" Connie asked.

He nodded and drew a cigarette pack and matches from his pocket. She lit one and handed it to him, then lit one for herself. She breathed out a coil of smoke and felt some of the tension trickle away with it. "I was rude earlier, I'm sorry. I am very grateful for your help in the street. It's just that I was . . ."

"Forget it. You wanted to save that man, but you can't save everyone."

Her gaze roamed around the room of wounded people. "I can save some," she said softly. She drew on her cigarette. "Tell me, do you believe in curses?"

"Of course. Don't you?"

She looked at him with surprise. She hadn't expected that from him. "Death seems to follow me. As faithful as a dog."

He looked at her with shrewd eyes. "Do you invite it?"

"Of course not." But she shrugged and gave Fitzpayne a self-conscious smile. "Do you know what one little girl called me today when I bandaged her arm? She said I must be an angel."

"Angels are supposed to bring happiness."

She grimaced. "Except for the Angel of Death."

He did something then that she wouldn't have expected of him. He took her chin in his hand and shook it hard, as if to rattle such thoughts out of her head. At the same time, his gaze fixed fiercely on hers and she was conscious of the feel of his callused fingers against her skin, an intimate touch from a man she barely knew. His strange, questing look searched her eyes.

"Why are you so angry with yourself?" he asked.

She jerked her head away. "I'm worried about my husband. He'll have heard about the attack on Palur by now and . . ."

"Don't fret over it. I sent a boy out to Hadley House to say that you and your son were unhurt."

The way he said it, as if it were nothing. It astonished her.

"Thank you. That was very kind."

Somewhere across the room a tiny baby started to bleat.

"Hear that?" he said sharply. "It's the sound of life, not death. Think of that when you are feeling buried under your curses."

"I delivered it."

"What?"

"The baby. Here in this basement, an hour ago." She laughed at his expression of amazement.

"Hah!" He clapped her on the back so hard it made her cough. "So you have broken your curse."

She stared at him. "What do you mean?"

"A life for a life."

She looked away. She didn't want him to see what his words did to her. She stubbed out her cigarette.

"I must go back to them," she said.

"You don't have to, you know. You look . . . as though you've done enough."

She glanced down at herself, at her bloodstained clothes. Her hand touched her hair and found it caked with dirt and grit from the explosion.

"Of course I have to," she said.

ɔ·ʕ

It wasn't the first time Connie had seen this amount of blood, the smell of it heavy in the air. The first time was in the hut, that last day with Sho when everything changed.

"What are you reading?" Sho's tone had been sharp when he woke. He had moved from sleep to total alertness in the course of one breath.

Connie was sitting fully dressed and cross-legged on the end of the bed in the hut. In her hand she had clutched the sheets of closely typed paper taken from his attaché case. Earlier she had focused on the features of her lover's face as he slept, on the familiar lift of his black eyebrow, the strong pad of flesh just beneath the cheekbone, the dormant line of his mouth. Her mind stumbled when she tried to reconcile the words on the paper with the face she thought she knew.

"I'm reading about what I did last week," she said flatly, "and the week before, and the week before that, and the . . ."

"Those are my private papers."

"And this"—she snapped them through the sultry air—"is my private life."

He sat bolt upright in the bed and stretched out his hand. "Give them to me." His voice was cold.

She uncurled from the mattress. "You've had someone spying on me."

"Not spying. Watching over you."

"Spying!" She lifted one of the pages. " 'Your fear that Mrs. Constance Hadley is having affairs with other men is groundless—based on what I have been able to observe.' " She tossed the document on the floor. "And this! 'Mrs. Hadley is, in my opinion, of stable mind and is well liked by the friends to whom I've spoken.' And this! 'She and her husband sleep in the same bed.' Which of my servants did you bribe to get that intimate tidbit?"

He sat very still. "I needed to be sure of you."

"Well," she said angrily, "you can be sure of this—that we are finished."

His skin grew pale as bone and his eyes changed as he moved smoothly from the bed to the door. He stood there naked, blocking her exit.

"No," he said quietly. "No."

Never in all their previous meetings together had he given any sign that she meant more to him than a pleasant afternoon's interlude. Yet now it seemed that their friendship lay in pieces, limp and colorless as the cigarette butts discarded at their feet. She saw his eyes slide to the leather attaché case on the floor, and something about the way he did it made her instantly alert. She darted forward and scooped it up.

He didn't move from the door. "Put it down, Connie."

She opened it. This time she looked in the zipped side flap and pulled out an object. It was a small shagreen diary. She flicked it open. Inside, every page was covered in tight, neat writing, mostly in Japanese script but some in English. She spotted Nigel's name. Her own. Her fingers turned another page. A description of the plantation smoke sheds, an account of the rubber process. Page after page of Japanese writing, then a sketch of the *Repulse* and of the dry dock in Palur harbor. Johnnie Blake's name beside the words *300 aircraft*. A list of regiments under the heading *Malaya Command: Indian III Corps, 8th Division (Australia), 11th Division, Malaya Regiment, 53rd Infantry Brigade.* Pages and pages of Japanese script.

Connie shut the diary with an angry snap, and saw on the back page in red ink the words: *300,000 whites tyrannise 100 million Asians* and underneath it, *KOTA BHARU is our way in.* Her blood grew cold in her veins as she realized what Shohei Takehashi was.

"A spy," she hissed. "You're a spy for Japan."

How much have I told him?

How many times had he listened at Nigel's table of talk of the rubber industry in Malaya? Or discussion of the airfields with Johnnie? Or the impregnable state of Singapore's sea-facing guns and its naval base.

Kota Bharu? Where the hell was that?

A knot of fear twisted in her stomach, and she dropped the book as if the pages burned her fingers. Sho's face was without expression as he stepped forward, and she thought he was going to pick it up, but instead his hand shot out and slapped her face. The blow almost knocked out her teeth, and something exploded high up inside her nose, sending tentacles of pain crawling through her face. Blood, warm and salty, trickled out of her nostril and down onto her lips.

Connie blinked, swore, and shook her head to clear it. But when he came at her again she was ready and rammed both of her fists into the center of his naked chest to push him away. She heard his lungs screech. She started to run for the door, but before she could reach it her hair was yanked from behind. She lashed out with a fist, but she stumbled as she was swung sideways by her hair like a rag doll.

She had a second for thought, a single spike of clarity. *Take care of Teddy. I'm sorry, Nigel, but take good care of my precious son.* Then the wall leaped forward and rammed into the side of her head. She felt her ear split. Blackness, thick as soot, stifled her mind and she forgot how to breathe.

CHAPTER SEVENTEEN

When Connie led Teddy out of the library basement after the air raid, the sight of the wanton destruction of Palur tore at her heart. Bodies were being extracted from the rubble, but ambulances were caring for the living, so the dead were laid out on the backs of trucks, each covered respectfully with a layer of sacking.

Fitzpayne insisted on accompanying Connie. "To see you safe," he said with a frown. "Looters are around."

Teddy clung to her hand. "What are looters?"

"People who take what is not theirs."

"Like pirates?"

"Sort of."

"Will they go to jail?"

"If they're caught."

All along the street people were bent over, sifting through broken masonry and girders. Looters? Or rescuers? Connie didn't know and didn't care. She just wanted to get Teddy home. Shadows had formed under his eyes that had never been there before.

"Look." Connie pointed up ahead. "There's our Chrysler." It was parked at the curb exactly where she had left it.

"I'll see if Ho Bah is there," Teddy said, and ran toward the car, eager for the journey home.

Fitzpayne glanced sideways at her. "Don't look so worried. He's young, he'll get over this."

"I hope so."

"I see your windscreen is shattered."

"Damn them! Damn all Japs to hell!"

He made no comment on her sudden outburst. Ahead of them, Teddy had reached the car. Connie saw his mouth open and shut, and his stringy legs grew rigid as he stared through the side window. She broke into a run.

"Oh, Ho Bah!" she moaned.

He was there. In the car. Lying slumped across the front seat, a bullet wound in his forehead, almost no blood, just a neat round hole. Teddy uttered a single harsh cry when she wrapped her arms around him. Fitzpayne lifted the *syce*'s scrawny old body and placed it on the rear seat of the Chrysler. Connie covered it gently with a rug from the boot while Fitzpayne swept the glass from the shattered windscreen off the front seats. She climbed into the front passenger seat, pulling Teddy onto her lap, and Fitzpayne took the driver's seat.

It took a long time to drive out of Palur. Roads were cratered, streets blocked by collapsed buildings and fallen telegraph poles, but with patience and care Fitzpayne eventually made it onto the road that ran through the plantation to Hadley House. On the front seat Connie cradled Teddy's head on her shoulder and told her son how proud of him she was. He didn't cry. But all the way home his teeth chattered fiercely.

᎐·Ꮹ

After the fight with Sho in the hut, Connie had come back to consciousness with a start. Her head hurt. When she opened her eyes she realized she was sprawled on her back on the floor of the hut, her hands roped together in front of her. Her whole face throbbed and her nose was blocked with blood, so she breathed softly through her mouth. Her heart was banging in her chest. Shohei Takehashi was sitting on the bed fully dressed, studying her with an expression that was so sad it frightened her. She thought about sitting up but wasn't sure she could make it yet and didn't want him to see her fail, so she stayed where she was.

"Sho," she said. Her voice came out thick but steadier than she expected. "You said you loved me."

"I do."

"Then let me go. I will tell no one what I saw in your diary."

He smiled, a slight twitch of his lips. "We both know that isn't true."

"If you let me go I will come with you to Japan."

For a moment something flared in his dark eyes, something like triumph. He had gotten what he wanted. "How can I trust you?"

When he moved off the bed and crouched close beside her, she quickly pushed herself upright. She didn't want his help.

He stroked her hair. "You look a mess, my sweetheart."

The room and his face were swaying in and out of focus. "Please, untie me."

He continued to stroke her hair but all the time shook his head slowly. She knew then. Knew that the hardness in his eyes and the sad shake of his head were not about the rope around her wrists. She was too much of a threat to him now—he intended to rid himself of her. With quiet determination she forced her legs into action and managed to stand. He rose to his feet and stared at her cautiously.

"Sho, there's no need to make this worse than it is."

She tried to remember where her car keys were. How far down the jungle track was the Chrysler parked? Could she run?

Yes. Yes, I can run. I can run for my life, for Teddy's life.

"Sho, don't do this. Let's both leave our relationship here and walk away."

"I can't walk away from you, Connie. You have bewitched me, and because of you I made mistakes. Because of you I wrote too much in English in my notes. Maybe"—he leaned forward to caress her damaged face, but she backed away—"maybe somewhere deep in my heart I wanted you to know."

"Why would you want me to know?"

"Because then I would have to kill you, and that's the only way I can be free of you."

He said it calmly. No fuss, no threat. As if he were talking about kissing her.

"I'm leaving, Sho. Don't try to—"

Before the words were out of her mouth he had a knife in his hand. She had no idea where it came from, but its blade was wafer thin, the kind of stiletto that she imagined assassins of popes had used in Italy through the centuries. She could picture the steel sliding neatly between her ribs. She drew a deep breath and prepared to scream, to batter him with her roped wrists and hurl herself out of the hut. She stood little chance, she knew that, but she wasn't going to stay here and do nothing.

It was the Malayan jungle itself that came to her aid, the jungle she hated so much. A troop of gibbon monkeys came crashing down from the trees, howling and screeching at each other as they hounded an intruder out of their territory, filling the air outside the hut with their noisy aggression. Sho turned his head and glanced out the window at them, but the moment his attention shifted, she raised her hands and slammed them between his shoulder blades to force him out of her path. He grunted and stumbled. She raced for the door, knocking against him as she ran. Out of the corner of her eye she saw him lose his balance and topple forward, but she didn't slow down till her hand was on the door.

Then a sound stopped her. Through the fog of pain and rage and fear, it penetrated. It was a thin, eerie scream. She looked back. Sho was lying flat on his face, a crimson flower blossoming around him, and from his throat came a sucking, gurgling noise that turned her stomach.

Run! Don't stay!

But she stepped back into the room. Warily she bent over her lover and turned him over. The knife was sticking out of his throat, his hand still clutching the ivory hilt, and blood was pumping in a torrent over his shirt front. He had landed on the blade when he fell.

"Sho!"

She tore her blouse over her head, thwarted by the rope on her wrists, and jammed it against the wound, but air continued to bubble out of it, gurgling as he fought to breathe. Quickly she withdrew the knife from his throat. It slipped out with a soft squelch that was to haunt her dreams every night for months to come. With her blouse clamped tight to try to stem the blood, she leaned close, her heart frantic in her chest, and she placed her lips on his. She breathed out into his mouth, again and again.

"Breathe, Sho!" she cried. "Breathe!"

But there was no response. His body shuddered, then lay still. Within seconds she saw all signs of life slide out of his eyes. They became nothing but black holes in his skull, and she knew he was dead.

"Sho!" she screamed.

Yet she kept breathing air into his mouth. Harder and faster. As if she could force life back into his limp body against its will.

"Sho, don't go," she whispered.

She wiped blood from his lips and tasted it on her own teeth as she drove air relentlessly into his lungs, hearing it escape in a whistle from the hole in his throat. Eventually, her chest heaving with exhaustion, she sat back on her heels and stroked his lifeless cheek.

"Sho," she said softly, "I can't let you take my son from me."

9·G

Connie sat on the floor beside Shohei Takehashi's body for three hours. The blood dried around her, turning as black and sticky as molasses. She felt his skin grow cold despite the heat of the afternoon, his flesh starting to shrivel on his bones as she fanned away the insects. A yellow lizard sidled across the dark patch on the boards beneath him, lifting its feet daintily one at a time. Glossy-backed flies came in swarms, drawn by the stink of fresh blood, and she flapped them away from Sho's throat, but they settled on her own face instead.

Finally, she rose to her feet and wrapped a pillowcase around Sho's head. She used the blade, holding it awkwardly, to cut the rope around her wrists and then, tucking his feet under her armpits, she hauled him on his back out of the hut. His head bounced down the three steps, *thump, thump, thump.*

Her knees grew weak beneath her, but she dragged him to the river's edge. If she rolled the body into the brown, muddy river it might be devoured in hours and vanish. But it might also float like a log and wash up somewhere downstream where it could be found by villagers or fishermen. She squatted beside him with her face in her hands, rocking back and forth, a low keening sound escaping from her throat. She knew that if she told the police what she had done, she would lose her son forever.

She pushed herself to her feet, entered the hut, gathered up all their belongings including the attaché case and diary, and made a bonfire of them. Then she scattered the ashes on the water's surface in a kind of burial service for her Japanese lover. Several times in the past month she and Sho had watched a monitor lizard, a huge seven-foot carnivore, emerge from the mangroves and pace out the beach as he marked his territory. She acted rapidly now. With the knife she made a diagonal cut across her left arm, and when the blood was flowing fast she threaded a trail of scarlet droplets all the way from the mangroves to the body of Sho on the riverbank. *Come and eat me.*

Her hands were shaking as they held the keys to her car, and to Sho's Ford. She set off walking down the track, unaware of the tears streaking her face.

ɔ·ɕ

Nigel had been standing on the doorstep waiting for her when at last she drove home from the jungle that day.

"What in God's name has happened to you, Constance?"

"I went for a walk. I climbed up the rocks around Malu, trying to find somewhere cool to sit and catch the breeze up there. I fell."

"You look as if you've been hit by a bus."

"I must go and wash. I don't want Teddy to see me like this."

"I'll call Dr. Rossiter."

"No, don't. I'm all right."

"No, I insist."

"Nigel, please."

"Look at you. You're hurt. I'm telephoning—"

"No. This once. Just . . . let me rest."

"Constance, other people's wives don't arrive home covered in blood. Why is it that it is always you who are different, always you who never fits in?"

"No, Nigel, you're mistaken. I'm not the one who is out of step with the rest of the world. It's the rest of this damn world of Malaya that's out of step with me."

৩·৫

This time, when Fitzpayne drove her home from the raid in Palur, it was Johnnie Blake waiting on the doorstep, shading his eyes against the sun's glare with his good arm. Fitzpayne made no move to climb out of the car.

"Thank you, Fitz," she said gently.

"Take care of that son of yours."

"I will."

"I'll leave the car behind the stables."

"No, take it. Use it to go back to town; I don't want you to have to walk the eight miles. You've done more than enough today, and anyway there might be another air raid." She peered sadly over her shoulder at the rug on the backseat. It was rumpled where the car had jolted over ruts, and the *syce*'s hand had fallen into view. "Ho Bah will be buried on the estate here. We'll give him a good funeral, won't we, Teddy?" She ruffled her son's dusty hair.

Teddy didn't reply. The boy suddenly tore himself from her embrace and leaped out of the car as if he couldn't bear to sit in it a moment longer. He rushed past Johnnie into the house. Everything seemed to be falling apart.

৩·৫

"Constance!"

Nigel was standing in the drawing room, propped up on a wooden crutch. His other arm encircled his son, crushing the slight figure to his chest, and Teddy leaned against him, face buried, his small shoulders quivering. At the sight of them so close, Connie felt a wave of love that stifled any words.

"Constance!" Nigel said again.

His face was gray, and he needed a shave. It was unheard of for Nigel not to shave. The expression on his face shocked her. It was one of utter anguish, and she quickly crossed the room to him.

"I'm so glad to be home," she said truthfully.

He let the crutch fall to the floor with a clatter and draped an arm around her shoulders, drawing her into a tight circle with himself and Teddy. Nigel's chest was heaving. Connie rested her cheek against his, felt the roughness of his stubble and rubbed her skin over it again and again.

꧁·꧂

That night, a storm hit. Rain sheeted down, hammering at the shutters and drowning any expectation of another air raid. The wind hauled at the trees, ripping off branches and hurling them through the blackness with cracking and thumping sounds that made Connie's heart pound. She couldn't sleep, with or without the storm. She paced the bedroom. Damn it, she wanted a cigarette. A small lamp cast a dim light on her side of the bed, and shadows sneaked around the room, creeping up on her like thieves. Nigel lay on his back under the mosquito net, eyes closed, his breath rising in a regular, shallow rhythm as though fast asleep, but she didn't for a moment believe it. Quietly in bare feet she padded over to his side of the bed, lifted the net and slipped under it. She sat on the edge of the sheet, careful not to touch him.

"Nigel," she said.

No response.

"Nigel, we have to leave."

His eyelids didn't rise but a low murmur escaped his lips. "No."

"It's too dangerous to stay." She spoke softly. "I've thought it all out. We have to shut down the estate and leave Palur."

With a sigh he opened his eyes, and for a long moment he stared up at her. She had no idea what was in his mind. "And where would we go?"

"Singapore. It's safer there. They say the Japanese will never get that far."

"No, Constance. I'm not abandoning my estate."

"They will come, Nigel. They will kill us."

"No, you're wrong. I told you before that they'll need the rubber, so they won't harm us."

"Maybe not you, but they won't need me. Or Teddy."

In the uncertain light she saw his mouth tighten. "They'll never get this far south. Our forces are the best in the world, Constance. Have faith in them." He tried to smile. "Have faith in me."

"You must understand that I won't risk our son's life in exchange for a pile of rubber."

"I can't, Constance. I can't abandon everything my father and grandfather built up here. This is my home. This is your home, and this is Teddy's home. I can't give it up."

"Can't? Or won't?"

Abruptly he closed his eyes, shutting her out. She placed her hand flat on his chest to remind him she was still here. His heart was thundering under her palm.

"Tomorrow, Nigel. We go tomorrow."

ꝺ·Ɛ

The night was long, the images of the bombing and the injured still rampant in Connie's head. Four times she went to check on Teddy and found him tossing and turning, his limbs throwing off the sheet with restless jerks. She held him. Kissed his damp forehead and prayed that the scarlet buttons on the safari jacket would stay out of his head. Dawn came with a bright-red haze that seemed to set fire to the treetops as she stood at her bedroom window.

"So." Her husband's voice startled her. She didn't know he was awake. "Where are you thinking of going?" he asked.

She didn't turn from the window. "I told you—Singapore."

"The roads and rail have been bombed. Already they say our troops are finding bridges blown."

"I know. That's why I plan for us to sail there."

"On *The White Pearl*?"

"Of course. If she's not damaged. Nigel, we have to go, you know we have to. For Teddy's sake."

"You could go alone with him."

She swung to face him. Behind the shroud of the mosquito net his hair was rumpled, his cheeks florid and lined with the folds of sleep. "And leave you here?"

"Yes."

"I won't go without you."

He laughed, a bark of sound that had an unpleasant edge to it. "Why not?"

"Because you're my husband."

Their gaze held across the room. They both knew her words were not true, not in the real sense of *husband*.

"Damn it, I can't sail *The White Pearl*, not with this bloody leg. And you can't handle her on your own."

"There's Johnnie," she pointed out.

"He's not exactly in top form, is he? Not with his bum shoulder."

"I've asked Harriet and Henry to come with us."

"You've what?"

"I know they're not sailors. But there's someone else who is, and I could ask him to accompany us as well."

"Who?"

"Johnnie's friend, Mr. Fitzpayne."

"Not that upstart who—"

"He knows boats, Nigel."

Silence edged into the room. Connie wanted to stride over to the bed, to shake her husband, to kiss his rough cheek and make him see sense, but instead she remained where she was. "I won't let Teddy be taken by the Japanese," she declared.

Nigel threw back the netting, his features jumping into clearer definition. "Very well, Constance, I agree to go."

She started toward him, relief flooding through her.

"But not today," he continued, stopping her in her tracks. "Not tomorrow. Nor the day after. Not until we know more about what is happening up in the north. If the imperial Japanese forces are driven out of Malaya— which I'm convinced they will be—then we stay. Agreed?"

"Agreed." Her eyes didn't move from his face. "But if things become worse for our troops . . ."

"They won't, I promise you."

She left it there. It was enough. For now.

༈

The SS Jaguar hated the sodden roads, despite its powerful 3.5-liter engine. It slid and scraped in the mud from last night's rain, bucking through the ruts however carefully Connie steered over them. She was driving to Palur to check on *The White Pearl*, to see for herself whether any of the bombs had blown the yacht to pieces at her moorings. The prospect filled her with rage.

On either side of the road stretched the plantation fields, waterlogged and sullen. Leaves and branches lay scattered over the ground, but overhead the sky was a solid gray sheet with a breeze that was listlessly stirring the clouds. It tugged at Connie's hair through the open window of the car, but at least the air was cooler today and she sensed her mind becoming more agile, felt her thoughts clarify as she picked her path into Palur.

"How's Teddy today?"

She glanced across at the passenger seat. Johnnie Blake had insisted on coming along as her chaperone, even though he couldn't drive with his damaged shoulder. She found she was glad of his company. It staved off the worst of her mind's imaginings.

"He's very quiet. Too quiet."

"It must have been hell for the kid yesterday." He rested a hand on her arm for a moment and then removed it. "And for you."

"Will you speak to him?"

"To Teddy?"

"Yes. Will you talk to him about how you cope with it, with the violence of war? You're a pilot and he has always hero-worshipped you. Now that he's seen some of the ghastly reality of war and that the airplanes he loves so much are for inflicting death, he needs you to tell him it's all right to be frightened. That it doesn't make him a coward."

"Oh, Christ, poor little chap."

"I've tried, but he won't listen."

"Of course I'll talk to him."

"Thanks, Johnnie."

He swivelled in his seat to face her, shifting his shoulder in its sling, and out of the corner of her eye she saw him smile. "Would you like me to talk to you, too?"

She laughed, a little bitterly, and corrected the front wheel as it slithered sideways in the mud.

ꊩ·ꊩ

Many of the streets in Palur were closed. Damage to buildings and roads was severe. There was a nervousness in the town, a watchfulness, a quickness as people tried to resume normal life, but all the time they kept one eye on the sky above them. The planes would be back. Everyone knew it.

By doubling back on herself time and again, Connie was able to weave the car down to the river, but the sight that greeted them made both Connie and Johnnie shudder. Huge craters had been gouged out of the quay, jetties destroyed, boats smashed to kindling, masts sprawled like broken limbs. Cargo ships were still on fire where they rode at anchor out in the deep channels of the river, and the gawky legs of the derricks lay like drunks on top of trucks. Over everything hung a shifting curtain of smoke.

"No farther!" A policeman held up a white-gloved hand.

"I'm trying to get to my—"

"Sorry, madam." He leaned his Ronald Colman mustache through the side window. "We've got an unexploded bomb down here on the quay. No one is allowed any closer."

"But you don't understand, I must—"

"Leave it, Connie," Johnnie said.

"No, I have to find out if *The White Pearl* is—"

"Leave it, Connie."

"No, I can't. I'm not going to let some blasted Jap bomb stop me getting to her."

"Don't." Johnnie removed her hand from the steering wheel and held it quietly between his own. "Enough of this. The yacht can wait."

She made herself breathe deeply, regaining control. She reversed the car, parked it at a safe distance, and then climbed out.

"I'm sorry, Johnnie. You're right. I didn't mean to . . ." Connie stopped.

Directly in front of her stood the rows of godowns, the warehouses that stored the country's goods waiting to be shipped all over the world: the tin, the rubber, the timber, the spices, the rice and the palm oil, the bananas and pineapples and a multitude of other wares that she could only guess at. In pride of place at the center of the warehouses stood the Hadley Estate godown. Except that it no longer stood. It had turned into a smoking, smoldering black mass that stank so bad, Connie had to clamp her hand over her nose.

"All Nigel's rubber," she whispered. "Oh God, this will break his heart."

"He'll be insured," Johnnie said in a curiously flat tone.

"That's not the point. His rubber is his life, it's what he eats and breathes. It's his . . ." Her words died as she dragged her eyes from the smoking ruin and looked at Johnnie.

Tears were running down his cheeks.

9·C

There was worse to come, far worse. Flash fire had ripped through the shanty huts at the railway embankment and reduced them to nothing. Only the rain of last night had rescued a lucky few. The fire brigade had been too busy trying to save the godowns to bother with the filthy hovels. How many had died? How many had run?

"They're like rats," Johnnie said quietly. "They abandon one place and immediately build new nests in another. Many will have survived. Don't worry."

But Connie did worry. She tramped through the filth and the ash, and she saw the misery and grief of people picking over the ruins of what had been their home. She asked again and again for the Jumat twins, but nobody knew. Nobody cared. The acrid air stung her eyes, but she wouldn't give up until she had scoured every corner of the wretched place. Johnnie stayed at her side throughout her search. At one point she found a native man squatting in the charred remains of a shack, covered in ash and cradling the blackened bones of a child in his arms. His eyes were milky white and he was crooning a low chant.

"You!" he called out to Connie.

She detached herself from Johnnie and approached him. The skin on the old man's cheeks hung loose, as if attached by no more than a few flimsy stitches. "You lose them," he muttered, and held out his filthy hand to her. She took it in hers.

"What do you mean?" she asked.

"You come before."

How can he know? He's blind.

"Do you know the Jumat twins, Razak and Maya?" she asked with sudden hope.

He drew her hand to the burned bones cradled in the crook of his arm and brushed her fingers over them. She shivered but did not withdraw her hand. Yesterday this child was running in the sunshine. He bent his head and pressed his lips to the fleshless skull.

"This Maya's," he whispered.

"Maya's child?"

"Ya." He nodded. "Yes."

Connie felt a rush of sorrow for the young girl. She'd had a child— and yet there had been no sign of it in their shack.

"How old?" she murmured.

He held up three fingers. Three years old. So Maya must have been twelve when she became pregnant, no more than a child herself.

"Where is she? *Mana?*"

He uttered a weird, undulating sound. "She dead."

No, please not dead. Not Maya. "And Razak?"

"He gone."

"Where?"

"To hell." The man chuckled and rubbed his fingers over his cheeks, tracing uneven paths through the ash on his dark skin.

Connie pressed her purse into his hand and he kissed her fingers, his lips dry and parched. She left the shantytown, her hands trembling, her feet finding a path through the charred ruins.

"Look!" Johnnie declared. He had climbed up onto the embankment where the railway track ran. "I can see *The White Pearl*'s mast." He smiled reassuringly down at Connie. "At least she hasn't sunk."

Ɔ·Ƈ

"Mr. Fitzpayne, good afternoon."

It had taken Connie two days to track him down to a dingy bar on the edge of town. She was surprised to find him in a rough place like this, one with sawdust on the floor and native girls painted to look like dolls behind the bar. There was an unsavory feel to the smoky atmosphere, where men with hard faces and even harder fists leaned over their beers and spoke in undertones. They spat on the floor and cracked their knuckles to show satisfaction. Shady deals were made. Men were hired and fired. She could smell the greed dripping as thick as grease down the walls when she walked in, and feel the many eyes that stared not at her but at the gold watch on her wrist, at the pearl necklace around her neck.

"Mrs. Hadley!"

Fitzpayne rose to his feet. He had been seated at a table with two other men and a bottle of whisky. He swayed slightly before he recovered himself, and with disgust she realized he was drunk, though it was only four o'clock in the afternoon.

"Mrs. Hadley, I didn't know you were a patron of Goodrington Bar."

He looked at her with a faint rumble of laughter in his chest, and she knew he was mocking her. She swallowed her annoyance. She did not intend to be sidetracked.

"Mr. Fitzpayne, may I speak to you in private, please?"

She stared pointedly at his two companions. One of them had a thick unruly beard, and the other had recently been in a fight, judging by his crooked nose and swollen eyes, but they just stared straight back at her, curious grins creasing their faces.

With a loud laugh Fitzpayne kicked the chair from under the bearded one. "Out! This lady needs a seat."

The two men vanished, and one of the painted Malay girls brought a fresh glass to the table when Fitzpayne snapped his fingers at her. He held out a chair for Connie.

"Do sit down, Mrs. Hadley."

She hesitated.

"You've hunted me down this far," he said in a low voice, "so you might as well spit out whatever you've come to say."

"I didn't expect to find you drunk."

He treated her to a broad grin. "We all have our moments of weakness." He sat down. "Even you, Mrs. Hadley."

Connie was sorely tempted to walk out. "I have a proposition for you."

He raised one of his heavy eyebrows. He was mocking her again.

"A business proposition," she added quickly and sat down.

"I see." He poured a shot of whisky into the fresh glass and pushed it toward her. It didn't look very clean. "Go on," he urged. "Tell me what this proposition is."

"I would like to employ you to skipper *The White Pearl*. My husband is injured and cannot sail her."

The eyebrows descended into a thick black line of aggression across his face. "Then why the hell isn't he the one sitting here in a lowlife bar asking for my help, instead of you?"

Connie flushed. "I told you. He's injured."

He leaned forward, elbows on the table and carefully scrutinized her face, feature by feature. She felt the color in her cheeks deepen.

"What about you?" he asked in a voice she barely recognized as his. "Are you injured?"

"Of course not."

"I think you are mistaken," he continued in the same voice. "Yesterday when the bombs rained death down on Palur, everyone was injured. Including you." He sat back in his chair and folded his muscular arms across his chest. "Including your son."

Connie banged a hand on the table. "I am not here to discuss my son."

He watched her for a long moment.

"So?" she said sharply. "Will you accept my proposition?"

"Where are you intending to sail to?"

"Singapore."

He nodded slowly. "There may be problems."

"What do you mean?"

"In case you haven't noticed, there's a war on."

She had expected so much more of Fitzpayne. With an effort, she kept her expression polite. "Good-bye, Mr. Fitzpayne. Thank you for your time." She started to rise from her chair.

"Whoa, now," he said as smoothly as if she were a skittish foal, and he pressed her down into her seat. "No need to be in such an almighty rush."

"You are drunk. No use to me. This has been a wasted journey."

He laughed under his breath, picked up her drink, and held it out to her. She shook her head. "I haven't said," he continued, "that I won't skipper your precious yacht for you. Here, drink my drink, and smoke one of my cigarettes"—he threw a pack of Players on the table—"while I consider your proposition."

His eyes were not gray today, but a misty purplish color that reminded her of a winter morning at home in England, the air so chill it could make your bones ache. She looked at the glass of whisky still in his outstretched hand. She hated whisky. Nevertheless, in one swift movement she took the drink, swallowed it down in a single shot, and felt it take her insides apart. With steady hands she extracted a cigarette and lit it with one of his matches. He smiled and refilled his own glass but passed no comment.

For five minutes they sat there in silence. She smoked her cigarette, and when any of the other drinkers gawped at her too long, she scowled at them. But she grew mildly alarmed whenever she moved her head too fast because the edges of the table blurred, as though they too had been burned in the fires that had raged through Palur. It was the damn whisky. She avoided looking at Fitzpayne, but as each minute limped past she could taste the foolishness and feel the heat of anger crawling up from the soles of her feet. There were others she could ask; she didn't need this man, she told herself. For heaven's sake, people would jump at the chance to escape from Palur on *The White Pearl*. So why was she putting herself through this?

But the unaccustomed alcohol had dulled the ache that was as much a part of her daily life as eating and smiling and cleaning her teeth. The usual throb of it was hiding under the whisky. Instead, a whole new section of her brain had yawned open, startling her. She blinked at its dazzling clarity, bright as newly polished crystal glass. And it was this core section of her brain that brought the truth leaping to the front of her mind: She trusted this man.

The realization jolted her, and she ground out her cigarette stub in the tin ashtray. *She trusted Fitzpayne.* She certainly didn't always like the man or his strange moods, and there was something odd, something distinctly wrong about the way he seemed to pop up in her life repeatedly. But if she and her family were going to be sailing into danger, she was convinced that this was the man to have on deck beside them.

"Well?" she said sharply. "Your five minutes are up, Mr. Fitzpayne."

He put down his drink and his full lips spread into a slow smile. "I just wondered how long you'd last."

"Does that mean you'll sail the boat?"

"Of course. You and I both knew the moment you put forth your proposition, Mrs. Hadley, that the answer was yes."

"Damn you," Connie said, and poured herself another shot of whisky.

Adam had burst somewhere inside Connie's head. Life came flooding back. She hadn't even known she was dead before, dead and buried deep in the red soil of the Hadley Estate. She stood now at the rail in the bow of *The White Pearl*, watching sunlight dart and skim off the water like drunken fireflies, and breathed in great lungfuls of life. Not the usual niggardly sips that left her wanting more, but an uncontrolled rush of it that swept her head free of debris and loosened a tight knot at the base of her skull.

She had brought her son this far, away from the reminders of the bombs. The next step was to open up a future for him that would widen his horizons beyond the mind-numbing rows of rubber trees, *Hevea brasiliensis*.

"This is short-term, old thing," Nigel had insisted. "We're not running away, we're just keeping our son safe until the bombing ceases and the enemy is defeated."

Not running away. Sometimes in the night Connie lay awake wondering who exactly the enemy was. It was the sinking of the great warships, the *Prince of Wales* and the *Repulse*, by Japanese torpedoes, followed by the abandonment of Penang by the British, that had finally tipped the balance. It galvanized Nigel into action. She had maneuvered him into leaving, but even now she clutched at the yacht's rail in case he tried to snatch it from her at the last moment. The sails swelled in the wind like elegant wings as *The White Pearl* flew west toward the sea, carving a crisp channel through the muddy waters of the river. The jib and bowsprit pointed the way, as if they knew exactly where it was heading and how many hopes were carried in the fragile curve of the hull.

Connie remained motionless at the rail, one of Johnnie's cigarettes between her fingers. Nigel was seated on one of the benches on deck, his injured leg propped up, one mistrustful eye on Fitzpayne at the helm, but all the time she felt him watching her. As though he didn't trust what his wife would do next. At her side, a small shoulder nudged against her ribs.

"Teddy." She smiled down at her son. "Look, there's a hawk fishing over there." Low over the water drifted a bird, its gray wings outstretched, as lazy in its movements as an old man.

Teddy's eyes followed the hawk, and for a moment they gleamed bright as two new copper coins and Connie's heart lifted. Since they were caught in the bombing of Palur, her son's eyes had turned the color of mud and not even the blunt-nosed terrapin she brought home for him had rinsed away their misery. But now *The White Pearl* was working her magic.

He leaned against her as he continued to watch the bird's flight. "Mummy, why didn't Jack come?"

"Because his parents decided to stay a bit longer."

"But they will die," he said.

"No, of course they won't, darling. Don't worry, they'll leave when they think it's right."

"But now is right." He looked up at her, searching her face. "That's what you said."

"It's true. Now is right for us. If we waited any longer, *The White Pearl* might be damaged in one of the air raids."

He nodded solemnly. "And Chala," he muttered. "She didn't come either."

"Oh, Teddy, don't blame her. She loves you dearly, but it was too big a step for her to leave Palur. Don't forget that many Malayans never travel beyond their town or their *kampong* all their lives."

He nodded again. She bent down and tickled him until he giggled, and somewhere below deck Pippin barked at the sound of it.

"Only four days to Christmas," she reminded him.

"Will Father Christmas come to our boat? There's no chimney."

"Of course he will. Don't frown like that. He has a special sleigh fitted with floats for children who live on boats."

"And reindeer are good swimmers."

"But we'll be in Singapore by then, anyway. It should only take us three or four days, depending on the winds."

"Where will we live in Singapore?"

"I've arranged rooms at a hotel for us." She changed the subject. "Would you like me to ask Daddy if you can borrow his binoculars to watch the riverbanks?"

"Yes! Yes, please."

Connie walked over to where Nigel was sitting.

Nigel was pretending to read a book, *Brave New World* by Aldous Huxley, and for a moment he said nothing when she leaned against the rail beside him, her face offered to the breeze. Under Fitzpayne's instructions, Henry Court was making a decent job of learning to hoist sail, hauling the halyard while Razak made the line fast around a belaying pin—*sweating and tailing*, as Fitzpayne termed it. But Connie was amused by the way Henry made great show of his newly acquired abilities, while Johnnie Blake, using his one good arm, went about his tasks quietly and with far greater skill.

Connie loved the movement of the waves and the tremor of excitement that rose up from the soles of her feet as she let herself sway with the roll of the deck. Her exhilaration at being on the move—not static any more, not chained up in a cage—with the wind tugging at her hair and the air no longer stuck to her skin with sweat made her more generous to her husband's ill humor. His frustration at being on *The White Pearl* but unable to sail her was making him sullen.

He lifted his head from his book and looked at her from under the peak of his hat. "Boy all right?" he asked.

"Improving, yes."

"Good." He scowled up at the empty sky, wary of what might come out of it.

"May he borrow your binoculars? He'll take good care of them."

Nigel was a man who hated to lend his personal possessions, even to his son, but one glance at Teddy's hopeful expression in the bow and he relented.

"They're in my locker in our cabin."

"Thank you, Nigel," Connie said happily. "Maybe we should buy him a pair of his own for Christmas when we reach Singapore."

"Maybe." He turned his attention back to his book.

ꙮ

"It's hot down here," Connie commented.

She had ducked through the hatchway and climbed down the companionway stairs that led into the saloon. Harriet Court was sitting at the central table playing cards. She had changed since she had been on the boat; her boisterous laugh had vanished and her mood, though not exactly unfriendly, was definitely private. Connie had the feeling she was regretting her decision to come on the boat, and no amount of urging could shift her from the table to venture up on deck. She just sat in the saloon playing Patience, hour after hour, and eating her way relentlessly through the small supply of biscuits.

"How can you eat so much and stay so thin?" Connie laughed.

She sat down on the padded bench opposite Harriet, beside the through-deck mast at the front of the saloon. She liked this spot. It felt as if it were where the boat's heart was beating, in the glow of the richly varnished timber walls. The seats were covered in a dark red material that the sunlight from the coach roof picked out and turned to the color of blood. She nudged the pack of Bourbon biscuits farther from her friend's reach.

Harriet dealt a card and snorted with irritation. "To hell with it. Nothing is going right."

"Cheer up, Harriet. Tell me what you're worried about."

Harriet looked up from the ace of spades, pushing her bangs off her face, her eyes suddenly amused. "It would be quicker to tell you what I *don't* worry about."

"All right, so what is it you *don't* worry about?"

Her friend propped her small chin on her hand and considered her answer for a full minute before she said, "I don't worry about my marriage."

Such easy words. They made Connie want to lay her head on the table and weep with envy.

"Lucky you," she smiled.

Henry Court could be loud and pompous at times—in fact, he often reminded Connie of a cockatoo, the way he liked to stick out his chest and ruffle his hair into a crest—but his heart was in the right place: deep in Harriet's pocket.

"Come up on deck," Connie invited.

"No, thanks." She shuffled the pack. "Tell me more about your Mr. Fitzpayne."

"He's not *my* anything. We've hired him for the boat, that's all. I know nothing of his background."

"Maybe you should find out. He doesn't look much like hired help to me."

"No," Connie said thoughtfully. "He doesn't."

"So why is he doing this?"

Because I asked him.

"Who knows?" she said lightly. "I think he just likes boats."

She stood up, tucked the biscuits back in the tin, and left Harriet to her cards, while she went in search of the binoculars.

ૐ

Maya wanted to die.

Had a knife been within reach, she would happily have slit her own throat. She was lying on her front in a stinking black hole, and inside her head her spirit was weeping and begging to leave. Beside her in the dark lay Razak. His arm was around her shoulders and the side of his head was pressed tight against hers, anchoring her to him, refusing to let her tiptoe out of this life and into the next. *Oh my twin brother, that is unfair. Let me die.* But he possessed half her soul, and he was refusing to let it go. She made no sound, so that even her breath left no trace in this world, but she was shivering violently, worse than when she had the fever.

She knew what this was. It was a punishment. All the time Razak had been right and she had been wrong. *Piss on her spirit.* Those were the words she had uttered about her mother, as carelessly as she would throw out the night slops on a rainy morning. *Piss on her spirit.* Aiyee! Such words of shame. She had shown no respect to the dead, and now her mother was taking revenge.

Mama, forgive me.

Claws seemed to rake her gut, and she had to squeeze her eyes shut to keep in the tears. Her mother's spirit was disemboweling her, making her suffer torment. She smelled the filth of her own vomit and begged again for forgiveness.

Never would she have thought her mother's spirit was so powerful, that one so useless in life could inflict so much pain in death. *I will avenge you, Mama. I swear on my life. Not for money, but for you, Mama. I know now that I was wrong to laugh at your curse.*

The moment the words formed in her head, daylight swept into the stifling hole like the breath of an angel. A voice said, "Good God, what have we here?"

It was the white lady. She dragged them across a room and up some steps, a smile on her face. Why wasn't she raging at them? Why did she laugh? The brightness of the day jumped on Maya's eyes, forcing her to close them after all that darkness, but in the split second that her eyes were open, she saw enough. Terror took a bite out of her throat.

"Razak," she whispered, and sought her brother's hand.

Water swirled all around them. They were bobbing up and down on the wide river, the land on each side just a thin green strip in the distance. That was why the lady laughed. She was marching them to the edge of the boat; she was going to throw them headfirst into the brown waves.

"No! *Tidak!*" Maya whimpered. Not to the lady, not to the greedy spirit of the river. But to her mother. "I'm sorry."

Immediately the white lady stopped pulling them across the deck, and the man from The Purple Parrot, the one who was *mem*'s husband, was sitting in front of them.

Mama's spirit is powerful beyond imagining. I bow down to it.

"Look who I found stowed away in the aft locker," the white lady announced.

Faces came and peered at them, so many faces. Maya wanted somewhere to run, but there were no back alleys on a boat, so she stood staring down at her feet, feeling the rolling movement beneath them as though she were riding on the back of a whale.

"Maya ill," Razak said urgently. "Need help."

"Oh, Maya." It was the white lady, her voice soft. "Here, drink this, you'll feel better." She thrust a flask into Maya's hand.

Water. It touched her lips and Maya could not stop herself; she gulped it down. Her insides begged to drown in the stream of water, but abruptly she stopped drinking and looked at the smiling lady with horror as she felt her stomach heave. She rushed past the husband to the rail of the boat and vomited up the water into the river. *Poison?* Had the white lady poisoned her? She clutched her stomach. Behind her, someone laughed and she looked round into the face of Iron-eyes, the man who had come to find them in the jungle. He steered a huge upright wheel with one hand.

"The girl is seasick," he said, "and we haven't even reached the sea yet."

ว·ç

Maya squatted down in a patch of shade. She was sitting on the warm boards with her back propped against the side of the boat, feeling its leaps and shudders and shakes as it stamped its feet on the waves. Her chin was perched on her knees and her arms encircled her waist, holding herself together. Death wasn't dancing so close any more, so she studied the boat and its passengers through half-closed eyes.

It was no different from The Purple Parrot, she decided. A huddle of people pushed together, eyeing each other uncertainly, while above them the giant white wings of the boat muttered and talked to each other like an audience, even clapping lightly at times. Except that in The Purple Parrot the hunger in the room was for sex, but here on this water-house the hunger was for something far more dangerous. It was for a future. Didn't they know that you had to get through today first, and then tomorrow? And before you knew it, the future was behind you. So what was the point of worrying about it?

Maya tipped her head forward and let her hair fall across her face in a long black curtain. She knew the other passengers were casting suspicious glances at her: the golden-haired one with the bandaged shoulder and the mask of laughter, the stocky one with the red cheeks who didn't like boats but liked his own voice. Only *Tuan* Hadley wouldn't look at her. But he had summoned Razak from her side and was teaching him a game played with flat round counters on a black-and-white board. The little son, the one who wore his young heart on a thread around his neck for all to see, was standing next to Razak's shoulder, whispering urgent advice. All three spoke in Malay. She felt left out.

But it was the man with the iron eyes of a hawk that made her nervous. He stood at the large flat wheel, in control, and seemed to grow bigger and bigger the more she looked at him until he filled the whole boat.

୬·ଜ

"Biscuit?"

The boy was holding out a small brown rectangle. Maya looked at it with distaste.

"It's a Bourbon," Teddy said. "They're my favorite." He noticed her reluctance to take it and added shyly, "If you don't have one now, Mrs. Court will eat them all down in the saloon."

Dimly Maya recalled a woman when *mem* had hauled them out of their hiding place and through the shiny wooden room, who had dark hair cut like a helmet and who had stared at her with the look that Maya was used to from Europeans. As if they'd just stepped off a clean sidewalk into horseshit.

"She eats," the boy said.

"Don't you?"

"Not like she does."

What did he mean? That this woman eats with tiger teeth, or rips her food apart with her fingers?

He squatted down in front of her and balanced the biscuit where her chin had lain on her knee. "So you'd better eat it now. Understand?"

"Yes."

She had no idea what he was talking about, but took the biscuit anyway. It had writing on it that she couldn't read. She sniffed its edge and it smelled sugary. The thought of eating it made her stomach turn.

"You like the boat?" she asked, to take his mind off the biscuit.

"Yes, she's beautiful."

"She?"

"All boats are called *she*."

"Why?"

"I don't know." He frowned, creating the same crease between his eyebrows that his father wore. "Maybe because they're pretty."

Maya stared around her. "Pretty? How is it pretty? It is wood and rope. And white sheets. It does its job. Like a servant."

"Some servants are pretty." Teddy grinned at her. "You're pretty."

She scowled at him. Either he didn't know what pretty was, or he was lying. "Razak is pretty," she said, and for some reason she didn't understand the boy laughed till he tumbled over on his back. He righted himself again and started telling her what everything on the boat was called: the bow, stern, aft, hatchway, anchor buoy, cabin, bilge, galley, boom, sheets, forestays, hawsers, halyards, a hank and a hound and a helm . . .

She put her hands over her ears. He laughed and tugged them away.

"A yacht can be gaff-rigged or bermuda-rigged—*The White Pearl* is bermuda-rigged." He pointed up. "See? A triangular sail without a top spar."

She covered her eyes.

"There's the bobstay and the bowsprit," he told her, turning away to point forward.

She threw the biscuit overboard behind her.

"And the lavatory is called the head."

He turned back, noticed the biscuit had vanished, and produced another for her from his pocket. It had a coating of fluff.

"Good, aren't they?" His eyes were bright with friendship.

She put the biscuit in her mouth. He watched her chew and swallow it but was called back to the black-and-white board by his father, so he scampered off. Maya clamped both hands over her mouth to hold everything in and heard a deep chuckle up ahead. It was Iron-eyes. Standing beside the wheel—what did the boy call it . . . a hank? Or was it a helm?—he was laughing to himself and watching her.

The boat gave a sudden lurch. Maya leaped to her feet and vomited the biscuit over the rail, then sank to her knees, head in her hands, and moaned. A gentle hand started to stroke her back and *mem*'s voice murmured something soft and comforting that made the clenched muscles of her stomach start to relent. The pain eased, but the stroking of her back continued and she let it go on and on, despite the howls of protest in her ears from her mother's spirit.

꒤·꒦

In the tropics, the sun sets like a stone. The sky can be on fire with scarlet flames torching the clouds, but the next moment the blaze has been doused and only gray ash remains. It was a daily disappointment to Connie that the display was so brief. On the water it was even more spectacular, the way the waves caught fire around the boat. She leaned over the rail, feeling the wind freshen, watching them flicker and fade. A flock of large bats darted over her head and swooped low over the water on the port beam. She followed them, mesmerized by their agility through the air, and tried to imagine what it must be like to possess that kind of effortless freedom.

"You'll get bitten by mosquitoes if you stay there," Fitzpayne's voice warned her.

The other passengers had gone below for their evening meal of fresh fish, mushrooms, and fried rice prepared by Harriet, but Connie wasn't hungry. She was too on edge. Fitzpayne stood at the helm in front of the tiny open-ended chart house—she was beginning to think he was welded to it—letting the boat run downriver. The staysail, mainsail, and mizzen were set close-hauled to the easterly wind, and as she glanced at him over her shoulder, his broad shoulders were silhouetted against the darkening sky.

"We could heave to," she suggested. "It would give you a rest."

"I thought you hired me to get you to Singapore as fast as possible."

"I did."

"So we sail on."

She didn't argue, but neither did she go below.

"She's a delight to handle," he told her with a smile of pleasure, as his experienced eye scanned *The White Pearl*'s sails. "In a reasonable wind like this she is lively and fast, light on the helm." He laughed, an intimate sound that she knew was meant for the boat, not for her. She could see how much he loved it, the way he ran his hands over the wheel.

The silence of the approaching night hung over the water like mist, and for a while she didn't speak, letting the tranquillity of the evening and the gentle motion of the boat seep into her mind. For the first time in a year that had been savaged by nightmares and self-recrimination at what she had done in a hut in the jungle, she felt a thin membrane of peace wrap around her thoughts.

"He won't go any farther. You must know that."

Fitzpayne's voice broke into her thoughts.

"Pardon?"

"Your husband," he explained.

As he hardened up on the wind, she set about tightening the sheets. "You think Nigel doesn't want to sail any farther? Of course he does, he's going to sail to Singapore, all of us are. We'll all be safe there. We can start again, and wait for this dreadful war to be over."

In the yellow rectangle of light thrown up on deck from the saloon below through the glass of the coach roof, Connie saw his wide mouth take on a skeptical tilt.

"You have no more intention of staying in Singapore than I have," he said.

"I don't believe I've ever discussed my intentions with you."

He laughed at that, a low sound that was swallowed by the descending darkness. "Your husband won't leave Malaya."

"You don't know my husband."

"I assure you that I've known men like him. They are wedded to what they are, and they regard themselves as indispensable to the empire."

"Maybe they are."

"Their beloved empire is about to come crumbling down around their ears, and they are blind to it. You are right to want to return to England."

"Who says that's what I want?"

"Isn't it?" He laughed easily, not expecting an answer, but his gray eyes remained fixed on hers. "Isn't it?" he repeated in an undertone designed for his own ears rather than hers.

"Mr. Fitzpayne"—Connie flicked out her hand at a greedy mosquito that was dancing around her head—"did you know that the mosquitoes that make that horrible whining noise are harmless? It's the silent ones you have to watch out for, those that make no noise at all. They're the ones that can give you malaria and make you sick. They are the danger, the ones you have to beware of."

He regarded her intently. "No, Mrs. Hadley. I didn't know that."

೨·ಢ

Below deck, *The White Pearl*'s interior was arranged into three cabins, all fitted out to the same high standard as the saloon. The large master cabin was used by Nigel and Connie; the next one farther forward also had a double berth and was allocated to Henry and Harriet. The third one lay aft and contained a pair of bunk beds. Teddy had scrambled eagerly on the top one and dumped his satchel of possessions on it, marking it as his territory. Johnnie Blake would be occupying the lower berth, but when Connie went to settle her son down for the night it was still empty because Johnnie was with Nigel and the Courts, playing bridge in the saloon. Connie hated bridge. It was an activity that seemed to her to be spitefully designed to cause friction and avoid real conversation.

Aft, there were two more narrow bunks tucked into an alcove behind a curtain, where the crew or servants would normally sleep. Fitzpayne had opted for one of these but clearly had little intention of making use of it, and the other one Connie had offered to Razak. Maya wouldn't venture down the stairs, so Connie had provided a blanket and a bucket for her up on deck.

"Thank you, *terimah kasih*," Razak said politely, but lowered his long eyelashes so that she couldn't see what thoughts shimmered behind them.

Connie climbed up onto Teddy's top berth, knocking her shin on the wooden lip along the edge of it, designed to keep its occupant from falling out in rough seas.

"Look what I've brought for you." She waved a book and a pencil at him. "It's a diary."

Teddy examined it, running a finger over the cover.

"There's a page for each day," she encouraged. "For you to write whatever you like."

"What should I write?"

"Oh, I don't know. Anything that comes into your head. You could list what you've seen on the river each day and—"

"And the spider that made Mrs. Court scream?" Teddy giggled.

"Exactly!"

"It has a leather strap." He tested its buckle around his thumb.

"That's to fasten around the diary when you've finished each day, so that no one else can read it."

"Not even you?"

"Not even me." She nodded seriously. "A diary is private."

He slipped his young arms around her neck and kissed her cheek. She hugged him, inhaling the sweet, warm scent of her son, then read him a chapter of *White Fang*. His eyes were closed, the rhythm of his breathing slow, when she finally climbed down from the bunk and crept to the door.

"Mummy," he whispered after her, "when I grow up I want to be a pirate."

კ·Ⴚ

Connie unwound the bandage from her husband's leg and gently removed the dressing. It was stained with yellow pus. She smiled in the hope of making him think the injury was improving and proceeded to bathe it with antiseptic. Nigel was lying flat on his back on the bed, feigning indifference, but in the yellow glow from the gimballed kerosene lamps on the wall, she could see the strain in his face.

"Johnnie's on deck with Fitzpayne at the moment. The wind has backed a little south of east. But don't worry," she said, "you'll be leaping around up there too in no time." A stupid comment. But she wanted to see the muscles of his cheeks relax.

Nigel didn't even lift his head off the pillow. "Don't patronize me, old thing. I'm not Teddy. How is it?"

She flushed and studied his leg. "The top half of the wound is healing well," she told him, "but the bottom half—that's where the parang cut to the bone—is still swollen and infected. But less inflamed than yesterday." The last part was a lie.

"Good." That was all. He waited for her to bind it up again.

She cradled his calf in the palm of one hand as she put on a clean dressing and bandage, and thought about the fact that until this accident, she hadn't touched his leg for years. She'd forgotten the feel of it. The strength of the muscle, the springiness of the hairs on the skin of his shin in contrast to the silkiness of those on his calf. The skin tanned from all the years spent in shorts.

"I think that we should put off the girl."

Connie almost dropped his leg. "You mean Maya?"

"Yes."

"No, Nigel."

"She hates sailing. Damn sick all day. Time to tell her to bugger off—in the morning."

"Nigel, don't be ridiculous. She's miles away from home now. We can't make her disembark in the middle of nowhere and just dump her on a stretch of beach. What on earth is the matter with you? Why do you dislike the girl so much?"

"She's trouble, Constance. I can feel it. I don't want her on my boat."

"On *my* boat," she said quietly. "You gave *The White Pearl* to me as a wedding gift, remember?"

He gave a stiff nod but made no comment. She finished the bandaging and patted his knee.

"I feel responsible for the pair of them," Connie explained as she blew out the lamp on his side of the bed. "I was very touched when I found that they had stowed away on my boat, because it means they feel they can come to me when in trouble. In place of their mother."

She left her own light on, intending to read a while, and hung her robe on a hook behind the door. She was wearing a flimsy nightdress. It would be heaven to wear nothing in bed because the air was stifling down here in the cabin—all portholes were secure when sailing—but she knew Nigel would hate that. The bed was far smaller than the one at home . . . God forbid that he might be forced to touch her in its narrow confines. She slid into the bed and felt her husband shift his body nearer to the far edge.

"Tell me what the matter is, Nigel," she murmured.

They both spoke in low tones because the walls within a boat's hull were notoriously thin.

"I know," she added, "that you're unhappy at leaving the estate, but your manager, Davenport, will run it as best he can until you're back."

"Until *we're* back," he corrected.

"Of course."

There was a pause while they listened to creaks and rattles as *The White Pearl* flexed her joints in response to a change of tack. Connie could picture Maya hanging her head over the black waters.

"But you like the boy," she said, dropping her voice further. "You don't object to Razak."

To her surprise there was a long silence, and she saw Nigel close his eyes as though the lids were too heavy and he was drifting into sleep. Yet after several minutes he spoke again.

"The boy is a decent enough fellow and means no harm. I believe the girl does."

"But if Maya were put off the boat, Razak would go too."

"You think so? I'm not so sure. He likes it here on the yacht and is excited about seeing Singapore. He told me so. Teddy likes him too."

"Nigel, Razak is her twin brother. Of course he won't desert her."

"That's a damn shame. I hope you're wrong."

The flatness of his tone made it clear that the conversation was ended.

"Sleep well, Nigel." She picked up her book.

"Fat chance of that." He suddenly twitched his head on the pillow so that he was looking directly up at her. "What is your real interest in the girl? It's not just because you killed her mother, is it?"

Killed her mother. It was the first time he'd said the words so brutally. Connie felt something raw open up inside her.

"It's about having choices, Nigel. We all like to feel we can choose. Poverty robs people like Maya and Razak of that chance to make choices, Maya most of all because she's a girl. She may reject education or my help to find a job, but I want to show her that she has the right to—"

"This isn't about her, is it?"

"What do you mean?"

"It's about you." His brown eyes grew fierce, though he spoke in no more than a whisper. "It's about the fact that you refuse to behave like other women, that you want control."

There was a moment of silence between them, like a transparent wall of ice, and Connie felt the sweat freeze on her skin. "Yes," she said softly. "I want to feel in control of my own life. To know that I am responsible for my decisions, just as you are for yours."

"Don't think for one moment that I will let you take control of my son's life."

"*Our* son."

He turned his head away from her. "Read your book."

·CHAPTER NINETEEN·

It was three o'clock in the morning. Connie sensed a shift in the wind and knew Fitzpayne had hoisted more sail. She raised her head off the pillow, listening hard. The boat was holding steady before a following wind and moving fast. Beside her, Nigel was snoring—but discreetly—forced by his leg to sleep on his back, so she dressed in the dark, made a pot of tea in the galley with scarcely a sound, and climbed up on deck.

The night air rushed at her, slapping her in the face. It woke her out of the numbness that had gripped her ever since she and Nigel had had their words. *My son*, he'd said, in a way that told her loud and clear that he could take the boy from her if he chose. She stood on deck, adjusting to the roll of long, unfettered waves, and knew they had reached the sea. She could smell its breath and taste the salt on her lips. They were carrying full canvas aloft, and a host of silver-winged moths had clustered around the lamp at the stern like a shimmering coat of new paint.

Johnnie lay dozing on one of the benches, but Connie knew he must have worked hard earlier to hoist so much sail. Fitzpayne stood at the helm taking a bearing, and in the moment when he was unaware of her presence—because of the noise of the wind overlaying her footsteps—she saw his profile clearly. In the reflected light from the lamps, she was struck by how it seemed to have changed in some subtle way, as though the bones had realigned overnight.

Had *The White Pearl* done that to him? Was it the water flowing beneath them, and the wind streaking through the rigging high above them that had stripped the stiffness from his manner and the tension from his movements? He swayed with the deck as though he were a part of it, and his hair was no longer swept back in a hard line but blew at will in dark brown tendrils across his face.

"Tea?" Connie offered.

She startled a laugh out of him. "Thank you."

"Don't you ever sleep?"

"I think it is Flight Lieutenant Blake who is need of his berth. He has crewed well for me tonight."

"Taking my name in vain, old chap?" Johnnie sat up and flexed his shoulder in its sling, shaking the knots out of it. They all spoke softly so as not to disturb those sleeping below.

"There's a cup of tea for you down in the galley, Johnnie," Connie said. "You must be exhausted. Get some sleep, it's my watch now."

Johnnie stood and yawned. "Are you sure?"

"Of course I'm sure. Go and rest that poor shoulder of yours."

"Give me a shout in a couple of hours and I'll be—"

"Go!"

He laughed, touched her arm gratefully, and vanished through the hatchway.

"Poor Johnnie," Connie murmured. "He hates being stuck here with his bad shoulder just when all his comrades are taking to the skies." She tipped her head back to stare up at the great arc of black clouds and to listen to the swell of the sea breathing in her ears. "I'll take her for a spell," she said. "Put your feet up on the bench."

Fitzpayne hesitated. She could see in his face that he intended to decline, reluctant to yield mastery of the yacht. But as though remembering who owned her, he suddenly released his grip on the wheel and stepped to one side. Connie took the helm.

"Hold her on a heading ten degrees south," he said.

She glanced at the compass in its brass casing in front of her, lit by a small oil lamp, and nodded. She could feel the pull of the current as she held her steady. In the darkness there was nothing to see but the bow lamp up ahead, and the shadowy shapes of the mast and the dinghy stowed on top of the coach roof. Oddly, she loved the isolation that the night granted, relished the freedom of seeing nothing and being able to steer her life in any direction she chose. Around her, the waves were black except for the gleam of breaking crests.

"You've changed."

Fitzpayne's voice came out of the night at her though she could barely make him out in the shadows, just the tip of his cigarette like a firefly at rest.

"No, I haven't," she responded.

His quiet chuckle was stolen by the wind. Surely he was the one who was different, not her. A sail flapped noisily for a moment, distracting them both as the wind veered, and she heard him tightening one of the stays on the port side. The firefly leaped overboard and drowned.

"You've changed," he said again softly. "Since you've been on the boat."

"No."

"Yes, you've come out of your shell."

"Was I ever in a shell?"

"Yes." He lit another cigarette. "One with damn great cracks in it, but still a shell to hide behind."

"I think you are mistaken."

"Do you?"

He approached her, his bare feet silent on the boards, only the movement of the new firefly in his hand announcing his whereabouts. When he came within the circle of dim light around the compass, he handed her the cigarette with a courteous tip of his head.

"You laugh differently, you move differently, you smile as if you mean it. I can see now," he murmured, "why . . ." He stopped himself abruptly.

"Why what?" Connie asked.

He shrugged and withdrew into the darkness. "A night like this sometimes tempts words out of us that are best left unsaid."

"Tell me something about yourself, Mr. Fitzpayne. You know too much about me."

"More than you think, maybe." It was a whisper. For a second Connie thought she had misheard, especially when he continued as though he had said nothing. "There's nothing much to know about me. I deal in boats, as I told you before. Very dull."

"What brought you out to the Far East in the first place?"

There was a pause and the boat sighed. "You and I both came here," he said quietly, "looking for the same thing."

"What was that?"

"For excitement. For a sense of freedom."

She laughed. "Well, I certainly failed to find them. What about you?"

"I've had my share of them in the past. Now I'm living a quiet life."

She didn't believe him but let the lie float away on the breeze. "I don't imagine Singapore will be quiet."

She drew on her cigarette and pictured the crowds of refugees like themselves who must be pouring into the city, fleeing from the advancing enemy troops. Nigel was determined that he would eventually return to the Hadley Estate with his family intact and in tow, to take up where he had left off with his rubber, but she had no faith in such illusions. The world he had reveled in was shattered forever, and whatever replaced it would be a totally changed social structure, she was convinced. Whoever ultimately took control of Malaya—whether Japanese or Europeans, or maybe even the gentle Malays themselves—the struggle would be intense and the price high. But she had no intention of being a part of it.

Nigel had shut up the house with deep regret, had even spent days burying some of the more valuable possessions in secret hideaways on the estate, but Connie had taken almost nothing. Just a handful of clothes. A couple of gold rings. A pearl necklace. They were her insurance, and she would wear them all the time, even in bed. She didn't trust Sai-Ru Jumat's evil spirits. Especially when she recalled the gray lines of sorrow on her husband's face when he locked the front door of Hadley House for the last time and cradled the key on his palm as though it were something precious. Her heart went out to him. This was where he belonged, this hot, humid, unbearable country. She understood that, understood how much he was surrendering for the love of his son.

When *The White Pearl*'s sails unfurled and carried them away from Palur, Connie knew that Nigel's heart was wrenched from his chest and his sense of self dislocated. So she forgave his moods and his sharp words and tried to curb the rush of pleasure that overwhelmed her each time she looked ahead along the fine lines of the boat's bow and saw a world waiting for her out there.

"Mrs. Hadley."

Connie gave a start. Fitzpayne was scrutinizing her carefully, and she could feel the energy of him, sharp and focused.

"A boat is not a place that offers much privacy." His voice was low, tucked in among the sounds of the rigging. "There are things that need to be said between us."

"Mr. Fitzpayne, the only thing I need is to get us away as far and as fast as I can."

He nodded. "You have a fine son. I can understand your rush to take him somewhere safer. The question is, where?"

"To Singapore. We agreed."

"You're right to leave Palur. The Japanese will sweep down through the peninsula of Malaya like a knife through a peach, destroying Percival's army. Yamashita's force will show no mercy to any British who are foolish enough to remain behind."

She shivered, despite the warm night air. "I have friends still in Palur."

"You can't save everyone, Mrs. Hadley." She heard, rather than saw, a slight smile in his voice. "And our journey south may not be smooth sailing."

"I am very aware of that."

She glanced warily up at the mute black sky. The sky had become something she didn't trust any more, and for a moment they listened together for the sound of aircraft engines, but there were only the murmurs of the boat and the purring of the sea.

"I feel responsible," Connie admitted. "Responsible for the lives of the people on this boat, because I suggested this method of escape."

She heard his impatient release of breath in the darkness. "Each one of these people—except your son—made their own decision to come on board *The White Pearl*. They are responsible for themselves. Don't forget, had they stayed in Palur, they might already be dead."

"I know." She gave a slight tilt of her shoulders. "But still."

Suddenly he leaned forward, his face close to hers, and she could feel his breath mingle with the breeze on her cheeks. "Listen to me," he said.

"What is it?"

"Can you shoot?" he asked.

"Yes, a shotgun. In England I used to . . ." She let the words trail away as she realized what he was asking. He didn't mean *Can you shoot a pheasant?*

She looked at him steadily. "Yes, I can shoot."

Without a word, he drew an object from his waistband under his black tunic, took one of her hands in his and placed something metal and heavy in it.

"It's loaded," he said. "Keep the safety catch on until you need it."

Her throat grew dry and her heart jumped at her ribs. "Thank you," she said, and was astonished to hear her voice as calm as if she were thanking him for a cigarette.

The metal that had lain next to his flesh felt warm against her palm, and the gun's weight was greater than she expected. She glanced down at it. *Is this why men start wars? Because once you have a weapon in your hand, you long to use it?*

"Thank you."

"One more thing. We don't know how long we'll have to be on this boat. You should start to ration the food."

꒦·꒷

"Mummy, come and look at this."

"At what, darling?"

"A boat." Teddy was whispering behind his hand the way he did when he had a secret to tell. "Come and see."

She had been halfheartedly completing a crossword on deck under the shade of her parasol, but abandoned it readily for her son. Nigel and Johnnie were below, playing chess in the saloon, keeping an eye on Harriet. Connie had announced over breakfast that food would be strictly rationed from now on, only to have Harriet flare up at her in annoyance. So Nigel had been appointed as official watchdog over supplies: one biscuit per person midmorning. But it was the water supply that concerned Connie most. If they were caught on the boat for any length of time, who knew when they could next take on fresh water? So from now on, washing water was restricted, and clothes and dishes had to be washed in seawater.

On deck, Teddy had wedged himself in the stern, scouring the horizon with his father's binoculars all morning and jotting down notes in his diary with his new pencil, licking the point each time he started afresh, just the way his father did. Connie wondered what on earth he found to write about, but she didn't intrude. Henry was taking his turn at the helm trying to hold course, as awkward as a duck in mud, while Fitzpayne called out instructions and sheeted the jib to leeward. The wind was fitful today, and Connie had to hide her impatience at their slow progress. She made her way aft to Teddy's perch and looked out over the water in the direction that his small arm was pointing.

"I can't see anything, sweetheart. Anyway, we've spotted quite a few boats in the straits already. Lots of other people are also on the move to sail somewhere safer."

Teddy frowned, and she noticed how tanned his skin was becoming, the freckles like corn dust on his nose.

"This is different." He was whispering again. "It's one of the *pinisiqs*, and it has been trailing behind us all morning."

"What on earth is a *pinisiq*?"

"Oh, Mummy! It's one of the native boats, the kind they carry cargo in."

"Really?"

"Yes. They have sharp bows and are fast. With the mainsail on a standing gaff."

"What a lot you know, Teddy."

He shook his head at her, losing patience. "Look!" He pushed the binoculars into her hand.

Immediately the waves seemed to dash up into her face, and she backed off a step. Every lacy white edge and green sinuous valley of water leaped into life with utmost clarity. She swung the binoculars up toward the horizon, and after a minute of hunting she found a long bowsprit with three foresails far in the distance.

"That's miles away, Teddy."

"But it's always there." His brown eyes looked up at hers with concern. "It never comes closer and it never disappears." He leaned his weight against her hip, and she had to bend to hear his final words. "I think it's chasing us."

Suddenly Fitzpayne appeared at her elbow and crouched down, so that he was on a level with Teddy. "You have sharp eyes, young man."

"Is it chasing us?"

Fitzpayne chuckled to himself and placed a hand on the boy's shoulder. Connie noticed that his hands were large, far broader than Nigel's, and seemed to swallow her son's small bones.

"No," he said, "she's not chasing us. Most probably trying to ship her cargo to Singapore before the Jap planes start crawling over the sky. It will be dangerous to trade from now on, so there will be shortages of everything."

"Maybe they're pirates," Teddy suggested.

"No," he smiled, "not even Indonesian pirates are stupid enough to risk Jap torpedoes."

"Maybe I should have a cutlass."

"A cutlass?"

"Or a knife in my belt." Teddy twanged his elastic belt hopefully, and its snake buckle popped open. "In case we are attacked."

"*Tuan* Teddy," Fitzpayne said in a stern voice, "the trouble with carrying a knife is that one day you'll end up killing someone."

Connie looked hard at Fitzpayne and then walked back to her crossword, drawing her parasol low over her face, safe from prying eyes.

ꙅ·ꙅ

Too much thinking. That was the trouble with the boat. Maya could hear the thoughts of everyone rustling and scratching, jostling each other, rushing in purple and red streaks up and down the deck, tumbling down the stairs into the bowels below. Too many thoughts. Too heavy for the boat.

By day, she refused to lift her head above the height of the sides of *The White Pearl*. If she looked the waves in the face she knew they would open their mouths and swallow her, so she crouched down on her blanket in the sharp end of the boat behind the dinghy on the funny roof of the saloon. It was best here, tucked away where Iron-eyes couldn't see her if she kept her head down, but the voices trickled between the open slats that allowed air into the saloon below, and she heard things. Things she wasn't meant to hear.

She heard the *mem* with hair as black as tar crying, "We're all going to be killed." Her man, the one with the loud voice and the big belly, told her, "Buck up," and Maya wondered what it meant. She heard him mutter to *Tuan* Hadley that he wouldn't let his wife parade around on the boat in just shorts and a thin sleeveless shirt like *Mem* Hadley did, and she heard the heat in *Tuan's* voice when he swore, "Damn her! Why won't she do as she's told?"

The tall one was different, the one with hair the color of sunlight and his arm bandaged to his chest as though holding his heart together. He was beautiful. He didn't ignore her or look at her as if she were a scrap of river flotsam. He smiled at her, and when she smiled back at him, instead of the scowl she gave to everybody else, he offered her a sip from his hip flask.

"It'll settle your stomach," he promised.

It was like dragon's breath scorching down through her body, but he was right, the sea's claws stopped raking her insides for a moment. She took another mouthful of it and felt her head fill with goose down.

"Better?" he asked.

She nodded.

"It might help if you looked out at the sea. That's what we tell new pilots who feel sick: Keep an eye on the horizon."

"You pilot?"

"Yes."

"You hurt in plane?"

"This?" He frowned at the sling. "Yes. Damned nuisance."

"You safe here."

The blue of his eyes darkened to the color of the sea. "Yes," he said. But the word sounded dead in his mouth.

"You not happy you safe?"

"No."

Yet he laughed. Maya could not understand it. The coils of the white man's mind twisted in strange directions. Like the way they played with the dog, rolling a ball along the deck for it to chase, instead of plunging the creature into a stew pot. A noisy little bunch of teeth and tail. Whenever it came near her, she hissed at it.

"Maya," the pilot said, "this isn't easy for any of us."

He was the only one of the white men to use her name. As if she were a person, as if she mattered. She put her lips to the hip flask again, and as she tipped her head back to drink, he said, "I'm sorry about your mother." She swallowed awkwardly, spluttering some of the liquid down her chin, wasting it. Why did this golden-hair care about her mother? She gave him back his flask, her eyelashes lowered, but he hadn't finished.

"How is your brother feeling? Both of you must be sorrowful at your loss."

She shot a look of surprise at the pilot, then gave him a shy smile. "You kind man."

He was blushing like a girl. "If there's anything," he said, "that I can do to help you—or your brother—let me know."

He walked away, and she peeped around the corner of the saloon roof to watch his long legs saunter down to the other end of the boat, the breeze ruffling his blue shirt, his hair flicking up in the sunlight. He looked like a tropical fish.

୨·୧

Maya tried to sleep, but the waves were kicking at her, drowning her dreams. When she opened her eyes, Razak was seated cross-legged on the deck beside her, watching over her, and there was a stillness to him, a contented shine to his beautiful face that alarmed her.

"My brother," she said as she sat up and stretched her limbs to rid them of the torpor that had slunk into them. This boat living was dull and her legs longed to run somewhere. Anywhere. "I am grateful that you find time to sit with me."

"Maya, you are always my sister."

"But your new friends please you more. *Tuan* Hadley with his black-and-white board. The boy with his dog and his satchel full of toys. The pilot"—the mention of him brought a smile to her lips—"with his talk of planes and his stories of dinners with sultan princes. You like them better."

He leaned forward and rested his head against hers. The warmth of it filled the cold corners inside her.

"Maya, they will throw me into the stinking harbor as soon as we reach Singapore. But this is a magic time that the spirits have granted us on this boat. We must use it well."

"Use it? How? Razak, I am dying here. Our mother's spirit has poisoned me so that I cannot eat."

He stroked her hand with his delicate fingers. "It is the sea, my sister."

"I know," she whispered. "But our mother's spirit hides itself in the dark waters. That is why I cannot look at the waves."

"If you eat, you will think better."

"Already too many thoughts ride on the narrow back of *The White Pearl*."

That night Fitzpayne ordered sail to be shortened. "There's a hard blow coming," he warned.

Connie knew that the might of the wind exacts a toll on those who treat it lightly, and she was grateful that when the first squall hit, Fitzpayne had already reefed the mainsail and was setting the storm jib.

"Mrs. Hadley, I would feel better if you were safe down below. It's not going to be pleasant up here."

"Mr. Fitzpayne, I am the only experienced sailor you've got, so you're stuck with me. I'm not frightened of bad weather." She gave him a quick smile. "Anyway, it's miserable down below in heavy seas."

He looked relieved, and she realized that he knew he would need her during the long hours of darkness that lay ahead.

"Don't say I didn't offer you the chance," he laughed as a wave smashed against the deck, making the boat shudder and sending up spray over them.

It wasn't long before torrential rain hurtled down on the boat as though trying to drown it. The weight of it battered the hatches and the deck with a noise so loud that Connie and Henry Court had to struggle to hear Fitzpayne's commands. Kitted out in oilskins, they tightened the stays in the darkness, while sea spray whipped across the deck and tumbled along the scuppers before running back into the sea. The wind had veered and came roaring across the island of Sumatra from the vast expanses of the Indian Ocean, pitching *The White Pearl* over on her port bow and dragging at her lines till they howled in protest. Fitzpayne had to fight to keep her on course, but Henry was terrified to move because the deck tilted at such a ferocious angle that it threatened to tip him into the foaming sea.

Nigel, Teddy, and Johnnie had been ordered to remain below, making certain that everything was battened down tight as the wind strengthened and the seas grew higher. A nonstop thrumming and vibration raged in the rigging, fighting with the hiss of advancing breakers and the thud on top of the dinghy and cabin roof each time a cascade of water crashed down on it.

Connie took a moment to go below to check on Teddy, but she needn't have worried. He was tucked up in his bunk, fighting to stay in it, eyes wide with excitement. It matched her own—except hers was laced with an awareness of what could yet happen to them in this storm.

"So, sailor, not sick yet?" she smiled at him.

"No," he answered, pride in his young voice. "Everyone else is. Even Daddy."

"So I hear. The saloon is a shambles."

She held tight to the lip of his bunk to stay upright as the sea rolled under them.

"Can I come on deck?" he begged.

"No, sweetheart, not this time. It's too dangerous."

He wrapped an arm around her neck. "I like danger, Mummy."

"There's enough danger to go around for all of us, these days. Don't worry, you'll get your share, I'm sure."

He grinned at her, but she didn't want her words to be true, not ever. She stuck her head in the saloon, where only Johnnie had enough strength to greet her with an uneasy grimace, and she poured them all some water, spilling half of it. The smell of vomit was strong, and she hurried back on deck. She offered to relieve Fitzpayne at the helm.

"It's cold and exhausting work," she shouted against the wind. "You've been at it for hours."

"Thank you, but no."

She was grateful that he didn't say what they both knew—that to hold a steady course in such seas could be beyond her physical strength.

Instead, she gave him Nigel's hip flask of whisky and went to lash down a stay that had broken loose. She didn't see how Henry let a wet sheet slip from his fingers, but it snaked through the rain and caught Connie across the neck, knocking her to her knees. A wave broke over her. She pulled herself to her feet, sucking in water instead of air, and she had to wipe salt from her eyes.

She and Nigel had occasionally sailed in bad weather before, but nothing like this and never at night. Yet when she looked at Fitzpayne gripping the helm, the hood of his oilskin was gone and his head was tipped up to the heavens. The rain drove down on him with full force, but his whole face was fiercely alive. The bow yawed suddenly as they slid into a trough and Connie stumbled, crashing against the mainmast and fastening both arms around it. She peered through the darkness for Henry. Where was he? His lurching figure had vanished.

"Henry?" she screamed.

"Below!" Fitzpayne shouted back against the screech of the wind. "I ordered him down. He's a danger to you."

"And Maya?"

"I threw her down the steps."

Poor Maya. She must be terrified.

Razak was the only other figure still struggling on deck, his dark face barely visible through the rain, but he gave no sign of fear. As a giant wave reared up and towered above them, Connie yelled at him to hold tight to something. Instantly Fitzpayne put the helm up and ran dead before the wind to take it true on the stern, but when it crashed down on top of them, battering their senses, it was her own grip on the mast that loosened. She was flung aft and would have been slammed against the mizzen if Fitzpayne had not reached an arm out of the darkness and seized her. He pulled her close, and she felt her fingers grasp at his slippery oilskin. He kept her upright until she found her feet on the heaving deck.

He said something that she didn't hear—but she could read his lips, even in the blackness of the storm: *I don't want to lose you.*

"You won't get rid of me that easily," she shouted, "but maybe we should heave to and try to sit out the storm."

"I'm running for shelter," he bellowed in her ear.

"Where?"

"A creek I know."

She nodded as rain gushed off her nose and chin. "Be quick."

He laughed. Actually laughed, showing large, capable teeth. She could feel the joy and exhilaration surging within him. If her hands had not been clinging to his chest, she would have hit him.

꒷꒦

How he found the creek, Connie would never know. It was an impossible task—Fitzpayne must have possessed a sixth sense in his brain, like birds. He eased the sheets and altered to a new course in the darkness, running before the storm with the wind on the quarter, until Connie felt *The White Pearl* take a breath and make for the briefest of breaks in the solid black line of the coast.

Along much of the shore of the Malay Peninsula, the jungle and endless mangroves shouldered their way right down to the water's edge, unwilling to yield even a strip of beach to the greedy sea. But a small, determined river had wound its way through the inland mountains down to the coast, bringing with it the mud and smells of the jungle through which it had carved a path. Where it flung itself into the sea, its current had excavated a shallow, sickle-shaped bay in the northern bank, so that at times like this, when the sea had lost its mind, it could sit quietly behind the narrow strip of mangroves that divided the bay from the raging waves and bide its time.

It was in this bay that *The White Pearl* found shelter in the lee of the land. She seemed to shake herself and settle at anchor with a discreet sigh that allowed Connie's pulse to quieten. She scrambled down the steps, her oilskins dripping puddles on the floor, to check on the five passengers below. The saloon felt dismal, not just because of the rain and the storm, but because Connie could sense their fear, fine droplets of it in the air. Harriet and Maya were still sunk with their heads in bowls, while Maya was huddled in a corner, her skin the color of seaweed. Connie gently touched her head and heard her answering wail of misery.

The others were seated on the padded benches around the table.

Astonishingly, Teddy was there, asleep, curled in a ball with his hand still clutching his father's so tight that she could see red weals on Nigel's fingers. Nigel was talking in an undertone with Johnnie opposite him but stopped abruptly when she walked in and looked up guiltily. Had he been talking about her? Telling Johnnie things that should not be told? She felt a coldness slide inside her. The dog, snuggled up on Nigel's lap, was the only one who greeted her happily.

"We've taken shelter," Connie announced. "Mr. Fitzpayne has found us a small creek, and we'll wait out the storm here."

"Thank God!" Henry responded. "About bloody time! I thought he was going to drown us." He was sitting stiffly, eyes fixed ahead, knuckles white where his fists clenched the table.

Harriet lifted her head from her bowl with a watery smile. "He doesn't mean it, Connie. He's . . ." She shrugged, as though words were alien things she couldn't handle right now, and returned to her bowl.

Johnnie pushed himself to his feet, stumbling as the hull bucked under him, and he held out a hand to Connie. He took her wet arm and steered her into his seat at the table. "You must be exhausted. Sit down, I'll make you some strong tea. You need it. We're grateful to you, Connie, for all your labors on deck." But his tone sounded more depressed than grateful. "Nigel and I were saying earlier what bloody useless crocks we are, just when . . ."

"No, Johnnie, don't. Neither of you can help it."

For the first time Nigel spoke. But instead of looking at her, he was gazing down at his sleeping son and the way his small fingers slotted so trustingly in among his own. "There are a lot of things we can't help."

༅·༖

The energy of the storm was still in Connie's blood, and the voice of the wind was in her ears when she sat alone at the table in the saloon. The others had gone to their beds. Nigel had carried his son to his bunk, but Connie wasn't ready to turn in yet. She had no idea what time of night it was, or how long she had to wait for dawn.

Her mind wouldn't keep still. It was as if the waves had washed through her brain and stirred up her thoughts with their salty fingers.

For no reason at all she kept seeing Shohei Takehashi's face as clear as the full moon, leaning over her shoulder, not open mouthed with teeth streaked with scarlet, as it had been when she had enclosed it in a pillowcase. No. It was smiling, respectful, and patient, as when he first said to her, "Will you dance?" Quiet, silken words that had tempted her soul.

What if she had said, *No. Thank you, but no*? Would she be different now? Would she be a person without an iron spike in her chest, maybe even one who could sleep at night? She couldn't remember what that felt like. A person who could talk and laugh without . . .

"Here, this will calm you down."

Fitzpayne placed a glass of amber liquid in front of her. It immediately started to slide sideways as the table tilted with the movement of the sea, and Connie wrapped a hand around it to keep it steady. She hadn't been aware of him descending the steps, but when she looked up at him she had a feeling he had been standing there for some time, watching her.

"Drink," he said. "It will help you sleep."

How did he know?

ꝑ·ꝗ

Connie woke. Her neck was stiff, her shoulders ached, and for one alarming moment she had no idea where she was. A wet tongue licked her cheek, and Pippin's unwholesome breath puffed encouragingly in her face.

"All right," she groaned, and with eyes narrowed to slits she struggled to sit up, which only encouraged the dog to perch on her lap and sweep its warm tongue over her chin. She fondled his little head and recognized that she was still in the saloon, though her brain seemed to be performing some kind of thumping war dance. Hell, she had fallen asleep on the bench in her wet clothes. Her mouth tasted like sand, dry and scratchy, and riddled with salt. Daylight was streaming down on her from the hatches above, but it was a dull, leaden light that told her the storm clouds still lingered, the creek water choppy under the boat. Where was everyone?

There was no clattering on the hatches, which meant the rain had ceased, so at least that was something. She meant to stand up. To find where Teddy was, and to see if Nigel's leg needed attention. But instead she let her forehead drop to the table, the wooden rail digging into her ribs, her hands curled around Pippin on her knees, and she sat like that without moving while her thoughts tried to rearrange themselves. Everything had knotted into a confused tangle but slowly, thread by thread, she started to tug them apart.

"More whisky?"

She jerked upright. "What?"

"I thought you might need a hair of the dog." It was Fitzpayne. He was holding out the bottle and trying not to smile too much.

"What?"

He sat down on the bench opposite her and the boat swayed. Only then did she notice the empty glass at her elbow. It had a dry amber crust at the bottom. He tipped an inch of whisky into it.

"Drink up," he ordered. "You'll feel better after that."

Dimly she recalled sitting here on the bench last night after the others had gone to bed. Images, blurred and watery, started to come into focus: Fitzpayne's broad features opposite her, his weathered hand pouring whisky after whisky into a glass. How many times? Once? Twice? More? His thick eyebrows rising when she confessed to him she had once swum naked across the river in Palur and back, at night under the stars. Why, oh, why on earth had she told him that? His gray eyes had been fixed with amusement on hers, and he had started to ask questions.

What questions? What answers had she given?

Damn the man! And damn herself!

"No more whisky," she said huskily.

"As you wish," he responded with a chuckle, and drank it down.

"I shouldn't drink." She rubbed her throbbing temple.

"Why not?" He laughed, but softly, as though aware of the shooting pains in her skull. "You had been working damn hard all night. Whisky relaxes you, and that's exactly what you needed."

She sat up straight and studied the face of this man who thought he knew what she needed. It lacked the handsome charm of Johnnie's, and was not distinguished like Nigel's. But now that his bad-tempered scowl had been banished—it disappeared the moment he set foot on *The White*

Pearl—there was an energy to his face that was attractive. But the complex layers of his gray eyes worried her, the watchful intelligence behind them. What had made him go out of his way last night to get her drunk when she was too weary to resist? What was his purpose? And what had she told him?

Connie felt foolish and embarrassed.

"Mr. Fitzpayne," she said quietly, "I trusted you."

"I know, and I value that."

"So please tell me, why are you really here?"

"Mrs. Hadley." He leaned across the table, and for the first time she could make out the tiny lines of exhaustion that crept around his eyes. "I am here because you are trusting me to sail you and your boatload to Singapore. No other reason. Don't worry, I'll get you there, come hell or high water." He laughed, a strange, disturbing sound, less of a laugh than a collision of thoughts. "I think we experienced both hell and high water last night, but we're still here. Still in one piece. That's what you want, isn't it?"

"Yes."

"So relax. Everyone is relieved this morning just because they're still alive. You should be, too."

She rose to her feet, pausing while her head went for a spin around the room. "I must find my son."

"He's fine. Your husband has got him gathering firewood on shore."

She nodded, a wary movement, and made for the stairs. She suddenly realized she was still wearing her oilskins, so she peeled them off and felt a need to climb up into the fresh air, but halfway up the stairs she ducked her head and looked back at Fitzpayne. He was still seated, his muscular forearms resting on the table, her empty glass in his hand. His eyes were on her, but it was impossible to read their carefully guarded expression. She wondered if he saw on her face that same curtain that was drawn tight, protecting the secrets that flitted like shadows behind it.

"Fitz," she said, "thank you."

"For what?"

She smiled at him and headed up on deck.

CHAPTER TWENTY-ONE

I hate this fucking jungle."

However much Kitty moaned or mutinied, cried or cursed, Madoc didn't let her stop. He made her walk every hour of daylight. Only when the very last glimmer had spilled from the sky and the darkness of the jungle erupted into life did he allow her to collapse in a shuddering heap on the tarpaulin that he spread on the earth.

"Madoc," she hissed at him through clenched teeth, as he lit a strip of bark with one of their last matches, "if I have to spend one more night in this bloody jungle, with no food and no dry clothes and no bed and no shelter, with no relief from the bloody mosquitoes, I swear to God I will start cooking you limb by limb, and will eat your heart while it's still beating, because I can't—"

"Hush, Kitty," he murmured as he lowered himself down on the tarpaulin, lifted her thick legs one at a time onto his lap, and started to hunt out and scorch the plump bodies of the leeches that were buried in her flesh.

"A fire tonight, Madoc. Please, just a small one." She gripped the back of his neck with a hand that was infected and shook his head back and forth. "Please. To cook something. To dry my clothes, as well as to scare off the animals that come so close I can smell their greedy breath."

"No."

"Please."

"No."

"Blast you."

Gently, by the flimsy light of a burning length of bark, he dabbed antiseptic on the bleeding holes in her skin. She didn't wince and didn't moan, just kept her finger and thumb digging into his neck like a death grip. She was shivering. But he wouldn't relent.

"No fire, Kitty. The Japs could be close behind us."

"You're crazy. They couldn't have got this far south yet."

"Don't underestimate them. They move fast." He gave a tight grimace that he was glad she couldn't see. "They have bicycles, don't forget. They will be advancing relentlessly, invisible in the jungle until they slide a bayonet into your guts."

"Shut up, Madoc!"

"I'm sorry, Kitty."

Abruptly she released her grip on his neck. "One measly bloody fire, that's all I ask." She collapsed onto her side with a defeated groan and lay silent.

Around them, the noises of the night were deafening, a vibrating rowdy crescendo of chirrups and whistles, roars and growls, booms and squeaks. It acted like a drum inside Madoc's head, deadening his thoughts, as he pulled a small bundle from his pack and unwound the cloth that was wrapped around the bundle. He took out two items.

"Here, Kitty." He held them out to her on his palm, as he used to offer an apple to the milkman's horse when he was a child. "Eat something."

"Piss off."

"You have to eat."

"Cook them first and then I'll eat."

Madoc looked at the two pale grubs as big as white mice on his hand. They had soft, glistening bodies that tasted foul, but they were food and they weren't poisonous. In his pack lay a large dead lizard that would taste like chicken if it were cooked.

"I'll eat one if you eat one," he urged.

She didn't reply. The black mound of her bulk—that, back home, could fill a room with her boisterous breasts and carthorse hips—seemed diminished here, and Madoc experienced a strange feeling that he was losing her to the jungle. It was eating her, devouring her damp, creamy flesh, sucking the life out of her the way the leeches did. The thought distressed him. Since the destruction of his bar and his home, he had kept them traveling south day after day, endlessly hacking their way through dense forest, avoiding trails and any *kampongs*, the native villages that they stumbled across.

"They will have food," Kitty had wailed.

"When the Japs come," he told her, "they will hunt down any whites hiding out in the forest or in the villages, and if they hear that we have been in the area, we won't stand a chance."

She looked at him, her face caked in muddy streaks. "They really frighten you, these Japs."

"They scare the shit out of me. You saw what they did to Morgan's Bar. They want me dead."

She had kissed him smack on the mouth. "They'll have to kill me first."

Now she was threatening to kill him herself if he didn't light her a fire and roast the lizard. Softly he stroked her dirty hair.

"Sleep," he whispered. When she was rested, she might eat.

He knocked out the stub of flame. Instantly all existence vanished, and there was only the total darkness of the grave. He shuddered, unable to see his hand in front of his face. He curled up behind Kitty, his stinking body merging with hers, and pulled the tarpaulin over them, tucking it tight to keep out the spiders and snakes and whatever else stalked through the trees. In one hand he clutched his knife. He didn't expect to sleep, but just the familiar warmth of his wife's flesh next to his relaxed him a fraction. His throat was dry and tense, the taste of anger in it bitter as the grubs. Christ, he would kill his own mother for a cigarette.

That was when the rain came.

ᗐ·ᑫ

"Kitty! Kitty! Wake up."

Madoc held a hand over her mouth to keep her quiet. Her eyes popped open, and for a moment her sleep-sodden brain must have thought she was at home in bed because she smiled at him.

"Kitty, come and look," he whispered.

Realization turned her eyes the color of dirt. Without a word she dragged herself to her feet and followed him along a path he had hacked through the undergrowth earlier with the parang, snaking up a steep hill. Everything was saturated. The earth was slippery beneath their feet, and it was tough going. He held her hand and pulled her over the roots and mud slides, puffing and panting, as the sky turned from unrelenting black to a dull, lifeless gray and a silvery mist crept up the slopes like a sneak thief.

Near the top of the hill, a rocky outcrop covered in moss and lichen was home to a whole colony of bright green lizards waiting patiently for the heat of the day to warm their blood. They were as sluggish as snails in their movements and Kitty eyed them with interest, hoping for breakfast, but Madoc drew her around the outcrop to the other side.

"Look!" he said, and pointed.

In the distance beyond the trees lay the sea, whipped up into rolling breakers by last night's storm. But much nearer, on the edge of the shoreline that was hidden from them by the forest, a thin gray ribbon rose above the canopy of the jungle. It was smoke.

ϱ·ʕ

"The fools have lit a fire."

Madoc could almost hear Kitty's brain clicking into life beside him.

"Breakfast," she murmured. "Cooked breakfast."

But it wasn't the fire that Madoc was staring at as they stood under cover among the palms on the forest ridge. He had eyes only for the boat. She was a two-masted yacht with elegant lines, riding at anchor and lifting her bow in the rough waters like a racing hound sniffing the air, eager to set off. Madoc clenched his fist as excitement screwed up his gut.

"Fuck me if there isn't a God in heaven after all!"

"Let me take a look at you."

"What?"

Kitty flicked her gaze over him from head to foot, frowned, and then stuck a finger in one of the holes in his shirtsleeve and tore it so that it flapped loose and forlorn.

"You're certainly dirty enough," she decided. "Like a bloody chimney sweep." Nevertheless, she rubbed more earth through his hair and snapped off a couple of shirt buttons. Satisfied, she nodded. "What about me?"

Madoc inspected her filth and sweat, the hunger in her eyes and the way the wind off the sea was whipping her wild gray mane into a frenzy. He smiled.

"Kitty, you are perfect."

ᘖ·ᘉ

It was a strange little group, Madoc noted as he and Kitty approached. Eight of them: three men, two women, two natives plus a boy. And a dog. Seemingly all marooned by the storm on this slender spit of land between the sea and a small horseshoe bay at the mouth of the creek. Behind them the waves crashed against the mangroves with ferocious determination, trying to tear their long limbs apart. The noise of it was a constant roar in the background. This side of the spit, the water swirled in and out of the sinuous roots as though in search of their weak spot. Madoc wondered how long it would take him to find the weak spot of this group.

It was the dog that spotted them first as they walked forward. It raced toward them, a high-speed black torpedo, barking a warning, but then it stopped short ten feet from them, stiff-legged and teeth bared.

"Hello, boy," Madoc said, and held out his hand with a grub on it but the animal wasn't fooled.

It growled. Madoc halted. He wasn't comfortable around dogs.

Kitty advanced toward it with a cheery, "Piss off, mutt!" She gave it a tweak of its ears that made its tongue sneak out and lick her hand. "Bloody useless guard dog you are," she scolded, and the dog hurtled around her heels.

"Hello there!" Madoc raised a hand as he called out to the man approaching them across the ribbon of white sand.

He recognized the type, even from thirty paces away. He'd crossed paths with them all his life. The arrogant set of the shoulders, the clean-shaven chin held a fraction higher than was natural, so that he could stare down his nose. The crisp cut of his cream flannels, ready to stride out for a game of cricket at a moment's notice even in the middle of the bloody jungle. The Panama hat at an angle that said, *I am better than you*, one of the rulers of the colonial territories. Only the limp betrayed weakness, and fleetingly Madoc wondered how he'd come by the injury.

"Hello!" he called again as he and Kitty closed the gap, but the man didn't lift his hat to them as courtesy required had they been equals. He didn't offer his hand either.

"Good God, man! Where the blazes have you come from?"

"We've been escaping through the jungle."

"From the Japs," Kitty added drily, as though the man were stupid.

"Are they so close?" He glanced with alarm at the mass of solid jungle behind them.

"No, we've kept ahead of them. My name is Morgan Madoc and this is my wife, Kitty."

Madoc watched the man incline his head in polite greeting, as if at a tea party. "I am Nigel Hadley."

"We need help." Madoc spelled it out for him.

In the background, Madoc spotted a couple of the others detach themselves from the group and approach, a tall man with his arm in a sling accompanied by a slender woman with blond hair and an energetic way of walking—unlike most women of her class, who never deigned to move faster than a bored snail.

"Come along," Hadley said, "come and meet the rest."

When the man and the blond woman reached them, there was an exchange of "Good heavens" and "Bloody hell!" and "Are you all right?" All the time Madoc saw the woman's quick blue eyes skipping between Kitty and himself, taking in the insect bites on her face and the lines of exhaustion.

"You poor thing," she said quietly.

She took his wife's filthy hand and threaded it through her own arm, leading her at a slow, considerate pace over the shifting sand, ducking her head against the wind. "You must be starving," she said. "Come and have something to eat. Take her other arm, Johnnie." She turned to the cricket man. "Nigel, do give Mr. Madoc a hand. He looks quite done in."

Madoc noticed the man she called Nigel give her a long, angry look once her back was turned. So that was how the land lay. Madoc smiled to himself. Maybe he'd already found the weak spot.

Ͽ·Ϲ

They were trying to fry ham and eggs on the fire, but they were burning them. How could people who could run a bloody empire not know how to cook eggs?

Madoc sat on the sand drinking tea out of a dainty porcelain cup and kept a civil tongue in his head. Best to see the lay of the land first. He didn't yell at them to put out the fire. He didn't argue when told the stiff gale would probably blow itself out overnight. He noted the small breakfast rations handed out to each person, and the way the dark-haired white woman looked as if she wanted to snatch the plate from his hand. The young kid with eyes as bright as bullets plonked himself down next to Madoc, clutching a pencil and notebook, and started asking all the questions that the men, who all seemed to have brooms up their arses, were too polite to ask.

"Did you see any Japanese?"

"What kind of airplane strafed your home? Did it have twin engines?"

"Did you see any leopards in the jungle?"

"How did you navigate?"

"Were there lots of snakes?"

"What did you eat?"

"Did you have to swim a river?"

Each answer was jotted down in the notebook. After a long pause, there came a whispered, "Were you frightened?"

"Teddy," Constance Hadley chided fondly as she tended Kitty's infected bites, "leave poor Mr. Madoc in peace."

She gave Madoc an apologetic smile, and in that brief moment he was surprised by what he saw in her face. This was not a woman at peace. This was a woman chafing against something. She reminded him of a magpie with a broken wing he'd once rescued. It used to wander grace- fully around the yard on its slender feet, but all the time it uttered a sharp, choked cry, desperate to fly.

"What do you reckon, Madoc?" Kitty muttered.

"They won't leave us stranded here, they're British," he chuckled as he sipped his tea and wished like hell that it had a splash of something stronger in it. "They do the decent thing."

"That Henry Court fellow isn't so keen."

"Nor Hadley."

He eyed the group, who had withdrawn in a huddle to the water's edge to discuss the situation, leaving Madoc and Kitty seated beside the fire with the charred food. It was clear that the discussion was heated. Only the native girl stayed away from it, prowling up and down the spit of land in her sarong like a young jungle creature waiting to sink its claws into something.

"So what do you reckon?" Kitty asked again between mouthfuls of egg.

"Three against two. The kid and the native boy won't get a vote."

"For us or against us?"

He shook his head. "It looks like it's going against us."

"Oh, hell!"

"I think the flight lieutenant and Mrs. Hadley will vote to take us on board. But the others are scared shitless at the idea of us contaminating them and overcrowding their precious boat."

Kitty stirred a piece of ham through the sulfurous smears on her plate. "There will be plenty of room for us on deck."

"They don't want us eating their food either. Did you see the look the dark-haired woman gave your plate?"

"Bastards."

As the wind chased the smoke from the fire into their eyes, Kitty gave him a long look. "All right, Madoc, what are you looking so pleased about?"

He leaned his shoulder against hers. "Kitty, my sweet, I have hot food in my belly, you safe at my side, and we're about to sail on a boat that would fetch a pretty penny for someone who knew where to sell her."

Kitty's eyes widened. "Madoc! Back off. We're in enough trouble."

He stared out at the sleek yacht, rolling and yawing as the waves churned beneath her. A male figure that Madoc hadn't seen before was standing at the rail, and the native kid was rowing out to him in a small boat.

"Luscious, ripe, and ours for the taking."

"Watch yourself, Madoc! Don't be a bloody fool. We're probably not even going to be invited on board."

He leaned forward, picked up the butt of a cigarette that had been discarded in the sand, and lit it from the fire. "You underestimate Mrs. Hadley."

"What do you mean?"

Madoc was always careful of what he said about other women to Kitty. Her tongue could be sharp.

"Just that she is . . ."—he hesitated, seeking out the right word—". . . unfettered."

"Rot! All women of her class are in chains. They wear them as naturally as they wear their hats."

"Not this one." He took a last drag on the cigarette butt and flicked it into the fire. "It seems to me that she's dumped her chains in the sea. That's why her husband looks at her as if he's chewing on a porcupine."

For a long while Kitty said nothing, just stared into the flames while the wind snatched at her hair and threw small whirlwinds of sand at her. The growl of the breakers masked the voices of the group at the water's edge, and Madoc felt the familiar sensation of a bubble expanding in his chest until it was almost painful. The nerves of his fingertips started to dance and prickle. A sure sign: The game was on. Winner takes all. His hand slid down to his pack and fingered the Russian pistol inside it.

Suddenly Kitty started to laugh, and the tense hunch of her shoulders vanished. She sat up straight and skimmed Mrs. Hadley's china plate across the sand in a gesture of abandon, and then she gave him the sideways look that always stirred his loins.

"Go for it, Madoc."

੭·੬

"Mr. Madoc."

"Yes, Mrs. Hadley?"

"I am worried about your wife."

"So am I. She's not well." Madoc cast a look of concern at Kitty, who had slumped on the sand in a passable imitation of someone struggling against total collapse. "She doesn't have a fever," he assured the woman as she bent over and felt Kitty's forehead. He couldn't have her thinking there was any risk of infection.

She crouched down and rested a hand on Kitty's shoulder. "It'll be the shock," she said quietly. "Losing everything."

"And starvation. She hadn't eaten in days until the meal you gave her."

Her face under the wind-tossed hair was mobile, her full mouth wide and expressive. As a rule, Madoc didn't take to blondes. Their skin was always far too pallid for his taste, but there was something about this woman. Something that drew his interest. Beneath her gentle hands and her soft voice, he was aware of a strength that made him cautious. He recognized it at once because it was the same quiet quality that Kitty had, a kind of taut steel mesh under the pliant skin. The woman's blue eyes possessed a single-mindedness that her long golden lashes couldn't hide, however hard she tried.

"What's going on here?"

Nigel Hadley had rejoined them and was staring uncomfortably down at his wife's head bent over Kitty. Behind him stood the other couple—the Courts, the wife clutching a biscuit in her hand. For one surprised moment he thought she was going to offer it to Kitty, but no, she sank her teeth into it and licked the crumbs from her lips.

"If your wife is exhausted, Mr. Madoc," Hadley said, "maybe she would prefer to stay on shore and rest, rather than take the risk of rough seas on the boat. Don't you think so, Constance?"

"No, I don't." Still crouched beside Kitty, Constance Hadley gave her husband an uneasy stare. "I think it would be inhuman to leave her here."

"For God's sake, Connie"—Henry Court pushed the cushion of his stomach forward, the way Madoc had seen lawyers do when making a point against him in the dock—"have you thought this through and considered what might happen?"

"What is it you are frightened might happen, Henry?"

"The food," her husband interrupted. "We have to watch out for our rations, otherwise—"

"Otherwise Harriet might eat them all," Connie finished, and watched the color rise in her friend's cheeks.

"Now listen to me," Henry Court started, "I demand an apology for—"

"I can cook for you on your boat." It was Kitty's voice, a sad, bleating sound. But she had lifted her head from her hands and was giving Nigel Hadley her most convincingly docile smile. "I'm a good cook. Ask Madoc."

Oh Kitty, I love you.

Instantly there was a murmuring between the two men, and their hostility slithered away.

"Perhaps we should find room for them after all, Nigel," Court said, unconsciously resting his hand on his stomach. "Can't just leave them here for the Japs."

Madoc had to bite his tongue to stop a laugh.

"Well, well, damn me if it isn't Morgan Madoc, the wharf rat!"

Madoc swung around to see who had spoken behind him. The rowing boat was lying like a tired turtle on the sand, and deep footprints led from it to the man who addressed him. Broad-shouldered, dark-haired, eyes the color of a freshly sharpened blade, the kind of man Madoc had spent a lifetime avoiding. In his hand he swung a parang that glistened in the morning air.

"Fitzpayne," Madoc said. This was all he needed right now.

CHAPTER TWENTY-TWO

Happy Christmas!"

"Don't, Connie. This is not a happy Christmas," Harriet pointed out morosely.

"Of course it is," Connie insisted. "Come on, Harriet, don't be so gloomy. Yes, there's a war on but we're all safely together and still alive. We're stuck here for at least another day—which is not what any of us hoped for, I know, but let's enjoy it."

She beamed at the three other females, seated in the rough shelter in which they had spent the night. "It's Christmas 1941. A Christmas none of us will ever forget."

She reached into the cardboard box that she had ferried from the boat with Fitzpayne at the oars the previous day, and brought out three small packages that were wrapped in silky green leaves. She presented one to Harriet, one to Kitty, and one to Maya.

"Happy Christmas," she said again, and added, "Let's wish for peace to all men."

They looked at the presents, astonished, but a ripple of self-conscious pleasure spread from one to the other.

"Thanks," Harriet said. She sat up straighter and unwrapped the leaves.

Inside lay a tablet of verbena-scented soap, a lace-edged handkerchief tied around six sugared almonds, and a tortoiseshell comb with a narrow silver backbone, one of a set of four that Connie's grandmother had sent her for her thirtieth birthday. Harriet lifted the soap to her nostrils, closed her eyes, and inhaled its scent. "Now I remember what real life smells like," she said, and uttered one of her old laughs.

The gifts were the same for Kitty and Maya. Kitty opened hers and nodded quietly to herself. She lifted her head and looked steadily at Connie. "You are a generous woman," she said, which embarrassed Connie.

Maya tore off the leaves and stared at the soap, handkerchief, and comb with round, baffled eyes. "*Terimah kasih*," she muttered, "thank you, *mem*." She stroked a finger over the smooth, pastel-pink coating of a sugared almond before popping it into her mouth, then ran the comb through a strand of her black hair, flicking it neatly over her shoulder as she finished. She grinned at Connie, showing small white teeth. It was the first time Connie had ever seen her smile.

"Happy Christmas to you, Maya."

ᎧᎬ

"What the hell are you doing, Kitty?" Madoc demanded in a low voice.

"I'm making a Christmas pudding for her." Her plump arms were elbow-deep in raisins and flour and God only knows what else, trying to avoid the drips from the tarpaulin roof.

"You're supposed to be ill."

"Go away."

Her mosquito-bitten face looked suddenly deflated, and it dawned on him that she had been enjoying herself and he had spoiled it.

"Be careful," he whispered. "Don't appear so bloody happy."

She gave him a look that could have curdled milk, so he decided to risk the rain rather than her tongue. It was sheeting down outside, as only tropical rain knows how, drenching him to the skin in seconds and battering his scalp with the force of a thousand tiny hammers. He ducked into the men's shelter and shook himself, smelling at once the aromatic smoke of a fine cigar. It made his lungs ache for one.

Constance Hadley had presented each of the men, including himself, with a gift of a Havana cigar and a handful of sugared almonds. The almonds he passed on to the Hadleys' kid, but the cigar he appreciated. He would enjoy it after his Christmas dinner—or *luncheon* as they insisted on calling it. It was dinner to him and Kitty, and always would be.

Yesterday the men had built two ramshackle shelters to wait out the storm, using tarpaulins from the boat with branches and fronds from the forest. They were tucked in close to the jungle's edge to escape the worst of the wind. The larger one was for the four women to sleep in, and the smaller one was for the six men and the boy. It seemed cockeyed to Madoc, but he was told in no uncertain terms by Nigel Hadley that "the ladies need space." He didn't ask what for.

He glanced around the shelter now. The boy was off with his mother, but on a blanket on the ground Hadley and the native lad were bent over a Snakes and Ladders board, while the pilot played poker with Henry Court. The cigar smoke was issuing from the mouth of Razak, who was trying to blow smoke rings, much to the amusement of Hadley who let out a great guffaw each time the Malay boy spluttered and coughed. The wind swirled the smoke through the shelter, chasing away the insects, and buffeted the tarpaulin roof.

"Where's Fitzpayne?" Madoc asked.

"Checking on *The White Pearl*," Hadley replied, without lifting his head. "Working the bilge pump."

Madoc itched to take a closer look at the yacht, and he had offered to row Mrs. Hadley out yesterday when she wanted to fetch some blankets, but Fitzpayne had stepped in and put a stop to it. He had rowed her out himself. Madoc had been left on the shore to stare disconsolately after them as the turbulent seas threatened to swamp the rowing boat in the rain. Damn Fitzpayne. He wouldn't mind seeing the man's dark curls vanish under those waves.

The shock of finding him here had been a blow to his plans and he would have to tread warily. Fitzpayne was no fool. They had first run into each other on the wharves of Kuala Terengganu on the east coast of the Malay Peninsula when Madoc was doing a spot of opium running down from Shanghai, at the same time as getting well paid for smuggling a cabinload of refugee Russian girls to the Philippines. He and Fitzpayne ended up on opposite sides of a knife fight, and Madoc still bore the scars. Why the hell did he have to turn up here?

He found a corner of the blanket to sit on, keeping a respectful distance from Hadley with his long, disdainful face, but close enough to snatch up the cigar when the native lad decided to discard it. He stamped his heel on a battalion of foraging ants and let his thoughts climb aboard *The White Pearl*.

ᗡ·Ϭ

Connie felt good about welcoming Kitty into the group. There was something about this woman she liked, despite her excessive amount of soft bare flesh and her bush of wild gray hair that made her look like one of the crazy fire-walkers that Connie had seen when she and Nigel stayed in the Station Hotel in Kuala Lumpur last year, en route to the Batu Caves. Kitty, she felt instinctively, was a person worth having in your corner, which was more than she could say for Harriet. She worried about her friend. Harriet seemed to be transforming into a different person from the one she knew in Palur.

Fear does strange things to people. The carefully constructed defenses can collapse and the creature beneath emerges, wild-eyed, claws sharpened. She thought about the way Nigel looked at her now—almost as though she were a stranger. Was she the one who had changed? Or was it him? He studiously avoided her company and spent most of his time with Johnnie, Teddy, and Razak. Less time with Henry, who was becoming more obnoxious with each passing day, as fear and hunger tightened his belt.

It pleased Connie immensely that Nigel and Teddy both enjoyed Razak's company. They were teaching him all kinds of things—maybe too many card and board games for her liking, but it made her laugh when the native boy shouted "Snap!" at the top of his voice and whooped with delight at winning. But she could see Maya withdrawing, becoming more and more isolated, and that worried her. She had tried to include the girl in her own activities, but Maya would just gaze up at her from under her thick black eyelashes and shake her head.

But today was Christmas Day. So while Kitty hovered over her pans bubbling on the fire, and Harriet sat with glazed eyes as Teddy explained to her the inner workings of a combustion engine—Connie had given him *The Wonder Book of Motors* for Christmas—she asked Maya to chop a couple of onions.

Connie held out a small knife to her. "Come and help."

The girl stopped combing her hair and staring out at the ceaseless rain. She rose from her knees, eyes jumping from the knife to Connie. "Yes, *mem*," she said.

As they worked side by side chopping the onions and peeling a head of garlic, the sounds of the storm raged outside their makeshift home and made the interior feel oddly intimate. Smoke from the fire swirled around them, and they had to lean their heads closer to make themselves heard above the snapping and cracking of the tarpaulin.

"Do you like cooking, Maya?"

The girl shook her head and concentrated on slicing the onion.

"I'm useless at it," Connie laughed.

Still mute.

"I think we're lucky to have Mrs. Madoc today, don't you, Maya? The men will be pleased to have a good hot meal."

The girl shrugged. She wasn't making it easy.

"Maya, I went looking for you among the shacks in Palur after the fire."

Maya's sharp little knife paused. "Why you do that, *mem*?"

"Because I was worried about you. I wanted to know that you and Razak had escaped the flames and were safe."

"I all right."

"Yes." Connie watched the girl's blade resume its staccato movements. "But a man told me you were dead."

"I not dead."

"So I see."

"Who silly bugger tell you I dead?"

"A blind man."

"Oh, him. He big liar. I run from flames, run, run, run. They not bite me."

"I'm very relieved that you did. Did most of the others run with you?"

"Yes, many many."

Connie nodded, put down her own knife, and turned to face the girl. "The blind man had a child that died in the fire. He said it was yours."

Maya's eyes widened with shock. "Aiyee! I tell you, he big liar."

"So it's not true?"

"No." She stabbed the point of the knife into the next onion. "I never have child." She shook her head vehemently, sending long black strands of hair leaping across her face in protest at such a thought.

Either she was telling the truth. Or she was a damn good liar.

ᴐ·ᴒ

Christmas luncheon was an odd affair. Nigel took control, just as though he were seated at the head of the table at home instead of hunkered down on palm fronds spread out over wet sand. He always delivered a speech, and today was to be no exception, though he had to raise his voice to compete with the howling of the wind. He thanked Kitty graciously for the splendid curry and rice she had created out of tinned beef and spices.

"Not our usual roast turkey, I admit," he conceded, "but a fine repast, Mrs. Madoc, given the circumstances. And a magnificent pudding."

Fitzpayne had come and extinguished the fire the moment the cooking was done, stamping it to ash, so the air was at least free of smoke. They were all decked out in Christmas hats. Not the usual paper crowns that were the traditional headgear at an English table on Christmas Day, but intricate garlands of greenery woven by Teddy. Connie could see a small spider spinning its web in Harriet's hair, but she made no mention of it. They all sat in a circle and sang Christmas carols when the meal was finished, which brought emotions roaring to the surface.

"Silent night, holy night," they chorused together. "All is calm, all is bright . . ."

It isn't silent. It isn't calm. Connie could not bring herself to mouth the words when it was so patently untrue. All was anything but calm and bright. Life was stormy. Dislocated. Perilous. Teetering on the edge of . . . of what? A tremor shook her, and she saw Harriet lower her face into her hands and moan, "My home, my sweet home is gone forever."

"It's the end," Henry muttered, and he didn't mean the end of the song.

To Connie's surprise, Fitzpayne shook the moment out of its downward spiral by immediately starting up with "O come all ye faithful, joyful and triumphant . . ." in a rich booming voice, and the others joined in eagerly, banishing the rank breath of the forest and the yearning for past Christmases.

"Joyful and triumphant." Connie sang the words and heard them reverberate in her head. The irony of them made her laugh.

ᕘ·ᕬ

As the light began to fade, Connie grew restless. The festive bonhomie petered out over halfhearted games of I Spy and Ludo, so a bottle of brandy came out in an effort to raise the spirits of the group. But Connie had no wish to drink. She stood by the flap of tarpaulin that acted as a door, feeling the shelter shudder and tremble as the wind battled to bring it to its knees. The urge to run down the sand, row out to *The White Pearl*, and hoist her sails even in the storm-force gale was so overwhelming that Connie had to hold on to one of the supports to keep her feet from taking off.

The sky was a surly gray, the clouds bruised and menacing. At least no pilot in his right mind would choose to fly in such conditions. The rain was starting to ease, but the force of the wind was enough to knock her teeth out. A world of green darkness loomed behind them, and already jungle trees were being uprooted by the storm and collapsing on the narrow beach like dead soldiers.

Connie longed to be on the move. She had learned that much about herself on the boat—the joy of outrunning her past. A hop or a skip forward, a jink to one side, a sudden burst of speed. All the debris of her mind was left in a squirming heap behind her. If she set off on *The White Pearl* and never stopped sailing, she was convinced the nightmares would vanish. The constant sounds in her head, the thud-thud-thud of Sho's skull on the steps of the hut and the crump of a car bumper into warm flesh would cease. The slow, soothing rhythm of the sea would calm her nerves, the smell of salt and seaweed would erase the stench of blood in her nostrils.

"You're getting wet."

Connie blinked, startled, and found Fitzpayne at her side.

"It will be dark soon."

"Your husband has his torch, and the rest of us have candles."

"Candles? This wind will blow them out in seconds."

He smiled at her, a warm, interested smile. "Then your husband will be the only one fortunate enough to possess a light," he said.

She felt her cheeks grow warm and was grateful for the gloomy light. He was studying her, amused.

"Do you have a cigarette?" she asked.

He offered her one and cupped his hand around the match for her, his head so close to hers she could smell the brine in his hair. The wind was whipping it around his face.

"Is *The White Pearl* all right?" she asked as she inhaled the smoke and nicotine into her lungs. "She's taking a pounding out there."

"She's in good shape. Strongly constructed."

They gazed out through the veil of rain across the small bay, where the yacht's white hull flashed in the water. Together in silence they admired her, thankful for the spit of land that gave her protection from the worst of the wind.

"Thank you for bringing her—and us—to safety here," Connie said.

He looked at her sharply and shadows draped themselves over his face, so that she could barely see his expression. He spoke in a low voice, despite the wind.

"Don't think we are safe, Mrs. Hadley."

"The Japanese will be marooned by the storm, just as we are, surely?"

"The danger is not just outside."

"What do you mean?"

"That there is danger within."

For a moment she thought he meant her. That she was the danger. She shook her head mutely.

"Morgan Madoc," he murmured. "I advise you not to trust him."

"Why do you say that?"

But before he could reply, a cry came from behind them in the shelter. Harriet had vomited all over her own lap and was mopping at her mouth with her new lace handkerchief. Connie went to her at once and wrapped an arm around her shoulders. Tremors shook Harriet's frame and she released a visceral moan like a sick animal, her hands clutching her stomach. She stared accusingly at Kitty, who was bringing a wet cloth to her.

"What the hell have you done to me?" Harriet demanded.

Kitty stood flat-footed, cloth in hand. "What?"

"You've poisoned me."

"Of course she hasn't." Connie moved quickly. She took the cloth and started to clean up the mess. "The rest of us aren't sick, and we all ate the same food. You must have eaten something else, or you've caught a chill."

The men watched helplessly, uncomfortable when it came to sickness.

"Harriet," Connie soothed, pushing back a damp lock of hair from her friend's forehead, "it's just a stomach upset, maybe even a delayed kind of seasickness." It didn't sound convincing. There were smears of blood on the lace handkerchief in Harriet's hand.

The sound of the wind rose. The shelter shook and the tarpaulin threatened to tear loose. Connie's ears filled with a roaring, and too late she realized it wasn't the wind.

ϑ·ᘓ

No, no, no, no.

Maya crept from her corner and squatted on her heels beside the dark-haired *mem*. She took the woman's limp fingers between her own and crooned a lilting Malayan melody under her breath, as she would to a child.

"No sick," she muttered, "no be sick."

It was the wrong one. The wrong *mem* was sick. They must have swapped plates. There was so much noise in the shelter, the *tuans* shouting and the wind bellowing, that it made Maya's thoughts cramp into a tight ball.

"No be sick," her lips mouthed again.

The woman bent over and retched miserably. Maya saw the telltale traces of leaves in the trail of curry that spilled onto the ground, the shiny green shoots she had torn up so small they could hide themselves inside a curry and no eyes would spot them. She stared accusingly at

Mem Hadley—why wasn't she sick? Why wasn't she the one vomiting her guts out?

"*Mem*," she muttered to the sick woman, "I sorry."

But the sounds outside and the panic inside snatched her words and threw them away. The woman's skin had turned the color of chicken shit and her eyes were starting to roll in her head. *Oh no, no, no. It wasn't meant for you. Why you swap plates with Mem Hadley?*

Someone seized her wrist, pulling at her, shouting something urgent in her ear. So much sound in the shelter, it deafened her. And the dog yapping. Without seeing or hearing, she knew it was her twin tugging at her, but she didn't meet his eyes. He would know. He would realize what she had done, that she had slunk into the forest in the rain and found the plant with the hard shiny leaves that her mother used to use to put an end to sick animals or to old people with milky eyes who were ready to escape this world. She didn't look up at him. She didn't listen to his words. Instead, she bowed her forehead flat to the ground and begged forgiveness for her mistake.

That was when she felt the sick *mem* give a small jerk, as if she had been kicked. Maya lifted up to look at her face. The woman's eyes were wide open, tears on her dark lashes, strings of vomit trailing from her chin and her mouth shaped into a perfect circle. But in the middle of her forehead lay a tiny scarlet petal. Maya couldn't understand for a strange, twisted moment where it had come from, and then she started to scream.

ꕤ·ꕤ

Teddy! Connie's first thought was for her son.

But she saw him safe on his father's shoulder, racing out of the shelter as it exploded to shreds around them. Rain flooded in, while a noise like a giant buzz saw tore at her eardrums and rattled the ribs of her chest.

"Harriet," she whispered to the woman leaning against her.

Connie still had her arm around her friend's shoulders, but the dark head lolled in her direction as if trying to listen to her quiet words beneath all the blast of sound.

"Harriet," Connie said again, "we have to go."

But she knew her friend wasn't listening. She'd seen the neat bullet hole in the center of her forehead, and the dark underbelly of the airplane that had strafed their camp on Christmas Day. But her eyes seemed to have disconnected from her brain, so she continued to sit beside her friend, talking to her, urging her to stand, refusing to believe. Dimly she was aware of the native girl, a small, silent presence, hunched up on the floor in a tight ball, her hand clutching Harriet's. Everyone else had vanished.

"Come on, Harriet," Connie whispered, "let's get out of the rain."

Arms suddenly wrenched Connie to her feet, so that Harriet tumbled flat on her back on the ground, rain instantly washing her face clean, flooding her open eyes like tears.

"Leave her!" Fitzpayne's voice yelled in Connie's ear.

"No!"

"It's too late."

"No, she might still be alive."

He pulled at her arm. "Quickly, the plane is coming back."

The rattle of machine guns spitting bullets was charging down the beach.

"Run!" Fitzpayne shouted.

"No."

With a curse he bent, threw Harriet Court's limp figure over his shoulder, and yanked Connie's arm almost out of its socket as he started to run. They scrambled into the dense tangle of trees where the jungle offered safety, the native girl shrieking at their heels. In the deep gloom of the forest Connie knelt on the sodden earth, rocking Harriet in her arms, only releasing her when Henry Court pushed her away roughly with the words, "Stay away from my wife. You caused this. We would never have been here in the first place if it weren't for you."

Connie bowed her head and remained on her knees at a distance. He had said out loud the words that were already in her head.

Four days.

Four days pinned on this slender spit of land. The daylight hours were spent out of sight under the trees, no one—not even Pippin—allowed to venture onto the beach. The hours of darkness were passed in a single rickety shelter of branches and fronds combined with what remnants of the tarpaulins could be salvaged.

A fierce argument took place about whether to bury Harriet now or to wrap her body in a blanket and take it back to Singapore for her funeral in consecrated ground. In the end, the Malayan climate won. The body had to be buried immediately before the heat and humidity set to work on it. The ceremony was short and simple, conducted with dignity by Nigel in the pouring rain, and a wooden cross that had been constructed by Fitzpayne was hammered into the earth to tell the worms where she was. Carved into the crosspiece of timber were the words *Harriet Arabella Court 1905–1941*.

9·6

It started on the evening that Fitzpayne rowed back from *The White Pearl* with Johnnie and Morgan Madoc. Still on board the yacht, Nigel and Razak were leaning against the rail awaiting their turn to be ferried ashore, small figures in the distance. That was how it was in Connie's head now: everything in the distance. All five men had been working on the yacht since daylight. She stood in the dark line of trees and watched the oars dip in and out of the waves with an easy rhythm as evening shadows created deep troughs around them. A flight of swallows swept low over the creek, while the sun painted the sky a triumphant gold that spilled onto the men in the boats.

Connie envied them. But it was better this way. She needed to remain in the forest each day, watching over Henry. Together they sat next to his wife's grave in the rain and the wind, while the other men of the group worked on repairing the damage to the yacht. During a second low pass by the Japanese fighter, its guns had ripped holes in the hull of *The White Pearl* below the waterline. Despite the heavy weather, Fitzpayne had labored hard to keep her seaworthy, patching up the damage with fresh timber and the pitch and oakum they carried on board. Razak was kept busy pumping out the water that had flooded her below deck. It pained Connie to see the yacht so forlorn and listing like an old woman, but her grieving was for Harriet, for her friend who had trusted her enough to join them in a race against an advancing army.

This evening the sun had at last beaten back the clouds and the temperature took a sharp jump so that the trees were wreathed in sinuous trails of mist that made the barks and cries that echoed in the forest sound eerie and disembodied. Connie found herself listening for the rising whoop of Harriet's laugh among the *che-che-che* calls of the drongo birds and the long piercing whistles of the mynahs. It was only the sight of Teddy that kept her alert and watchful.

Ever since Christmas Day her son had been withdrawn and had focused a hundred percent of his attention on his jam jars of spiders and beetles and moths, studying them through the magnifying glass, like a miniature professor with his brown curls sticking out at wild angles, bits of leaf and fern caught in his hair, and all the time he jotted down notes in his diary. But the expression on his face looked baffled, tired of the complication of people and hungry for the simplicity of the creatures in his jars.

Connie sat and talked gently with her son, but he wasn't ready to communicate with anything more than a mute shake of his head or a nod of his chin. When his father invited him to join himself and Razak on *The White Pearl* with Fitzpayne, he turned it down with an indifferent shrug of his narrow shoulders. That gesture, so adult and so unlike Teddy, made tears spring to Connie's eyes. Equally he ignored Kitty Madoc's efforts to draw him out with snippets of rice cake and honey. It was the little native girl who seemed the only one able to get through to him. She brought him a snake. A dead one, but still a snake. Teddy was crouched under a banana palm, watching an army of a million red ants mountaineer over a branch he had laid across their path, when she came up to him and dropped the dead reptile at his feet. It was three feet long with red flower markings along its green back. He handled it delicately and told her it was a paradise tree snake.

"It's a flying snake. It flattens its ventrals and glides from tree to tree."

"Full of poison?" the girl asked.

"No, it's harmless. It feeds on lizards. It's beautiful," Connie heard him say. "But what I'd really like is a king cobra."

"King cobra eat you," Maya told him.

Neither of them laughed. Solemn young faces. It was as if they already knew perfectly well that life was about creatures devouring other creatures. About men killing other men. It came as no surprise. And when the rowing boat approached, dipping and bobbing through the sheet of gold that the setting sun had spread out over the water, Connie felt a change in the group of survivors. It was then that it started, the sense of time running out. As though a clock were ticking inside her head.

ϑ·ε

"Kitty, I'm in love," Madoc confessed.

"I can see that," Kitty chuckled as her head swiveled back and forth, inspecting the elegant fittings of the saloon. It was the first time she had been on board *The White Pearl*.

"Isn't she the most desirable creature you've ever seen?"

"Stop drooling. It's a rich man's boat, so what else do you expect?"

"A rich woman's boat, apparently."

"You mean it's hers?"

"Yes."

"Nice work." Kitty pulled a face.

"That Jap plane did some nasty things to her."

"Do you mean to Mrs. Hadley or to the boat?"

They exchanged a look. "That's debatable," he muttered. "She's taken the death of Mrs. Court hard."

"It just goes to show," Kitty said as she inspected the tiny galley and patted the gimballed stove with approval, "that money doesn't buy you happiness. What that woman needs is a damn good—"

"Ssh, Kitty." He put his fingers to her lips and raised his eyes meaningfully to the hatches above. "On a boat," he said in an undertone, "nothing is secret. The walls are paper thin. Everything can be overheard."

"Everything?"

"Everything."

She started to chuckle again as she opened the storage lockers to assess their contents. "Is that so?"

϶·ϵ

Henry Court gave up his cabin. Real civil of him, Madoc thought, and accepted it for Kitty and himself with alacrity. Kitty said it was because the poor man couldn't bear to sleep in his dead wife's bed, but an occasional ghost didn't matter a damn to Madoc—he already had a trunkload of them. Henry now chose one of the narrow bunks behind a curtain instead, and Razak took the lower one. Fitzpayne didn't seem to need to sleep but said he would opt for a bench in the saloon if he did. The native girl still crept around on deck like a dark shadow, setting the hairs on the back of Madoc's neck on end.

They had hoisted sail at first light under Fitzpayne's command, an uncertain wind from the south making progress difficult, but Madoc gave a satisfied grunt each time the headwind caused them to tack and steer off course. He was in no hurry to reach Singapore, no hurry at all. He'd watched Constance Hadley and Henry Court hang over the stern as they sailed out of the creek, their gaze fixed on the patch of jungle where Mrs. Court lay buried, unwilling to lose sight of it until the very last moment. It was absurd really, because it didn't matter how deep they stuck her; the forest animals would get the body in the end. It was the law of nature out here.

"Take the helm, will you, Madoc?" Fitzpayne interrupted his thoughts.

"Happy to oblige."

Madoc didn't let a single word of discontent pass his lips in Fitzpayne's presence, not even when he'd been knee-deep in the muck and filthy water in the bowels of the boat to help Fitzpayne patch the holes. Despite their efforts at repair, and the sailcloth pulled tight over the pitch, the boat was still taking on a certain amount of water, which slowed the speed even more, but Madoc wiped the smile off his face and took the helm. Even wounded, she was a joy to handle.

"Madoc," Fitzpayne said under his breath, "keep an eye on the Hadley boy while you're on deck."

The kid was up in the bow scarcely speaking to anyone, just glued to the binoculars—very expensive, Madoc noted—scanning the skies with them and turning at regular intervals to sweep the horizon behind the boat. To the west, the long outline of Sumatra was just visible behind a veil of mist, its humpbacked silhouette green and shadowy in the distance. Gulls wheeled overhead, and the cool, early-morning air tasted clean and salty after the humidity of the jungle. Madoc heard light footsteps on the companionway and saw Constance Hadley emerge. She held a hot drink and a cigarette in her hand, both of which she offered to him with a smile. Her blue eyes were cloudy, her face thinner than when he had first met her.

"Thanks," he said, and nodded toward her son. "Your kid likes to watch things, doesn't he?"

"Yes. He's very observant."

For a second Madoc felt unsettled. Exactly how observant was this boy? What had he noticed? Madoc had never had much to do with children and they made him uneasy. More footsteps announced the appearance of the flight lieutenant on deck. Madoc had noticed before that the pilot liked to pop up unexpectedly around Constance Hadley, under the pretense of exercising his damaged shoulder and of getting her to rebind it. But she kept him at arm's length. She was fond of the pilot, though, that much was obvious, but keen to draw a line in the sand between them.

It was the husband who was entertained by Johnnie Blake most evenings, laughing over cards or arguing over the toss of dice while the native lad grinned and learned the tricks of gambling. That was the trouble with Englishmen of their class: They were always more at ease in male company than female. In their book, women were for the bedroom and the ballroom. The fools had no idea what they were missing. It wasn't just the curves of Kitty's body that Madoc relished, it was also the curves of her mind.

"Spotted anything interesting?" Constance Hadley had moved forward and was talking to her son.

She balanced herself well with the movement of the deck. Her skirt and blouse were dark today, a black ribbon tying back her fair hair, the nearest she could get to mourning weeds. It occurred to Madoc as he watched her lean over Teddy that there was something of the ballet dancer about her, that same elegance of feet and hands. He and Kitty had once shared digs with a troupe of dancers—the memory made him laugh. Thieving little bitches they turned out to be.

"Aircraft!"

The boy's young voice rang out clearly and his hand pointed east. Madoc flinched. He couldn't help it. Airplanes did that to him ever since the attack on his bar—it made no difference whether they were British planes or Jap ones. The crippling roar of an aircraft engine was branded into his brain.

He peered hard into the glare of blue sky. "Can't see any."

"Six of them."

The boy had the advantage of the binoculars.

"Ours or theirs?" Flight Lieutenant Blake asked.

There was a pause while the kid studied them. Why the hell didn't Blake snatch the binoculars from him and look himself? Too bloody polite for his own good.

"Ours. Bristol Blenheim bombers," Teddy answered.

"Sure?"

"Twin engines. Single tail."

Madoc held the bow steady to help the identification and had to admit the kid seemed to know his stuff.

"Good man," Blake said.

The boy gave a self-conscious little nod, pleased, and Constance Hadley shot Blake a grateful look. So that was the way to get to her—through her son. Madoc stored the information away and was turning it over in his mind, debating how to use it, when Fitzpayne suddenly materialized at his elbow, silent as a bloody snake. Madoc yielded the helm without a word, and at that moment the planes roared overhead, making his teeth shudder, and every eye watched the formation's progress south.

"They'll be heading for Tengah Air Base," Blake surmised. "Or maybe Seletar, if it hasn't been too badly bombed for them to land." He spoke casually, but no one on deck was fooled. The man was aching to be up there.

"Probably on the run from the Japs," Madoc muttered.

The blow to his stomach knocked him sprawling flat on the deck and drove the air from his lungs. Heads turned to stare in bafflement. He glared up at his attacker, but Fitzpayne was back at the helm, gaze fixed straight ahead as though he hadn't stepped away from it for a second. Fast as a cobra strike.

"Are you all right, Mr. Madoc?" Constance Hadley asked, bemused. "What happened?"

"He tripped," Fitzpayne answered for him. "Over his big mouth."

Blake stepped forward from the bows to confront Madoc. "They're not on the run, Madoc. They are British pilots defending Malaya and risking their young lives to save people like you."

Madoc muttered something inaudible, gave Fitzpayne a hard stare, and turned to go below. Fuck the lot of them. As he jumped down the stairs he heard the bastard call out to everyone, "We'll be in Singapore tonight. Let's get more canvas aloft."

"But there's the native *pinisiq* again," the Hadley kid yelled. "It's chasing us."

Fitzpayne's voice rumbled, "It's just a local trading boat, Teddy. Nothing for you to worry about."

But Madoc had sharp ears. They had no trouble detecting a lie.

꿍ᐧᢕ

Nightfall descended like a blackout curtain. Singapore was flickering in the distance, drawing moths to its flame. Pinpricks of light sparkled across the waters of the Malacca Straits from the bow lights of boats bound for the city's protective harbor. It seemed that others had also chosen to flee by sea during the hours of darkness, before the fist of war closed around them, but the moon was already rising and pointed them out with a silvery finger, turning them into milky ghosts.

Connie felt *The White Pearl* shiver under her feet, as though the boat sensed they were approaching their journey's end. The night was hot and clammy, bats flitting through the rigging like lost souls, the slap of the waves against the hull marking a steady rhythm that should have calmed her thoughts but didn't. She took the helm and smoked too many cigarettes.

"Nervous?" Fitzpayne asked.

She had been aware of his presence, leaning against the mast in the darkness, as though their journey together were already over, and he was done with them. The thought disturbed Connie.

"No, not nervous. Thinking about what lies ahead."

He turned to her, his face pitted with shadows. "Singapore lies ahead."

There was a moment when the fungal smell of the verdant jungle wafted on the breeze, bringing with it a sense of wildness and freedom, and a part of Connie choked at the thought of being trapped in Singapore.

"Yes," she said softly.

"Where will you stay?"

"I've booked rooms at Raffles Hotel. I don't even know if it's still standing, or whether it has been bombed in one of the air raids." She paused. "What about you?"

"I won't be lingering in Singapore. Just long enough for a bath and a drink, and then I'll move on."

"Where will you go?"

"To one of the islands I know."

"Which one?"

"There are thousands of islands here, many small and secretive, and even the Japanese won't bother to capture them all."

The way he said it—as though it were a certainty—made her skin crawl. "You think their troops will definitely get this far?" she asked.

"Don't you?"

Before she could answer, the wind jumped and gusted down from the ancient hills of Sumatra to the west of them, so that the yacht heeled hard to port. When *The White Pearl* abruptly righted herself, Fitzpayne stepped closer, offering a hand to steady her at the helm. She didn't take it.

"Tell me, Mr. Fitzpayne, where do you come from?"

He laughed, a warm sound in the darkness. "We are soon to say good-bye. Why ask now?"

"Because I want to know."

There was a moment's hesitation while he decided how much to say. Or not to say.

"I was born on a beach by the ocean's edge here in East Asia," he said as he exhaled smoke into the wind. "My parents were"—he smiled at her almost shyly—"adventurous. They came from Hull in England, but together they trawled all over Asia."

"People who like to push the limits."

Again he uttered a soft laugh. "That's true."

"And you?"

"What?"

"Do you like to push the limits, Mr. Fitzpayne?"

He let himself sway backward, leaning away from her. "I like," he said, "to push others to their limits."

It was an unexpected admission. "But why?"

"That's when you learn the truth about people." He drew on his cigarette, the tip dancing in the darkness. "When they are stripped of their pretenses, their defenses down, you learn exactly what they are capable of."

Does he suspect? What I am capable of? Is that why he gave me the gun?

"And what do you do then?" she asked. "When you know the truth about someone."

"The truth is always cleaner than a lie." He touched the back of her hand on the helm and added in a quiet voice, "Lies weaken a person. They are the bedfellows of fear."

A cold sensation spread from somewhere under Connie's breastbone and rose up into her throat until she felt an overwhelming need to vomit it out, to rid her mouth of the rotting taste of fear and lies. She turned her face to him and opened her lips to say the words that were embedded in her tongue. *I killed a man.*

But that was when the drone of airplane engines shattered the tropical night. Before the words could emerge, the first bombs started to fall on Singapore.

♉·♉

A tidal wave of sound hit *The White Pearl*. Connie felt the boat quiver as plane after plane roared overhead. Tracers streaked across the night sky like fiery veins, crisscrossing the darkness as RAF fighter aircraft tried to shoot the imperial Japanese bombers out of the sky.

Connie stood at the rail, clutching her son's hand. They watched helplessly as the city was pounded again and again, as bombs hit their targets, fires flared into life, and the boom of explosions ripped through the night.

"They are giving the Keppel docks a hammering," Johnnie said. His voice was tight.

Connie's mind filled with images. Of ordinary people. People going about their business along the Tanglin and Orchard Roads. Sitting in the Alhambra cinema or the Roxy, watching Humphrey Bogart in *The Maltese Falcon* and eating ice cream. Where was the governor, Sir Shenton Thomas? Where were the air-raid shelters? Ack-ack guns started to roar defiance.

"Mummy, look!"

A plane exploded, falling out of the sky, and beside her Johnnie flinched. Flames leaped up from the ground and she could feel her son's excitement radiating from his skin. Fitzpayne was sailing *The White Pearl* as hard and as fast as he could, catching every scrap of wind in the sails.

He had doused the bowlight, and around them other boats were doing the same. Only the moonlight saved them from collision.

"That is the end," Connie whispered.

"End of what?" Teddy asked.

"The end of Singapore for us."

He twisted his face up to look at her, his brown eyes searching her face. "Why?"

It was the newcomer, Madoc, who answered. "Because there's no point us going there any more, sonny," he said. "The Japs will pour their troops and their guns and their tanks into the city in no time. We're done for in Malaya."

"That's enough," Connie said sharply.

"But it's true," Madoc's wife said in a sad murmur. "We're finished."

Teddy's head swiveled to face Johnnie Blake as a gigantic explosion somewhere in the docks slammed against their eardrums. "I thought we would beat them," he said accusingly.

"We didn't stand a chance." Johnnie looked down at her son. "Not a chance." He shook his head in despair. "No decent planes . . ."

"But what about the Brewster Buffalo?"

"No, Teddy. It's no match for them."

"Johnnie," Nigel interrupted, "no need for this."

But Connie knew there was a need. They all had to face the truth now—even her son. The sea around them was littered with the lies of the past.

"What about General Percival and our army?" Teddy whispered, eyes fixed on the fireworks in the sky. "Couldn't they . . . ?"

"No," Johnnie said savagely. "Percival was given a ragbag of ill-trained divisions from India and Australia to back up our boys in the Eleventh Division in action at Jitra and Slim River. Look at Singapore now! I can imagine General Percival in his operations room in Sime Road listening to those bombs falling and cursing his ill luck. I wish to God I were up there tonight in one of those creaky old Buffaloes."

"I'm very glad you're not," Connie said clearly. She turned away from the sight of British colonial power on its knees. "Let's get out of here."

꠵·꠵

"What now?" *Tuan* Hadley demanded.

He sat at the head of the small table in the saloon, his fists clenched tight in front of him. Maya observed him closely. How could a man's face grow so old so fast? Like the Tamils who worked in the quarries and trudged home covered in a second skin of gray dust. That was what *Tuan* Hadley looked like now.

"I know an island." It was Iron-eyes who spoke.

Maya listened with sharp ears. He was leaning his big shoulder against the shiny wall, his eyes half hooded like a tiger's when it hunts. *No, no, Iron-eyes. You don't eat me. I run fast.*

"I know an island," he told them again, "that should be safe."

"There are thousands of islands here," the *tuan* with the fat belly and the dead wife pointed out. "Which one?"

Iron-eyes gave a slow smile.

You no fool me. You smile like a tiger smile.

"It's not far—away from the mainland, east of here toward Borneo. Many of the islands are uninhabited, but this one has a small number of people on it. We could fix up *The White Pearl*'s damage there, get her properly repaired, and take on supplies. It would give you time to decide what you want to do from here."

His eyes skimmed each person in the shiny belly of the boat, touched on Razak, then on herself with the smallest of nods. *Why nod at me, tiger man? Because you know I not trust you?* Last and longest he looked at *Mem* Hadley. The weight of iron slid from his eyes and in its place tumbled a dark blue sadness. Sadness as heavy as the weight on Maya's heart because now not only her mother was gone, but her country was gone too.

Mem was the only one who seemed to understand this. As they sailed away from Singapore, she had come to Maya and wrapped an arm around her shoulders, drawing her close.

"I'm sorry, Maya," she'd said softly. "This is a terrible blow to you."

Maya could feel the warmth of her embrace and hear the kindness of her words, and they filled a cold and lonely place in her heart that ached hard right now. Her eyes filled with tears. For a long moment Maya forgot to hate her. She had let her head rest lightly on *mem*'s shoulder and held on to her hand with eager fingers. She'd breathed quietly and imagined what it must be like to be this woman's child. But all the time her own mother's angry screech wailed in her ears at the betrayal.

ჟ·ჳ

Sweat and fear had started to stamp their feet in the room. Maya could smell them. Next to her stood the *tuan* with the dead wife. His hand left a damp patch on the map when he placed his palm on it.

Iron-eyes spread out a giant map—he called it a chart—on the table and everyone gathered around, shoulders touching, eyes jumping from place to place. Nervy as frogs. He pushed his finger over a pretty expanse of blue and jabbed it on blobs of green, some long and thin, others fat and round, bundled up against each other. Then there were pink sections and yellow sections, and strange-shaped squiggles that she knew were writing.

"Understand?" Iron-eyes checked his listeners.

Everyone nodded agreement. Maya didn't understand, not one word. Yet she nodded too. But Razak had the courage to ask, "Is the blue bit the sea?"

Beside her the fat *tuan* laughed, and Maya wanted to slap him.

"Yes," Iron-eyes said. "That's correct."

The sea? So much sea? She was sure he must be lying.

"This," he said with his finger on a skinny slice of pink, "is Malaya."

Maya gaped. Now she was certain he was lying. That skinny pink tongue could not possibly be Malaya. Malaya was huge, with forests that were endless. Beaches that made her legs ache they were so long, when she tried to walk them in search of a turtle.

"This is Malaya," Iron-eyes repeated and she realized with shame that he was saying it just for her and Razak. "This is Singapore." A stubby little leaf tucked against the tip of the pink tongue. "And these are the islands of Sumatra and Java. As you can see, they are only a step away."

A very tiny step on the chart, so small she could make it without the boat, without even getting her feet wet.

"But that means General Tojo will invade Sumatra and Java as soon as they have taken Singapore," Fitzpayne added.

"Just a minute there," the pilot interrupted. He shook his head and stabbed a finger on the chart, right on the long green bean that Iron-eyes claimed was Sumatra. "The RAF has 225 Bomber Group over there with seventy-five Blenheim and Hudson bombers. Plus 226 Fighter Group with two squadrons of Hurricane fighters. They'll make a decent fight of it."

There was an awkward silence in the room. Everyone wanted to believe Golden-hair. The sea grumbled impatiently outside and gave the yacht a jolt to hurry them up. Maya felt her stomach heave.

Iron-eyes took a moment to light a cigarette, to look away from them packed around his chart, and said through the smoke, "We all know that Royal Dutch Shell Oil has its main refinery in the city of Palembang in southern Sumatra. To seize oil refineries is one of Japan's primary objectives in sending its invasion forces to this region." With impatience he threw away the box of matches still in his hand. It knocked against a lamp and made it spit oil. "Of course they will damn well invade Sumatra, and your paltry collection of bombers and fighters is not going to stop them, I'm afraid, Flight Lieutenant Blake."

Mem Hadley stared at him, and something Maya couldn't read flickered in her blue eyes. "So what do you recommend we do?"

"It leaves us with Borneo—which we think has probably already been invaded—and New Guinea, a journey of several hundred miles. I am suggesting we take this route"—his finger crossed the blue, dodging between the blobs of green and yellow—"to avoid Japanese detection. We will travel at night. For all we know the Japs may get there ahead of us."

Tuan Hadley was nodding. So it must all be true. Maya nodded too and darted a look at the circle of faces. Most were transfixed by the paper chart on the table, but the new man, the one with rabbit teeth and the fat wife, was gazing around the saloon the way a dog does when it takes possession of a new kennel and cocks its leg to mark its territory. The only other person not studying the mysterious chart was *Mem* Hadley. She was staring out one of the moon-shaped windows, her cheeks flushed and her eyes on fire with anticipation. Whatever lay ahead, she wanted a bite of it.

ꟼ·Ϥ

"What are you doing?" Maya prodded her brother in the ribs.

"Polishing shoes."

"You're not his servant."

"He feeds us and he keeps us safe from Japanese bayonets. He doesn't throw us to the sharks."

Maya crouched down beside Razak on the deck. He was sitting cross-legged in the cool air of early morning, his black hair gleaming where the first rays of sunlight ran fingers over it. Everything wanted to touch her beautiful brother. Around him in a circle sat ten pairs of shoes, five black leather, four brown, one as creamy as milk. She reached out and touched that one—it felt as soft as a piglet's ear.

"Don't," Razak frowned.

"I'm not hurting it."

"It's polished."

"Do these all belong to *Tuan* Hadley?"

"Yes."

She slid her hand inside one that wasn't polished, and it gobbled up her whole fist as though she'd pushed it inside a whale. She lifted the shoe, inspected its stitching, its flat obscene tongue, the tiny air holes in the side, the laces squeezed into a tiny metal clamp at each end. She turned it over and studied its smooth, buttery sole. The shoe was heavy and stank of white man's sweat.

"Why does anyone need so many shoes?"

Razak fixed his eyes on her with reproach and removed the shoe from her hand. "Because he's an important man."

She leaned forward and spat on one of the polished shoes. "You forget, my foolish brother, you forget why we are here."

"We are here," he said, his face suddenly stern, "because our mother willed it."

"We are here," she corrected, "because I willed it. Our mother cursed this woman who killed her, and her spirit will only rest when we have carried out that curse. I was blind before, but now I have eyes wide open." She made herself push the memory of *Mem* Hadley's protective arm from her mind.

Her brother made a noise through his nose. Maya's spine quivered. It was the noise of disgust an Englishman would make. He quietly picked up the shoe, wiped her spittle off it, and replaced it in the polishing row.

"We were wrong before," he said. His dark eyes turned on her, an intense gaze that made her shift her position uneasily. "I didn't understand. But now I do. Our mother may have given us little when she was alive, but in death she gave us this gift." He waved an expressive hand around the boat. "This life. I am learning so much."

"What kind of thing?"

"*Tuan* Teddy is teaching me to read English."

She felt a snake of jealousy coil around her gut. "We are nothing to them, less than ants under these big-boat shoes of his."

"I am learning to play white men's games."

"What good is that to us?"

"White men play their games for money."

His words felt like a beetle's horny back stuck in her throat. "You refused to take *Mem* Hadley's money when she offered it before."

"Little sister"—he touched her cheek gently—"your head is still full of river mud. This"—he gestured upward to the great white sails and down to the shoes on the deck—"is what our mother's spirit has bequeathed to us. She knew when she stood in front of the car, when she felt it crush the life in her and when she uttered the curse, she knew she was giving us all this."

"Razak, have you been chewing on the crazy weed?"

"No. But I know *Tuan* Hadley's mind. He says we have to leave Malaya until the war is over."

"How long?"

"He says a year."

She screwed up her nose. "He doesn't know the Japanese."

"Then, he says, we will go back. He promises to give me a good job."

"As a rubber tapper. A tree-milk drinker. You will die out there in the—"

"No. A good, important job. He says he will train me."

"And me?"

For the first time uncertainty flickered in his black eyes. "You must go where I go. It's what our mother's spirit whispers to me. You are no longer sick on the boat and that shows she is pleased."

Maya snatched up the tin of shiny polish on the deck, stuck her finger into its greasy depths, and drew streaks of black down her own cheeks, across her forehead, and along her nose. She took hold of Razak's chin and did the same to him. When they were both daubed with war paint, she whispered into the delicate curve of his ear, "Razak, you forget who you are."

CHAPTER TWENTY-FOUR

The heat was ferocious; it hammered on Connie's skull despite her straw hat, and the air itself seemed exhausted. They had sailed through the night, the seas growing heavier, so that the boat pitched as Connie took soundings and Madoc trimmed the sails. Fitzpayne guided them by a chart that seemed to exist only in his head. He wove a stealthy pathway, twisting and turning among an archipelago of more than fifty islands that were hunched and brooding slabs of blackness looming out of the sea. The canopy of their dense forests was stitched together by the moonlight. Sometimes the belly-roar of a wild animal or a screech from a night bird would ring out and make Connie's hands pause in whatever task they were performing.

Shortly before dawn, she collapsed into bed beside Nigel, weary enough to sleep without dreams for once. When she woke she found daylight waiting for her and the boat almost empty, only Fitzpayne and Teddy sitting on deck and fishing with long lines in the swirling blue waters. The others were ashore. Fitzpayne had tucked *The White Pearl* into the mouth of a narrow river and furled her sails, nestling in close to the thorny rambutans and the feathery fingers of the casuarinas. No passing aircraft would notice her daytime hideaway.

"Caught anything?" Connie inquired of Fitzpayne and her son on deck.

Teddy held up two fish by their tails for her to examine. "It's a red tail gourami," he told her, "and look, a Javanese rice fish."

"Oh, how splendid. It comes with rice already cooked inside it, does it?"

"That's silly!" But her son laughed, and the sound of it warmed her insides. Too often that sound had been missing. "Mr. Fitzpayne has been teaching me to tie knots," he added with excitement. He abandoned the fish and picked up a length of rope from the deck. "Look, this is a bowline."

Deftly his young hands tied the rope while he murmured the ritual instructions, "Rabbit comes out the hole, goes round the tree and back down the hole." He pulled it tight. "See?"

"I am impressed."

A sudden shout from the shore made her look up. *The White Pearl*'s passengers were playing cricket on the frill of sand on the edge of the jungle. The sight of it made Connie laugh out loud. She'd had no idea that Nigel had smuggled bat and ball on board.

Behind her, Fitzpayne commented wryly, "Wherever Englishmen gather together, there will always be the sound of leather on willow. It's one of the laws of the universe."

She laughed. This morning he was unshaven and clothed in an old black shirt and trousers that were turning green at the knees, with a wide leather belt holding a Malayan kris knife at his waist. All he needed was a cutlass between his teeth to look like a South Seas pirate. A shout of "Well bowled" caught her attention.

"Look, Kitty Morgan is in wicket!" Connie exclaimed.

"She's better at catching than the men."

Nigel was limping after the ball before it rolled into the water, while Pippin roared in circles around him in a frenzy of barks.

"How is your husband's leg these days?"

"Improving."

"Good."

For a moment she wanted to tell him that one part of the wound looked bad, swollen, and ulcerated. But she didn't. Nigel would hate it.

"Why aren't you down there scoring runs with them?" She smiled at him. The horrors of last night were being carefully overlaid by a fragile structure of normality: a smile, a game of cricket, a fishing rod. Only Maya prowled alone, like a stray at the water's edge.

"Not my game," Fitzpayne commented, and nodded toward where Teddy was reeling out his fishing line again. "Anyway, your son refused to go ashore."

Connie frowned. Teddy adored cricket, but he wasn't even watching the players. She glanced back at Fitzpayne and caught a momentary softening of the muscles of his face as he looked at her son. "He's finding it hard," she said under her breath. "There's something not right."

Fitzpayne's eyes narrowed. "There's something not right with us, either."

Us? Did he mean himself and her? Or all of them?

"There's a war on, you know." She raised an ironic eyebrow, and was relieved when he laughed.

"Mrs. Hadley, don't look so concerned about your son. Teddy will survive."

"Survival isn't enough," she said fiercely. "I want more for him than just survival."

"By his age I'd seen a dozen men die." His voice was gentle. "It will make him stronger—inside. Where it matters."

"He won't talk about it."

"Let him deal with it in his own way. He'll come to you when he's ready. And if he doesn't, well, then you know he's learning to grow up."

"I don't want him to grow up. Not yet."

"He'll learn from his experiences. Don't try to prevent him."

Connie studied his face, seeking out the man behind it who had convinced himself that seeing death makes you stronger. "So what is it that you think he will learn?"

"How to face reality. Not to run from it."

Connie snorted. "There's nothing wrong with running from reality sometimes."

Fitzpayne came forward. He didn't touch her. But it almost felt as if he had, as though a part of him reached out and steadied her.

"I'm sorry," he said, surprising her.

"For what?"

"For agreeing to sail you to Singapore."

She stood there, held his gaze and didn't let him see how much his remark had stung. "I'm not," she said firmly, and turned away. "I must go and see what new fish Teddy has managed to hook."

But her eye was caught by a lonely figure on the riverbank. Maya had moved to a secluded stretch that was hidden from the cricketers by a kink in the shoreline, and she was stepping out of her bright sarong and *kebaya*. She stood naked, slight and fragile, dappled by brilliant pools of light that danced up from the water's surface. She stretched her slender arms up toward the heavens, then plunged into the river with an almighty splash, before bursting back onto the shore and shaking herself, so that her long wet hair flicked out in an arc around her, creating a brief enchanting rainbow.

It was too private a moment to linger on. Connie stepped away from the rail and headed over to Teddy, but when she glanced back at Fitzpayne, he hadn't moved. His gaze was fixed on the native girl.

ꮙ·ꭼ

In the late-afternoon heat, they slept in their cabins. The boat itself grew quiet, silencing its sighs and creaks as though preparing for what the night ahead would bring. Connie dozed fitfully. The air was thick and weighed down by flies, but just as she was contemplating sliding out of the bed and going up on deck, the noise started.

Soft at first. A faint moan. A regular *arr-arr-arr* sound. At first Connie thought it was a sob. Someone crying. She looked at Nigel's back lying beside her, but it was stiff and silent in sleep. Or was he awake, listening to the noise as closely as she was? The moan grew louder and she thought of Johnnie, of his damaged shoulder, of the pain he never mentioned and the sorrow of watching his comrades shot out of the sky. She sat up.

At once, the regular *arr-arr-arr* speeded up and a lower-pitched groan joined it. Abruptly Connie knew where it was coming from. Her cheeks flooded with color and her ears burned, but she didn't cover them with her hands. She sat there, gazing down at her own pale thighs and listened to the Madocs' coupling as intently as she would to a piece by Brahms. Twice she looked round at her husband, but he hadn't moved a muscle.

Her heart rate climbed as the sounds grew more intense, and she imagined the blood pumping around her body, charging through her veins until she felt the heat of it between her legs and released a whisper-thin moan of her own.

ϑ·ϛ

Madoc did not like the mood on the boat. He didn't like the way Fitzpayne had these people eating out of the palm of his hand. What was he up to?

The White Pearl had set off just before sunset. The wind had dropped and the sails hung with a lethargy that was at odds with the restlessness of those on board. They wanted to move on fast to the island that Fitzpayne had promised would offer a safe breathing space, and a meal that wasn't rationed on the plate. That was where Madoc planned to make his move. Just the thought sent adrenaline thundering through his bloodstream, and he felt the familiar ache. That addiction to danger, the kind of danger that he needed like other people needed air.

Around them other boats were on the move, all with the same idea: to flee the relentless advance of Admiral Yamamoto's Japanese aircraft carriers with their strike planes. The sky seemed to have been steeped in blood by the setting sun, and it made Madoc uneasy—he could imagine how much blood was staining Malaya's soil right now. Yet tiny *perahu* boats, doggedly plying their trade, still darted out to the fishing grounds, and a few sailing boats were still bound for Singapore in the vain hope of gaining a berth on one of the departing troopships. But most were like themselves—scattering outward across the South China Sea to seek safety. Throughout daylight hours Japanese planes droned across the sky, forcing Madoc and his fellow passengers to withdraw into the forest, to clamber over the roots of the mangroves and retreat into its dark world like creatures of the night.

But now, below deck, Madoc couldn't stop his hands from touching the inlays in the varnished wood, the gleaming brass fittings, the inviting curves of the table and benches. They drew him to them.

"Madoc!" Kitty hissed at him. "Stop it. It's not yours yet."

"Do you have it ready?" he asked.

She rolled her eyes at him. "Of course."

Lodged in the deep pocket of her voluminous skirt was the Tokarev pistol. It was too bulky for him to carry, even in his waistband, without someone spotting it as he worked at hauling the sails.

He stepped close to her and stroked her throat. "Watch out for yourself, Kitty."

She roared with laughter. "You're throwing my own words back at me, you wretch."

But he meant them. He shifted his palm over her mouth to quieten her. "I'll watch out for you, Kitty," he whispered.

ᔭ·ᖋ

The lone aircraft came streaming down out of nowhere. In the west, the sky was growing darker, but in the east it still clung to its peacock blue, and it was from there that the earsplitting note arose.

"It's a Hurricane," Teddy yelled.

All on deck watched the battle rip across the heavens. A Japanese Zero had latched onto the British plane's tail, and its guns spat out repeated flashes of fire. The Hurricane slipped and slithered through the air, turned on a wingtip and lost height, spinning and twisting to shake off its attacker.

"Hell, look at that!" Nigel roared. "The Jap plane is faster, more agile."

The Hurricane's tail was hit. Johnnie stood in grim silence.

"Here, use these." Teddy thrust the binoculars at him.

But the pilot gave a tight shake of his head. "No."

"You'll see better."

"I've seen enough." Yet his eyes clung to the plane.

Connie could not imagine what kind of terror must be stalking the Hurricane pilot's heart, but he continued to duck and weave out of the line of the Jap's fire.

"Higher," Madoc bellowed up at the sky. It was streaked with a tangle of white trails like a giant spider's web. "Get higher, man, for Christ's sake."

"He's trying," Johnnie muttered, his lips bloodless.

Abruptly the British plane plunged into a downward spiral.

"He's crashing," Connie gasped.

"No," Fitzpayne said. "He's playing dead. What do you think, Blake?"

"Please God!"

The small group stood transfixed. They watched the British pilot hurtle toward the waves and certain death, but they released a great whoop of joy when the nose of the Hurricane suddenly popped up, dragging its frame back into the sky on shuddering wings. With one elegant switchback maneuver, it came swooping down behind the Zero and opened up its guns.

Before their eyes, the delicate metal ribs of the Japanese aircraft burst open and half its tail rocketed away in a thousand pieces. Nigel and Henry, along with Madoc and Kitty, sent up a gigantic cheer that made the hairs on Connie's arms stand on end. Even the quieter voice of Razak echoed it, and he waved his hands above his head in victory. Johnnie didn't utter a sound, and Teddy looked stricken. Maya sat on the deck with her head in her hands and refused to watch.

It was Fitzpayne, gripping the helm, who shouted the warning. "He's coming for us!"

"What?" Henry was still grinning, his hair flat with sweat.

"The Jap."

"But he's dead in the sky."

"Come about!" Fitzpayne shouted. "Double quick!"

Connie and Madoc leaped to the ropes. Their hands worked fast as Fitzpayne jibed quickly, changing course. Connie's fingers did what she told them. But at some deep level her mind sank into despair because she remembered how Sho had told her about this—about the way a Japanese warrior would rather die in glory, taking his enemy with him, than live with the shame of defeat. Defeat, he had assured her, was the ultimate degradation, and Japanese troops were drilled in the belief that honor lies in committing *hara-kiri*, the taking of one's own life, rather than be captured. *Shohei Takehashi, did I dishonor you? Such a shameful, paltry death.* She wanted to sink to her knees, to accept this ultimate revenge that Sho's people would inflict on her for what she had done to him.

But instead she seized Teddy, who was standing open mouthed. He was staring up at the aircraft that seemed to fill the sky with its pale gray shattered body and its scarlet nose that made it look as if it had already tasted blood. For a moment the shriek of its engine seemed to fracture her thoughts. She wrapped her arms around her son and raced to the rail, poised ready to jump. She looked around quickly for her husband. "Nigel!"

But he was a lone figure standing in the bow of the boat, his fists raised in defiance. The plane's scarlet roundels loomed toward him. Even with her heart thundering and her son's arms tight around her neck, she registered that magnificent and foolish image of her husband. It astounded her.

A flash of blue dashed past her, and she reached out a hand to grasp it.

"Maya," she said urgently. "Jump. Now."

But the girl squirmed in her grip and whimpered.

"She can't swim," Teddy yelled.

"We'll hold her up." Connie swung up on the rail. "Now! Everyone off! Jump!"

Below her, the ocean lay as blue and silky as Maya's sarong, the dark outline of a massive fish flickering down in the depths, and she prepared to jump. At that moment the boat suddenly leaped forward. There was no wind. How in hell's name did Fitzpayne manage to find just enough to fill a sail; how in hell's name did he steer her in that split second to safety? With an earsplitting roar the Zero smacked down onto the ocean in the exact spot that they had occupied, and a wall of water rocketed up into the air before crashing down on the deck. The tip of one wing scraped the hull, and Connie felt the vibration of the impact through her feet.

She clung to her son, drenched to the skin, and saw his dog washed from one side of the boat to the other, its feet scrabbling, its ears plastered to its skull. For one second Connie thought they were going to capsize, as the clear blue water came rushing up toward her. But no. *The White Pearl* proved the strength of her keel. She rocked back the other way but continued to pitch and roll violently as the waves surged. Everyone fought to hold on to something.

Then Connie saw it: the plane, wallowing alongside the boat like a pale gutted shark. One wing had snapped off, but the other wing stretched out on the surface, keeping it afloat, and the hoops of the Zero's metal formers were revealed like skinned ribs along its frame. Its cockpit cover had vanished. Inside sat the inert figure of its pilot, pinned to his seat by the webbing of his safety harness, his shoulders slumped against the straps. Flying goggles obscured his eyes, and one of the lenses was cracked. Seawater was swilling around his knees as waves flooded into the cockpit.

Connie knew he was dead. Blood had drenched the front of his flying suit across his chest, and as the level of the water rose, it stained pink the white scarf that hung from his neck. Death had come stalking her once more. She could hear its dry cackle whispering in each fold of the waves. There was a burble from the ocean's depths as the weight of the aircraft's engine started to drag it down, nose first.

It was then that one of the pilot's gloved hands rose slowly from the water and tugged his goggles down to his neck. A pair of almond-shaped eyes glared up at her. They were black and accusing. Without a moment's hesitation, she released Teddy and Maya and leaped over the rail, plunging into the water. As it closed over her head she heard Fitzpayne's voice roar, "Connie! Don't!"

꒐·꒦

The ocean flooded Connie's senses. She was swept down into a blurred world, where sparkling columns of blue light fell as tall and straight as church pillars into the shadowy depths far below her. Creatures moved down there, but they paid her no heed. It was a silent world, where all sound ceased. She had an intense feeling of dislocation, as though the world above had fractured and she had slipped through a crack.

Her hair and her skirt floated around her in the warm blue waters, drifting like weeds. She stretched out her hands to the sides to slow her descent, and as the water spilled through them she knew that this could be her moment of redemption. To redeem a life for a life. She could let herself drift down forever, down to those shadowy depths and those creatures with sharp dorsal fins and even sharper teeth that would strip flesh from bone with one bite. Her moment to repay.

But with a series of quick, decisive kicks she drove herself up toward the dazzling ceiling of light that beckoned her back into the world above.

꒷·꒦

She swam with determined strokes to reach the plane. It had drifted away from the boat. Its damaged tail was rising out of the water as its engine dragged the nose deeper, and Connie could see the pilot's white face. His lips were moving in silent prayer, yet his hands made no attempt to release his safety harness as the seas rose around him. Connie gripped the edge of the cockpit and felt it lurch, threatening to roll on top of her.

"Quickly," she said. She grasped the strap of the harness.

"*Iie!* No!"

His gloved hand knocked hers away.

"You must get out," she shouted.

"I die." His lips spoke the words calmly, but his dark eyes were anything but dead. They spat fury at her.

She wasted no more time on words. The flimsy lightweight aircraft was on its way down. The scarlet cowling over the engine started to dive deeper, releasing great gusts of air bubbles as it sank. Connie fought with the harness fixings, leaning in toward the pilot as the water rose to his neck. He made no sound. Her struggles must have been excruciating for his wounded chest, but he uttered no cry of pain or even a grunt of anger. The water covered his chin and lapped up over his bottom lip, but his gaze was fixed rigidly ahead, seeing only what was inside his own warrior head.

"Help me," she screamed at him.

But he didn't seem to hear her. The ocean rushed at him and engulfed his mouth. He closed his eyes. Frantically Connie pulled and tugged at the harness under water until finally she felt it pop open, and she managed to drag the straps from his limp shoulders just as the plane nose-dived straight down. It wrenched Connie with it.

Fear tore a precious ripple of air from her lungs. She clamped her mouth shut and pulled with all her strength at the pilot's body, but he was trapped. His legs were pinned. She kicked and yanked again, felt his uniform split, but she could not dislodge him. The brilliant kingfisher blue of the water was abruptly replaced by a somber murkiness where the columns of light didn't reach. Her lungs started to burn.

Give up.

Her mind spoke to her.

Give up, or you'll die with him.

Her fingers gripped harder. She jammed her feet on the bulkhead behind the cockpit, her hands locked under his armpits, and fought to lift him clear.

He's dead already, her mind insisted.

She didn't listen. Strange lights began to flash and loop in front of her eyes, and she knew her brain was starved of oxygen as the plane drifted deeper. She hauled harder. Suddenly one of his legs was released. She felt it give. With a great flood of relief she fought for the other one but it was jammed firmly in the crushed space. Black trickles of something like tar bubbled inside her brain and she felt her muscles grow weak.

Give up. Or die.

Her lungs were on fire. But floating into the narrow tunnel of her vision Connie suddenly saw another pair of hands appear, yet her sluggish brain did not dare trust her eyes. The dark bulk of someone's shoulder. Where had that come from? As she yanked one last time, draining her limbs of effort, the other hands—square hands that she recognized—reached in and dislodged the second leg.

It felt like flying. As though she had shot upward, when in reality it was only that she had stopped descending. Her hands clutched the limp body of the Japanese pilot and, even now, even with her brain shutting down and her legs barely moving through the water, she knew that this was the moment to grasp her redemption. But she had to breathe. To open her mouth and suck in . . . something. Her lips parted; she couldn't stop them. Every instinct told her to keep them shut, that water would flood in, but still they opened in their desperation to find air.

The hands seized her. A strong grip took hold of her head. For one panicked second she tried to shake them off, but they were clamped on each side of her skull. Fitzpayne's face blurred in front of her. His lips pressed hard against hers, sealing the water out while ripples of air trickled into her lungs. She breathed.

CHAPTER TWENTY-FIVE

M adoc," Kitty said, "get down there."

They were on deck and an early-morning mist was keeping the salt air cool. She nodded toward the open hatch through which the rumble of male voices drifted, along with threads of cigarette smoke.

"For God's sake, find out what they're deciding," she told him.

Kitty had been bad-tempered ever since Mrs. Hadley and Fitzpayne had dragged the Japanese pilot on board last night. *A Jonah*, she called him. *Why didn't they let the bastard drown?* Madoc wondered that himself.

"Where is she?" he asked.

"Where do you think? Hadley is furious."

"So would you be if I dumped your enemy in your bed," he pointed out. "And then spent the night nursing him, so that you had to kip on a bench in the saloon."

"It's not just that."

"What do you mean?"

"Haven't you noticed?" She lowered her voice to keep it from Fitzpayne at the wheel. "The way he hates her to pay attention to other men, especially the flight lieutenant. But Fitzpayne and Henry Court as well. Even you, for Christ's sake!" She shook her head and glanced up at a booby wheeling freely up above them, its wings outstretched on a warm current of air. "She's very careful to concentrate on her son or even on the surly little native chit when Hadley is on deck as well."

No, he hadn't noticed that.

ᕴ·ᕯ

The men were arguing in the saloon. Madoc slid in quietly, but he needn't have worried; they didn't take a blind bit of notice of him. They were seated around the table with faces as solemn and self-important as a war cabinet, and you would think they were trying to hammer out a bloody international peace treaty rather than just decide the fate of one murdering little Jap prisoner.

"Get rid of him!" Henry Court thumped the table with his fist. "I wouldn't have let him on board at all if this were my yacht."

Hadley looked at him coldly. "Well, it's not."

"He could be the same pilot who killed my wife."

"Henry," Johnnie responded with a tight expression on his face, "a pilot fights for his country. When we are at war it means we drop bombs and fire bullets so that the enemy dies. It isn't personal. This pilot tried to crash his plane on us because it was his duty to do so. Don't take it personally."

"My wife is dead, damn you. Are you telling me I shouldn't take that personally?"

"I'm deeply sorry about Harriet, you know I am. But—"

"We will get rid of him," Hadley interrupted, but it was obvious to Madoc that he was acutely uncomfortable dealing with the situation his wife had put him in. "Just as soon as we can."

"She should have let the yellow bastard drown," Court insisted.

"Maybe he can be of use to us," Madoc said casually.

All eyes shifted to him. "How?"

"Maybe he possesses information that we could extract from him about where the enemy troops are, how far they have invaded—in Malaya and in this bloody maze of islands. Even where they have cached weapons and fuel." He shrugged as he propped himself against a support pillar and lit a cigarette. "Just a thought."

Flight Lieutenant Blake frowned, creasing his fine features. "He won't talk. We must hand him over to the proper authorities."

"We could *persuade* him," Madoc suggested.

Blake looked sick. But Hadley and Court both brightened.

"He is the enemy," Hadley reminded them all. Below them rumbled the sound of the native boy working the bilge pump.

ᛒ·ᛒ

Connie heard the anchor being lowered, condemning them to another day of inactivity. Fitzpayne was right to keep them hidden during daylight hours, as the Japanese planes seemed to have relentless mastery of the sky now, but the waiting and the delays stretched her nerves taut. Her mind was unable to travel beyond the figure on the bed.

She watched him breathe, her eyes focused on his narrow chest. Such slight bones; he was scarcely more than a youth. His chin was hairless, his skin as smooth as ivory, yet his hands were broad and capable, his fingers large-knuckled like a farm boy's. *Is that what he is?* A farm boy torn off his land and thrown up into the sky by his glorious Emperor Hirohito?

She had bandaged his chest, a large dressing pressed down on the wound. Blood had flowed onto the bedsheets, but the damage to him was less severe than she had feared. A large flap of skin had been gouged from his chest, hanging on by a narrow thread, crinkled and slippery. She had to flatten it out and douse it with antiseptic, and as she did so she could make out the white bones of his ribs, gleaming scarlet. But they seemed intact, and though his lungs were choked with seawater, they had recovered quickly when she breathed into them. His right collarbone was broken, rising at an odd angle, and his forehead had been scraped and bruised under his flying helmet.

But he was alive. And she intended to keep him that way. So she watched him breathe, hour after hour.

ᛒ·ᛒ

A knock sounded on the bedroom door.

"Come in," Connie said.

The door opened and Teddy scampered in, his eyes darting from her to the Japanese pilot and back. There was something wistful in the turn of his mouth, a quiver of loneliness, and she wrapped an arm around him, drawing him to her side. Behind him in the doorway stood Fitzpayne.

"It's too hot in here," he announced.

He was right. She was drenched in sweat.

"How are you?" he asked.

The question surprised her. She'd expected him to ask after the pilot. "I'm fine."

Fitzpayne smiled. "So a bit of drowning does the intrepid Mrs. Hadley no harm."

"Apparently not."

Teddy patted her arm. "You're well, aren't you, Mummy?"

"Yes, I am. I am also grateful to you, Mr. Fitzpayne, for—"

"It was nothing," he said quickly. "I couldn't resist the chance of seeing Henry Court's face when you dragged a Japanese pilot on board." He chuckled. "So, is he awake?"

All three stared at the inert figure on the bed.

"I think so," she said, "though his eyes are shut."

"Has he spoken?" Teddy whispered.

"Yes, several times. He suddenly flicks open his eyes, gives me a black stare without blinking for minutes on end, and then hisses something at me."

"What does he say?" Teddy asked.

"I don't know. I don't speak Japanese. But it's not good, that much I can recognize. He hates me."

"I've got an idea," Fitzpayne said, and pulled a length of rope from his pocket. "Let's all go up on deck where there's a breeze. You need some fresh air."

Connie reluctantly shook her head. "I have to watch over—"

"Your patient is coming with us. That's what the rope is for."

The eyes of the Japanese on the bed opened a narrow slit, and Fitzpayne barked out instructions in an unfamiliar language.

"Is that Japanese you're speaking?" Teddy asked, impressed.

"*Hai.*" Fitzpayne bowed politely over his hands, exactly as Sho used to do. "Yes, it is."

He dangled the rope in front of Connie and raised one of his thick eyebrows questioningly. She turned to regard the pilot.

"*Hai,*" she said at last. "Yes."

᛭

Throughout the afternoon, waves of aircraft droned overhead. Teddy stayed glued to the binoculars and his high, excited voice called out at regular intervals.

"Six Brewster Buffaloes. Two Hurricanes."

"Eighteen bombers. Japanese."

"Ten Zero fighters. Japanese."

"Four Bristol Blenheim bombers. One C-type flying boat."

The sight of them glinting like shoals of fish in the arc of blue beyond the trees induced a somber mood on deck. *The White Pearl* was yet again tucked out of sight. She had nosed her way into a tunnel, where a silt-laden river was overhung by the jungle canopy with long sword-shaped leaves rustling and birds whistling. A set of leopard prints stood out clear and fresh in the mud on the bank. Again Fitzpayne had been patching up the damage to the hull with oakum and pitch, caused this time by the Zero's impact. Connie had watched him work, sweating in the heat. She thanked all the gods of Malaya that this resourceful man had agreed to sail *The White Pearl* from Palur. Whatever his reasons.

"I say we should dump the bastard here. He'd be picked up soon enough. The Jap troops are swarming all over these bloody islands."

Henry and Nigel were arguing. Henry wanted to get rid of the Japanese pilot immediately, but to Connie's surprise Nigel declined to do so.

"We hand him over to the proper authorities when we reach somewhere suitable," Nigel insisted.

"And in the meantime, he eats our food and we have to watch out that he doesn't murder us in our beds. You know how sly Japs are."

"Henry," Connie pointed out, "he's tied up. There is no danger. He is injured, and Fitzpayne says this island is uninhabited. He would die here."

"So? One less to worry about."

"Henry," Nigel said curtly, "the man will be dealt with according to British prisoner-of-war standards. We all know the inhumane things the Japanese troops did when they invaded China, but I will not stoop to their level."

Henry stalked off across the deck, but Connie walked over to the bench to sit beside her husband and lightly touched his shoulder.

"Thank you, Nigel," she said.

He looked up at her for a moment, squinting against the sunlight, the lines on his face growing deeper as he did so. "I want you to be happy, Constance." He didn't smile as he said it, and she felt the sincerity of his words.

"And you, Nigel? Are you happy?"

His lips came together in a fixed line. "Of course. Except for this damned war."

Ɛ·Ɛ

"*Bushido*—it is the code of the samurai warrior."

Connie was bandaging Fitzpayne's hand, listening to his explanation of the Japanese pilot's behavior. A chisel that Madoc was using had slipped and gouged a chunk of flesh from the base of Fitzpayne's thumb, forcing him to come up on deck. Kitty had apologized on her husband's behalf, but Fitzpayne had given her a black look and suggested she save her apologies for something accidental rather than intentional. And Kitty, instead of protesting her husband's innocence, burst out laughing, shaking her full bosom and wiping sweat from under her arms.

"I'll smack his bottom," she chuckled, and ambled below.

To Connie's surprise, Fitzpayne had watched her broad hips squeeze down the stairway and grinned. "She's too good for that no-good drifter," he laughed.

"She's a great help," Connie said, "to him and to us."

He nodded. "She can cook, and she knows how to haul a rope. Under all that flesh there are muscles a man would be proud of."

The Japanese pilot was sitting in his patch of shade next to the mast, staring at Connie with implacable hatred. His hands were lashed together in front of him and his ankle was tethered like a goat to the mainmast.

"*Bushido*," she echoed. "The Way of the Warrior. Tell me about it."

"It's the ancient code of the samurai warrior and is still taught to Japanese children from an early age," Fitzpayne explained. "It emphasizes loyalty, honor, and obedience."

When he spoke about such things, Connie liked the way his face became more expressive, more mobile. She continued to wind a bandage around the bones of his wrist, aware of the weight of it in her hand. "Those are qualities we all wish for in our children."

"Yes, the Japanese place great worth on filial piety and self-sacrifice."

"Ah, self-sacrifice." She glanced at the dark head beside the mast.

"Even now they believe that their Emperor Hirohito is a god in human form. They worship him and feel honored to die for him. For them, life is a constant preparation for death, and to die a good death with one's honor intact is the ultimate aim of life."

Connie thought of Sho, heard the thud of his head on the steps. A bad death. And now this pilot, desperate to die.

"No wonder he hates me. I have robbed him of his glory," she murmured, and tied the ends of the bandage together. For a moment Fitzpayne left his hand lying in hers.

"Don't think of that. It is a young man's empty-headed idealism. When he is old and gray he will bow down and kiss your feet with gratitude."

"You speak Japanese fluently."

He reacted as if she had accused him of something unpleasant.

"I lived there for a time," he said coolly. "Not long. My Japanese is poor."

It didn't sound poor to her when he shouted orders at the pilot.

"I see," she said.

But she didn't see. Didn't understand why the warmth had gone.

"The monsoon rain is coming," he said abruptly. "You'd better get below. We'll sail before dark."

ᗭ·ᑕ

He was right about the rain. Vast, merciless sheets of it pounded the river into a swirling torrent, stirring up the mud and hammering *The White Pearl* until her masts shook in their sockets. But Connie liked monsoon rain. She welcomed its total commitment, no half measures. It was all or nothing. She pulled on her yellow oilskins and took a stretch of canvas to the Japanese pilot, for him to huddle under on deck. She offered him a cigarette, but he refused.

You are a prisoner of war," she told him. "There is no dishonor in that."

But his hatred crawled all over her like lice.

"If you change your mind," Fitzpayne called out through the downpour, "and want me to toss him overboard, just give a shout." He was encased in his own oilskins, glossy as a seal. "After all, maybe Henry Court is right, maybe this is the Jap pilot who killed his wife."

"A life for a life, is that what you think? That it's a fair exchange?"

"Something like that."

"That's harsh."

"So, what do you believe? That a person should turn the other cheek and embrace the enemy?"

"No." She had to shout above the noise of the rain. "But none of us knows what goes on inside someone else's head." She paused and stared out across the churning river mouth, at the dark swaths of jungle. "I don't know what goes on inside your head," she finished.

He laughed, a great roar of sound that startled a gibbon hanging by one skinny arm from a branch in the pouring rain. It startled her too. "You wouldn't want to know, I assure you," he told her. When he was amused, the hard edges of his jaw and even the deep sockets of his eyes seemed to soften. "It's as dark and unruly in there as that patch of jungle you're staring at. Too muddy for your pretty white hands."

She looked down at her fingers. At the newly formed pads of muscle and the roughness of their skin from handling the ropes.

"Is that what you think? Pretty and white?" She said the last words with scorn. "I see them differently."

She saw them covered in scarlet. Ugly hands.

"What I think is that you should be kinder to yourself."

Such unexpectedly gentle words from him. They caught her by surprise, and she felt something loosen inside her. Her gaze studied him through the veil of rain.

"Why are they doing it?" she queried. "You know this part of the world. Why did the Japanese launch into this war? I know they are winning at the moment and are seizing oilfields, but . . ." She shook her head. "It's suicidal. How can they possibly expect to defeat the might of the British Empire and the United States in the long term?"

He accepted the change of subject with a shrug of his bright yellow shoulders. "It's exactly the long term that they are aiming for."

"What do you mean?"

"They want to launch a savage blow against white feudalism. To demonstrate to the Western world who is the natural leader of the Asian races in the future." He glanced northward through the drenched green hills, as though drawn by the force of Japan's will. "They will win in the end, the Japanese. Whoever is victorious in this war, it marks the end of Western dominance in the East."

"Good riddance to us, I say."

He laughed again, an edge to it this time. "Your husband may not agree with you there."

Connie said nothing. Because there was nothing to say.

I HATE RAZAK.

Below deck, the words jumped out at Connie from the page in big thick capital letters, black and spiky. Her hackles rose. What had Razak done to warrant such an outburst in her son's diary?

She knew she shouldn't be reading it at all. It was private, and she was acutely aware of that fact. She had promised him she wouldn't do so when she gave the notebook to him, but he had left it on deck when Fitzpayne summoned him down below to study the charts. He had scuttled at Fitzpayne's heels, forgetting his diary, and the rain had seeped into its pages. Connie held it between two fingers, dripping, and knew that Teddy would be mortified, so she had slipped down to her cabin to dry it off.

She took a towel and mopped the covers that were already beginning to crinkle. Poor Teddy, he would be so cross with himself and the rain. She undid the strap that held it closed and dabbed at the worst of the damage. On some pages, the penciled words were already fading into illegibility. She had flicked through quickly and smiled to herself. So many pages covered in small, careful handwriting. How industrious her young son had been.

I saw a school of jellyfish. White like milk.

Had he? He didn't mention it.

I like it when the wind roars like a tiger in the sails. And later: *Maya is scared but I told her* The White Pearl *will not capsize because it has a giant keel. The mast would brake first. That's what Daddy told me but Maya started to cry and that made me feel bad.*

Oh, Teddy, my sweet boy. Connie blotted the towel on several more pages, trying not to read their content. *The best Christmas ever. In a kind of tent.* She laughed out loud, and made herself move on. *I spotted a dolfin.* That was when she saw it.

I HATE RAZAK.

They were the last words he'd written. She experienced a confused pulse of anger toward the native boy. What had he done? Hurt Teddy? With no qualms now about breaking her promise, she examined the previous page. The writing had grown tiny and cramped as though the words could barely breathe, and she had to peer closely.

I love Mummy. But I don't love Daddy any more. He has forgotten me. He plays Snakes & Ladders and Drafts and Hangman with Razak. Not with me. He gave Razak his speshal penknife for Christmas.

He what? Nigel would never allow *anyone* to touch the mother-of-pearl penknife that he had been given as a child by his grandfather. He carried it like a talisman in his pocket at all times.

He laughs with Razak.

It was true. Connie realized abruptly that Nigel had taken to laughing recently. She would hear his delighted chuckle ripple out while she was occupied reading her book or unfurling a sail.

He strokes Razak's hair.

Connie's cheeks flushed crimson.

I saw Daddy kiss Razak today. On the lips again. A long kiss. It's not fair. He wants him to be his son. I HATE RAZAK.

๑·६

Connie's grief for her marriage was like mourning a death. The terrible pain of loss. Great waves of sorrow were suffocating her. Her heart slowed to a sluggish, ill-focused beat, and it ached as though someone had stamped on it.

She wanted to shout. To scream. To give voice to the despair that was tearing through her. But instead she sat silently in the saloon, barely able to touch Kitty's excellent meal of fish and rice. When done, she said quietly, "I feel unwell," and vanished into her cabin. She sat and stared out through her porthole at the turbulent waves and when the sky flared scarlet, as the sun shimmied down toward the horizon, she didn't light the lamp. She lay in the dark, arms curled around herself in a tight ball on the bed.

Nigel had never wanted her. Their marriage was a sham. He'd wanted a son, that was all, and a wife figure to mask his true desires. Her husband had used her and cheated her. All the years that she had tried so hard to win his love, to gain his favor, he had been repulsed by her. How he must have loathed her, hated sharing a bed with her night after night—far, far more than she ever realized. A deep moan escaped into her pillow as a wave of humiliation swamped her. She buried her face. Burned into her brain was the look on his face each night when they were vainly trying for a second child, the effort he had to make.

She had heard about men whose taste was for boys, but she had never known one. There were always whispers in the club, discreet finger-pointing on the tennis courts. *See the good-looking chap knocking hell out of the ball, well . . .* Or even, *Don't look now, but the fellow at the bar is giving young Macauley the eye. Right under his wife's nose.*

She had paid little attention. But she was vaguely aware of the collective cold shoulder that British society out here turned on such men. *Deviant*, Harriet had giggled, and rolled her eyes. The careers of those men ended abruptly when the whispers started.

She didn't cry. The pain was far too deep for tears. Instead she forced herself to picture Razak, how beautiful he was, and how she was the one who had dragged him into their life. Was this the mother's curse? Was this what Sai-Ru Jumat intended when she said, *I curse you, white lady?* That her son would be her implement of vengeance?

ꝯ·ꝿ

Teddy came in to kiss her good night. As he slipped an arm around her waist, she knew that his father would never let him go.

"Mummy"—he kissed her damp cheek—"I'll read to you. Like you read to me when I'm ill."

So she lay on her pillows, eyes fixed on his face, while he read her a page from his favorite book on learning new skills, describing the technique required to build an igloo.

"Useful," she said when he'd finished, "if I ever go to Lapland."

He nodded, wanting to laugh but not quite able to.

"Don't worry, darling," she said, "I'll be right as rain tomorrow. Daddy will put you to bed tonight."

He scowled his father's frown at her. "Daddy's too busy. I can put myself to bed."

She kissed his salty hair, breathed in the sour smell of his jealousy, and felt his confusion mingle with her own.

ꙅ·6

It was hours later that Nigel came to bed. She was sitting up, alert, with the kerosene lamp casting a dull, oily glow in the cabin. She would talk to him. Quietly. Calmly. With no display of anger and no embarrassment. She had planned the words in her head. Outside, the wind was fretful but the creaks and shrieks of the timbers became less intrusive, as though settling down for a night's sleep.

"Feeling better?" Nigel asked politely.

"No."

"Aspirin?"

"No, thank you."

"That's a shame, old thing."

Connie turned to face him. "Nigel, I am neither old, nor a thing."

He paused in the process of removing his socks and looked at her, surprised. "Just a turn of phrase, that's all."

She opened her mouth to tell him that she knew now that he had never loved her, that he had tempted her out to Malaya with tales of exotic enchantment, that he had lied to her, deceived her. About everything. All to gain a son. But now that he was in danger of breaking his son's heart.

Yet when she examined his face, seeking out the liar, the deceiver, the heartbreaker, all her prepared words died in her throat.

She might have felt humiliated. She might have felt hurt and rejected.

She might have felt mortified that her husband preferred a Malayan youth to his wife. But it was clear from looking at Nigel that he was brimming with happiness. How could she not have noticed before? The darts of light in his eyes. The shine on his skin. The curve to his mouth. And the way his long features, usually so stiff and controlled, seemed to have rubbed up against each other and repositioned themselves, so that she would have sworn his nose was shorter, his chin blunter, the lines of his cheeks and his eyebrows more fluid.

Suddenly, just like her son, Connie felt a stab of jealousy, as sharp as a knife in the ribs. Nigel was in love. Nigel was happy. In the nine lonely years of their marriage she had never seen him like this, and she could not bring herself to snatch such happiness from him right now. He was trapped within his own desires, and her heart bled for him. So she closed her mouth and slid down under the sheet, careful not to let any part of her body touch his as he climbed into bed. In case the clash of skins sparked something in her that she couldn't control, and made her lash out.

"Good night, Nigel," she muttered.

"Good night, old thing," he said.

ϑ·Ϛ

A slender arrow of silver lay on the bedsheet. It was still dark outside, but a tiny slit in a cloud somewhere had allowed moonlight to sneak through and find a path to Connie's bed. She watched it edge its way up toward her. She lay awake, fingering the pearls that she wore constantly, some distant part of her mind paying heed to the motion of the boat to judge the height of the waves, and to the grumbling of the rigging to reckon the speed of the wind. But all her attention was on the silent form beside her in the dark. She listened to his breathing and counted the times he turned on his side with a sigh rumbling up from his dreams. At one point, a sudden movement of the boat jolted him from his sleep, but he chose to pretend otherwise. Nevertheless, Connie spoke to him softly.

"Nigel, do you like Razak?"

An indistinct murmur rose from her husband.

"Nigel, do you like him?"

"Razak is a nice enough young man." But he had hesitated too long.
"Do you love him?"

"What?"

"Do you love him?"

He sat bolt upright. "Constance, have you gone out of your mind?"

"Hush," she soothed. "I can see you love him. So can Teddy. That's why he's sulking. He thinks you have forgotten us."

Nigel released a loud explosion of sound, then lowered it to a throaty hiss as he clambered from the bed. He landed on his bad leg and stumbled in the darkness, cursing, but by the thin arrow of moonlight she could make out his features, contorted with anger. Or was it fear?

"Constance," he said in a low voice, aware of thin walls around him. "I demand an apology and a retraction."

"No, Nigel, I can't. I should have realized before. It's true, isn't it, that . . . ?"

"It is not true!"

"Oh, Nigel, you should never have married me. It was cruel."

"Don't be absurd, Constance."

"Please, Nigel, don't lie to me any more. Be honest with me."

"You are suggesting something that is disgusting and unnatural. As well as illegal, as you well know." His voice trembled. "The Malay boy needs help, and I am giving it to him. Isn't that what you wanted?"

Connie rolled over on her side, away from him. "No, Nigel, that is not what I wanted."

CHAPTER TWENTY-SIX

Madoc was worried about the boat. She was still taking on too much water, limping against a headwind. The rain didn't help. It lashed down on the deck, hammering at the timber planks as if intent on robbing Madoc of his prize. Nothing was visible. The solid sheets of rain swallowed the tops of the masts and veiled all land from sight, so that *The White Pearl* floated in stifling isolation, alone and disconnected. They were trapped in her own private world.

"What do you think?"

Madoc leaned against the rail alongside Flight Lieutenant Blake. The man was huddled in mustard-yellow oilskins, his gaze turned outward to the water, a closed expression on his face. Even so, he was a good-looking bastard. A bit too eager to please for Madoc's liking, but that was no bad thing. It might yet work in Madoc's favor. He noticed the blond pilot was munching on a biscuit—they were in short supply now, along with fresh water. He'd bet his good boots that the feral little native girl had smuggled it to him. Whenever Blake ventured up on deck, she scuttled around him with small scratchy sounds like one of the damn cockroaches.

"What do you think?" Madoc repeated.

"About what?"

"About our chances."

Blake continued to stare at the turbulent water. "I think," he said, with an attempt at an ironic smile, "that we are running out of islands to hide in."

"You're damn right there. Can't help wondering if this Fitzpayne fellow is leading us on a merry dance."

Slowly Blake turned his head, blue eyes narrowed. "A dance that ends where?"

"That's what I want to know."

"You don't trust him?"

Madoc shrugged. "Do we have reason to?"

"He's guided us to safety . . . so far."

"Barely." Madoc gestured with his chin at the Jap swathed in green canvas and tethered to the mast. "Your friend, Mr. Hadley, slipped up there. Not his best decision—to allow an enemy on board."

Blake frowned, but before he could comment Madoc said, "I get the feeling Fitzpayne is taking his time bringing us to this island of his, and I wonder . . ." He stopped and glanced over at the figure at the helm.

"Wonder what?" Blake prompted in a low tone.

"How many of us have to die before he feels ready to sail *The White Pearl* into safe harbor."

"For God's sake, man, that's going too far."

"Is it?"

A sudden squall of rain slapped them in the face and made them turn their backs to the wind, hunched inside their oilskins.

"What do you mean?" Blake muttered.

"I mean, the way he talks with the Jap. He squats in front of him when he thinks no one is about and speaks in fluent Japanese."

"So?" Blake demanded.

"So I'm beginning to wonder whose side he is on."

ᔅᐟᑐ

The rain had cried itself to sleep. At last the noise of it had stopped. Maya watched the steam rise off the deck as the sun's rays stroked the timbers with warm fingers, and it reminded her of the smoke from the fires that had danced from hut to hut in her street in Palur. Flames that crackled and devoured as Japanese bombs fell. She flicked a glance toward the Japanese pilot and felt an uncomfortable heat flare in her chest. He should be lying at the bottom of the ocean, wrapped in a coffin of seaweed.

She could see death on him, as gray and lifeless as cobwebs on his skin. Like the child charred in the fire, the one *Mem* Hadley saw in the old man's arms in the filthy street. *Not my child. My body gave birth to it but it was never mine.* She shuddered.

She had been little more than a child herself, and the baby was sold immediately by her mother to a couple who were barren. Her child, but not her child. After a day selling flowers on the streets, dodging the traffic, she would refuse to cross paths with it. She would take a snaking route back to her hut to avoid its bright little face. Maybe this Japanese pilot dropped the bomb that caused the fire.

She stared at him, the dull heat spreading tentacles through her chest.

She still recalled the look of sadness on *mem*'s face when she asked about the child, the softness of the words that carried so much concern within them. She felt them pull at her. Why was it that the only person who cared was the woman she had sworn to hate?

꩜

"Twenty-seven Mitsubishi bombers," Teddy shouted.

Maya looked up from her perch on the hatch. Like black bees strung out across the sky, Japanese planes were flying in formation overhead. In the far distance somewhere they could hear the growling and pounding of big guns. Lines of angry fire spat through the gloom as evening cast its gray net over the restless ocean.

The White Pearl spread her sails and Maya felt the familiar rocking motion start up under her feet as the waters took hold of the hull. It still made her nervous, but no longer sick. Once the planes had vanished in the direction of Singapore, she watched Fitzpayne ease the yacht from under the canopy of trees. Despite the boat's wounds, tonight she would reach his island of safety. That was what he had promised.

Maya didn't know why, but she trusted Iron-eyes' promises.

꩜

"Here, Maya. Drink this."

Golden-hair had brought her a cup of tea. She thought the British stupid to drink it all day. It tasted of dog's piss. But she looked up at him gratefully, tossed her dark hair over one shoulder, and put her lips to the cup.

"Why you kind to Jap?" she asked. Earlier he had taken a cup of tea to the prisoner.

"Because he's a pilot, like me. He was just doing his job, flying his plane."

"He bad. He try kill us."

"That's part of his job."

"His job to die. Good thing."

"No, Maya. He's young and has his heart set on serving his emperor with glory. Dying for him, if necessary. It's a concept we have all but abandoned in the Western world."

She didn't know the meaning of all his words, but she heard the edge of sorrow in his voice and saw the way his golden lashes seemed to grow heavier over his eyes.

"You good man," she told him, nodding vigorously. "He bad man."

He didn't laugh at her the way Iron-eyes would have done. Or turn away from her the way *Tuan* Hadley always did, as if she hurt his eyes. Golden-hair regarded her solemnly and then took her hand in his, the one not in the sling. It looked like a small, ugly brown leaf on his broad white palm, but he folded his fingers around it. He spoke. But her ears didn't hear. They were listening to the happiness singing in her heart, and all her mind could think of was that this strong, plane-flying hand of his wanted hers. She gazed at the bony rise of each of his knuckles and the veins pulsing with blood under the freckled skin.

"Maya?" He was waiting for a reply, but she had no idea what he had asked her.

She risked a smile at him. "You crazy," she said.

ɔ·ɕ

The White Pearl swept out into the open sea as if she owned it. Maya had seen white ladies enter a room like that, with head high and a spine as straight as a ship's mast, taking possession of the space around them instead of just passing through it the way Maya did. She admired those women, even though they had stolen her country.

"Maya!"

She lifted her head. Young *Tuan* Teddy was in the back—*no, think, what is it?* . . . the stern—of the boat, beckoning to her. She hurried over.

"Look!" he said. He pointed out to sea.

As though on command, the evening clouds that had lain stubbornly over the water picked up their grubby skirts and sneaked away below the horizon. Vivid red streaks from the setting sun painted the tops of the waves, and Teddy's cheeks turned crimson. Maya didn't know if his flushed cheeks were the work of the sun or the fear that leaped into her own heart.

"It's back," he whispered.

It was the native boat, the *pinisiq*, the one the boy had spotted before. This time near enough to be clearly visible to the naked eye, its long pointed nose sniffing them out.

"Is same one?" she asked.

"Yes." He looked at her as if she were simple. "It has the same patched sail."

"Tell *Tuan* Fitzpayne."

"Last time, he said it was just a trader ship going about its business."

"Maybe he right."

"Maybe he's wrong."

They stood side by side, staring at the craft in the distance. It reminded Maya of a mosquito, spindly and fragile but with a long point at the front and a nasty bite.

"Tell *Mem* Hadley."

The boy glanced across at his mother and shook his head. "Today she's not . . . concentrating."

Maya had no idea what *concentrating* was, but even so, she knew what he meant. *Mem* Hadley was different today. The skin of her face was dull and colorless. She kept looking at her husband, and when she spoke to him, her voice was gentle. She had played Snap with her son in a slow, distracted manner like someone who had only just learned the game. Now, aware of Maya's scrutiny, she picked up the rope she had been knotting and headed for the stairs, but just at that moment Razak came bounding up them. *Mem* Hadley jumped back the way she would if she'd seen a scorpion. Then she vanished below in a hurry.

Razak slumped against the rail next to Maya, his mouth sulky. "A white person's mind is like a lazy bird's nest," he muttered. "It falls apart when the wind blows hard."

Teddy was listening. He understood Malay. Maya saw him frown as he tried to shape the insult in a way that made sense to his young mind.

"What devil is in your tongue now?" she asked her brother.

"*Tuan* Hadley is . . ." He stopped.

"Is what?"

"He doesn't see me today. He turns his eyes away. Today I don't exist for him."

She pressed her hand flat on his chest, fingers splayed over his heart. She felt it beating wildly. "You are a fool, Razak. You will destroy everything for us."

She walked away. Sometimes her brother needed a slap.

Ꭾ·Ꮐ

A hand touched the calf of Maya's leg. She was scurrying past the prisoner when his fingers reached for her. She kicked the hand away.

"Maya."

The Japanese pilot's voice was low and nasal. She looked down at him, propped in a sitting position on the deck, his back to the hefty mast, his legs in uniform stretched out straight above fur-lined boots. He had cast off the tarpaulin to reveal the dressing on his chest. It was big and square and stained with dried blood. His black hair stood up on his skull like the bristles of a brush.

"What?" she said rudely.

"I speak you."

"*Tidak.* No."

"Help me."

"*Tidak.* No."

"Please. *Onegai shimasu.*"

His narrow face was tipped up toward her—*a boy*, she told herself, *he's only a boy*—and she saw clearly the shame that swirled in his eyes, shame at having to beg help from a girl. His chest heaved with each labored breath and his forehead was scuffed. Smudge marks sat in the hollows under his eyes like bruises. She didn't like looking at him.

"No." Her feet started to move away.

"I help you," he said quickly.

When she swiveled back to him, he was staring at her brother in the stern. She crouched, her eyes on a level with the wounded pilot's. "How?"

ꕔ·ꕔ

Maya tried to find her mother's face in the darkening waters, but it wasn't there. She listened for her voice when the waves fingered the bottom of the boat, but all she heard was the low hissing as the sea drew breath. Maya longed to know that her mother's spirit was at last pleased. She had made a deal with Jap man.

"What you want?" she had asked him.

He had smiled at her, but it was an empty smile. "I want help."

"You are bloody Jap fool." She shook her head at him. "No help."

He nodded, as though he had expected her bad words. "You help me. I help you. I see you and brother look at white lady. Daggers in eyes."

"So?"

"I want her dead. You want her dead."

"Dead?" She said the word under her breath. It tasted bitter and sharp on her tongue.

"When she gone," he finished, "we go from ship."

"Hah! Escape? You mad."

His face was smooth, as though he hadn't yet used it much. He knew nothing. The boat was a boiling cauldron, and he was stupid enough to think he could climb out without scalding his pretty pale skin. Just at that moment, the boy's dog came trotting around the corner from the hatchway, a fistful of flies crawling over one of its ears, its tongue falling out the side of its mouth as though seeking somewhere cool. Maya tried to shove the horrible creature away with her bare foot, but it danced back, claws scratching at the deck timbers, then jumped forward again, eyes bright in its shaggy face. It wanted to play.

"I here to avenge my mother," Maya hissed at the Jap. "The white woman kill her."

"So," he nodded, "we deal?"

Maya hesitated, and hated herself for it. It should be piss-easy to say *yes*, to say *let us harm the white woman, let us make her suffer*. Yet her tongue was slow with the word, reluctant to let it go. Her eyes scanned the deck, but there was no sign of *Mem* Hadley; she must be busy down below. *Tuan* Teddy and his father were reading their books in uneasy silence on a bench.

"Yes." She forced the word out. "We deal."

That was when she sought her mother's smile of approval in the waters and listened in vain for her voice in the waves.

"But how you help me?" she asked.

His mouth stretched into the empty smile again. "Like this."

Fast as a snake, his hand whipped out and caught the small dog by the scruff of its neck. It whimpered. Suddenly he was standing and swinging his fettered arms back over his head. He paused a second, then sent them hurtling forward and at the last moment his fingers opened. The dog sailed through the air in a long arc over the sea like a blackbird that had forgotten to spread its wings. Maya saw its pink tongue open, its white teeth flash in protest, and heard a spine-chilling howl leap from its jaws, a sound too monstrous for its tiny lungs. She rushed to the rail to see it splash down into the sea, but instantly it bobbed to the surface like a cork.

"No, Pippin, no!" Teddy's voice screamed. "No! Daddy, it's Pippin!"

Maya could see the dog's front paws scrabbling on the water, its eyes wide with panic as the boat started to recede. The black head was vanishing in the vast rolling sheet of the sea, and as a wave broke over it, she heard a bark of desperation.

"Pippin!" Teddy screamed again. "Daddy, help him!"

The sight of the boy's face twisted in terror did something painful to Maya's insides. She leaped to her feet, and in that fleeting moment, three things happened.

The boy clambered up onto the rail, preparing to leap down into the waves to his dog.

Tuan Hadley kicked off his shoes.

Mem Hadley raced up from below through the hatchway, Iron-eyes roaring behind her.

CHAPTER TWENTY-SEVEN

Connie's chest hurt with relief. Her son's scream had chilled her soul, but when she burst up on deck she saw that he was alive. His limbs were intact. No blood. The boom had not slammed into his skull, cracking it wide open. But he was balanced on the edge of the boat, about to jump.

"Teddy! Don't!"

She rushed forward, but Nigel was already there. He pulled the boy back down onto the deck and with a curse dived off the side of the boat.

Why? Why was her husband plunging into the waves?

Her hand gripped her son's shoulder. "What's happened?"

"It's Pippin!"

He pointed. The sun had sunk below the horizon, the sky fading toward night, so that the troughs within the waves were daubed with shadows. She couldn't see the dog. She raced for the life belt that hung on the side of the hatch and skimmed it out toward her husband, but already the boat was carrying them away from him. He raised a hand in thanks and struck out toward the canvas ring, but the brutal reality of the ocean's power was all around him and it lifted the hairs on the nape of her neck. Only then was she aware that Fitzpayne had seized control of the helm from Henry and was shouting, "Come about!" Henry and Razak leaped to the ropes as he spun the wheel, drawing the mainsail across the boat so that the bow swung gracefully round, circling back toward the life belt.

"We're coming, Nigel," she called out, her heart pounding. *I'm coming,*

Nigel, I'm coming. She glanced down at Teddy. His anxious gaze was fixed on his father.

"Don't let Daddy drown."

"I won't."

"Scout's honor?"

It was their phrase. When something really mattered.

"Scout's honor," she echoed.

She spotted the dog then. The damn dog. It was swimming frantically toward Nigel and when it reached him it lavished kisses all over his salty cheeks, making Nigel laugh and take on board a mouthful of water. Connie drew a deep breath. It was going to be all right. She was impressed by Nigel's calm. No panic. Easy in the water. A steady leg kick—despite his injury—to keep him treading water as he held on to Pippin and waited for the yacht to reach him.

Had he swum toward the boat, had he not waited with an Englishman's certainty for it to come to him, the outcome might have been different.

சூ·Ᏻ

Madoc pulled on his trousers and hurried up on deck to see what the hell all the commotion was about. His quick eyes took in the scene at once: Hadley in the water, the life belt a vivid white circle on its darkening waves, the sails shortened as the boat drew close. Night was falling fast. Everyone had sprung forward and they were now lined up along one side—like sitting ducks, their backs to him. They were calling out to Hadley and tipping the balance of the boat, so that it rolled awkwardly to starboard. Fitzpayne had lashed the wheel and with a neat flick of his arm threw Hadley a line that landed smack in front of him. He grasped it firmly. Only then did Madoc notice the dog's sodden black head next to him.

"What the hell's going on?" he demanded, aware of Kitty arriving quietly at his side.

"Nigel dived in to get the dog," Henry Court replied over his shoulder.

"Daddy has saved Pippin's life," the boy said proudly.

"How on earth did the animal end up in the water?"

Flight Lieutenant Blake frowned. "Yes, that's a good question."

Madoc was struck by how gray his face looked. Maybe it was just the shadows.

"That man did it!" the boy shouted.

All eyes flicked to him.

"The Jap, he did it. I saw him." Teddy's young face was screwed up in anger. "He threw Pippin overboard."

Constance Hadley promptly marched over to the prisoner. "Is that true? Did you throw the dog overboard?"

"*Hai.* Yes."

Her hand came up and slapped the Jap pilot's face. It resonated through the quiet evening air. She immediately resumed her position at the rail beside her son and called out to her husband, "Nigel, we'll soon have you back on board."

"Grab hold," Fitzpayne shouted. "We'll haul you in."

Even now, Hadley was behaving like the perfect English gentleman. Women, children, and bloody animals first. While the fool was tying the rope around the dog's middle, Madoc seized his moment—when everyone's attention was focused on the water and their backs were turned—to step away from the edge and remove the Tokarev pistol from Kitty's skirt pocket. Land was no more than a mile or two away, not too far—for those who could swim.

"No," Kitty hissed at him.

She seized his wrist and wrapped the fingers of her other hand around the muzzle of the gun.

"No, Madoc."

He tried to shake her off, but she was strong. Their hands fought a silent battle.

"No shooting," she insisted under her breath.

"No shooting. Just persuasion to join Hadley in the water."

He felt her fingers start to loosen. But a small brown hand suddenly slid between them and a penknife blade was stabbed into his arm. He made no sound as blood oozed from the shallow wound, and Kitty laughed.

"Thank you, Maya," she said, and pocketed the gun once more.

Madoc stiffened and stared into the native girl's furious black eyes.

He knew that one day he would have to rid himself of this interfering little sewer rat.

୨·୧

"Teddy, get your arms set to take Pippin," Fitzpayne ordered as he pulled on the rope, hand over hand.

"I'm ready."

The light was going. Connie could sense the nervousness around her on the boat. No one said it, but the words passed from head to head unspoken: *Leave the dog, Nigel. Get back on board.* Yet she felt immensely proud of him. He had demonstrated his love for his son, for everyone to see. Teddy could never believe now that his father loved Razak more than he loved him. She experienced a great rush of gratitude to her husband.

"Come on, Nigel," she shouted encouragingly.

The sky and the sea were beginning to merge in the coming darkness, and the current was slowly drawing him backward. Her husband's familiar face was bobbing like a pale ball on the surface of the waves next to the life belt, his hair plastered in strands to his forehead. She smiled at him and waved. He smiled back and kicked harder with his good leg. As Pippin plopped wet and ecstatic into Teddy's outstretched arms, Razak shouted something in Malay. Connie didn't understand. But she saw Fitzpayne react. He was untying the rope from the dog, but he stopped and lifted his head. She felt her own heart pause. His eyes scoured the waves and then he moved fast.

"Hadley," he called out, "catch the rope. Be quick."

His voice was sharp. Urgent. Connie felt alarm crawl up her spine. The rope snaked out once more and landed in the perfect spot for Nigel to seize hold of it. He started to tie it to the life belt through which he had his arm looped, but Fitzpayne didn't wait.

"Hadley, just hold the rope, for God's sake, and we'll pull you in."

His shout was impatient and he gave the rope a strong tug that yanked Nigel toward the boat. Connie's eyes stopped watching her husband and examined the waters around him. That was when she saw it: the tip of a thin black fin. Like a blade slicing through the waves behind him. It was circling in a leisurely manner, as if it had all the time in the world.

"Nigel! Hurry!" she cried out.

He heard the fear in her voice. They all did. Nigel quickly spun himself round in the water and caught sight of the fin only yards away.

"Shark!" Johnnie bellowed, snatching at the rope. "Get out of the—"

Later, much later, Connie learned to turn down the volume on Nigel's scream in her head. But that first time she heard it as the shark attacked, it felt as though the sound of it split her skull apart.

So fast. So brief. So rough.

Suddenly Nigel was jerked from the water. He shot sideways ten feet, arms flailing, his body shaken back and forth like a rag doll. Connie clutched Teddy to her, burying his face in her dress. For a split second Nigel rose up above the water and she screamed as an arc of blood soared into the air before he was abruptly hauled below the surface. Blood-stained water closed over his head. Silence now. One solitary hand flapped briefly in the curve of a wave, a final farewell. Nothing more.

But his scream was trapped inside Connie's head, tearing at her skull.

৯·৫

Six hours. Circling and circling the area. Through the darkness they searched the secretive surface of the ocean, risking torches, chasing shadows. The moon rose. Its brittle light turned the water into hard metal, impenetrable and unyielding.

There was no Nigel. They all knew that he was gone, but it wasn't until Fitzpayne, his face set tight as a fist, finally caught the tip of a boat hook into the floating sleeve of a shirt that had once been white, that Connie could bring herself to nod her head, the signal to hoist the sails. Treacherous muscles. To give the nod. Bones that betray.

As *The White Pearl* moved off before the wind, she didn't abandon the spot where she was standing when her husband screamed. She stood there all night, listening to him.

৯·৫

"I'm so very sorry."

It was Fitzpayne. He was standing at Connie's side at the rail. How long had he been there in the darkness? He was generous enough not to look at her, giving her that much privacy, and she was grateful. Instead, he stared out at the black, rolling seas and made a sound like the wind through his nostrils, exhaling hard.

"You did your best," she said. The words felt stiff in her mouth.

"The boat was too slow." He shook his head. "She is sluggish to respond because she is damaged. I couldn't . . ."

"You did your best," she said again.

"Not enough. The sea is unforgiving of mistakes."

"The only mistake was Nigel's."

For a long time after that, they remained silent. Between them stood her son, asleep on his feet, his hands clutched around Connie's waist, her arm looped around his shoulders, holding his weight against her body. His head lolled against her ribs, warm and heavy. Clouds marched across the night sky, throwing a shroud over the moon and stars, so that only the thinnest beam of light sneaked through. Connie watched it bounce like a silver pebble skimming across the waves.

"Do you know what I want to do?" she asked fiercely.

"Tell me."

"I want to plunge my hand into the ocean and wrench him back to life." She lowered her head and inhaled silently through her mouth, so that he would not hear the ragged edges of her breath.

In the darkness he stroked her hair, his hand cupping her head. It was a gentle comforting touch that brought forth a great shudder of grief from her. He left his hand there, until she was still once more.

"Let me take the boy," he urged.

His arms lifted Teddy effortlessly without waking him, and Connie was thankful that her son could find such oblivion.

"I'll carry him to Madoc's cabin, if you prefer," he said. "They can move into the master bedroom."

Her heart tightened. How could he know of her reluctance to enter the room where she and Nigel had shared a bed in case her husband's salt-stained figure rose from the sheets, covered in trailing seaweed and pointing an accusing finger at her?

"Yes," she said. "Thank you."

"You still have your son. He's safe."

"Yes."

She walked behind him toward the hatchway, her eyes fixed on her son's bare legs hanging over Fitzpayne's arm, and her feet moved as though they belonged to someone else.

Suddenly she said hotly, "The sea is a monstrous thing."

Fitzpayne stopped. Without turning he said softly, "I know." The gentleness of his voice made her want to cry. Then he descended the steps.

She hesitated, unwilling to leave the deck. Down below, she knew she would suffocate. The waves would seep in and smother her nose and mouth. She made herself listen to the familiar slapping of the water against the hull and gazed out over the dark, heartless sea.

"Good-bye, Nigel," she whispered, and hurried down to her son.

ꝯ·ꬶ

A knock on the door made Connie turn her head. It took an effort. The joints of her neck felt stiff and rusty, she had been sitting so rigid on the bed. She had no idea for how long. Hours? Days? No, not days. Teddy was curled up beside her like an exhausted kitten, his head on her lap.

The knock came again. Her fingers touched her son's damp hair as if she could keep the noise from penetrating, but he didn't stir. Between his eyebrows, a miniature version of his father's frown-crease rumpled his smooth skin and she ironed it gently with her thumb.

She didn't want to talk to anyone.

She heard the rustle of a sleeve against the door as an arm was raised to knock again, her senses too acute, everything painful, even the light falling in a puddle from the kerosene lamp and the grating whirr of a fly's wings, the creak of the timbers. The sounds seemed to grind against each other in her brain. Before the knock could be repeated, she slid out from under Teddy's cheek and moved to the door, the words *Go away* forming on her tongue. She opened the door.

It was Henry, the last person she expected. He looked red-faced and awkward.

"Yes?" she asked.

"I want to . . ." He stopped. Started again. "How are you?"

"I'll live."

He chewed at the inside of his cheek, searching for the words he had come to say. "When Harriet died . . . you were a real help to me. I know you want to be alone, but it's not always best."

"I have Teddy with me."

"I know."

They stood staring at each other's shoes.

Henry burst out suddenly with, "I admired the way you slapped the blighter."

"You would have done the same for Harriet."

He nodded. But grief had changed her. She didn't notice Henry's mottled cheeks or the way he unconsciously stroked the bulk of his stomach for reassurance, which had always irritated her before. All she saw was the loneliness he was trying to hide, the dark anger deep within him, and the anxious downturn of the edge of his mouth. She touched his arm and felt the hollowness of it, as though Harriet had been the marrow in his bones.

"Constance, I want to kill him, but I don't have the nerve." Henry's hands were shaking. Abruptly he walked away.

ᘐ·ᘓ

Dawn spilled its light into the master cabin. Madoc could hear Fitzpayne working the bilge pump hard below him. Still taking on water, then. He sat fully clothed on the edge of the bed and listened for other sounds. No sobbing from other cabins, no gnashing of teeth. All good signs. Nobody out of control. Madoc had had only two hours' sleep, but he could feel his blood pumping fast. Today would be his day—he could feel it in his bones.

With a grin he reached over and smacked Kitty's broad rump. "Wake up, wife. Just because we're in the master bed doesn't mean you can snore the day away."

She grunted, opened one eye, and dug a finger into his ribs. "Piss off." She rolled over, turning her back on him.

He had to admit that Kitty was not at her best first thing in the morning. He lifted her skirt from where it lay on the floor, but it was not weighed down in one spot the way he expected it to be. He shook it, frustrated.

"Where's the gun?" he hissed.

"It's not there."

"Where the hell is it?"

"When you need it, it will be ready for you, Madoc. You won't need it today."

"So you're a bloody crystal-ball gazer all of a sudden, are you? Able to see what's waiting around the corner?"

"Don't shout."

He seized her shoulder and shook it, though not hard enough to hurt her. She sat up, her breasts exposed, and he could smell the sleepy musk of her body. He whispered harshly, "I need it, Kitty. Today we'll be landing at Fitzpayne's bloody island. We'd have been safely there by now if he hadn't wasted hours in an insane search for a dead man. God only knows what will happen, and I need to be ready to—"

"Let's see how the land lies first, shall we?"

"No. This is our chance, Kitty. Don't wreck it for me."

"For us."

"That's what I meant."

"Madoc, I'm watching your back. I don't want you fed to the sharks like Hadley." She paused, prodded back an unruly swath of her hair, and muttered thoughtfully, "Madoc, will you search insanely for my body when I die?"

His heart slammed against his ribs. The thought of a shark's jaw scything its way through Kitty's flesh did something bad inside him. He pushed her back on the goose-down pillows and sank his teeth gently into her throat.

"Kitty, tell me where the fucking pistol is," he growled against her skin. "Or I will throw you to the sharks myself."

౨·౬

"Razak."

Her brother didn't lift his head from his knees. Maya tugged at his hair. "Razak, don't be like this."

He moaned.

"The *tuan* is dead, Razak. But *Mem* Hadley will still look after us. She won't . . ."

He moaned once more. They were crouched on deck, hidden away from the Jap, and Maya took a firm grip on her brother's black hair, raising his head. He was crying. Huge tears streaked his face and dripped onto his knees. They frightened her.

"Razak," she said in a small voice, "our mother will be satisfied now. This revenge will lie sweet as honey on her tongue." She stroked his cheek. "Be happy."

He leaned his head against hers. She could feel its pain pass through into her own skull and settle there like river mud. She wrapped an arm around her twin and held him close, crooning softly.

"Now," he whispered to her, "you must stop hating."

୬·୧

It was scarcely light, yet everyone was on deck, everyone except Constance Hadley and the boy. There was a restlessness on board, people constantly moving around as though they could outpace the thoughts that stalked them. Madoc felt tense. The yacht was limping badly, cumbersome to handle, and on the horizon the native boat could be seen drawing ever closer.

Hadley was gone. Madoc had to work at keeping the smile off his face. Expressions on deck were somber. Fitzpayne was grim and silent. Madoc felt sorry for the wife and the boy, no question of that, poor kid, but he was glad they were keeping below deck. He didn't like the reminder that the sight of them gave him—like Henry Court, whom he avoided like the plague—that husbands or wives could die on you. Could leave you alone and unloved. *Oh Kitty, don't you ever fucking die on me.*

The argument with her this morning had been short-lived because she was right, damn her. He was going to have to wait until the boat was fixed before trying anything, but the idea of this island of Fitzpayne's made him nervous. Nervous as hell.

୬·୧

Connie waited. In the cabin she made no sound, though she could hear the footsteps above her on deck and the low rumble of Fitzpayne's voice giving orders. She was waiting until she was certain that Teddy was asleep once more.

His young face on the pillow looked flushed and vulnerable, but at least in sleep his body stopped shaking. Earlier he had woken in the darkness and she had rocked him in her arms in the hot little cabin, talking to him, telling him the only one to blame for his father's death was the Jap. Not Teddy, not Pippin, not Daddy, not Mummy. Not those handling the boat. Just the Japanese pilot who tossed the dog overboard. He was the one to blame.

Not you, my beloved son, not you.

Fitzpayne had questioned the pilot in Japanese and asked him why he did it. "He said it was because the dog was annoying him," Fitzpayne had reported. But Connie had looked into Fitzpayne's eyes and seen in them the knowledge that the dog was thrown into the water as a deliberate act of revenge, a gesture designed to hurt *her.*

"No one could have predicted Daddy would leap in to rescue Pippin," she assured her son. "He was very brave."

"He's a hero," Teddy had sobbed.

"Of course he is. He loved you so much."

"I hate all Japanese."

How could she blame him? They had taken his home and now they had taken his father. So she waited, stroking her son's sweat-soaked hair, and only when she was sure he was fast asleep did she open the leather bag at her feet. Inside lay the gun Fitzpayne had given her the night of the storm.

ɘ·ɕ

War had altered her more than she believed possible. Connie stepped out on deck into the early-morning light, drew the damp air into her lungs, and contemplated killing a man. This time it would not be an accident, not a push that turned into a stumble and an unintentional killing. This time her heart was choked with murder.

She strode across to the base of the mainmast and placed herself in front of the prisoner she had saved from the sea, but this time she didn't see a young man dragged away from his parents' farm, or even a patriotic servant of Japan intent on fighting for his country. No, not this time. She saw the sullen head and black, hateful eyes of the man who had killed her husband, and so she lifted the gun in her hand and pointed it straight at his heart.

He leaped to his feet. Said something in Japanese.

She wasn't aware of the shout from Johnnie Blake, or of Fitzpayne lifting his head where he was seated on the deck filleting fish with Kitty. She heard only a roaring in her ears—was it the wind in the rigging?—and saw a long narrow tunnel of vision with the Japanese pilot's face at the end of it.

"You killed my husband." She spoke calmly. "A life for a life."

A split second of panic passed over the prisoner's face before he regained control of himself. He became very still, nodded once, and slowly closed his eyes, long black lashes settling on his cheeks. His lips moved silently, and she realized he was saying a prayer. What was in the prayer? A plea for blessings on his soul? A sorrowful farewell to his family? A final vow of allegiance to his emperor? Or was it yet another impassioned curse called down on her head? The roaring grew louder in her ears, more insistent; not the wind, no, not the wind. It was the sound of her own blood in her ears, and she felt another pulse of the rage that had driven her to point the gun.

Her finger curled around the trigger. She took aim at his chest, aware of the weight of the gun in her hand, of the hardness of the metal against the skin of her fingers, of her hunger for vengeance.

"A life for a life," she said for the last time.

"Go ahead. Shoot him."

There was a hesitation in her finger as Fitzpayne's words pierced the noise in her head.

"Shoot him if you think it will make you feel better, Connie."

Connie. He had never called her Connie. Always Mrs. Hadley. Maybe if he had called her Mrs. Hadley this time, she wouldn't have listened because it wasn't who she was any more. On the periphery of her vision she could see him leaning against the mizzenmast, fish scales on his fingers and a long-bladed filleting knife in one hand. Around him other figures moved, but they were out of focus and she had no idea how many were gathering. But the face of the Japanese pilot was pin sharp. Every detail—his narrow bones, his pale skin, his smooth slippery eyelids—all were branded into her brain as she prepared to fire.

"Do you know what killing a man does to a person, Connie?" Fitzpayne asked, as casually as if inquiring if she knew the time by her watch.

Yes, I know. I know what killing a man does to a person.

"It isn't good," he said gently. "Not good at all. Take my word for it, this man isn't worth it."

The Japanese pilot opened his eyes and fixed them on Connie.

"It's worth it to me," she said fiercely.

"It won't make you feel better, and it won't bring Nigel back. But if you're really determined to see this Jap dead . . ."

Her finger tightened.

". . . I'll do the job for you," Fitzpayne finished. He held out a hand for the gun. "It won't be the first time I've killed a man."

The sounds in her head were growing louder, more jumbled, and were joined by shouts and movement around her. Suddenly the Jap wasn't looking at her any more but staring open-mouthed over her shoulder.

"Connie?" Fitzpayne was right next to her. Everything steadied. "You won't be needing this now." He curled a hand over hers on the gun and flicked a glance behind her.

She spun around and saw a flurry of grubby sails and the long, pointed bowsprit as the native boat, the *pinisiq*, that had dogged their wake for so long drew alongside, as silent as a shark. Grappling hooks were hurled over *The White Pearl*'s rail, attached to scrambling nets that stretched up from the deck of the *pinisiq*, which sat lower in the water. Someone screamed. They all knew there was only one brand of voyager that boarded a boat with such arrogance: the pirates of the South China Sea.

CHAPTER TWENTY-EIGHT

Madoc seized the Tokarev pistol from Kitty's pocket and brandished it in front of the pirates. The waters round here were riddled with them, sea scum that vanished among the thousands of islands like rats down holes. Their reputation as thieves and killers was legendary. He pushed Kitty behind him and took aim at the first head that rose above *The White Pearl*'s rail. It was brown-skinned, tufty-haired, and as wrinkled as a stale apple.

"Get off this boat!" Madoc shouted at him.

Blake and Henry Court stood shoulder to shoulder, ready to make a fight of it, but Madoc fired a warning shot. The bullet skimmed the cheek of the tufty man, whose face screwed up into a snarl. He wiped away the trickle of blood and licked it from his knuckles, his eyes startled. Across his back hung a rifle.

"My next shot will split your dogshit brain," Madoc warned in Malay, "if you don't—"

A blade, stinking of fish, slid under Madoc's throat. Christ! His body went rigid, and then he heard Fitzpayne's voice soft in his ear. "If you pull that trigger again, Madoc, I'll cut your tongue out before our friend over there even hits the deck."

Madoc hesitated.

"I'm telling you for the last time, put the gun down, Madoc. There's no need for it. Give it back to your woman. She has the sense to know when to keep it out of sight."

"Fuck you, Fitzpayne. What the hell are you doing?"

Fitzpayne released an unpleasant laugh. "Just do as you're told and don't make trouble for everyone. Drop the gun."

Madoc did so, and it clattered on the deck.

"Kick it away."

Madoc kicked it, but not too far. He wanted to spit, but his mouth was as dry as a whore's heart.

"Now we talk to them," Fitzpayne announced calmly.

It was Constance Hadley who surprised everyone by stepping forward, right up to the man still perched on the rail. She stripped the gold watch from her wrist and held it out to him. Madoc could see no sign of the gun she had been clutching earlier.

"Here," she said, "take this. If you leave us alone, we'll give you our valuables."

As if Tufty-brain knew what *valuables* were! But he sure as hell recognized the worth of a Cartier watch when he saw one, and his hand snatched it from her, sliding it into a pouch at his waist. He grinned, showing off a battalion of gold teeth. He'd have the pearls off her neck next. During this exchange, Fitzpayne removed the knife. Maya was crouched behind the helm, peeking out with a look on her face that was half fury and half terror, but her brother seemed less concerned. He was regarding the other boat with keen interest.

"Fitzpayne!" Kitty called.

She had darted forward, quick on her feet despite her bulk, and snatched up the pistol from the deck. She held it with both hands, its business end pointed unwaveringly at Fitzpayne's back.

"Fitzpayne, if you ever put a knife to my husband's throat again, I swear to you I will put a bullet in your fucking balls."

Fitzpayne didn't even turn, but the sound of his chuckle drifted behind him. "I don't doubt it," he said as he moved past Blake and Court toward the scrambling nets, where the watch stealer was poised. "Now, fellow passengers, let me introduce you to my friend, Nurul."

"Wake up, Teddy."

Her son's eyes opened reluctantly. His lashes rose, slow and heavy, the movements of his limbs like a broken doll, but when he looked into his mother's face he sat bolt upright in bed.

"Mummy, what is it?"

Connie sank onto the edge of the double bed. "You remember the boat that you said was following us?"

He nodded.

"Well, it seems you were right. It has caught up with us and come alongside."

His eyes grew huge. "Who are they?" he whispered. When she hesitated, he added quickly, "Pirates?"

"They call themselves traders, but they look like pirates to me."

"With cutlasses?"

She could feel his excitement, and because for a moment it overlaid the savagery of his despair at the loss of his father, she couldn't begrudge him it. "Rifles, actually."

"How many?"

"Six men that I've seen. One has a mouthful of gold teeth, and another is wearing a bandolier of bullets that looks as if it weighs more than he does. But it seems that they are friends of Mr. Fitzpayne."

"Friends?"

"That's what he said."

Her son's mouth gaped open. "What are they doing?"

"He has gone on board their boat at the moment and is talking with them, while two of them have come on board *The White Pearl*."

"With their rifles?"

"Yes, but only hanging on their backs, so don't worry. They look . . . friendly enough."

She was lying. One was a tall and rangy native with a doleful mouth and nervous eyes that darted around like a scared rat's. The other was squat and mean-looking. He constantly chewed on a wad of tobacco, and his hands never strayed far from the kris at his belt, a knife with a vicious blade that curved like a wave. Both looked ragged, their rough shirts bleached by sun and salt, but she had to admit they made no aggressive moves, just stood quietly eyeing *The White Pearl* as though she were a woman.

Teddy jumped off the bed. He pulled on his shorts and shirt, eager to be involved, but she made him sit beside her and spoke to him quietly.

"Teddy, this isn't a game. Not a pirate story in a book."

"I know." His young face looked hurt. "I'm seven now."

"You must remain down here. It's safer."

"No, Mummy, please."

"We don't know yet what they might do."

"I'll be good, I promise, I'll be quiet."

She took his precious face in her hands. "I know you will. That's why I want you to hide. They won't even know you're here."

"No!"

"Yes, Teddy."

"No!" He gripped her hands and pulled them from his face. She was astonished at his strength. "Mummy, I don't want to lose you too. Let me stay with you." He burrowed his shoulder tight against her. "Please, Mummy, please."

She wrapped her arms around his slight frame, rocking him, rocking herself. "All right, Teddy," she murmured into his hair, "we'll do this together."

They sat locked together, listening for noises from above, but there were no voices, no footsteps, no sounds of life except the shriek of gulls as they wheeled overhead.

"Teddy," she said softly.

He tilted his face up to hers, and with her thumb she smoothed out the neat little furrow between his eyes once more. It felt gritty with sorrow. She managed a smile for him.

"Teddy, these men could be"—she didn't want to say the word *dangerous*, so she changed it—"could be unpredictable. Do nothing to antagonize them, nothing to annoy them. They are not in any way like Long John Silver or Captain Hook. Do you understand?"

"Don't worry, Mummy, Mr. Fitzpayne will make his friends be nice to us."

"Of course he will."

He gave her a tentative smile. "But Daddy wouldn't like them on our boat, would he?"

"No, I don't think he would."

She cupped his chin in her hand. "Teddy, there is no second chance in life. We have to get this right."

༄·༄

On deck, nothing was happening. *The White Pearl*'s sails lay furled, and the boat rolled like a drunk on the great swell of the waves that barreled in from the Pacific Ocean. The sun broke free of the horizon and began to haul itself up inch by inch. Today it seemed a huge effort. Fitzpayne was pacing the deck of the *pinisiq* in deep discussion with Nurul, the man with the gold teeth who had come on board. The other boat's hull was longer than *The White Pearl*'s, with raw, salt-stained timbers and a patched mainsail. The expanse of its deck was divided up by two large hatch covers, and Connie wondered what lay beneath them in the hold—something heavy enough to make the *pinisiq* ride low in the water. Maybe Fitzpayne was telling the truth when he maintained it was a trading vessel, sailing out of sight of Japanese attack planes, dodging between islands as they were doing themselves. Maybe.

Or maybe not.

She approached Johnnie and Henry Court, aware of the Japanese pilot eyeing her warily from his usual position at the base of the mast. She couldn't bear to look at him. She had put Pippin on a lead and placed the end of it firmly in Teddy's hand.

"Johnnie, what's going on?"

"We think Fitzpayne must be making some kind of deal with them."

"What kind of deal?"

"We don't know. But we're guessing it's to his advantage, not ours. These men mean trouble for us, that's obvious."

Henry leaned forward, his forehead moist, and in a low voice suggested, "Let's make a run for it. While this Fitzpayne chap is on their boat, let's hoist *The White Pearl*'s sails and make—"

"No," Connie said sharply. "I hired him because he knows these waters. We don't know them at all. I trust him."

"Nigel didn't," Johnnie pointed out gently.

"That's not fair, Johnnie. Nigel is not here."

"I know." He shook his head, his lips tight. "I'm so very sorry."

She nodded. *Sorry* was a slender word.

"Listen to me," Henry insisted, "we have charts. We can navigate ourselves away from here."

"Henry, talk sense. *The White Pearl* is taking on water. She's unstable and slow and in serious need of repair. The other boat would overtake us easily."

"So what the hell is your Fitzpayne talking about to men of that kind? I don't like it."

Connie didn't like it either, but she didn't rise to the provocation. "We shall have to ask him," she said sourly. "I'm sure he has a good reason."

But when Fitzpayne leaped back over the rail, she had her doubts. She had a strange sense of losing the man with whom she had shared cigarettes and sat up drinking whisky after the storm, a feeling that the figure standing before her now—with his dark hair turning to copper in the rising sun and a new, unfamiliar energy to his limbs—was a stranger. Someone who had been hiding inside the man she thought was her friend. Was this the real Fitzpayne? Wilder and more unpredictable, someone she didn't know? *I trust him*, she'd said, but now . . .

He stood on the deck, legs astride, balancing effortlessly on the balls of his feet as each wave swept under the boat, thumbs tucked into his belt, and waited for the barrage of questions.

"Who are these men?"

"What do they want?"

"For God's sake, are they really your friends?"

"Can't you get rid of them?"

But Connie said nothing. She saw the exhilaration in his face, the desire to push ahead with whatever plan he had hatched with his gold-toothed friend, and she knew that whatever they said—Johnnie or Henry or Madoc—he was set on a course.

"So what next?" she asked quietly when the others had finished. It wasn't the past that mattered to her now, it was the future.

He smiled at her. "Next, we change boats."

"No," Henry said vehemently. "I'm not leaving *The White Pearl*."

"I knew you'd say that."

"Well, you were damn right," Johnnie jumped in. "We're not leaving this boat."

Fitzpayne plucked a cigarette from his lips. "Just calm down."

"Have you betrayed us?" Connie asked flatly.

"Of course I haven't." His words were stiff and angry, but his expression was gentle as he looked at her. "The skies will be packed with Jap bombers today, heading for Singapore. Every inhabitant who possesses a boat will be taking to the water to flee the attacks. It'll be like shooting fish in a barrel for the Japs. No chance of escape. Boats like yours," he chose his words carefully, "sleek, elegant craft that shout of white ownership, will be first in the gunners' sights."

"We could hide. Like we did before, in an inlet somewhere."

"No."

"Why not?"

"Don't you realize?" Fitzpayne looked with exasperation at the faces around him. "This boat of yours is sinking. I have done the best repairs I can, but it's not enough. So I have come to an agreement with Nurul that we will exchange boats. We board the *Burung Camar* and sail at speed with a following westerly straight to the island where there is protection for you, while Nurul and part of his crew take *The White Pearl* into hiding. From the island I will send a vessel under cover of darkness carrying sufficient equipment for more repairs to *The White Pearl*, so that she can creep to us one night when she's patched up."

"Why would Nurul help us?" Connie asked.

He laughed, with no attempt at making it convincing. "I've promised him you'll pay him well for his services."

She shook her head. "How do we know we will ever see *The White Pearl* again?"

The question hung between them in the overheated air. His expression of impatience barely altered, except for a shift of focus in his eyes as he stepped closer to her on deck. He said quietly, "I give you my word."

"That's all very well," Henry blustered, "but can we trust it?"

Connie ignored him. "What is the real reason?" she asked. "If it is so dangerous to be in a white man's boat in these seas, why would Nurul take such a risk?"

The slate-gray eyes grew paler as Fitzpayne's eyelids lowered and his lips parted in the beginning of a smile that he refused to let out. "Nurul does it because he is my friend, and because I ask him to." He shrugged his shoulders in mock disdain. "Of course, the money helps."

☙

They argued in private, Connie as the official owner of *The White Pearl* and Fitzpayne as official navigator, both enclosed in the confines of the master cabin. Words were spoken in undertones, fierce and hostile. For Connie, Nigel seemed to rise up in the bed, observing them with his lips pulled into a disapproving line.

"You're one of them, aren't you?" Connie accused Fitzpayne. "One of the pirates, part of their thieving band. I must have been mad not to suspect earlier."

"I work with boats, as do they. They are traders."

"Buying and selling boats, you told me." She flicked her head aside, strands of hair clinging to her damp neck. "You lied to me."

"No, it's true."

She wanted to shake him, to place her hands on him and shake him till the truth rattled through his teeth. She wanted him to say that he hadn't deceived her, that she could trust him with her life and with her son's life, and that he wasn't just an opportunist making money out of her. She wanted him to make her believe him. But instead, he nodded and offered no explanation for his association with Nurul and his thieving band.

"Connie, you and your son have suffered a terrible blow, and it seems to me that it would help if you . . ." He stopped, his mouth tightening over the unspoken words, and she realized he was conscious of a line between them that he was wary of crossing.

"What?" she asked. "If I what?"

"If you get yourself and your son off this cursed boat just as fast as you can."

He turned away from her and ducked his head to gaze out one of the portholes. He scanned the sky for several moments while she stared dumbly at the flat wall of his back in his black shirt, her mind spinning. Was that it? Was *The White Pearl* carrying Sai-Ru Jumat's curse? Connie touched a finger to the gleaming timber wall and felt the heat of it slither under her skin. She snatched it away. What did he mean? Cursed by bad luck, or cursed by this relentless war, or cursed by her own ill-chosen actions? She was suffocating in the silence. With a quick stride he came toward her and the room seemed suddenly too small, too intimate. Neither of them let their eyes stray toward the bed where she had lain with Nigel. Fitzpayne stood close, so close she thought he was going to hold her, but he kept his arms at his sides.

"Well?" he asked.

"I'll go with Teddy. And you? You'll come on the other boat?"

"I assure you, I have no intention of leaving you."

"Good," she said. "Thank you."

He lifted her hand, turned it palm upward, and dropped her gold Cartier watch onto it.

CHAPTER TWENTY-NINE

"They're from Sumatra," Fitzpayne informed Connie, as if that explained everything.

He was referring to the three members of the crew who were sailing the *pinisiq*. He took her by the arm and gave her a quick trawl of the deck, showing her the small hut in the stern where the crew ate and rested. Its roof was low and rounded, made of *attap* fronds.

"No cabins, I'm afraid. When it rains hard they sleep in the hold with the cargo. You have to rough it here."

He looked at her as if he expected an objection, but she made none. She peered into the shadowy interior of the hut. A hummingbird, bright as a rainbow, fluttered in a bamboo cage that hung from a beam, and she lowered her head intending to enter, but three millipedes the length of her hand were crawling along the wall toward her hair. She stepped back. Fitzpayne laughed but didn't release her arm.

"What's in the boat's hold?" she asked.

"Trade goods."

"What kind of goods?"

He gave her a look, but she didn't realize what was coming.

"Rubber."

"Rubber? Hadley rubber?"

"Could be." He laughed again, softly to himself.

She pictured one of the commercial boats carrying Hadley rubber to the port of Singapore for shipment for the war effort, for tires and cables. Boarded by grappling hooks and nets, the cargo stolen and the boat sunk. It had happened before and driven Nigel to bouts of fury.

"I see," she said, teeth clamped together. "What does the name of their boat, the *Burung Camar*, mean?"

"The Seagull."

She nodded. "The robber bird."

He turned her by her elbow to face him. His expression was amused, but there was a tentativeness at the back of his eyes and she realized he was unsure of her reactions, as though she too had changed since the swap of boats.

"Learn not to ask questions," he said firmly. "That way, you'll stay alive longer."

"Is that what you do? No questions, no lies?"

"It's safer."

"Safer? Nothing at all about this godforsaken patch of the world with its man-eating mosquitoes and its bombs is safe!"

"You're probably right," he said with a shrug.

But she wasn't fooled. She'd watched him on the boat. There was nothing remotely casual about the way he had the men jumping to do his bidding, loading on full sail, snatching every scrap of wind from the sky. Or in the way he let his eyes take a break from scouring the clouds for any sign of aircraft to gaze out over the stern.

"Is it Nurul?" she asked. "Are you worried?"

"He is my friend. Of course I worry for him."

That scrawny scrap of a pirate with a gaping mouth like a frog's, flaunting his gold teeth in the sunshine. The one who took her watch, the one who climbed onto her boat with a rifle on his back. He was this man's friend. How did that happen? He was stuck on a white man's yacht that it seemed the Japs would just love to shoot out of the water—because Fitzpayne had asked it of him.

"He looks to me like someone who knows how to deal with trouble," she said, and touched his arm. "Don't worry about him."

He looked down at her hand. "To be responsible for someone's death kills a part of your heart. If you do it enough times, there is nothing left of you. Just the outer shell that eats and breathes and fools people into thinking you're still there."

"Fitz," she said sternly, "I'm trusting you." She banged the flat of her hand against his chest. "There's still a heart in there, I can feel it beating like a damn bilge pump."

She waited for his deep laugh, but it didn't come. Instead, he lifted his hand and placed it over hers on his chest.

"Connie, I'm sorry I couldn't save him for you."

"Don't."

"It will always be there with us, that failure."

"It was the shark. Not your fault."

His lips curled into a slow smile. "You're not a very good liar, are you?"

She exhaled heavily to rid her lungs of the shakes and took her hand from under his. "Just give me a cigarette."

Ͽ·Ꮹ

The native boat moved differently through the water, more like a lean, long-distance runner than the showy sprinter that was *The White Pearl*. Despite the cargo in her hold she scythed through the sea, the westerly wind full in her triangular sails, her rigging muttering with a high-pitched whine of impatience. Connie stood on deck watching the bow wave as it curled away with a flash of white froth across the deep blue water, like a woman showing off her petticoats.

She knew Nigel would be angry if he were at her side. But something inside her was uncoiling, she could feel it, and she lifted her hand to shield her eyes from the glare of the sun as she stared hard, past the *attap* hut on deck to the gleaming stretch of endless blue water that lay behind them. Somewhere back there lay *The White Pearl*. She had abandoned it and everything it stood for, after a fierce argument with the others on board.

"You can remain on her if you wish," she had declared, "but I'm leaving with my son. I trust Mr. Fitzpayne when he says a Western yacht is far more of a target than a native vessel. Surely even you can see that it makes sense."

Yet she was actually surprised when Henry Court and Johnnie followed her over the side onto the *Burung Camar*, Henry with sullen, barbed remarks but Johnnie in silence. He didn't meet her eyes. She knew he was as acutely aware as she was of their mutual treachery to Nigel. He had removed the sling from his shoulder but carried his arm awkwardly, and his lips were pale as though his suffering were squeezing the blood out of him.

"I'm glad you decided to come," she told him.

"Nigel would never forgive me if I let you go off alone."

"Johnnie," Connie said gently, "he's not here anymore."

He leaned forward, kissed her forehead, and sat down on one of the hatches as suddenly as if the strings in his legs had been cut. She lowered herself beside him, the wood uncomfortably hot against the backs of her legs.

"He would forgive you anything," she told him. "You know how fond he was of you, how proud he was of everything you did. He would pick up that photograph of you both that he kept on the piano, smile, and say, 'What's old Johnnie up to now, I wonder?' Then he'd raise his glass to you."

"Did he?"

"And whenever you wrote a letter, he kept it in his shirt pocket until the writing blurred with sweat."

"He never told me that."

"He would forgive you anything," she said again. "Even kissing his wife."

She felt Johnnie's arm tremble and when he turned his face to hers, tears were running down his cheeks.

"You only kissed me that night because I belonged to him, didn't you?" She spoke carefully. "I understand, Johnnie, how much you loved each other and"—she stroked his fingers on the hatch—"I'm grateful that he had you to care for him."

Johnnie's blue eyes stared at her, self-conscious and awkward.

"Really I am," she said. "You loved him more than I did."

つ·ᓂ

Maya saw *Mem* Hadley make Golden-hair cry. It hurt her to see it, stinging like a wasp inside her chest. How did *mem* have such power over him? Maya studied her keenly to spy out her secret, but all she saw was tenderness. In the way her fingers touched his hand, in the turn of her eyes when she looked at him, and in the lilting sound of her soft words. Maya watched intently to learn how it was done, but a wave of guilt suddenly sent a shiver through her that made her teeth chatter. She forced herself to look away. This white woman was an intruder, an interloper, a killer of mothers. What was this power she possessed to climb right inside a person's head?

With a hiss of anger and a shake of her head, as though she could tip *mem* right out of it, she scampered into the cockroach-ridden hut and put a pan of water to boil on the rickety oil stove. Tea. That was what cured a white man's ills; that was what Golden-hair needed.

The boy, *Tuan* Teddy, was seated inside the hut on the stained mat playing with the pirate boat's monkey, a tiny scrap of a thing with huge, dung-colored eyes in a naked pink face with ferocious teeth. It wore a leather belt round its middle and a miniature silver bracelet on each wrist. The boy's dog was regarding it with nervous eyes. Maya had been astonished that *Mem* Hadley had let her son keep the dog after it caused the death of her husband. Maya would have tossed it to the sharks, but white minds were strange countries with tangled, baffling pathways.

It struck Maya as odd that the no-good, weasel-faced Madoc and his fat wife chose to stay with the yacht as well, instead of coming on the *Burung Camar. Mem* Hadley had thanked him and said she was grateful to have someone to keep on eye on it. Aiyee! Weasel-face was getting ready to bite off her fingers. Maybe the Jap planes would blast his skinny bones out of the water when the yacht set sail again. They wouldn't know that Iron-eyes had insisted that the Jap prisoner remain on *The White Pearl* as well until it was repaired.

"You need milk."

Maya was pouring the hot water into a tin mug. She sprinkled black tea leaves on top and looked over at the boy. "What?"

"You need milk in the tea," he explained kindly.

"No milk here."

"Any sugar?"

She inspected their tin box of provisions. "No sugar." She rummaged through it, and held up a squat jar. "Honey?"

"That will do."

She stirred four spoonfuls into the hot water. It didn't look quite right. The tea leaves were floating on top like ants.

"It's for *Tuan* Pilot Jo-nee," she told him.

The boy laughed, came over, and stuck his finger in the honey jar. He took turns licking it with the dog and the monkey.

"Lucky Jo-nee," he said.

Ɔ·Ϛ

The island looked like a crab, except it was green. It was covered so densely with jungle that it formed a carapace that was impossible to penetrate. Maya viewed it with apprehension. It had a high hunched back that rose in the center, and outcrops of land stretching off to the side like claws, ready to clamp onto invaders.

"What is so special about this island that makes it different from all the others?" Razak asked in her ear. His voice sounded sad, and she knew he was missing *Tuan* Hadley. She hadn't told him about her deal with the Jap.

She took his hands in hers. "I don't know. I am sick of new things, my brother. Every day they come at me like arrows, and I hurt all over. I want to sit in a hut on dry land and eat fish and pawpaw stew and speak to no one."

"Except Golden-hair."

Her cheeks flushed, and she glared across the waves at the island. An army of black clouds was marching toward them. It would rain soon.

"Maya," Razak whispered, "he is not meant for you, any more than *Tuan* Hadley was meant for me."

Tears stung Maya's eyes, and the wasps stirred in her chest again. "Who says?"

Her brother's arm curled around her shoulder and drew her to him. "I say."

The ache in her head was comforted by his protection, knowing that he would guard her from the arrows of newness. But the ache in her heart was too big to mention, in case words gave it the power it needed to eat her alive.

ϑ·Ϛ

A solid wall of trees barricaded the island. No white sandy beaches laced its shoreline, and there appeared to be no inlets or inviting creeks where wildlife came to search for turtle eggs. Darkness moved like a living thing behind the tree trunks as Fitzpayne expertly steered a course through the waves that crashed against the mangroves. The long bowsprit heeled to starboard, and the deck trembled and creaked as the rising wind tussled with the rigging.

The air was thick and oppressively heavy, so that when the rain started it came as a relief. Connie didn't mind the soaking. She felt a restless energy that matched the rain's and preferred to stand out on deck rather than in the hut as it pitched and rolled in the grip of a fierce current. Her eyes strained to make out the features of the island, but the curtain of rain made everything obscure and greasy, except for the veins of lightning that flared out of the sudden gloom.

Abruptly, Fitzpayne swung the wheel hard to starboard, and for a moment Connie was convinced they would be thrown against the gray trunks and pitched into the ocean. She seized the rail, but without warning the boom of the waves ceased. The air around her changed color; it became green and shimmering as though they were underwater. Astonished, because she had seen no gap, she realized that Fitzpayne had unerringly found a hidden narrow inlet, and they were gliding under an arc of dark green foliage high overhead.

"What is this place?"

"It has many names in many tongues." Fitzpayne's eyes scanned the riverbanks, where nothing seemed to move except the rain. Yet she could sense his pleasure, as though this place meant something to him.

"What do *you* call it?" she urged. And when he didn't answer she added, "Home?"

He laughed, and there was a certain contentment in the sound. "It's as good a name as any."

ꙅ·Ɛ

The place wasn't at all what Maya expected. She stood nervously on the jetty with the waters snarling at her below the planking, and she wanted to throw herself onto the muddy path, cling to its solid earth, and swear she would never set foot on anything that moved ever again.

"Look up there," Razak said, his eyes bright with excitement.

"No!"

"It's good, sister."

"No!"

"We will be as free as monkeys up there."

"I don't want to be a monkey."

She stamped her foot on the jetty to remind him she was made to be on the ground, but he laughed, entranced by the network of ropes and walkways that was strung through the trees like spiderwebs.

"Come along, Maya." A hand took her wrist. It was *Mem* Hadley. "Let's take a look at this new home of ours."

The rain was easing back to a sullen drizzle, and *mem* gently coaxed her across the planks to solid land. Maya sank gratefully to her knees in the mud, patting its sodden surface with her palms as if it were a dear friend. *Mem* didn't laugh at her but stood quietly beside her, inspecting this strange green world they found themselves in.

"Teddy will love it here," she smiled.

"Yes, *mem*."

"Razak too, I think."

"Yes, *mem*. They foolish men."

Mem Hadley gave a soft laugh, and there was a sound in it that Maya had not heard before, a clear, ringing sound like a bell that swings free of its rope. How could a face look so sad but a voice sing so happy in the same person? Inside Maya, a tight fist that was lodged somewhere below her throat—that had been jammed there ever since *Tuan* Hadley was gobbled by the shark—relaxed its grip a fraction at the sound of it. But she was certain *mem* would not smile at her like that if she knew the real reason that the piss-brain Jap threw the dog in the water.

"*Mem*," she looked around warily, "we in bad shit."

ꙅ·Ꙅ

We in bad shit.

Such frightened words. Connie felt a surge of sympathy for the young native girl. In the back streets of Palur, Maya might have been quick and feral and alert to its dangers, but here in the tangled world of the jungle she was as awkward and ignorant as Connie herself. The long-limbed trees and the grasping fingers of the lush foliage reached out for them; the jungle's rank breath hung over them.

Connie understood why Fitzpayne had brought them here to an island that hid its face away from the outside world, but as she stared beyond the narrow river where all manner of different boats already rode at anchor, she felt a stab of alarm. The high canopy that masked them from the sky was not made up of just the boughs of trees that towered sixty feet, even a hundred feet, over the silver thread of the river. There were nets up there, slung from the branches on one bank to those on the other, allowing the creepers to weave their stems in and out of the netting, climbing and twisting until a green mat blocked out the sky. It felt like a prison.

From the riverbank no buildings were visible, just a network of rope pathways high up in the trees, but as Fitzpayne led them in single file along a narrow track deeper into the forest, Connie became aware of movement and sound around her. She hung on tight to Teddy, with Pippin tucked under her arm. Figures peered down at them from above. Shouts reached them, and hands were raised in greeting to Fitzpayne. They followed dim green tunnels that converged in a sudden and unexpected explosion of light as a clearing opened up before them.

Connie wiped sweat from her forehead. The humidity here was something solid; she had to drag the air into her lungs by force. Still the green light, still the netting and matted foliage overhead, but it came as a relief to see an open space. She was finding the closeness of the trees claustrophobic and the smell of rotting vegetation suffocating.

"This," Fitzpayne announced to his group of six followers, indicating

the single large building in the center of the clearing, "is the Kennel."
His eyes darted from person to person, gauging reactions, and lingered
longest on Connie's son's face.

It didn't look like any kennel Connie had ever seen. She glanced up
and caught sight of a man perched on one of the rope walkways forty feet
up under the canopy, a rifle in his hands. It was pointed directly at them.

"May we go inside?" she asked. She didn't want Teddy to see the rifle.

"Let's take a look," Johnnie said.

"Be my guest. But you may not like what you see," Fitzpayne warned.
He led them up a set of steps and under a lintel carved in the shape of
a lizard.

The building was constructed of bamboo, up on stilts and with a
roof of dripping fronds, every upright post carved with intricate designs
of animals and insects. It smelled strongly of wood smoke. The single
room was about sixty feet long, and whatever Connie expected to find
inside, it was nothing remotely like the scene that confronted her. The
noise of it hit her first, a howling of banshees. A band of twenty or more
children—of varying ages and all shades of skin color—were standing
in a circle, bare feet leaping up and down on the timber floor, shouting
with frantic excitement. Small fists punched the dusty air.

At the center of the circle between the dark heads Connie caught
sight of a flash of golden brown and a flurry of a glossy green wing. With
a sickening lurch she realized what was taking place here: a cockfight.
A tall skinny native kid with a bare chest and one milky eye was holding
a pile of coins cupped in his hands and grinning widely. She turned away.
Her distaste was reflected in the faces of Johnnie and Henry, and together
they stepped back quickly toward the door, but she could feel her son
tugging to draw closer to the circle of boys.

"No, Teddy," she said sharply.

"Savages!" Henry declared.

But Fitzpayne laughed disparagingly and tossed a silver coin to the
skinny boy who snatched it out of the air. "On the small drab bird."

"Yes, sir, Mr. Fitz." The boy automatically bit the coin with his strong
white teeth to test its worth.

One of the cockerels screamed piteously, and Connie saw that the spurs on the back of the birds' legs were elongated with metal tips. Blood spattered the boards underfoot. She swept Teddy away. It annoyed her that Fitzpayne encouraged the fight.

The losing bird, the one Fitzpayne had bet against, uttered a piercing shriek as its golden breast was ripped open and feathers flew. The feathers fluttering in the hot and humid air, a tantalizing lure, were too much for Pippin. He had endured the shouts and the scent of blood with restraint, but the feathers broke him. He leaped out of Teddy's arms, leash flying behind him, shot between the bare legs, and hurled himself at the bright green throat. A quick snap, and the bird hung loose from his jaws. There was a roar of fury. The children fell on the dog. Teddy went for them, fists flying, and with a curse Connie leaped in among the small assailants to extract her son.

"Stop it, you savages!" she shouted, dragging a ferocious urchin off Teddy's back.

She waded into the squirming bodies, knocked heads together, scooped up Pippin, and dangled the animal high in the air above the children's heads. The tall skinny boy picked out a pebble from his pocket and launched it at Teddy's head, but her son was too quick. He ducked and the pebble whistled past, catching Henry Court on the elbow, but Teddy jumped forward and his fist landed a solid left hook on his attacker's jaw. The boy bellowed.

"Enough!" Fitzpayne roared.

He strode into the melee, delivering well-judged kicks and cuffs until order was restored.

"Well," he growled at them, "that's a fine way to greet our guests!"

But Connie could see the grin lurking at the corners of his mouth. What was it with men and fisticuffs? Johnnie was smiling too, nodding approval at Teddy, who emerged with a bleeding lip and a torn shirt, his face still crimson with rage.

"Here," Connie said crossly, dumping Pippin in his arms. "Take better care of your dog."

"No dogs," the skinny child yelled, clutching his ribs.

"What?"

"He's right," Fitzpayne allowed. "No dogs are permitted on this island. They are too much of a sign of habitation, and they're impossible to keep quiet."

She stared at him, stunned. "You knew that when you brought us here."

He turned to her son. "I thought your dog would make a good breakfast for someone."

Teddy didn't scowl or protest. To Connie's astonishment, he squared up to Fitzpayne and burst out laughing, a joyous young sound that she hadn't heard in a long time.

"Pippin will eat that boy for breakfast if I order him to!" he declared.

"Then you'd better keep the creature on a tight leash," Fitzpayne muttered, and ruffled a hand through Teddy's messy hair. Finally he allowed his grin to surface. "Come!" he ordered.

ᗺ·ᘜ

Connie liked living up high. It gave her a different perspective on the world. Everything on the ground looked small. Up here, under the treetop canopy, she felt the sea breeze cool against her cheeks and heard the birds so clearly that at times she thought they had perched inside her head by mistake. On the sea she had felt small, a tiny speck in a vast expanse that any wave could dash from sight at a whim, but up here she felt tall and all-seeing. Oddly powerful.

Nigel would have hated the weirdness of it. Stuck in a bamboo hut forty feet up from the ground, while a tropical storm lashed down on the flimsy roof and a monkey sat chewing on a pawpaw fruit at eye level with her. Connie had made herself a brush out of spiky twigs and was growing used to sweeping out invading spiders and millipedes, lizards and frogs and even thin, whippy snakes that made her shout for Teddy.

Getting Maya aloft had been a problem. Maya had sobbed and begged and swore she would sleep in the Kennel, but no. It was another of the rules. *Nobody sleeps on the ground.*

"Why not?" Connie had asked Fitzpayne.

He had shaken his wet head, spraying rainwater like a dog. "Because if anyone slinks onto the island uninvited at night, the place must look deserted. By day we have lookouts and sentries to watch out for intruders, but at night it's harder to spot them."

A rope ladder hung down from one of the trees to reach the huts in the leafy canopy. Maya swore she would rather die.

Fitzpayne grinned at Connie and gestured to the bag on her shoulder.

"Do you have a scarf in there?" he asked.

She rummaged and pulled out a silk blouse. He took it from her and let the material flow through his fingers. It was a strangely intimate moment, as though he were handling her, rather than her blouse. He tied the blouse around the eyes of the wretched Maya, tossed the girl over his shoulder, ignored her kicking feet, and bounded up the ladder with ease. Connie wondered what on earth it must feel like to be man-handled so roughly. Nigel had never stepped beyond the bounds of courtesy, not once. But Nigel wasn't here.

"Up you go, Teddy," she called.

He scampered up as nimbly as a gecko, Pippin draped nervously around his neck, and she followed after them, careful first to tuck her skirts into her underwear to give her some privacy. Henry came puffing up behind her, then Johnnie, awkward with one arm. Razak brought up the rear. The rope walkway swayed alarmingly when she stepped on it.

"All right?" Fitzpayne asked.

"Of course."

"You'll get used to it."

"How long do you intend to keep us here?"

"As long as you like, Mrs. Hadley." He dropped Maya on the walkway and led her, whimpering, through the branches at a speed the others had to struggle to keep up with.

"Damn the man," Henry muttered behind her. "He's enjoying this."

"We won't be here long," Johnnie assured him. He was scanning the sky through the branches and netting. It was like looking through the bottom of a green bottle. No sound of aircraft engines, not yet.

Connie could hear the restlessness in his voice, and she could only guess at his yearning to return to his squadron. He never mentioned the subject, and he carefully sidestepped any questions if she raised it, but she saw the look in his eyes when he gazed skyward. At least he had an aim, a future to dream of. That was more than she had.

CHAPTER THIRTY

*M*em." Maya eyed the silent figure warily.

The two of them were in the hut. Maya hated it. It was not natural to live in the sky, but she could only go up or down the silly-pissy ladders when Razak helped her by carrying her on his back. She would shut her eyes tight and pretend she was asleep. She had been astonished when Iron-eyes had dumped her in this hut with *Mem* Hadley and her son, and declared that they must share it. *Mem* had not murmured, but Maya was embarrassed.

She had glared at Iron-eyes. "Not right," she told him. "Not right at all."

"Maya, just do as you're told for once."

He had marched off along the rope path, sweeping aside the branches that hung in his way, leading Jo-nee and the fat *tuan* to a hut in another tree, and showed little patience for their caution. *Mem*'s hut was tiny, just long enough to lie down in, and had three rattan mats on the floor for them to sleep on. That was all. A slatted bamboo blind covered the window hole, and another was gathered above the door frame. Maya inspected *mem*'s face for disapproval but found none.

"This is exciting, isn't it?" *mem* said to the boy, who was still clutching his dog as though frightened that the other wretches might climb up and eat it.

"Yes!" he agreed with an eagerness that startled Maya. "We're living in a treehouse."

His mother laughed, but she looked as if something still hurt bad inside her. She took the dog from him and set it down on a mat. Its black eyes shone in the gloom and it gobbled up a passing butterfly.

"Now, you must both behave."

Maya thought *mem* was talking to her and she nodded obediently, but no, she realized *mem* meant the dog and boy. *Mem* bent down, kissed her son's wet hair, and stroked the dog fondly. Maya wondered if she sat quietly on the mat next to the dog whether *mem* would stroke her head, too. Since *Tuan* Hadley's death, Maya could feel herself bound to this white woman. Sometimes she could even hear her mother's evil cackle of laughter when the winds blew in the trees. Sai-Ru Jumat was wicked in life, and now she was wicked in death, goading her daughter, never giving her any peace.

Maya slumped in a corner and wished Razak were not so far away. She knew he would be racing up and down, exploring, while she was marooned up here, with *Mem* Hadley. It was as if her life and *mem*'s life were hooked together now, as tight as one of the rope ladders.

ɔ·G

The aircraft came, a whole swarm of them buzzing like hornets. They flew low with machine guns blasting at some unfortunate boat caught out on the open sea. Maya jammed her hands over her ears and bent double, with her forehead touching her knees.

"Teddy," she heard *mem* say with no shake to her voice. Why was she not frightened? "You must remember never to use your father's binoculars here."

Her son carried them around his neck, and he fingered their casing constantly as if it were part of his father. "Why not, Mummy?"

"Because they may glint in the sunlight and give away our position to an enemy plane."

"Oh, I didn't think of that." He stared solemnly at the binoculars.

Maya would have snatched them from him and thrown them out of the hut. Bad binoculars. *Mem* trusted him too much. It occurred to Maya that *mem* was good at trusting.

"All OK here?"

Maya's stomach did strange things. She looked up quickly and smiled at the figure in the doorway. It was Jo-nee, his golden hair the color of seaweed in the green light.

"Yes, we are fine, thank you, Johnnie," *mem* replied.

"Hear that machine gun?"

"It's horrible. It could easily have been us in the boat if Fitzpayne hadn't brought us here."

The sound of a heavy bomber droned overhead.

"They are out in force today," *mem* said.

"It's bad news for Singapore, I'm afraid, Connie."

"Fitzpayne told me that the retreating British army is blowing up bridges to slow the Japanese advance down the peninsula to Johore."

Golden-hair shook his head. "That's not going to stop them."

"Nothing will."

"No British tanks, and not enough bloody planes. What was General Percival thinking? He's let us down badly and now we've lost everything."

Maya listened and could not understand how they could stay so quiet. If she were them, she would scream and cry and slit the throat of every Japanese on earth.

"And you, Maya?" He stepped into the hut, lowering his head because he was so tall. "Are you OK up here in your eyrie?"

He smiled, and she smiled back shyly. "What is *eyrie?*"

"It's the home of an eagle."

"Hah!" She looked out the doorway at the swaying branches and immediately felt dizzy, but she copied *Mem* Hadley and kept her voice calm. "But I not eagle or monkey. I ground-rat." She twitched her nose at him and made him laugh.

"I'm going down. Do you want me to help you descend the ladder?" he offered.

"I no fool, I stay here. No ladder." She glanced at *mem*, who was standing by the window hole, gazing out with a face that had gone far away. A big speckled spider was walking slowly around her hand on the ledge, interested in the pale white skin. "I look after *Mem* Hadley," Maya said in a small voice.

Jo-nee looked at *mem*. "Thank you, Maya. She needs more help than she will admit. Come on, Teddy," he added brightly, "let's go and see what we've let ourselves in for on this island, shall we?"

They vanished, and the hut became drab and gloomy again. For a long time neither Maya nor *mem* spoke, and a blade of green light slid through a gap in the roof fronds. It edged its way toward Maya's bare feet, and she drew them away. When it cut a slice off *mem*'s shoulder, she shuddered.

"*Mem*," Maya said when her thoughts became too heavy to hold inside any more, "I sorry you sad."

The blue eyes looked round at her, surprised. "Thank you, Maya." She ran fingers through her blond hair as if to brush out the memories that left such shadows on her face. "In wartime, many people grow sad."

"Shark not know it wartime."

Mem laughed. "You're right. But if it weren't for the war, my husband wouldn't have been on the boat in the first place." She paused and lifted a grasshopper from the hem of her skirt. "There are always *ifs* in life, Maya. If there weren't a war, if we had stayed in Palur, if I hadn't rescued the pilot from drowning, if I hadn't driven the car the day your mother crossed the street . . ." She stopped and smacked her hand on her knee.

Maya didn't know if she was squashing an insect or squashing her thoughts. For a while, no words came out, but Maya could feel the little hut waiting for more. She could feel her own ears wanting more.

"Tell me, Maya, what would you like," *mem* asked suddenly, "if you could choose anything?"

"Bowl of rice and chicken satay."

Mem smiled. "No, I mean, what would you like for your future . . . if you get out of this alive?"

"That easy. I like plenty food. And a bicycle."

"A bicycle?"

"So I not walk-walk-walk all time."

"And where would you ride this bicycle of yours?"

"All places."

The blue eyes studied her gravely. "You don't ask for much, do you, Maya? You are not greedy like some. Nothing else?"

Maya lowered her eyes. *Mem* was looking at her too hard; she might see too much. Maya picked at a patch of dry mud on her ankle and scratched it away, but she couldn't scratch away the words that climbed onto her tongue. "I ask I be pretty and gold-haired and white like you. But nobody listen."

"Oh, Maya."

A shout somewhere farther along the walkways made them both look up, and their gaze met and held.

"You *are* pretty, Maya. Your skin is . . ."

"Horrid dark."

". . . your skin is like velvet. It's beautiful. But more importantly, you are clever and you learn fast. You should be proud of yourself."

"Why *Tuan* Jo-nee Blake so sad?"

Mem blinked, caught off balance by the switch of subject, but in Maya's head it was the same subject.

"Johnnie is sad because he can't fly his plane. And because he and my husband were close friends, long before I met either of them. They were at school together, and he misses Nigel now."

"Razak miss *tuan* too."

Mem Hadley's face closed up tight, like the lid of a box slamming shut. Maya could tell that *mem* did not like Razak. But suddenly she whipped the silk blouse out of her bag once more. "Maya, come on, it's time that you and I both faced our fears. The blindfold for you and for me . . . I am going to speak with your brother."

꩐·꩐

Connie strode along the narrow trail, mud churning beneath her feet. It was a dark brooding place that Fitzpayne had brought them to. Its steep slopes were crowded with dense jungle that towered over the narrow gorge carved out by the river. The pervasive sound of bird calls, monkey shrieks and booming bullfrogs bore down on her, trapping her under the green netting, and all the time she heard the pattering of Maya's small feet on the track. It struck her as strange how she and the young girl seemed to need each other now in an odd sort of way, and she found it comforting to have her muttering behind her.

Figures flitted in and out of the trees. Some were on the forest floor, but most were high on the walkways or leaning out of the window holes in the huts up there, smoking cigarettes and watching her. No one came near her, no one spoke to her. Had they been warned off?

She saw no women.

She retraced the track back to the Kennel, but the children had vanished and in their place a group of seven Chinese men were squatting in a circle on the floor, industriously mending fishing nets, fingers shuttling back and forth at high speed. One halted his work long enough to beckon to her. They wore ragged tunics over loose trousers, and the black watchful eyes of all of them fixed on her as she approached. They chattered away in Chinese and nodded to each other. Maya mewed nervously and hung back in the doorway.

Connie stood over them and smiled politely. "I'm looking for a young Malay man who came here with me. His name is Razak. Do you know where—"

"Missee," the oldest Chinese spoke. His face was crisscrossed like old leather, but his eyes were sharp. "We sail tonight. We go west to Ceylon. You come?"

"Pardon?"

"You come with us." His lips spread in a thin smile. "We save you." One of the others murmured something to him.

"And your girl," the old one added, glancing across at Maya.

Dust hovered in the humid air along with the stink of fish. Connie took a step backward. "No, thank you."

"We pay." With a flick of one hand he lifted a cloak at his side to reveal a silver box. "We pay missee good," he said.

He was so polite, Connie could scarcely believe he was offering to buy her.

"No." She took another step away from them.

He chewed on his bottom lip and covered up the box once more. "Your Razak is with Fitz. Much work in pit." He gestured off in the direction west of the Kennel.

"Thank you," she said, bowed courteously to her would-be purchasers, and left before Maya could even think of saying yes.

ᗡ·ᗡ

She found Razak with Fitzpayne in the pit.

Only Fitzpayne's head and naked shoulders showed above ground level; the rest of him was immersed in a hole in the forest floor about six feet square. His hair was spattered with wood shavings, and sweat gleamed in a green shimmer over his skin. He was wielding a pickax when he caught sight of Connie striding up the trail toward him, and he stopped in midstrike, the pickax's metal head poised in the air. She became aware of her skirt sticking to her legs, and under her breath she cursed this damn climate. Beside him stood Razak.

"Mr. Fitzpayne, you are . . ." She was going to say *busy*. She could have added *working like a native*. But her eyes registered what else lay in the pit other than himself and Razak: vicious rows of sharpened stakes pointing up toward the sky, their tips honed into lethal spears lying in wait for the unwary. The blood in Connie's veins, so hot a moment ago, turned cold, and her tongue froze to the roof of her mouth.

He dropped the pickax and jumped easily out of the pit. Up close she could smell the sweat and the timber on him, and the earth beneath his fingernails. For a moment she thought he was going to touch her, but he stayed his hand before it made contact with her arm.

"Are you all right?" he asked with concern.

"Of course. I've just been hurrying in the heat." She pulled the brim of her straw sun hat down so that it shaded her eyes.

He moved back, and for one nightmare second she thought he would fall into the pit. "Fitzpayne, careful!"

But all he did was offer a hand to Razak to haul him up. Razak was also stripped to the waist, and Connie was again struck by how beautiful his body was. *My poor Nigel, it must have been unbearable for you.*

"What are you doing?" she asked Fitzpayne. As if it weren't obvious.

He shrugged, his muscles flexing under his damp skin. "Preparing."

She didn't ask for what.

"Have you settled into your hut?" he inquired. The change of subject wasn't exactly subtle.

"Yes." She laughed. "Thank you, it didn't take long to unpack my belongings: a book, a hairbrush, and a change of clothes. Oh, and a needle and thread. I intend to turn my skirt into trousers."

He glanced at her legs, his gaze lingering on them. "I can find you some trousers . . . if you wish," he offered.

He was embarrassed. That surprised her.

"I certainly won't be running along this path too often," she assured him, and took another look at the pit.

"There are others," he warned.

Visions of spikes plunging through her son's young chest rushed into her head.

"Where?" she demanded.

"Don't look so worried. It's safe. They are boarded over at the moment."

Once more she had that odd sense that he was about to touch her. "I wish to have a word with Razak, if you can spare him for a moment."

"Of course." He bounded back into the pit and hoisted his pickax. "Attend to *Mem* Hadley, Razak."

Another man emerged from the forest with more stakes over his shoulders. He was of Indian blood with thick curly hair, and Fitzpayne introduced him as Supp. His long, sleepy eyes turned on her and Maya with an interest that he made no attempt to disguise until Fitzpayne clipped the tip of his friend's boot with his pickax. It made him curse.

"Take no notice of Supp," Fitzpayne smiled. "He possesses no manners."

"It strikes me that this island of yours is noticeably short of women."

"There are a few women here," he said, the smile still caught on his lips. "But yes, this island is short of women like you."

Connie wasn't sure what he meant.

৯·৫

"Razak."

"Yes, *mem*."

"I have something to ask you."

"Yes, *mem*."

Connie had not spoken to Razak since the day of Nigel's death. Her anger at him had blocked the words, but now she could smell the sadness on his young frame, as acid as stale sweat.

"Did you order the Japanese pilot to throw the dog overboard?"

His large round eyes looked stricken.

"No, *mem*, no. I . . . no, *mem*, no . . . I . . ." He choked back tears. "No," he said finally. "No. Why I do that?"

"To hurt me. To hurt my son."

"No, *mem*. I not hurt you. You belong to *Tuan* Hadley."

She believed him, believed that he would have done nothing to hurt Nigel. Suddenly she was able to see the figure before her not as the malicious hand of his dead mother, but as just a sad young boy, dazzled by her husband's power and wealth and attention. Just as she had been dazzled all those years ago by Nigel's promises of the exotic.

"I'm sorry, Razak," she said softly.

He lowered his head, and a tear that gleamed green in the strange underwater light slid down his cheek. "I sorry too, *mem*."

CHAPTER THIRTY-ONE

Madoc liked having *The White Pearl* to himself. Kitty had gone ashore to stretch her legs and to get away from him. She wore a beautiful pair of high riding boots that had belonged to Nigel Hadley and relished stamping on leeches that wafted up from the leaf mold.

"I'll stamp on your fucking head too, Madoc, if you don't talk sense," she had growled at him before stalking off the boat.

They'd had a row. He hated quarreling with Kitty. He couldn't bear to see the way her eyes aged physically when they argued, the spidery lines around them growing deeper. He was waiting for her to return. The boat was well hidden in the mouth of a narrow muddy river, tucked under some areca palms, while on the opposite bank lay a fringe of sand, where their three companions were digging for bait.

He had to admit that the damn pirates knew these islands the way he had once known the streets of London, every twist and turn and secret back alley. He spat down into the water. When his path had crossed Fitzpayne's before in Shanghai, Madoc had come off worse in a difference of opinion over shipping Russian girls to brothels in the Philippines. He'd had to leave Shanghai after that, in a hurry. This time he was being more careful. He'd started playing cards with Farid, the pirate from Batavia, the one with the nose like a camel's and the simple mind. Bit by bit he was gleaning snippets of useful information from him, and next session he was planning to gamble a box of Hadley's Havana cigars, but he didn't tell Kitty that. Madoc was willing to be patient. Oddly, it was Kitty who was in a God-almighty rush to take the boat and skedaddle as soon as the hull was patched up.

"No, Kitty. Let's get her properly repaired in that bastard's island workshop, and then—"

"Then they'll be too many for us. We'll never get *The White Pearl* away. Can't you see that, you pea-brain?"

He'd sighed. "No, Kitty. When she's in good trim we can make a run in her, southeast to Australia or, if you want, west to Ceylon and India. New territory for us, a new life, where—"

She had slapped him, a round-armed flat of the hand. "Don't push your luck, Madoc. We can handle these three pirates; the odds are in our favor, even though the boss man, Nurul, watches you like a hawk. Even now, while he's working on the beach, he has one eye fixed on you and I'm bloody certain he will want to know what this row is about. I bet you he'll sidle over the minute my back is turned, offer you a beer, and get you talking. Just make sure you think before you speak."

Now Madoc scanned the edge of the forest for any rustle of branches, any sign of her return, a flicker of her white cotton blouse, but the black mass of trunks had swallowed her. He worried about snakes and poisonous spiders, but she would have slapped him a bloody sight harder if he had dared forbid her to go off on her own. He looked down at the bottle of Tiger beer in his hand. Damn her, she'd been right about Nurul. Nevertheless, he smiled to himself and lit another of Hadley's Dunhill cigarettes from the butt of the old one. There was something Madoc didn't intend to tell his wife. After a few beers the gold-toothed pirate had confessed a weakness for blondes, and for one blonde in particular— the one who had given him her Cartier timepiece.

Watch your step, Fitzpayne, or you may find the blade of a Malayan kris so deep in your back you'll be eating your own fucking heart.

Ꭹ·Ꮹ

"Mr. Fitzpayne, I'd like to see over this island of yours . . . if you have time."

"I wondered when you'd ask."

Fitzpayne finished sharpening the tip of a wooden stake and placed it on top of a pile of them. Other men who were working beside him had melted into the forest at Connie's approach, glancing back at her with distrust, their faces dark-skinned and suspicious.

"They don't like my being here," she commented.

"Of course not."

"Why?"

"Because you are a foreigner and therefore an enemy."

"But so are you. A foreigner, I mean."

He nodded and reached for his shirt on the ground. The muscles of his stomach gleamed flat and hard. "Out here in East Asia we are all foreigners," he said, "and we have to give them reason to want us here. Reasons to trust us."

As he slipped his shirt over his head, there was a sudden roar of aircraft engines, and without comment or even glancing up, Fitzpayne pulled her deeper into the shelter of the forest. Her mind seemed to flatten, skidding away from her.

"It's all right to be frightened," Fitzpayne said gently. "It's wartime. Everyone is frightened."

Her back was jammed against the bark of a tree that was crawling with ants. One hand was shaking.

"Where's Teddy?" she whispered.

"He's safe."

"Where?"

"I'll show you."

ᗘ·ᘐ

It was like walking into hell. The smoke, the heat, the resounding noise that made the air in her lungs vibrate and the stench of hot metal. All rushed at Connie the moment she stepped into the massive underground chamber.

"Our workshops," Fitzpayne announced.

There was an arrogance in his words. Connie studied his face by the uncertain light of the kerosene lamps and saw pride in it. This place might be communal but it was his doing, she had no doubt of that. It was a long, arched cavern with earthen walls. Blacksmiths' furnaces lined one wall where men with glistening backs bent over anvils and hammered molten metal into shape with blows that exploded in Connie's ears. Flames sent twisted shadows crawling up the wall.

"Doesn't the smoke from these fumes give you away?" she asked.

"No. It is vented into a side chamber and released only at night. That's when the cooking fires are lit too—in the Kennel after dark."

"I'm impressed," she shouted above the noise. "No wonder you want to bring *The White Pearl* here."

"Come with me."

He took her hand and led her toward a heavy door in the side wall. It swung open into another cavern, clearly an additional workshop, but this one was stacked with timber. Fitzpayne shut the door firmly behind him to keep out the smoke and pointed out two tapering masts that ran along the center on trestles with men sanding them down to a smooth finish. Elsewhere, saws rasped teeth against seasoned wood, and Connie noticed the ribs of a rowboat held into curves by metal clamps.

"This is where we are making the repairs to send out to Nurul for your yacht, enough to bring her here for a proper overhaul." He frowned at her. "Don't look so worried! She'll soon be—"

"She doesn't feel like *my* yacht any more. The connection has gone."

He straightened his shoulders, and she had a sense of him shifting a weight on them, one that sat uneasily. "Perhaps it will come back. When all this is over."

"When all this is over we will no longer be the people we were."

He nodded a quick decisive gesture before he turned away. "Take a look at your son."

"Teddy?"

She followed the line of his hand. Buzzing around the workmen like industrious bees were four young boys, each with a broom made of twigs in his hand. They wore cloths tied around their heads to combat the sawdust in the air, no shirt but short trousers chopped at the knee and rope sandals on their feet. Three of the boys were brown-skinned, but one was white and had his back to her.

"Teddy?" Connie said softly.

Her son was sweeping up a pile of wood chippings and heaping them into a burlap sack. He moved eagerly, and she could tell he was enjoying himself, rummaging in the dirt and the mess. From a woven rattan basket that hung on his chest poked the black head of Pippin, his tongue licking sweat from Teddy's salty skin.

"Good heavens!" She turned to Fitzpayne. "How did that happen?"

"A boy needs to work for his supper here," he smiled.

"So young?"

"The younger the better." He glanced to one side, where the tall skinny boy from the fight in the Kennel was extracting nails from old timber with a pair of pliers. "It's the only way he'll be accepted here."

Connie felt a warm sense of gratitude to this man, who seemed to understand more about bringing up her son than she did herself.

"And Johnnie?" she asked. "Have you got him and Henry digging pits for their supper?"

He laughed, relaxing, and she realized that he had feared she would snatch Teddy out of there. Didn't he know her better than that?

"Near enough," he chuckled. "They're both in the Kennel, stripping fibers from climbers to plait ropes. Blake's arm is up to that."

"And Maya?"

"That little wildcat took one look at the box of fish I told her to gut and vanished."

Connie nodded. "That sounds like Maya. So what about me? What work are you setting me to do to earn my supper?"

He observed her, arms folded across his chest and one thick eyebrow raised, his black stubble glistening in the lamplight. He shrugged. "You can sew, so you said."

"Damn you, I can do more than sew."

"What?"

"Something more useful."

"Can you cook?"

"No."

"Can you chop down a tree?"

"No."

"Can you repair a net?"

"No."

He seized her elbow and steered her down a small dark tunnel and out into the fresh air. It was pouring with rain. In less than five seconds they were soaked.

"Then you will sew," he told her. "I will tell the men to bring you what needs doing."

"What about the other women on this island?"

He gave her a slow unamused smile. "They cook. And certainly there is no other honey-haired beauty with a throat the color of her pearls."

He walked away into the forest, leaving Connie standing alone on the trail in the rain, and she wondered how on earth she had managed to annoy him this time.

꒐꒦

There were rules on the island. Any infringement of them was punishable by death by hanging. No argument, no discussion. No judge, no jury. A rope over a tree. Quick. Instant.

No swimming in the sea in daylight hours.

No boats in and out, except at night.

No guns to be discharged.

No telescopes.

No mirrors outside huts.

Fights to be conducted with fists, knives, or boat hooks. *Boat hooks?*

Cooking to be carried out only in the Kennel.

Blackout to be observed. Blinds and shutters closed after sunset.

No torches.

No chickens, no goats, no pigs, no cows, no cats, and no dogs.

NO FIRES.

Connie looked at the list. How Fitzpayne had gotten around the dog rule for Pippin she couldn't imagine, but Teddy was keeping his pet firmly in his bamboo basket strapped to his body during the day, and allowed him a run only at night. Connie had to admit that all the rules made sense—to prevent discovery by the outside world. But the severity of the retribution made her nervous. She had never encountered such hard men before among the soft-fleshed colonials. It made her look at Fitzpayne more cautiously, knowing he was one of them.

The newcomers were marched into the Kennel as soon as it grew dark on the first evening and made to stand against a wall in front of a line of ten men, as grim-faced as a firing squad. The large room was smoky and hot from two cooking fires that burned brightly at each end, hovered over by a group of older women in dark headscarves. Between them, the intervening space was crowded with men, curious to inspect the Europeans. The smell of fish stew hung thick in the air and made Pippin drool down Teddy's naked chest. Teddy himself was standing upright, his head high. Connie was proud of her son's courage. She didn't take his hand, aware that he had chosen to stand between Johnnie and Henry, to be one of the men.

"No fire. No fire."

It was the fourth time the man had said it. He was a lean and wiry Mawken, with dark skin and rimless spectacles perched on his broad nose. He wore a brown shirt over a straight black skirt that came to his ankles, and he stood in front of his ten men with his chest puffed out, as self-important as a general in front of his troops.

"I am Badan." He thumped his chest. "I say no fire." His black eyes narrowed as he inspected each one of them at his leisure. When satisfied, he pointed a finger at Connie. "You understand?"

"Yes."

"You light fire, you die."

"It's a bit harsh," Johnnie commented mildly.

"That's the rule!"

Beside Connie, Maya squirmed and clutched Razak's hand. He was regarding the line of men with keen interest. Connie glanced around and spotted Fitzpayne through the smoke slouched against a wall, with a glass of something in one hand and a cigarette in the other. He was watching her carefully. She inclined her head to him, and he responded by raising his glass to her.

The bespectacled man, Badan, suddenly stepped closer, too close. Connie's heart bolted to her throat, but he didn't come for her; he came for Maya. He took a handful of her long black hair in his fist, making the girl whimper. He yanked her forward and there was a murmur of approval in the room.

"You," he spat at her. "You lit fire in hut."

Maya's eyes grew huge. "*Tidak!* No!" Her small hands entwined around his arm, beseeching him. "Let me go." She tried to sink to her knees, but he held her up on her feet.

"You lit fire. You cook water in hut." He dragged her to the center of the room and glanced up to where a thick greasy rope was looped around a roof beam overhead.

"*Tidak!*" she screamed. "No!"

"No, stop it!" Connie shouted, and darted forward. She seized Maya's wrist. "She did not light a fire. It was only a tiny oil stove that we brought with us, a small single flame to heat water, no real cooking. She made a cup of tea, that's all." The tea had been for Johnnie. "Leave her alone."

"She hang," Badan stated. It was said to the men in the room.

Connie could smell their hunger for the girl, more overpowering than the stink of the fish stew, and she felt a wave of fury so fierce it made her hands shake. Badan saw it and smiled with satisfaction because he took it for fear. Already someone was reaching up with a pole and unhooking the rope.

"Mr. Badan," Connie said, carefully emptying her voice of anger, "be reasonable. None of us knew of the fire rule then. It was a mistake for which we—and Maya—are deeply sorry. It will not happen again, I promise you. It was just to make a cup of tea on the little stove that we brought in our box of provisions."

She turned her attention to the line of ten men.

"I have whisky in my provisions box," she announced, and smiled at them.

One man wearing a dark green bandanna stepped forward, breaking ranks. "How much whisky?"

"Only one bottle. But it's good Scottish whisky."

Out of the corner of her eye she saw Badan take hold of the rope. On the end was a noose.

"And these," Connie said loudly.

Her hands went to her throat and detached the string of pearls. She trailed them through her fingers so that they clicked gently and caught the light, glinting like milky stars.

"They will buy whisky for all." She turned to Maya, took her trembling hand, and slowly poured the pearls into it. "Maya would like you to have them as an apology for her actions."

Maya stood rigid, teeth chattering.

"Nod to them," Connie muttered.

Maya nodded.

"Say sorry," Connie urged.

"Sorry." The word was the croak of a tree frog.

Connie saw the men's eyes fix on the set of perfectly matched pearls. "Agreed?" She smiled at the faces, her pulse so loud in her ears she couldn't hear their words but saw their lips moving and their heads nodding. She drew Maya toward her.

Badan snatched her back. "She broke rule," he shouted, and slipped the noose over the girl's neck.

Razak started to shout something urgent in Malay, but it was Johnnie Blake who stepped forward with an air of reasonableness and said pleasantly, "Look, old chap, I know your rules are important. You have to make sure any passing aircraft or boat doesn't spot smoke on the island, but the poor girl didn't know that she wasn't allowed to light a measly stove." He spread his smile to include the other men. "Let's be fair about this. She was just making me a cup of tea."

Badan tightened the noose and Maya screamed. The air seemed to thicken, and there rose a strange sound that resonated in Connie's head. It came from the crowd of men, shuffling their feet up and down on the dusty floorboards, and even the group of children huddled in a far corner had stopped their play and risen from their knees to do the same. She had no idea what it meant, but it felt bad.

"Stop it, you fools."

It was Fitzpayne speaking. He sauntered across the room, as though the matter were of no great moment. He was wearing a dirty shirt and he'd wound a strip of soiled cloth around his head, so that he looked more like one of them, an island pirate, than the skipper of *The White Pearl*.

With an easy grin to the ten men, he said, "But I have ten crates of whisky aboard the *Burung Camar*, just ready and waiting for a buyer."

"Where's it from?" someone shouted. "We don't want monkey piss."

"No, it's from a white man's cellar. He was stupid enough to take it away with him on his fine schooner on the Indian Ocean and"—his grin widened—"I decided to relieve him of the burden of it out of the kindness of my heart, to enable his yacht to sail away faster from the Japs."

Someone laughed. Someone else shouted, "I want to see the girl hang."

A rumble of dispute rippled around the room. Badan gripped the girl tighter. "She hangs."

"Very well," Fitzpayne said, unconcerned, and lit himself a cigarette. "You choose."

He flicked a glance at Connie and the pearls, then walked over to the wall, picked up a purpose-built wooden box lying there, and dumped it under the roof beam where the rope was attached.

"Go ahead. Don't let me spoil your fun," he said. "But ten crates of whisky would entertain you all night instead of for five minutes."

Connie immediately moved closer to the pirate in spectacles, took the string of pearls from Maya, and slipped them around his arm, fastening the gold catch so that they hung like a loose bracelet on the hand that clutched Maya's hair. A moment of silence took the room by the throat.

"Whisky?" Connie asked the men. "The pearls will buy the ten crates of whisky."

There was a collective murmur.

"Whisky it is," Fitzpayne responded. He waved a hand, and two men disappeared into the wet night to fetch the crates from the *Burung Camar*'s hold. "Let's have some music," he shouted. "Come on, Wong Yee, give us a tune. Chop-chop."

A young Chinese woman detached herself from the cooking pot, bowed politely over her hands, and let out a short burst of Cantonese that Connie didn't understand. She was wearing a long dark dress, and from within its folds she drew out a nose flute. She fitted it with deft skill to her left nostril and began to breathe. A thin silvery sound filled the room and hung suspended on the night air as the notes rose and fell in a haunting melody. Razak stripped off his shirt, stepped forward, and began to dance, a slow, graceful flow of movement with hands and fingers curved backward as they wove capricious patterns in the smoky room, creating a story. All eyes focused on him as his naked skin glistened like polished amber in the lamplight.

While everyone was watching Razak, Connie detached Badan's fingers from Maya's hair and slipped the noose off her neck. Fitzpayne removed the necklace from the pirate's arm and folded it out of sight in his palm.

"These are payment for the whisky, Badan," he said.

"Pearls worth more than your swamp whisky," Badan snapped.

"The deal is done."

"*Bajak laut!*"

To Connie's astonishment, both men burst out laughing. Instantly the tension and hostility dissipated, and when the pirate removed his spectacles to clean them, Fitzpayne gave him a comradely slap on the shoulder. Without a backward glance at Maya, as though the fuss had been over nothing, Badan ambled off toward the fish stew.

"What does it mean?" Connie asked quietly. "*Bajak laut?*"

He looked at her, but the laughter was gone. "It means *pirate*."

"And is it true?"

"That I'm a pirate?"

"Yes. Are you one of them?"

He leaned close. "If I weren't one of them," he said in a low tone, "you would all be dead by now."

"Would he really have hanged Maya for so little?"

"Of course."

CHAPTER THIRTY-TWO

On the island, Connie felt her mind slowly unhitch from the orderliness of her previous existence. Days passed; she wasn't sure how many. She grew lazy. And she went native. She donned the short oriental trousers that Fitzpayne supplied for her, and a drab green shirt that she wiped her fingers on whenever they were muddy—which was often. Around her head she twisted a strip of muslin from her skirt, which kept the sweat out of her eyes and made her less conspicuous among the dark-haired islanders.

She stood for hours looking out at the rain. It came down in great lashing torrents day after day, wrenching branches from trees and silencing the bickering of the gibbons. It dislodged her thoughts. It swept away images of her past, flushed them out of her mind, so that she had difficulty recalling the exact shade of brown of Nigel's hair, or the smell and texture of Sho Takehashi's pale skin, both of which she thought were indelibly imprinted on her brain. But this strange green world seemed to swallow her, to spill into her head. It swamped her old world in a way that at first startled her, but then pleased her.

Her anguish over past mistakes faded, and when she rested her head against the door frame of her hut up in the trees and came eyeball to eyeball with a speckled brown spider the size of her fist, she discovered that another kind of anguish had also faded. She knocked it onto the walkway outside and watched it run from the bombardment of raindrops. She slept on her mat whenever she felt like it during the day, or found a trail alongside the river when she wanted to walk, but otherwise she just stared out at the rain. She lost the rhythm of her days. She didn't go down to the Kennel for evening meals, but someone—Teddy or Maya—always brought her something from there: a chunk of fish, a scoop of rice or an *otak-otak*, which was new to her, delicious spicy fish patties wrapped in banana leaves and grilled over a fire. Sometimes she ate the food, sometimes she didn't.

Each morning she made an attempt at pursuing Teddy's schooling—a regime of reading, writing, and arithmetic—but as they bent over the books together, their eyes would meet in silent collusion and the lessons grew shorter and shorter. He would kiss her cheek and dart down the bamboo ladder with Pippin in his basket, with an alacrity that should have made her worried but didn't. It made her happy. Happy that he was happy. Every day more garments or sheets of canvas were brought to her to mend, but they gathered in a pile that grew steadily higher. Pippin curled up on it at night.

Slowly, a little more each day, Connie's past ceased breathing down her neck. As she lay awake on her mat listening to the rain or to the night murmurs of her son, she allowed nothing but the present inside her head.

ꃓ·ꃕ

"Are you sick?" Fitzpayne asked.

"No."

"Are you hurt?" He stood in the doorway of the hut.

"No."

Connie was stretched out on her mat in her shabby shirt and trousers, enjoying the sensation of the hut swaying in a high wind, forty feet above the ground in a storm.

"So what's the matter?"

"What makes you think anything is the matter?" she asked.

"Do you know what time it is?"

"As if that is important here." She rolled her head to the side and looked out through the window hole, where the green light outside looked fractionally brighter. "Noon?" she suggested.

"It's time you got up."

She laughed. The figure of Fitzpayne was backlit in the doorway, so she couldn't make out his expression, but his voice sounded amused.

"You haven't touched the sewing," he pointed out.

She closed her eyes. "I'm . . . stopping."

"Stopping what?"

"Stopping being Constance Hadley."

A silence filled the hut, a silence so huge she was astonished it didn't shoulder the roof off and leave them defenseless in the rain. Her eyes remained shut and she didn't hear his feet cross the boards, but she caught the scent of his wet hair and the faint sound of his breath, so she knew he had moved closer.

"I rather liked Constance Hadley the way she was," he told her quietly.

"She's gone."

"Gone where?"

"She has gone to live on *The White Pearl*."

Suddenly his foot nudged her ribs, startling her. Her eyes popped open. He was standing over her, a tall, powerful figure. "So who is this?" He nudged her again with his foot. His face still lay in shadow. "Who is this lazy creature, too bone idle to lift a finger?"

She smiled up at him. "This is Connie."

"Hello, Connie."

"Hello, Fitz."

"Are you the one who owns the kid who is running around like a savage and making the other ignorant urchins pay him in gifts to read stories to them?"

Connie leaped to her feet, eyes wide in horror. "What?"

"Hah! I thought that would get you out of bed."

꒷꒦

She found her son. And she found his stash. He was crouched with his new friend, the tall skinny lad named Akil who had caused him such grief that first day in the Kennel. They were under an old dugout canoe that was jammed over a cleft between two rocks, forming a shelter of sorts. She spotted them only because Pippin's black tail was swishing through the wet sand.

"Teddy! Come here at once."

For a moment she thought he was going to disobey her, but eventually, with a sullen droop of his head, he squeezed from under his hideout and faced her squarely. She took his arm and marched him out of earshot of the other boy.

"Teddy, what are you doing?"

"Nothing."

"I've heard that you are charging to read stories to the other children."

He scuffed his feet in the dirt.

"Is it true?" she insisted. "Tell me."

He shot a glance over toward Akil, who was now squatting under an umbrella of broad spiny leaves about ten feet away, a frown on his face.

Reluctantly Teddy nodded. "Yes," he whispered. "But I deserve it. I translate stories into Malay for them because their English is so bad."

"Teddy, these boys have so little. It's wrong to take from them."

He pulled his shoulder from her grasp. For the first time she noticed the muscles developing under his skin, the thickening of his upper arms from the physical work he was doing here, and she wanted to squeeze him to her and hold him tight. But she remembered the words she'd said to Fitzpayne about the old Connie having gone, and spoke in a stern tone.

"Show me," she said.

"Show you what?"

"What you've taken from them."

His shoulders slumped. "You'll confiscate them."

One of his father's words.

"Maybe. Maybe not. Show me."

He trotted off ahead of her, bare limbs streaked by the rain, and led her to an old metal box that he had hidden in the hollow of a fallen tree. Flakes of orange rust speckled his fingers like measles as he opened the lid. Inside lay a miniature morgue. A small bat, two chameleons, several geckos and lizards, horny black beetles, and even a yellow and red moth larger than her hand. No birds, she noticed.

"Teddy, why on earth have you acquired such a macabre menagerie?"

"To dissect them, of course."

"Is this all you took from the boys?"

"Yes."

But she knew her son too well. "Don't lie to me." She held out her hand. "What else?"

Slowly, miserably, he drew something from his back pocket and placed it on the flat of her hand. It was a shiny gold guinea. They both stared at it. He was his father's son when it came to business. Connie knew she couldn't take it from him.

"Teddy, do you like it here?"

"Yes."

"Why?"

He scratched at his wet hair. "Because I can choose what I do."

She felt a small but permanent crack open up between them. "So why the sad face?"

He lowered his eyes. "I feel bad."

"Why bad?"

"It's complicated."

Another of his father's phrases when he didn't want to explain something.

"Try me."

"I'm only free because Daddy's not here." His voice grew small.

Gently she stroked the wet strands from his face. "There is always a price to pay for freedom, Teddy."

He kicked at a log and dislodged a beetle, which he stared at with interest.

"You may keep the coin," she said. "But in exchange, there's something I want you to do for me."

༘·༗

"Good God Almighty! What kind of place is this?"

Madoc stood on the deck of *The White Pearl* and looked around him while the rattle of a chain sounded in the stern as Nurul dropped anchor. The busy walkways under the tree canopy made him think of the inside of a beehive, but this one was a strong, dense green, humming with energy. It was almost dark now. The sun had slid gracefully behind the island's hunched back as they entered the shadowy inlet.

"What do you think?" Kitty asked at his side.

"Interesting."

"See the rifles?"

Up in vantage points in the trees men stood watching their arrival, rifle barrels resting on their forearms. "Quite a welcoming party."

"I warned you," she muttered under her breath. "We should have made a run for it when we could."

He flicked a ragged moth from the tangle of her hair. "I admit I didn't expect this place to be so organized."

"Madoc," Kitty whispered. "Let's go tonight. Take the boat. They won't be expecting that."

"Smile nicely, Kitty. Our friend is here to greet us."

She swore and glanced over to the riverbank, where Fitzpayne was standing, arms folded across his chest. He wore a knotted scarf around his head and gnarled leather boots up to his knees, and though Madoc could see no gun, a heavy parang hung at his side. *The White Pearl* made the other boats look as dull as turtles, her elegance drawing envious eyes from among the trees.

Madoc slipped his arms tightly around Kitty's ample waist, and together they studied the shore, conscious of Fitzpayne's gaze. "We won't be here long, I promise you that. It occurs to me that there are people who would pay top dollar to know that this hideout exists."

She leaned her weight against him. "Take care, Madoc. Look at that bastard. Don't imagine that he won't have thought of that."

"That may be. But he doesn't know that I've discovered from Farid— Nurul's poker-playing pirate—where Fitzpayne hides a secret shortwave radio on board the *Burung Camar*."

The strength of her smile made Madoc decide that the loss of the cigars had been worthwhile.

৯·৫

"So you're still alive, I see." It was Fitzpayne.

"Still alive and kicking," Madoc responded.

"What about the Jap pilot? Killed him off yet?"

"Your friend Nurul certainly had a good try a few times, but no, he's still with us."

"I'll tell Nurul to throw him in the hold of the *Burung Camar*."

"Quite a setup you have here in the trees," Madoc remarked.

But Fitzpayne turned on his heel and strode off into the gloom of the forest, leaving Madoc and Kitty to follow behind. The evening air was thick with mosquitoes and felt like soup in Madoc's lungs after the clean breezes of the open seas, but he was too intrigued by what he was seeing around him to care about the discomfort. His eyes darted everywhere. Someone had designed a clever fortress here. Sentries loomed above him armed with rifles and sharp eyes. Kitty nudged him in the back from behind, as if to say *I warned you*. Fitzpayne was prepared for everything.

"How long has all this been here?" he called out to Fitzpayne as they fought for footing on the muddy trail.

"Long enough."

"I'm surprised I haven't heard whisper of it before. Such places are hard to keep secret."

"We have a way of keeping it secret," Fitzpayne said over his shoulder.

"What's that?"

"Anyone who talks is killed."

"Jesus Christ! Simple but effective."

"I advise you to remember that."

As he continued to walk behind Fitzpayne, Madoc let his fingers crawl over the Tokarev pistol tucked in his waistband, hidden away under his shirt. Something else that was simple but effective.

"I haven't seen any workshops," he said, peering into the gloom. "To repair the boats in. Where are they?"

Fitzpayne stopped so abruptly that Madoc almost crashed into him. "The trouble with you, Madoc, is that you ask too many questions."

"No harm meant," Kitty intervened pleasantly. "We're curious, that's all."

"Haven't you heard that curiosity killed the cat?"

With a sweep of his hand, Fitzpayne pushed aside the dense curtain of overhanging foliage that obscured the clearing beyond and led them up a set of steps into a long meeting hall.

"This is the Kennel," Fitzpayne announced. But as they ducked their heads to walk through the doorway, he lowered his voice and added, "Watch yourself here, Madoc. These are not men who take kindly to an intruder with a gun stuck down his trousers."

Kitty grabbed a handful of Madoc's backside and squeezed it so hard that it felt like a damn dog bite. "Stupid shit," she growled at him, and pushed past into the dimly lit chamber.

The shutters were closed, and a handful of native women were tending a fire to cook the evening meal. Huddles of men were seated on the floor, playing cards and mah-jongg or whittling shapes out of driftwood. But most of them just sat and smoked rough cigarettes or strange-smelling clay pipes and drank beer by the gutful. There was no welcome for him and Kitty, just the usual hard-eyed stares and suspicious muttering. That was OK. He didn't intend to hang around any longer than was necessary.

Down the far end, a bunch of kids sat in rows, dirty knees akimbo, reciting in unison something they were being taught. He spotted the Hadley boy among the dark heads, and Razak as well, but his attention was taken by the way Fitzpayne slipped easily into the inner life of the hall, greeting, laughing, and offering smokes. He became a part of it all as effortlessly as chameleons ripple up and down tree bark, almost invisible.

"Madoc." It was Kitty.

She thrust a sheet of cardboard into his hand. He squinted at it in the poor light and saw that it was a list of rules. He scanned them and frowned at Kitty, but she wasn't paying attention. Instead she was staring open mouthed at the children.

"Just kids," he said.

"Look at their teacher."

He looked, indifferent at first, at the slight, graceful figure sitting so relaxed on the floor in front of the children. She was leaning over one of them, listening with a solemn expression to what the urchin had to say. A length of soiled material was wound around her head, and she wore clothing that was too big for her. It was only when she raised her head to attend to another child that it dawned on him who she was.

"Constance Hadley!" He shook his head in disbelief. "She *has* changed."

"That's an understatement," Kitty chuckled.

"She's cut her hair."

"She looks . . . not European. Her bones all flow together, not stiff boards like the colonials. We've seen men go native out here, losing their Western ways, but never a woman."

Madoc's gaze swung around the noisy chamber, and he noticed numerous men staring openly at their children's white teacher, as they fingered their beards and watched the wisps of golden hair escape her headcloth and dance in the lamplight.

"She'd better be careful," he said under his breath to his wife, "or she will stir up trouble for herself."

Kitty slipped her arm through his, letting the side of her breast bump against him, reminding him to whom he belonged. "No fear of that," she said. "She has her protector."

"Who?"

She cast her eyes at the man standing in the shadows.

"Fitzpayne?" Madoc said, surprised. "Really?"

"Oh, Madoc, how can men be so dense?" She laughed, puffed out her cheeks and walked over to Fitzpayne. "What have you done to her?"

Fitzpayne didn't take his eyes from Constance Hadley, but his face seemed to loosen and he almost smiled. "What has she done to herself?" he asked softly.

ϑ·ϭ

Madoc cursed the moon. It was too bright. It shone like a torch down through the darkness onto the riverbanks, its slippery light penetrating the netting and foliage overhead. He stood tight against a trunk and listened.

Nothing. Only the slap of the water and the usual wild clicks and cries and whirrs from the jungle's night chorus. A wind rattled the leaves and tugged at the rigging of the boats. At least half of them had weighed anchor and gone, presumably moving on or maybe just out doing what pirates do, but *The White Pearl* lay at anchor downriver from the *Burung Camar*. Beauty and the beast. For an hour he remained in the dark shadows of his tree and waited until finally a sentry grew bored and showed himself. Madoc smiled with satisfaction as the man lit a cigarette—which clearly had to be against camp rules—but now that Madoc knew exactly where the watchful eyes were positioned, high up on one of the platforms, he moved upriver, forging a path through a thick stand of bamboo. He chose a section of the bank that was overhung by branches and slid silently into the water.

It was colder than he expected, but he set out with a strong stroke that carried him quickly into midstream. He hated the water. It was muddy and foul in his mouth, but worse was his certainty that it was packed with other creatures, and not ones he cared to meet. When the current hit, he went under, but he kicked strongly against the flow and bobbed back up to the surface. The moonlight fell as white as ice on his face, and he let himself be carried a few yards before striking out once more and finding an anchor chain to grasp hold of.

He clung there in the shadow of the boat, drew breath, and took his bearings. *The White Pearl* was directly ahead, the *Burung Camar* hiding just behind her, her mast as sharp and silver as a needle. He turned in the water to check the platform back on shore. The cigarette had vanished in the darkness. He felt his heart kick at his ribs but convinced himself that he was invisible to any watching eyes, nothing more than a dark ripple in the river.

He spat filth from his mouth as a wave broke over his face, and he swam with a sudden surge of energy in his limbs. He could taste greed, along with the filth, and this time he was determined to make Fitzpayne pay. The thought of his shortwave radio tucked away in its hiding place was too enticing to resist. When he reached the rope ladder that hung down the side of the *Burung Camar*'s timber hold, he hauled himself up out of the water.

CHAPTER THIRTY-THREE

Connie crouched in the shade of a crooked mangrove tree and poked a stick into a small pool of seawater trapped among its roots.

"Having fun?"

She looked up, startled, shielding her eyes from the early-morning sun. "Hello, Fitz." She smiled a welcome and then frowned at the end of her stick. "It's not working."

"What's not working?"

"My stick."

He laughed and squatted down beside her to inspect her pool. "What have you got in there?"

"A crab. A big one. He's hiding under that tangle of roots at the side." She prodded the stick into the hole, stirring the green water into life, forcing a sea snail to the surface but no crab.

"I've been looking for you," he said.

"Oh? What for?"

He removed the stick from her grasp.

"You're not bold enough," he said.

Not bold enough.

"With the crab?" she asked.

Their eyes held for a moment. His irises appeared almost blue today, warm and interested. She was aware of his shoulder only inches from her arm, a sliver of heat-laden air between them, and the way his legs folded up under him like a grasshopper's with long muscular thighs. His knuckles were thick and tanned by the sun as he held her stick.

"You should do it like this," he said, and gave three hefty jabs at the crab's hideout.

Instantly there was movement and a blur of scarlet shell as he yanked out the stick with the crab attached to the end. It was holding on for grim death with its one huge, overdeveloped claw, too angry to let go.

"A soldier crab," Fitzpayne declared. "They are fighters."

Connie heard the respect in his voice. "Is that what you are, Fitz, under the veneer of good manners? A fighter? Is that why you're here?"

He placed his hands on either side of the crab's shell, cupping it delicately so that it couldn't attack his unprotected fingers with its massive claw. "You and I are both fighters at heart, Connie," he said, but he didn't look at her. Instead, he raised the soldier crab aloft for her to examine its underside. Behind him, between the trees, the sea was a dazzle of peacock blue, and a stiff wind cast strings of foam over the surface of the waves. "We fight for what we want, each in our own way."

She reached out and touched the crab's hard shell, scratching her nail into a crack where its leg was jointed. "But everyone has a weak spot." She smiled at him again because she didn't want to argue. "And some of us are better than others at hiding it."

"So, what's your weak spot?"

"Oh, it's not so hard to guess."

"Your son, Teddy?"

"Yes."

"He seems to like it here. In no hurry to leave."

"I know. He's enjoying finding out what he's capable of."

"He's not the only one." She felt his gaze on her face. "But you know it can't go on forever, don't you?"

Connie flushed. Here she was, dressed in appalling clothes, poking at a crab and talking to a pirate about her weak spot, while Japanese planes cruised overhead at will. Of course it couldn't go on forever. On impulse, she removed the miserable crab from his grasp and tumbled it back into the water. "But I like it here, the way my crab likes his pool.

I fish for food, I sleep on a rough mat alongside the ants and wash in a muddy river. At the moment it's enough."

"And teach English to the kids, don't forget."

"Yes, that too." She nodded at him with a smile. "I enjoy that."

"And watch your son turning into a fine soldier crab," he laughed.

She reached for his hand. "Fitz, I cannot thank you enough for what you've done."

Her words seemed to float between them. She saw his expression change. Saw him retreat from her. Saw the tightening of the muscles in his face. Despite that, she raised his hand to her lips and softly kissed the back of it. It tasted salty and smelled of crab shell. Fitzpayne withdrew his hand at once, creating a distance between them, and rose to his feet. His movements, normally so agile, were stiff and awkward.

"I came to tell you something," he said in a formal tone.

Connie stood. She looked him straight in the eye. "What is it?"

"The Japanese pilot is dead."

He spoke with brutal calm.

"What happened to him?" she breathed.

"His throat was cut. In the hold of the *Burung Camar*. We don't know who, most probably someone who got wind of his presence and decided that the only good Jap is a dead Jap."

He gave her time, let her gather herself. She shook her head mutely. Neither spoke, but she leaned forward and let her forehead fall against his collarbone. She rested it there as his arm encircled her shoulders.

"Why should I care so much?" she murmured against him. "I tried to kill him myself, but"—she hesitated—"there were too many voices from the past."

He touched her hair. "Tell me what happened in the past."

So she told him. Not about Sho; no, not about him. But she told him about the car accident. It all came spilling out about killing Sai-Ru Jumat, about wanting to make up for it by taking care of the woman's two children, Maya and Razak. She struggled to explain that saving the Japanese pilot was supposed to repay a life for a life. To appease, to placate. To display her penitence.

"It was meant to make everything right," she whispered, "but instead it made everything wrong."

His arm still encircled her and held her against him, not close enough to hear the beat of his heart but close enough for some of the turmoil to be drawn out of her by the stillness of him. He talked quietly. About taking what she needed from the past and leaving the rest behind, about knowing her own weaknesses and, even more important, her own strengths. About making choices for her son and for her boat. Yet not once did Nigel's name pass his lips, or the concept of a tomorrow. Instead, his words brought her to focus on this moment, this place where they stood together beside a murky pool among the mangroves. Connected in some vital way she didn't understand.

He lifted her face from his chest and kissed her forehead, wrapping her in his arms without a word for so long that the shadows grew shorter and banished from her mind the awareness that another bad death had come stalking her.

꒰·꒱

It's not what your eyes see that matters. It's what your brain sees. Connie pushed her way through the jungle, and it struck her that its light no longer seemed gloomy to her. It felt soft and shaded. The beetles on the bark were no longer ugly and black, but iridescent creatures capturing a rainbow on their backs, and the branches no longer crawled with the menace of snakes and spiders but flourished with life.

It's what your brain sees that matters.

Sweat still ran down Connie's skin, cicadas still sounded incessantly in her ears, and a troupe of monkeys still squabbled unseen in the trees, as irritating as children fighting in a playground. But she smiled as she clambered over fallen trunks, her limbs full of new energy, and her brain opened up to the immense beauty of the island. For the first time she looked properly at the long, succulent leaves and the rich red soil under her feet. She inspected strange, fingerlike creepers that twisted up a hundred feet toward the light and gazed at the butterflies that spun through the air like bright confetti.

Her brain changed what her eyes saw. Somewhere at the core of her a heavy coffin lid had lifted. It was the lid she had slammed shut on her hopes and dreams, condemning them to the grave that was her marriage. But now it creaked open, and light flooded into those dark recesses. How could she not have known? So blinded by death that she could no longer see life, could no longer see love.

She still felt the weight of Fitz's arm against her shoulder blade where he'd held her, and still smelled the scent of his skin, as she'd breathed him in. Yet she could not reconcile the Fitz in the Kennel—the one who stole boats and drank with cutthroats who hanged people for fun—with the Fitz on *The White Pearl* who was generous and dependable. But as she walked, she smiled to herself at the memory of his eyes, as mutable as the sea itself, and the way the muscles along his jaw flickered when he was trying not to smile. During the storm at sea, his hand on her arm had lashed them together in a bond that she had not understood until now.

Abruptly a twig snapped nearby in the forest, barely audible, and she was convinced that Fitz had come back to find her. But instead, directly in front of her on the trail, stood Nurul. Pinpoints of sunlight sneaked through the tree canopy and speckled his mahogany face, glinting off the gold tombstones that beamed in his mouth as he grinned broadly at her.

"Good morning, *mem*. You lost?"

"No. I'm heading back to the camp now."

Nurul had been the one who broke up her moment with Fitz. He had approached them with a loud whistle among the mangroves and told Fitz something in Malay, something that sounded urgent. Fitz released her reluctantly and she'd stepped back, regretting his retreat.

"What is it?" Connie had asked.

"I'm needed in the workshop." He stroked her cheek briefly, a soft caress. "I'm sorry."

"You go," she'd said. "Go and fix whatever you have to fix."

"You'll wait here?"

"In my hut. It's more private."

He'd nodded, his hair tossed across his eyes by the wind. But it was clear he didn't want to leave her, and he lingered for a moment more among the mangroves, his eyes unable to abandon her face. "This is a greedy and savage war," he said. "Promise me, Connie, that you will take good care of yourself. Promise me now."

"I promise." She wanted to touch him again but didn't, not with Nurul listening to every word and watching every gesture. "Don't worry about me."

"Fitz," Nurul interrupted, flapping his hands in the air, "you need hurry."

Fitz vanished. In seconds his outline merged with the trunks as he strode away, but first he had stepped right up close to her and brushed her lips with his own. That was when she finally understood.

Nurul was standing in her way now, blocking the narrow trail, still grinning at her, and Connie was reluctant to go around him. It would mean forcing her way through the undergrowth on either side, with its leeches and vicious thorns.

"Has Mr. Fitzpayne finished already?" she asked.

"No, he work on *Pearl*."

Still the grin. Still the path blocked.

"Thank you for sailing my yacht safely to this island, Nurul."

"I happy sail."

Still the path blocked.

"May I pass, please?" she asked politely.

The teeth vanished back inside his head, and the lines on his face that a moment ago had seemed so friendly suddenly rearranged themselves and became arrogant. He swelled out his chest.

"I like you," he said in a solemn voice.

A blade of fear slid under her ribs.

"I am honored." She bowed her head to him.

"I like you much."

His hand darted out and seized a lock of her hair. She recoiled, snatching it away, and wanted to run back the way she had come, but she was wary of turning her back on him.

"Nurul, you are a good friend to Fitz."

He nodded. "He owe me."

"I don't think he would be pleased that you are—"

He pulled a narrow box from somewhere inside his trousers, and his eyes shone with pride. He held the box out to her. "You like," he said.

It was a midnight-blue velvet case for a piece of jewelry, green mold freckling its surface. She started to shake her head.

"No. Thank you, Nurul, but definitely no."

His face creased like old leather and he jerked the box open. It was the most lavish necklace Connie had ever laid eyes on, a set of shimmering diamonds the size of birds' eggs held in a filigree of white gold. Her eyes widened in horror.

"From a Russian princess," Nurul boasted. "Now for you." He pushed it at her.

"A dead Russian princess?"

He shrugged, removed the necklace from its satin nest, and lifted it to her neck.

"No, Nurul. Thank you, but no. I am not interested." This time she took several steps backward and continued to retreat down the trail, still facing the man who wanted to buy her with looted Romanov jewels. Did all these pirates believe women were for sale?

He was coming after her. "No!" This time she shouted it at him, her heart jammed in her chest, hot and unwieldy. Still she wouldn't turn her back on him. It was how she had always handled an ill-tempered dog—face it down—so that when Nurul shot out a hand to seize her arm, she was ready and slapped it away.

"Don't! Stop this! I am not interested in—"

He struck her. The speed of the attack caught her off guard. She reeled backward, her head ringing where his fist had slammed into her ear. Before she could recover her footing he was on her, throwing her against a tree, knocking the breath out of her, with his body crushing hers. There was a scornful joy in his black eyes as his legs forced hers apart while his hands pulled and squeezed and invaded. She screamed. But she knew that the jungle would swallow her voice. She raked the side of his face with her nails, but it didn't stop his fingers tearing open her shirt and seizing her breast.

He was too strong. Connie fought him, kicked and thumped and sank her teeth into his cheekbone, tasting blood. But still his hands moved relentlessly over her body, dragging at the waistband of her trousers. A fierce drumming raged in her head and she struggled to clear it, to think without panic because she wasn't going to win this battle on strength alone. She let her limbs go limp, allowed his mouth to take bites of her neck and his hand to crawl into her trousers, degrading her.

Then, when he was panting hard, she opened her mouth and screamed, "Fitz! Thank God you're here!"

It was enough. Nurul jerked back, half turned his head to look behind him. In that split second when his attention was elsewhere, she slammed her head against his nose with all her strength. Blood splattered over her skin and up into her nostrils. The pirate whinnied, high and ragged, his face a scarlet mask of fury, but before he could recover she crashed her knee into his engorged groin. He buckled, but still one fist gripped her wrist. She leaned over him, snatched his knife from his belt and drove the point of it so hard into the back of his hand that it stuck there, swaying. He made no sound, but his fingers slowly opened up to release her, and his eyes fixed on her with hatred.

Connie didn't wait to finish the fight. She turned and ran.

꒷·꒪

Still he came after her. She thrashed her way through the undergrowth, her heart juddering in her chest, her hands striking out at branches, indifferent to leeches and thorns or the snakes that slithered away from her running feet. She had to carve out a path for herself. But all the time she could hear Nurul baying behind her, his curses reaching out to her, and she was under no illusion what he'd do to her if he caught her.

But now the jungle became her friend instead of her enemy and opened up dark green spaces for her to slink into. Thick foliage enfolded her. Curtains of creepers hung down around her, silencing the noise of her movements, and when her feet found a narrow animal track, she raced along it with gratitude. Sweat poured from her skin, and her breath came harsh and raw in her throat. Was this what she had been reduced to? An animal hunted through the forest? Did it take no more than one brutal man to strip her of decency and the trappings of humanity that she had wrapped around herself so carefully for all those years on the Hadley Estate?

She paused in her flight, listening hard. Her hands were quivering. She could have killed him. When she snatched up Nurul's knife and plunged it into his hand, she could just as easily have plunged it into his heart, but she hadn't. She still had a hold on herself, on who she was and how far she could trust herself. Life was something so precious that she could not allow herself to treat it cheaply.

The images of death kicked into her head. Sho's body laid out for a monitor lizard. Sai-Ru Jumat's eyes opened wide and full of blood in the sunshine. The old man crippled in the street of Palur, Harriet with the crimson flower on her forehead. Nigel's hand raised above the waves when the rest of him had gone from her. Images that, during her idleness, she thought she had banished.

"Thank them, Nurul," she whispered, "that you live. When you could have died."

ꏞ·ꏝ

"Fitzpayne."

Connie spoke his name aloud. Not that he could hear it, but to comfort herself.

"Fitz, which way?"

She was lost. An hour? Two hours? More? How long had she been tramping through the jungle? She'd stopped checking for the sound of pursuit because Nurul had long ago given up on her and was probably hunched in his hut, pouring gin over his wounds. At one point when she stumbled across a mossy stream, she washed her face and found her cheek swollen and split where he had punched her. She'd squatted beside the trickle of water, peering upward at the snatches of blue sky that flashed between the foliage of the canopy, observing the progress of the shadows and trying to decide which direction was west.

"Fitz," she said once more to the green space around her, "you're the damn navigator, not me. Give me a clue."

In the end she decided to follow the stream. Common sense told her that it must reach the coastline eventually, and from there it would only be a matter of time before she found the camp.

ঙ·ৄ

The stream abandoned her. It plunged under a fall of rocks and vanished, leaving her alone in the forest. She continued to struggle in the direction she believed was west, and found herself talking aloud to Fitz. Telling him things. About the kite she flew off the cliff at Beachy Head and the desire she had to copy it, to spread her wings and fly in the face of the wind.

When she heard a dull booming sound, it took her a full minute to recognize what it was. Waves.

She ran.

"Fitz, look! The ocean. I'll soon . . ."

Her tongue caught on the words. She was higher than she'd realized. She must have been climbing all the time in the jungle, and was now poised on the edge of a low escarpment that overlooked a vast expanse of blue water and a white sandy beach that dazzled the eyes. She dropped to her knees, shuddering with relief. But her hands had to clamp over her mouth to silence the cry that sprang from her lips.

Below her, about five hundred yards away, stood row after row of men. They were listening in the scorching heat of the sun to the words of a squat figure who strutted in front of them, jabbing at the air with a sword. Every single man on the beach wore the uniform of the Imperial Japanese Army.

ঙ·ৄ

What was it with men and war? With guns and rifles? Violence seemed to draw them like wasps to a melon.

Connie wiped sweat from her face. She stared down in disbelief at the beach and at the two attack boats that lay at anchor offshore, as fear crawled like a cockroach down her throat. She ducked her head lower into the undergrowth and started to edge backward. She had to warn Fitz. Had to find Teddy, find her son. Get off this island. What had brought the Japs here? She heard her own breath coming in great gasps. She knew she had to get back to the camp fast.

Fitz, help me.

The warm steel of a bayonet bit into the skin of her throat. A hand seized her hair from behind and yanked her to her feet, and she caught the smell of stale sweat and leather. A voice jabbered something at her, words she didn't understand. The pressure of the blade eased a fraction and she slowly turned around to face the man behind her. The moment their eyes met, he released his hold on her and stepped back a pace, waving the bayonet under her nose.

She didn't know which of them was more frightened. He was a young Japanese soldier with a gentle child's face, his mouth soft and barely formed. He looked no more than fourteen and must have lied about his age to be taken into the army. His black hair under his cap was cropped viciously short, and his uniform appeared new and scarcely used, as though this were his first guard duty. He clutched the bayonet nervously in his hand while Connie fought to bring to mind the few words Sho had taught her.

"*Konnichiwa*," she said. "Good day."

His eyes narrowed. He retreated another step before releasing a torrent of words that meant nothing to her. She kept her attention on his eyes, dark and dangerous in their fear, rather than on the blade that still threatened her.

"*Hai*," she said. "Yes."

She moved forward as though to listen more closely, but he instantly backed off farther and started to pull his rifle from his shoulder. While he was half distracted by the awkwardness of handling both the rifle and the bayonet at the same time, Connie recalled the lesson she'd learned from Nurul and struck. Hard and fast, when he least expected it. Her fist smashed into his throat.

He tottered backward, screeching, but she knew she couldn't stop now, so she clamped her hands on his rifle and saw his terrified eyes widen with horror as she wrenched it from his grasp. She flicked the rifle over so that she was holding it by the barrel, raised her arms, and swung it at the young boy's narrow chest. But neither he nor she had the heart for this fight. He ducked in an attempt to evade the blow and she hesitated at the last second, which tipped them both off balance. All the rifle did was nudge him, and all the Japanese soldier did was topple over backward, but his heel became caught on a root half buried in the leaf mold behind him.

He fell awkwardly, and the snap of a bone was audible to both. He opened his mouth wide and let out a silent scream that would take its place alongside the other nightmare images lodged in Connie's brain, but she didn't waste a second. She snatched up the bayonet from the ground, slung the rifle over her shoulder and raced off into the jungle.

CHAPTER THIRTY-FOUR

Maya was searching for Jo-nee. Sometimes the bad thought came to her that he was hiding himself from her, that she was an ugly crab scuttling after a bird of paradise, but she emptied that notion out of her head and trampled it into the mud as she scoured the camp. He had spoken out, tried to save her. Risked his life for this crab when that no-good piss-pot Badan wanted to tighten the noose in the Kennel.

Jo-nee cared for her. Why else would he do such a brave thing? He must care. But he was white and English, so he knew no words for love. That was why she sought him out throughout each day and brought him things that she had snatched from the clutches of the forest: a guava fruit, a rowdy red flower, a butterfly as golden as his hair, the tail feather from a macaw, and best of all, a big brute of a lobster that she had stolen from a pot and that made him whoop with pleasure. He always accepted her gifts with a smile and an upward sweep of one golden eyebrow, but she was not sure he understood . . . that she was wooing him.

Always it lurked, like the shadow of a vulture's wing in the back of her mind, the fear that he hid from her. She had learned to scamper up and down the stupid ladders with her eyes good-tight shut, so that she could creep into the hut he shared with the fat *tuan* who was no longer fat, and leave a handful of nuts wrapped in leaves on top of his bedmat, or four cigarettes that she'd earned by letting one of the stinking pirates touch her breast.

She had in her hand now a tin mug of coffee beans that she had sneaked from one of the sacks being loaded onto a boat, and she beamed from ear to ear at the certainty that it would make him love her. Maybe just a tiny sand-grain of love. Maybe today enough to give her a kiss. She stuck her head in the Kennel. It was full of many voices and the dog barking, its claws scratching on the boards as it raced from one end of the chamber to the other. Boys shrieking like monkeys. So much noise but no Jo-nee, just *mem*'s son and a pack of native brats. They were rolling a ball of white latex up and down the floor and betting cigarettes on whether the dog would catch it before it reached the other end. She noticed the Hadley boy was puffing on the butt-end of a smoke.

"Out of my way, girl."

Maya jumped. It was Badan. He was leading a group of men with sacks on their backs through the door into the chamber. Razak was among them, but her brother didn't look at her, just swaggered past. She crept in behind them and scowled at Razak. She wanted to pluck him out from among them just as she would pluck the finest feather from a scraggy cockerel. All the men crewed on the same boat and had come to divide up the spoils from the previous night. Was that where her brother went? Was that what he did? They threw the bulky sacks on the floor and started to dig around in them, shouting and arguing, pulling out handfuls of silver knives and forks, which they played with like street urchins. One with tattoos where his ears should be started to juggle with some spoons but stopped when Badan tipped a sack of sugar on the floor. It glistened in the dim light.

That was when the dog lost interest in the ball it was chasing and came scampering over. Instantly the Hadley boy called to it, a sharp command that registered with the animal because its black ears twitched, but it wanted the sugar. The children all knew better than to go anywhere near it. Maya saw the small pink tongues dart out of their mouths, ready to lick the floor as soon as the men were gone.

"Piss on you!" Badan kicked the dog.

It yelped. *Tuan* Teddy shouted. But the dog dodged back to the tempting pile of sweetness, gobbling and snuffling, its black face covered in sugar. Badan bent to yank the dog away, but the moment his hand touched the animal it snapped its head around and sank its teeth into Badan's fingers. Quick. Efficient. A death bite, if its attacker had been a weasel.

Badan roared. One young man laughed. The Hadley boy leaped forward, but he was too late. Badan had the dog by the scruff, blood pouring from his hand, and raised it up in the air. Maya could smell fear. The young man's. The boy's. The dog's. She slunk back toward the doorway and gave a low whistle to attract Razak's attention, to draw him out of this place where shadows gathered. He glanced over to her, his black eyes anxious. But he didn't move.

Badan snapped the dog from side to side till its eyes nearly popped out of its head, and then he took it over to the hanging rope. The young pirate ran forward immediately, eager to help and to gain his master's forgiveness for the laugh. He seized the pole and drew down the rope, placing it in Badan's free hand. Maya started to shake. *Tuan* Teddy was screaming. Another of the pirates, one with a scruffy beard and long piglike eyes, was holding the boy, twisting his arms behind his back.

"No, no, no!" Teddy begged. "He didn't mean to bite, he . . ."

Maya crouched in the corner and covered her ears. Tears were flooding down the boy's face. Badan grabbed hold of the noose and yanked it tight around the dog's tiny throat. The creature growled, flashing its white teeth and snarling at the hand. Badan's face creased with satisfaction, and he uttered a contemptuous laugh as he looked at the boy, unmoved by his distress.

"Stop your whining, boy," he roared in Malay.

"Please," Teddy pleaded. "Please . . . I'll give you . . ."

"Shut up, whelp. You have nothing I want."

"But I do. I have something you want." Maya heard the words jump out of her own mouth and wanted to cram them back in.

Badan frowned and glanced around to find the speaker. Still he shook the dog back and forth by its neck, as his eyes found Maya. "Come here, girl," he ordered.

Her feet moved. Her brain had stopped working, but her feet carried her over and she stood before him, eyes downcast, heart flying out of her chest as though it would not stay to face what was to come. There were mutterings around her, but the pounding in her ears drowned out all other noise.

"What do you have that I would want?" Badan demanded.

Slowly Maya raised her eyes. In the room were men. Men were men all over the world. From the swirling panic in her head she drew the thread that led her back to The Purple Parrot and, humming softly, she started to dance. Not the graceful movements of Razak. Not the classical ancient sweeps of the hands and feet, the way maidens had danced for their lords and for their gods through the ages in Malaya. She swayed her hips, dipped a shoulder, undulated around Badan like a snake as she rolled up her *kebaya*, her cotton top, her eyelashes fluttering, her black eyes turning to smoke, soft and sultry. Her lips opened to him, pink and inviting.

She could feel his gaze on her body, thick as tar, and her throat refused to swallow. The boys stared—she could see the moist insides of their open mouths—and the men breathed hard, edging closer. She brushed against Badan's arm and walked her fingers through the trickles of blood up to his wrist. She twitched her chest muscles to a steady rhythm, making her small breasts dance the way she had seen the girls do in The Purple Parrot, until she could see the flesh around Badan's mouth grow slack with desire.

She reached for the rope. The dog's eyes were starting to bulge and small coarse coughs rose from its throat, but she scarcely heard them because there was a voice screaming inside her head, demanding to know why she was doing this. Why couldn't she just let the stupid animal die? But in her heart Maya already knew the answer—it was for *Mem* Hadley. For the white woman who had shown her how to love, she would do whatever she had to do. She grasped the rope, but it was abruptly ripped away, jerked from her hand as someone behind her seized her arm and dragged her backward. It was Razak, his face dark with fury.

"You shame me, sister!"

He yanked down her *kebaya* to cover her breasts and shook her ferociously so that her bones rattled like twigs and the thoughts in her head crashed into each other. Dimly she was aware of a sudden shouting outside in the clearing, of loud voices and rushing figures. Someone screamed. She tried to think straight, but the shame in her brother's eyes had scorched her mind to ash. Through the gray dust of it she saw Badan tighten his mouth and release his hold on the dog so that it swung loose at the end of the rope, its back legs kicking frantically. Teddy lunged forward, but too late. Badan tugged hard on the animal's tail and the small black body grew limp.

He did not even glance in Maya's direction but wiped his spectacles and hurried from the chamber with the men and the boys behind him to join the commotion outside. In the dim wretched place of death Maya watched the Hadley boy, his thin limbs stiff and spiky. He stood beside the dog where it hung like a piece of meat, but he didn't touch it.

"Pippin," he whispered once, but nothing more.

Mute and tearless. No longer a boy. Maya saw something die in him, and her chest hurt for its loss. Angrily she shook herself free from Razak's grip and was about to go to the boy when her brother spoke sharply with a nod toward the door.

"*Tuan* Teddy, it's your mother out there."

The boy's face crumpled for a moment, and then he gathered himself together, the way a newborn calf gathers its gawky legs under itself, and ran from the room. Razak followed. Maya was left alone with just the dead dog and her shame.

☙❧

They believed her. Connie had feared they would think she was lying—to frighten them. But they believed her when she stumbled into camp, scratched, torn, and frantic, drenched in sweat, and swore that assault boats had landed Japanese troops on the island. Immediately chaos broke out around her, people shouting and running in all directions, the dank green world bursting with sudden energy, and it took a while for her to recognize that there was order within the chaos.

A chain of men passed boxes containing God-knows-what down to the jetty in a disciplined line of hand-over-hand conveyance. Tea chests vanished on board boats, and sails were hoisted at a speed that spoke of the whole maneuver being well rehearsed. A brigade of men carrying rifles took up prepared positions around the camp, and machine guns appeared from under green canvas on specially reinforced platforms up in the trees. Through the heart of all the noise and activity strode Fitz,

a quiet, controlling presence. He ordered men to remove the covers from
the stake pits, to raise the tree ladders, to set the spring mechanism of
the capture nets. He sent some boats farther upriver and others out to
sea to make a run for it.

"How long?" he asked Connie. "How long have we got? How far away
are they?"

"An hour at most. I ran back as fast as I could but . . . not always on
the right trail."

She didn't tell him. About slashing out a path with the bayonet,
about her panic when she found the sun behind her instead of ahead of
her. Or about falling down a gully and fighting her way out through
giant ferns, red earth sucking like quicksand at her feet. But when he
gripped her shoulders tight and held her close, her body molded to his.

"Connie, you're exhausted."

"I'm fine. Go and do whatever you have to do."

"First I'll take you down to the workshops. You and Teddy will be
safer underground." He kept one arm in a protective loop around her
and headed toward Teddy.

When she arrived at camp, her son had run to her and flung himself
into her arms, his face buried in her filthy shirt before withdrawing
abruptly and without explanation. He stood silent and uncommunicative
in the shade of a rambutan while others hauled on a rope to raise a box
of hand grenades to one of the platforms. He didn't offer to help. Something in his young face had changed. She had been gone only a few
hours, yet she felt a lurch of sorrow at the disappearance of something
precious from her son's face. She would talk to him when the time was
right.

"Come quickly," she said to him. "Bring Pippin."

But he shook his head, and she assumed the dog was up in the safety
of the tree hut. In single file they ran behind Fitz along the trail that
skirted the river, and that was when they heard the sound. Fitz reacted
first. He swung around to her.

"Hide! Keep out of sight!"

"Planes," Teddy shouted. He scanned the sky.

Connie felt the air vibrate as the roar of engines enveloped the forest, swooping down on them, tearing at the treetops. Then the rattle of machine guns.

"Stay here," Fitz shouted, and thrust her with Teddy behind a broad tree. "Don't move from here."

"Fitz!"

He kissed her mouth. Quick and urgent.

"Fitz, don't . . ." She wanted to say, *Don't go. Don't die,* but she forced the words down and instead she took his face in her hands and smiled into his eyes. "Don't forget . . . I love you."

She saw something open inside him, some dark raw place that had been hidden away, and he leaned his forehead against hers.

"What is it?" she whispered.

He held her close. For one brief moment she stroked the long tendons at the back of his neck, and she wondered what demon her words had let loose within him.

"Fitz," she said, "take me with you."

"I can't. I can think of nothing better than having you with me all the time." He took her hand in his. "I am a greedy man, Connie, but I can't let you take that risk. You have your son to think of." He turned to Teddy. "Stay with your mother, Teddy, look after her until I—"

His final words were swallowed by an explosion that blasted the forest, tearing limbs from the trees.

"Bombs!" Fitz shouted.

More explosions. A tidal wave of sound. Screams erupted around them in all directions, and Fitz pushed Connie and Teddy to the ground at the base of the tree.

"Don't move!" he yelled.

Connie hooked an arm around his neck and placed a kiss, full of heat and fury, on his lips. And then he was gone.

Ϭ·Ϭ

The Japanese planes came one after another, a great flock of them. Connie dodged between trees, Teddy at her heels, his small hand gripped firmly in hers. She couldn't remain where she was, however much Fitz had asked her to, because to remain there would be to wait to die.

Around her the destruction was relentless. Trees were ripped from the ground, broken walkways dangled like cobwebs, and bullets tore holes in the forest. Each time a bomb exploded Connie felt cold with fear for Fitz, but she had to get Teddy to safety. She raced for the underground workshop, only to discover that a direct hit had blasted the chamber wide open and its contents of timber and workmen were strewn in a tangled mess over the forest floor.

"Teddy, hide here."

Connie pushed him into a thicket of bamboo, but as she checked each body, searching for a flicker of life, the small figure of Teddy bobbed up at her side, his need to be with his mother overwhelming all else. So she didn't shut him out. This was his world even more than it was hers. He helped her shift lengths of wood and seize hold of hands that were already turning cold. Not until every chance of finding someone alive was exhausted did they stop. Only then did Teddy start to cry, a shuddering release of grief as he told her that Pippin was dead too. She took him in her arms and tried to hide her rage.

How can I teach my son to deal with death when I can't deal with it myself?

She soothed his quivering back and spoke to him quietly about his father and about how much his father loved him, told him how proud he would be of his son today. And when the tears finally stopped, she kissed his sweet damp forehead.

"Teddy, my love, we have to leave now. We have to escape from here. But first we need to find Fitz."

They retraced their steps, and as they emerged from the trees she felt her son's hand tremble in hers. Ahead of them the river was on fire. The wingtip of an aircraft reached up out of the water like a plea for help.

"It's a Zero," Teddy whispered. "Shot down by the machine guns in the trees."

Its fuel had spilled onto the surface of the river and caught fire, sending flames streaking across the narrow inlet, so that several boats now burned. Smoke wreathed the air and a gray shroud had dimmed the sun. The acrid stench of it scoured their nostrils, and their gaze turned immediately to *The White Pearl*. Miraculously she was still riding at anchor, unharmed, but on deck Connie could make out movement, and when a gust of wind stripped the smoke from the yacht for a moment she saw at least twenty people crammed on deck—among them the bespectacled face of Badan.

"Look, Mummy!"

Teddy pointed to the stern, where someone was preparing to weigh anchor. It was Henry Court—he was running out on them.

"Wait!" Connie shouted across the water, but it was lost in all the noise. "Wait for Fitzpayne!"

But she knew it was too late. The yacht would glide downriver without her. She was no longer Mrs. Nigel Hadley, owner of *The White Pearl*; no longer the woman who had set out from Palur.

"Teddy," she said urgently, "where do you think Fitzpayne could be?"

"He'll be with the rifles."

"Where?"

"In the gun pit."

"Show me."

Together they started to run through the smoke but were stopped by the sudden sight of Maya. She was darting in panic back and forth along the riverbank in full view, her long hair loose and tangled, and she was screeching her brother's name. "Razak! Razak!"

"Oh, Maya, no," Connie cried. "Wait here, Teddy," she ordered, and started to run toward the girl, just as a Japanese plane swept down into the narrow river valley and opened up with its guns.

CHAPTER THIRTY-FIVE

Kitty couldn't swim. Madoc cursed her foolishness. He had told her a thousand times that it was dangerous to live in this land of infinite waterways without learning how.

"Only people who can swim end up drowning," she used to laugh. "People who can't swim—like me—never go in the water. Anyway, you can always rescue me."

Now, at the water's edge, it had come to that. She looked at him with steady eyes and said, "Don't let me drown." Then she wrapped her arms around the plank of wood he had thrust at her and threw herself into the river. She flailed like a newborn kitten, let go of the timber, and promptly went under, scaring the bloody life out of him. He grabbed a hank of her thick hair and yanked her back to the surface, his heart beating again only when he saw her gulp in air.

"Hold on!" he ordered as he jammed the balk of timber under her arms and started to kick out for the central channel, towing Kitty with one hand.

Her eyes were panicked.

"Kick!" he shouted.

She kicked, feebly at first, then harder. They began to move against the tidal current.

"Madoc."

"What is it?"

She was swallowing water and shaking her head. "I don't like this."

"Kitty, my love"—he lifted her chin higher, treading water at her side, frightened sick for her—"it's a bloody stink hole for all of us."

"No, I mean"—she spat out a mouthful of slime—"this." She nodded at the yacht just ahead of them. The wind had shifted, and *The White Pearl* was half hidden once more in the pall of black smoke billowing from the junk anchored alongside her, so that her gleaming white hull was masked from sight. But Madoc had spotted the men on board who were eager to make off with her, and now that he was this close, he could hear raised voices on deck.

"I can handle them, Kitty."

"No." She had stopped kicking. One hand clung to his shoulder, holding him back.

"It's ours," he snapped impatiently. "*The White Pearl* is meant for us."

"Not this time, Madoc."

"I tell you, it is."

"It's a death ship."

"Don't be stupid."

A wave hit him in the face. Kitty deliberately released her hold on the timber and grabbed at his neck, her full weight dragging him down. For ten seconds they were drowning, but he fought back to the surface, hauling her with him, and they both gasped air into their lungs. The timber was gone. His fear turned to anger.

"Stop it, Kitty! You'll bloody kill us both."

She shut her eyes, shivering. "A death ship," she repeated.

"Shit, you're spooking me."

He glanced back at the shore and saw the chaos there. He caught a glimpse of Fitzpayne charging out of the forest with a horde of native kids behind him. All carried rifles. Above the trees, another plane was beginning its run. With a curse he wrenched Kitty's arm from his neck and, keeping a firm grip on her, he veered away from *The White Pearl*. Instead, he swam a course straight for the *Burung Camar*.

ⱁ·Ɑ

Connie was knocked off her feet. Her ears hurt as she staggered upright again. Another explosion. She coughed as a rush of smoke swept into her lungs and her head jerked round to see *The White Pearl* disintegrate into ten thousand silvery pieces that hung in the air, suspended briefly between life and death, before descending into the water. It was a direct hit.

The White Pearl no longer existed, nor the people on her. Connie felt sick, appalled at the capacity of human beings to hurt one another. She thought of Henry on deck and was unaware of the tears on her face as she raced toward Maya. The girl was still screaming, still out in the open, while above her the roar of an engine sent waves of sound rolling through the trees. Connie clamped her hand on the girl's tiny wrist and dragged Maya off the sunlit bank of sand into the safer gloom of the forest.

Maya's scream went on and on and on, battering Connie's ears, but when she finally halted and they looked behind them, Maya uttered only a faint moan. Across the sand where her footprints had churned it up, a neat line of bullet holes traced a path. Abruptly Maya dropped to her knees on the dank earth and wrapped her arms around Connie's ankles. She kissed Connie's muddy feet, wiping her shins with her hair.

"*Terimah kasih, terimah kasih, terimah kasih,* thank you, thank you, thank you," she sobbed.

"Maya, don't."

"I be dead without you."

"You're alive, thank goodness."

"You save me."

"Please, don't, Maya."

"*Mem,* you save me, though I bad. I sorry, so sorry. You an angel."

"No." Connie jerked the girl to her feet. "I am definitely no angel. Now let's move. We'll find Razak now," she promised.

୨·ଟ

Fear robs you of self. Connie could feel her fear untying the knots that held her together. She stared at the devastation in the river valley and mourned the wanton loss of life. Fear and sorrow: They were two sides of the same coin. Fear for Fitz; sorrow for Henry. Together they untied the fastening that shaped her into a civilized being, and the rage that lurked inside, deep and primal, came roaring to the surface. She craved one of Fitz's rifles to defend her son.

Teddy had remained exactly where she'd left him, tucked inside a fold of mangrove—for the simple reason that beside him, one hand firmly on his shoulder, stood Fitz.

"Connie!" Fitz's face was dark and set hard. "You almost got yourself killed."

She heard the anger in his voice. She wanted to wrap herself around him and tell him she was still here, still alive—still his.

"I need to find Razak," she said.

"Razak?"

"Yes. I promised Maya."

He released his grip on her son. "You're too ready to make promises." He scowled at her and took a deep breath, his self-control costing him dearly. "But I have him safe." He was about to stride off without another word, expecting her to follow, but at the last moment he hesitated and stared at her. His thick hair was disheveled and wet, his shirt torn and bloodied.

"Come with me. Please, Connie."

As if she could say no.

᠑·᠖

Nurul sat in the middle of the rowboat, pulling strongly on the oars and bringing them closer to the *Burung Camar*. His hand was bandaged and he did not look at Connie. The aircraft attacks had briefly subsided, and in the lull Nurul had launched a flimsy boat that Fitz had hidden among the roots of a mangrove tree. Johnnie Blake was waiting there already with Razak, and as soon as he saw Connie arrive, he hoisted Razak onto his back and stepped down into the rowboat. It swayed precariously, and Maya uttered a soft wail. Razak had a gash on his back but he made no sound, just rolled his head to look at his sister as he took his seat in the bow.

"He's all right," Johnnie called out to her.

"He not right." Maya jumped into the boat, making it rock with a violence that meant Johnnie had to cling onto her to stop her from top-pling overboard.

"In you go, Teddy," Fitz urged the boy. "Take care of your mother."

"Aren't you coming out to the *Burung Camar*?" Teddy asked at once.

"No." Fitz looked at Connie. "Not yet."

Connie didn't move. He took her hand and she interlaced her fingers with his, fastening them together.

"Fitz," she said quietly, her chest tight and empty, "you must leave with us. It's too dangerous here. The troops are coming, I saw them, they will . . ."

Kill you. They will kill you.

She wanted to say things to him, but not that. "They will be here soon." She wanted to beat her fists on his stubborn chest and rip apart his iron will with her bare hands.

"Connie, I have to remain for the moment," he said. "Don't worry, I will join you shortly. There are people here who need me."

None of his words filled the dark spaces in her chest. But when he stopped speaking, she didn't say *I need you* and was careful to banish all jealousy from her voice as she asked, "How long? I will wait here."

"No, you must go."

How could she go, when half of her would remain here with him? But she didn't make it harder for him than it already was. She nodded and did as he asked. His eyes didn't leave hers as Nurul rowed them out into the river, and as the distance between them stretched, yard after yard, Fitz did not move away. He stood on the bank watching her, a lone figure slumped against a mangrove tree, and when the billowing smoke drifted across and stole him from her, it was as if her heart were held in darkness.

꒚·꒚

It was a sudden change in the wind direction—like the breath of the gods drawing away from the accursed Japs—that made Maya scream a warning. Later, she was sorry. Later she wished she had kept her mouth shut, or clamped her hand over the sound. But in the tiny rowboat with Jo-nee comforting her twin instead of her, she didn't think. She saw the Japs and she screamed.

The wind was swirling upriver carrying the smoke with it, so that the riverbank was suddenly bathed in bright sunlight, and that was when she saw the gray uniforms, creeping along the shore like rats. Iron-eyes was right in their path, but instead of keeping alert and watching his back, he did nothing but stare out over the water at *Mem* Hadley, waiting for her to reach the safety of the *Burung Camar* and hoist sail.

"They come," Maya wailed.

A small hand took hold of hers. It was *Tuan* Teddy. He squeezed it tight and whispered something to comfort her. The ferocity of his grip on her fingers startled her, and for a moment it squeezed out the terror. She heard *mem* cry out as she recognized the danger Iron-eyes was in and saw her leap to her feet in the boat. On shore, Iron-eyes had started running, but before he could warn those left alive in the forest that the Japs were here, a single shot rang out.

He went down as if he had been scythed at the knees. *Mem* Hadley made no sound, but Maya felt all the air sucked out of the boat.

"Go back," *mem* yelled at Nurul. "Go back for him. Now, go back now."

But Nurul shook his head and rowed on. *Mem* wasted no more breath on him.

"Johnnie, take care of Teddy," she said quickly. Then she kissed her son's head, dived into the muddy green water, and struck out for the mangroves.

"No, *mem*!" Maya cried. "It bad. Come back."

Tuan Teddy shivered, his fingers clutching the side of the rowboat as if they would take a bite out of it, while his mother's small blond head bobbed away from him among the burning boats. She was a strong swimmer. But Maya wondered what kind of strong heart she must possess to do such a crazy thing, and it made her want to cry. Not for Iron-eyes; not for *mem*'s son. But because to be loved so much must make your heart burst with happiness. To die so happy would not hurt.

ꀀ·ꀀ

Madoc watched it all happen. He stood on board the *Burung Camar* and acknowledged with a curse that he was not going to get the *pinisiq* under way before Nurul reached it.

"Patience," Kitty murmured in his ear. "Nurul is an easy target."

"Don't talk rubbish, woman. He is as sharp as one of the knives he's so fond of, and devoted to Fitzpayne."

"I'm not so sure."

He turned his head to look at her as she pushed back her wet hair. Still this woman could astonish him.

"Look," he pointed out, "Flight Lieutenant Blake is in the rowboat, as well as the Jumat kids."

He wished to hell that they had made a run for it earlier, but Nurul had stationed three men on the *pinisiq*, all with guns. He was no fool.

"Razak will come over to our side if he thinks we are winning," Kitty said confidently. "And Nurul won't need much . . . encouragement."

"What kind of encouragement?"

The rowboat bumped against the hull.

"That's for me to know," she chuckled, "and for you to find out."

As Nurul swung over the side, Madoc was tempted to stick a gun right in his shiny gold mouth.

Connie hid Fitz. Deep within a clump of tall, sharp-edged jungle grasses that closed over their heads.

"Quick," she said. "We must be quick."

Fitz leaned against her as she eased his shirt from his shoulders.

"For bandages," she said succinctly.

He nodded and extracted a knife from the sheath on his belt. "You shouldn't have come back."

It was the first time he'd spoken since she'd scooped him up off the riverbank. With one of his arms across her shoulders for support, she had half dragged him into the tangled world of the jungle, seeking sanctuary in its damp shadows. Every moment she had expected another rifle shot to ring out, or a bayonet through the ribs. But the sporadic gunfire from the few pirates left alive in the treetops forced the Japanese troops to keep their heads down for the vital few minutes she needed.

Connie worked fast, but her mouth was so dry her lips wouldn't unstick from her teeth, and something strange was going on at the back of her eyes. Green lights kept flickering like emerald fireflies, distorting her vision. She hadn't known that fear could feel like this, like an illness. Fitz was bleeding where the bullet had sliced through his thigh.

"The bullet has exited out the back," he told her. "I'm lucky."

Lucky? She lifted her gaze from the wound and fixed it on his face. His skin was taut. Dark smudges of pain lay beneath his eyes, and his pupils were black and sharp. But his mouth seemed to have crept out from under the iron control of his will and was half smiling at her. She took the knife from his hand.

"You know you shouldn't have come, Connie."

"How could I not?"

"I wanted you to escape with your son."

"Leaving you here to play with your guns without me?"

He laughed. As the sound seeped into her head, it diluted her fear. She cut the sleeves from the shirt and folded them into two wads. She pressed one hard on top of the wound on the front of his leg and rolled him over to look at the exit wound on the back of his thigh. She gasped. It was much worse.

"Hurry," he urged.

She jammed the second wad onto the wound, stemming the flow of blood. "It's not an artery," she reassured him.

"Nothing more than a scratch, then."

"Something like that." She bound the rest of the shirt around his thigh.

"Do you know what it is to die of loneliness?" he asked.

She looked at him.

"That's how I felt," he murmured, "when Nurul rowed you away from me."

She rested her fingers on his. "I came back. Doesn't that answer you?"

More shots rang out somewhere close.

"Hurry!" he said. "Nurul will come for us. He and I have a place to meet in any emergency. It's a promontory on the far side of the island."

In her mind she saw again Nurul's indifference when they'd been in the rowboat. "Maybe we could swim out together instead to the *Burung . Camar*. Teddy is on board."

Suddenly shouts echoed no more than a hundred yards from them.

"I'm sorry, Connie," Fitz whispered into her ear. "It's too late for that, the boats will be gone. Nurul knows better than to approach a shoreline thick with Japs. He will return to the promontory when it's dark. Help me up."

She took his weight. "Can't we stay here? Hidden in these tall grasses until tonight?"

"No, it's not safe. It won't take them long to find the blood trail."

She hadn't thought of that. She looked around her at the telltale scarlet smears. "Let's move."

"You have courage," he said simply.

It startled her. She saw in his face that he understood how much she had left behind for him, how desperate she was to return to Teddy. Together they started to move cautiously through the grass that waved above their heads in the humid breeze from the river, his arm heavy on her shoulders, her hand gripping his naked back. She wanted to tell him that she wasn't brave, but that she had left a man dead on a riverbank once before and she wasn't going to do it again. She wanted to tell him that this time it was different, that this time she had refused to let him die.

But she didn't mention any of these things. She let them lie like stones in the acid of her stomach and told him instead that if he didn't hobble a damn sight faster they would be fish food long before nightfall.

෧·෧

Fitz knew his jungle. It was his domain. He guided Connie down hidden gullies and through solid green walls of vegetation to find the faintest animal trails that made the going easier. The flies and leeches thickened as they pushed farther inland, and the air grew more humid until it had a body and weight that Connie felt she could cut into slices with Fitz's knife.

"You must rest now," she told him.

He glared at her from under his dark eyebrows each time she said those words, but she insisted.

"I don't want you to bleed to death on me," she said.

"I don't intend to die," he said. "Not yet, anyway."

Though he spoke quietly, there was something savage in his eyes. She knelt at his side. "What is it?"

He looked utterly weary, his eyes half closed as though he would shut out the world. She was aware of how many friends he had seen die that day.

"The Japanese did not invade this island by chance," he said. "They must have had a good reason to come here."

"What do you mean?"

"Something . . . or someone . . . led them to us."

"Who?"

"My guess is that it was that wastrel, Madoc."

"What? No, he would never do such a—"

"Hush." He placed a finger over her lips and smiled faintly. "You have too much faith in people, Connie." He stroked her chin with his thumb. "Not everyone is like you."

"Why would Madoc do such a thing?"

"You know I told you that your Japanese pilot was killed in the hold of the *Burung Camar* last night?"

She nodded.

"I think Madoc slit his throat."

Her mouth fell open. "No."

"I suspect he went out there under cover of darkness for the radio. And had to silence the Jap to keep him quiet."

"What radio?"

"Behind a panel in the boat's hold, I keep a shortwave radio. Madoc must have found out about it from one of the crew—I could tell this morning that it had been disturbed—and for some reason he decided to send out a message to someone."

"No, I can't believe it was Madoc. He would never betray us to the Japs. You know how he hates them. Maybe it was Nurul himself, and maybe he killed the pilot."

Fitz gave a short laugh. "No, not Nurul. Connie, it is the look in a man's eye that tells you what is in his heart, not his slippery words. I don't mean that Madoc would betray us to the Japs intentionally, but they monitor all radio traffic, and their direction finders trace transmissions. He could have radioed someone in Singapore and told them about this place."

Connie put her hand over her mouth. "You really think it was him?"

He leaned forward and placed his lips on the back of her hand. "Yes, I do."

ꝺ·ꝯ

"Poor old Henry Court bought it when *The White Pearl* went up," Johnnie Blake said with a somber tug of his earlobe. "God rest his soul." His eyes looked sick.

Bought it? Went up?

Madoc groaned. What the hell was the matter with people like Blake? Why the need to speak in code? What was wrong with saying it straight?

"A Jap bomb blew Court to pieces." Madoc spelled it out clearly for them. He saw the lad, Teddy, wince and his eyes fill with dismay. "Don't worry, kid, your mother will be OK. Fitzpayne will get her to safety, you can bet on that."

Like hell he will. They are most likely both already lying dead in the jungle with bullets in their backs and ants in their eyes.

"Please," Teddy begged, "we must sail back to the island."

"Too late for that," Madoc answered. "Look around you."

The *Burung Camar* was carrying full sail and, with an empty hull, was flying away from the island like a fox with its tail on fire. Nurul was squeezing every scrap of speed out of his boat to find somewhere safe to tuck her under cover before more Jap planes came screaming out of the sun. An unpleasant swell was running across their bow, but the fresh northwesterly filling the *pinisiq*'s eight sails drove them beyond reach of any binoculars on the island's shores, so that Madoc felt the hairs on the back of his neck settle down at last.

Nurul was a skipper of few words, which suited Madoc just fine. He told his passengers nothing. His crew of three consisted of Madoc's two gambling companions from his days with Kitty on *The White Pearl* while waiting for repairs, and also a new Javanese with a woman's golden skin and a huge belly that shook when he laughed. And he laughed whenever one of the white people spoke to him. Razak was the only one Big Belly deigned to talk to, so it was Razak who came to them with the information that they would be returning to the island at nightfall.

"No," Madoc stated flatly. "I'm not going back there. It's crawling with Japs."

A desperate "Yes!" burst out of Teddy.

Johnnie Blake came over to Madoc and drew him out of earshot. Madoc knew exactly what was coming.

"Look, Madoc, it's not just for the boy. Mrs. Hadley and Mr. Fitzpayne are part of our"—for one hideous moment Madoc thought he was going to say *our squadron*—"part of our team, and we don't ditch members of our team. It's not honorable."

"For Christ's sake, Blake, you and I know they are as good as dead by now."

"It's possible, yes. But I hope that's not true. They are both"—he struggled for the right word—"resourceful people."

Resourceful. Madoc could think of other words for Fitzpayne, and *bloody-minded* was one of them. The Japs were welcome to him.

"I suggest," Blake continued, "that we discuss it with Nurul. You speak Malay, so you—"

"Nurul is not the kind of man open to suggestions, Flight Lieutenant. If we want to change his mind, we have to kill him."

"Good God, Madoc. You are barbaric."

"I'm alive. That's what counts. And I intend to stay that way."

"You and your wife could always leave us. I'm sure Nurul would be more than happy for you to disembark on whatever island he seeks shelter in."

Madoc heard in the man's voice the desire concealed scrupulously behind the veneer of politeness—the desire to be rid of him for good. *Not the right class, old chap. A bit off-stump when it comes to values.* Bitterness burrowed into Madoc's flesh like the black head of a leech, and he looked around the deck for Kitty. She was farther aft, talking quietly with Nurul, their heads close together. She was taller than the pirate and twice as wide, but the wrinkles of his face were screwed up in an expression of pure delight. He kept casting sideways glances at Kitty's luscious breasts and darting his tongue across his lips, while Kitty rubbed her backside against the mizzen like a bitch in heat.

Madoc let his hand slide to the Russian gun hidden in his waistband;

it felt good to his fingers—hard, brutal, and unforgiving. Like himself. He smiled with satisfaction and knew that today was the day he would use it. So why, when he looked across again at Kitty and saw her jut her breasts almost into Nurul's gold teeth, did he feel sick in his gut?

ꬑ·ꬿ

"Shall I tell you why Nurul helps the God-almighty Fitzpayne?" Kitty asked. She was biting into a peach.

Madoc shook his head. He didn't want to know. And he didn't like the way Nurul was sharing not just his peaches with Kitty, but his secrets as well. How many secrets was she sharing with him in return?

"Don't sulk, Madoc. You look like a five-year-old."

She laughed easily, tipping back her throat, making Nurul lift his head at the far end of the boat as though his ears were fine-tuned to her voice. But Kitty's eyes didn't laugh. They were moody and withdrawn, and they frightened the hell out of Madoc.

"No," he said. "I don't want to know."

"Well, I'm going to tell you anyway."

The sky was vermilion behind her, setting fire to her hair. Nightfall was only minutes away, and Nurul was preparing to set sail from the river mouth into which he had squeezed the *Burung Camar* for what had remained of the day.

"He carried Nurul's wife," Kitty said.

"Who?"

"Fitzpayne. She was heavily pregnant and in terrible pain, and he carried her on his back for ten miles through the jungle to a hospital while Nurul was away at sea."

Madoc definitely didn't want to know.

"She survived," Kitty continued relentlessly, "and bore a healthy son. But five years ago they both died of malaria."

"So Nurul has no wife? He's probably on the lookout for another."

"Oh, for Christ's sake, Madoc, don't be so stupid."

But he wasn't being stupid. Something dark and chilling was going on behind his wife's eyes.

"What is it, Kitty?"

She looked at him in the descending darkness. "He says you betrayed us to the Japs."

"Kitty, that's insane. You know I'd never do that."

"I know." She looked away.

"So why the fuck do you believe him and not me?"

For a moment her gaze shifted to the native girl who was standing beside Flight Lieutenant Blake, massaging his bad shoulder with small eager hands.

"I believe him," Kitty said quietly, but he wanted her to shout and cuff him the way she'd done a thousand times before in arguments. "I believe him," she continued, "because he saw you."

"What?"

"He saw you swim out to this boat at night. The Jap pilot's throat was cut and the radio used, he says." At last she looked him in the eye. "Was it you?"

"Yes, I admit that. The pilot got in the way. I told you that we could get good money for passing on information to the British authorities in Singapore about what the setup was on that island."

"They traced it. Your transmission was traced. That's how the Japs knew where to come. It all happened because of you, all those lives slaughtered, so many children killed. So much death. All that destruction was caused because you would not be satisfied with just taking a boat to sail. You had to have more. It was just greed. Oh, Madoc, Madoc . . ."

Never before, not ever, had she spoken like that to him. It wasn't the words—sometimes they had shouted worse at each other—it was the desperate sadness in her voice, that look of finality in her eyes. It sent terror darting through his bowels. He gripped her wrist.

"Kitty, I didn't mean to. You know I hate the Japanese as much as you do, especially now." He stopped. She was shaking her head.

"Madoc, we have to let Nurul go back to try to find Fitzpayne and Mrs. Hadley."

"No, I won't allow it. We agreed, Kitty."

"I know it's risky, but enough is enough, Madoc." She touched his chest, just over his heart, and gave him an odd smile. "Let's salvage what we can from this. The kid needs his mother."

"I tell you, we're not going back there."

She stepped away from him into the velvet darkness that was creeping along the deck. "Nurul might have something to say about that. But," she shrugged, "he might reconsider if I ask him nicely."

"No," Madoc said sharply. "I don't want you near Nurul any more."

He didn't mean it to happen this way. He didn't want to do it without her by his side, watching his back. But without a word he walked over to where Nurul was busy coiling rope and listening to the Hadley kid who was speaking to him in low, urgent tones. Madoc drew out the Tokarev pistol and pointed it straight at the pirate's chest.

"Nurul, hoist those bloody wings of yours. I want us to set sail."

Nurul's sharp eyes shifted from Madoc to the gun and back again. His gold teeth flashed warily. "To where?"

"To India."

ි·ෙ

They climbed higher to cross the center of the island, and deep mist hung over everything like the breath of the earth itself, deadening the clamor of the jungle. It painted the leaves with a metallic sheen and muted the vibrant colors of the huge butterflies, turning them into ghosts that wheeled through the air. Connie adapted a branch into a crutch to aid Fitz, but she saw each step take its toll. It was time to rest again.

"Will the Japanese come this far?"

"Yes," Fitz said, "I'm afraid they will. I'm sorry, Connie." He turned his head to study her face. "But nowhere is going to be safe on this island now. The Japanese are very thorough. They are experts at jungle warfare."

Connie could hear the respect in his voice. They were seated side by side on a rock at the base of a stubby waterfall, their feet in a pool of green water. She had bathed his wounds again, her fingernails stained pink, and rinsed out the bandages that were soaked with blood.

"Your whole world has changed," he said softly.

Her arm slid around his back, holding him safe, feeling the heat of his skin seep into her own.

"Not just my world, Fitz. We all know it's the end of Western domination of the Far East. The whole empire is starting to crumble, so we are all going to have to change, whether we like it or not."

He touched his head against hers, and she became aware of him inhaling the scent of her, the sweat, the dirt, and the fear. "And do you like it, the idea of change?"

The question was not asked as if it mattered, just tossed out as though it were no more than a passing curiosity. But Connie knew that Nigel sat with them unmentioned. She knew just what the question meant and how much the answer mattered to Fitz. She entwined her fingers in his.

"I hate the deaths," she said fervently. "All the pain and the cruelty put me in a rage that makes me want to . . ." With an effort she stopped herself from giving voice to what the rage did to her. Instead, she leaned against his bare shoulder and said more calmly, "Time is striding on relentlessly, Fitz. We can't halt it. We can't pull it back and scream for it to stop. Everything is moving forward so fast, and there's no point in saying, *How dare you leave me behind?* We have to move forward too."

"Is that what you're doing? Moving forward?"

"I have to. I love my son," she said flatly, as if it answered his question.

"I know." He attempted to rise on his good leg, but she held him down. She could feel his exhaustion.

"Were you as rebellious when you were a boy?" she asked suddenly. "What were you like?"

He was amused by her question. "I was trouble."

"I can believe that. I know you said you were born on a beach, but where?"

"Out in the Philippines. My parents owned a touring circus."

"A circus?" She dipped her hand in the water and splashed it over him. "So you were the star trapeze act, I presume."

"Something like that. I used to dive from a high platform into a teacup of water." But his face abruptly closed and he spoke quickly. "My parents were both killed in a motor accident in Shanghai when I was twelve years old, and I was shipped back to England to my uncle, who educated me at Harrow. He tried, really tried, to turn me from a Malayan monkey, as he called me, into a civilized English gent."

"Not with much success, I see," she smiled.

He raised one black eyebrow at her, but the resonant boom of a naval gun out at sea knocked the smile from his face. She shivered, despite the stultifying heat.

"They're here in force," Fitz warned. He closed his eyes, and for a moment she feared he would tumble forward into the green pool at their feet and she wrapped herself around him.

"Hold on to me," she whispered.

His hand tightened on hers. "Connie, I learned yesterday that Singapore has surrendered. General Wavell ordered a scorched-earth policy to be adopted, destroying all factory machinery and burning the warehouses on the wharves to leave nothing for the Japanese invaders. They bombed the hell out of the city."

"Oh, God, poor Singapore."

"The Japanese Chrysanthemum Division—their crack troops—crossed the Straits of Johore and took the island of Singapore. At six o'clock yesterday evening General Yamashita accepted the surrender in the Ford factory." His voice grew hard; the words seemed to scrape against his teeth. "One hundred and thirty thousand British and Commonwealth troops surrendered. The worst military surrender in British history."

Connie felt a rush of shame. They both knew that the impossible had happened. A shudder of sorrow shook her, and Fitz held her head gently against his chest until it had passed. She helped him to his feet. She tucked herself under his arm, fitting perfectly inside the curve of his shoulder, and together they continued to fight a path through the jungle.

ઝ·ઘ

The rain came, great drenching sheets of it that made the ground slippery underfoot and turned any slope into a treacherous mudslide. The only relief was that it drove the biting flies into hiding and silenced the gibbons in the trees. But it didn't silence the Japanese troops, whose rifle shots punctuated the drumming of the rain.

"Connie, listen to me." Fitz rested against a trunk. He was breathing hard. She tightened her grip on his wet skin, and it felt hot. "Nurul won't risk setting sail until after dark." His voice was so low she had to lean closer. Water was streaming down his face in rivulets.

"How far from here is the promontory?" she asked calmly.

"An hour." He glanced down at his leg. "Maybe more."

"That's good. It means we have time to find shelter somewhere. You must rest your leg and get out of the rain, or . . ."

"Or what?"

They were speaking in whispers, though there was scarcely any need as the clatter of the rain was deafening.

"Or"—she rested her wet cheek against his—"or I shall have to strip your wet clothes off you."

He laughed, a small, intimate sound that warmed them both. She didn't ask why he was so sure of Nurul. She had to make herself believe what he believed—because her son was on board that boat and it was the only way she could get back to him. So she sat Fitz down under a tree—overriding his protests—and, using his knife, she hacked off an armful of giant fern fronds and *attap* leaves, which she proceeded to weave around him until he was enveloped in a cocoon of greenery. She wriggled her way in beside him, pulling the big glossy leaves over their heads, and for the first time she felt safe. It was an illusion, she knew. But it was an illusion she clung to.

The warmth and solidity of Fitz's body next to hers made her thoughts less ragged. She could consider her son without icy panic. *Nurul, I swear I would never have stabbed you if I had known.* Fitz sensed her despair and pressed her tight against him, as though he could keep her safe inside his own skin. But neither spoke. They rested, her hand protective on his wounded leg.

"Fitz," she murmured eventually, the rain dripping on her knees, "if you get back to the *Burung Camar* and I don't make it, will you make certain Teddy gets safely back to my parents in England? They live in Compton Bassett in Wiltshire. Their name is Harrington."

She felt a ripple of shock run through him. For a moment she wondered if she'd asked too much.

"I won't let you die," he promised. "Tell that to your son."

"But if I do?"

"You won't."

"Remember," she told him. "Harrington in Compton Bassett."

He made a sound of disgust, and she said no more.

ᴐ·ᴄ

Connie kept track of time. She counted out the heartbeats in her head. Fitz's eyes were closed and his breath was shallow, but she knew he wasn't asleep. Curled up in the green cocoon, she kept watch on the jungle through a spyhole in the vegetation, listening for signs of soldiers through the rain. Oddly, in spite of the dread of what lay ahead, and her desperate need for her son, an astounding thing happened. Happiness came raging in, and she fell asleep nursing it to her, her head on Fitz's shoulder.

She woke with Fitz's fingers on her lips, his soft hiss in her ear. Through the spyhole she glimpsed uniforms, gray and menacing. Her heart jumped and her first instinct was to run, but Fitz held her firm. She saw the knife in his hand, and in her head she cursed this gray-uniformed enemy who took no heed of rain or jungle, but marched with such relentless efficiency. The soldiers moved away but Fitz remained seated a long time before he dismantled their cocoon and limped deeper into the jungle, his face set, his arm gripping Connie.

CHAPTER THIRTY-SEVEN

A rifle was jammed into the back of Connie's neck. She didn't scream. Didn't move. A guttural shout behind her told her what she already knew—that it was a Japanese rifle.

Fitz, don't come back for me. Stay safe.

Terror darted up her spine, but she spoke calmly.

"Hello, *konnichiwa*. I am Connie. I . . ." Slowly, with infinite caution, she turned around.

၁·၄

The rain had stopped, and she had been hiding behind an outcrop of rock that loomed over the shoreline below, overlooking the promontory of land that stretched like a finger into the sea. The vivid colors and sounds of the breakers as they rolled up onto the dazzling white beach made Connie cry when it had first burst into sight, when she and Fitz emerged from the gloom of the jungle. Because it held the route to freedom and to her son.

"They've been here," Fitz murmured as they lay on their stomachs in the undergrowth. He pointed to a neat line of footprints etched in the sand below them.

"Nurul?"

He shook his head.

"The Japanese?"

He nodded, and when he saw despair sweep over her, he pulled her to him. "He'll come," he promised. "Nurul will come."

They had remained hidden until it was almost dark. He would not let her rebind his wounds but held her in his arms, her head on his chest, talking quietly until she knew the thoughts in his head the way she knew the thoughts in her own. That was how she knew that he regarded her present danger as his fault.

"It was my decision," she'd whispered, "to swim back to the island." Her tongue flicked out and licked the salt from his skin. "Not yours."

"I shouldn't have brought you to this island. I believed you and your son would be safe here, but I should have left you behind in Palur."

"I would be dead if you had. Not just because of the Japs."

"Sometimes dead is better than hell."

She lifted her head and looked up at his face. It lay in shadow, but she could feel his heart thundering in his chest. "Are you in hell, Fitz?" she asked gently.

He smiled at her. "No, Connie. This is the closest to heaven I'm likely to get."

"Don't be so sure."

She had pushed him down onto his back with soft whispers, the sandy soil steaming around them in the heat of the day, and she had kissed his mouth, then the hard tendons of his throat and the broad expanse of his chest. It tasted of salt and strength and something else, something stubborn. She slid her blouse from her shoulders and watched him as his hands tenderly caressed her breasts, exploring their creamy skin, touching the hollows and curves of her body. Teasing the secret and intimate sounds of pleasure from deep within her throat.

"Connie, this is not how I want it to be for us, snatched and desperate and—" He stopped.

At first she thought he was in pain, and she quickly lifted her weight off him, but he still didn't move. He was listening, alert and wary. She ducked lower to the earth as he rolled onto his front beside her. She could hear nothing but the growl of the waves on the beach and the birds' raucous calls after the rain.

"They're here," Fitz whispered.

"Where?"

"Behind us. In the jungle."

Connie's skin tightened. She rose to a crouch, pulled on her blouse, and took his arm. "Hold on to me."

For a split second he didn't react and she saw admiration in his eyes. She felt color rush to her cheeks.

"Come on," she hissed and yanked at his arm.

In silence, they threaded a path through the trees that lined the beach and down to the base of the promontory, where an ancient rockfall from the cliff had created a fortress of sorts. They dodged in among the boulders and buried themselves in the deep shade they found there. For a long time they waited, but all was quiet.

"Do you think they've gone?" Connie murmured.

"There's only one way to find out. I'll have to take a look."

"No, Fitz." She gripped his wrist. "No."

"Stay here. Don't move."

He kissed her, nothing more than a brush of her lips this time, and then he was gone. She stood immobile, cheek wedged against the warm rock, peering through a tiny slit that gave her a partial view of the beach as she begged God to guard Fitz, offering to deal—her soul for his life. *Please, please.* Minutes dragged past while shadows shifted.

That was when the Japanese rifle jammed into the back of her neck.

ɔ·ʚ

"Hello," she said. *"Konnichiwa."*

But this wasn't a young raw recruit like last time, terrified of the rifle in his hand. This one was a battle-hardened soldier with sharp features and a desire to kill her in his black eyes. He shouted something at her in Japanese and gestured with the tip of his rifle, forcing her to emerge from her hiding place. She did exactly as she was told, hands in the air, but as she walked in front of him across the white sand her eyes darted among the trees.

Fitz, don't come back for me. Stay safe. Take care of my son.

She was going to die. Now. Here. On this foreign beach. Alone and unburied. Food for the fish on the next high tide—or maybe the black ants would get her first. But instead of the terrified scramble of emotions she expected to find in herself, her mind was oddly calm. She saw everything around her with precise clarity: the long, glossy leaves of the nipa palms waving good-bye in the wind, a lizard with its crest raised in final greeting, the sea bright and glittering as it sighed its farewell, and on her hand a fingerprint of blood that belonged to Fitz. All were outlined in vivid colors, as if her eyes knew it was their last chance to view the world.

Once she was out in the open, other uniforms gathered around her, gray as lice. Ten, twelve, twenty of them, she lost count. They jabbed at her with rifle butts and herded her into the shade of trees like a calf into a slaughterhouse. They argued with each other in Japanese, their faces full of rage and exhaustion and lust, and as she listened to them the numbness of shock began to wear off. She felt a rush of nausea. She vomited over one man's boot and he kicked her, but not hard.

The soldier who had found her seemed to be claiming the right to shoot her. He kept lifting his rifle and squinting along its barrel at her, until the others eventually backed off and shrugged agreement. Her heart stopped beating. She shut her eyes and found Fitz's face there in her mind's eye, waiting for her. Fitz and Teddy, hand in hand together. A wave of intense sorrow shook her because she would never see her son grow into a man or . . .

More shouting. A sudden outburst of voices rose around her that sent her mind into chaos—because the one shouting the loudest, the one making the most noise, belonged to Fitz. But the words were all Japanese. Her eyes shot open and he was there, in front of her. Not in her mind's eye. He was real flesh and blood, and if she stepped forward she could touch him. She didn't understand why the soldiers didn't shoot him.

His words spilled out into the jungle, harsh and angry, his face rigid, and when he looked at her his eyes were indifferent, his mouth scornful. She could make no sense of the stream of Japanese that poured out, but over and over from his mouth she heard the words that turned the sweat on her skin to ice: *Constance Hadley. Takehashi.* And then again, *Constance Hadley. Takehashi.*

Shohei Takehashi had come back to haunt her.

CHAPTER THIRTY-EIGHT

Three days.
Three days of sweat and swearing.

Three nights of mosquitoes and raking the earth with her fingernails to try to dislodge the metal post to which her wrists were tied.

Once in every hour, day and night, the sentry outside marched in to ensure she was still tied up and that the metal stake was secure. The first time he walked in with a sledgehammer that dwarfed his fragile physique, she thought he had come to kill her, to pound her brains out in the dirt. But the blows were for the stake, not her head, driving it firmly back into place while he shouted at her in Japanese for loosening it.

They had put her in a green tent erected in the clearing where the Kennel used to stand before it was bombed. It was stifling and airless, with barely enough room for a person to stand. Not that she could rise from her knees. Her wrists were tethered to the stake at ground level, looped through holes bored in it with no more than an arm's length of free rope. Enough to allow her to reach the bucket that was emptied at the end of each day, or to lift to her mouth the single mug of fish broth that she was given at dawn every morning. A tin mug of water arrived at midday, and another at sunset. That was it.

Three days.
Of sweat. Of tears. Of rage.
The fear was always there, so solid and real that it became a

companion to her, one she loathed and taunted and derided to see how much punishment it could take before it slapped her in the face and brought her weeping to her knees. And all the time she pictured Fitz-payne's indifferent face swirling through her mind.

You betrayed me. You betrayed my son.

Her lips formed the words, but she put her hand over her mouth to keep them in. She rested her forehead on the ground and replayed each scene through her mind: Fitz laughing with her on the boat, Fitz teaching Teddy to fish and tie knots, Fitz asking, *Do you know what it is to die of loneliness?* His lips warm and demanding on her breasts. She scoured each scene, seeking clues until her thoughts grew weary and wavering.

ᘐ·ᘓ

Time after time inside the tent, Connie began to think of Sho; to question why Fitz would utter his name. As she grew more sleepless and hungry, her mind started to play tricks, and after three days of isolation she heard his voice. She was lying on the earthen floor in a pool of sweat, picking scabs from the insect bites on her arm, when she heard Sho say quite distinctly in English, "Constance Hadley is a dangerous woman. Beware of her. She is like that spider that kills its chosen lover after mating."

Connie sat up. She wanted to rip off her ears, to banish the sound of his voice from her head.

"Sho," she shouted at the dripping walls of the tent, "if you are here, this must be hell."

She tried to gnaw the rope from her wrists. Only when she tasted blood did she think to stop and wonder what demon had entered her soul.

ᘐ·ᘓ

They came for her, two smooth-faced soldiers no taller than herself. When one cut the rope that bound her to the metal stake in the ground, she didn't beg or cry or grovel at their feet, pleading for her life the way a part of her wanted to. She stood up straight and walked quietly between them, drawing into her lungs for the last time the wild scent of the jungle after the stale fog of the tent.

They gripped her arms, but instead of taking her to a killing ground, they marched her toward a large khaki tent set up near the riverbank, its flaps wide open to pick up any breeze off the water. The afternoon sun cast shadows from the trees across its surface, but once inside, she stopped dead.

"Sho?"

Her escort jerked her forward.

"Sho?" she whispered again.

On one side of the tent stood a table covered with maps and papers, alongside two folding chairs, one with binoculars on its canvas seat, the other with a pair of wooden crutches propped against it. But Connie registered it all only dimly because her mind was fragmented as it fought to make sense of what she saw directly in front of her. A large square of pristine white silk lay on the ground like a spill of milk. On it were arranged an ancient black clay teapot, two tiny handleless porcelain cups, so fine they were almost transparent, and a small bamboo vase containing one bright orange flower of a kind Connie had never seen before. Two men were seated around it, cross-legged on the ground, as though at a table. One was Fitz. The other was Shohei Takehashi.

Sho's voice spoke to her, a harsh order in Japanese. When she didn't respond immediately, one of her escorts jammed his rifle into the back of her leg. She stumbled forward and buckled to her knees. She heard a hiss of breath, but she didn't know from which man it came. She looked at them again now that she was closer and at eye level with them, and a pain roared into life in her chest. *Fitz, who are you?* His expression was grim and cold, his thoughts hidden behind eyes as dark as the clean black shirt on his back.

She clutched at reality. Dragged it into her head.

It wasn't Sho. It couldn't be. In the dim light of the tent she saw that it was *almost* Sho—but not quite. The man seated in front of her possessed the exact shape of Sho's head and jaw, the arch of his brow, the same almond eyes and full prominent lips. But now that she was close she could see that this man was older, his hair threaded with silver. A pair of deep lines scored the skin between his nose and mouth. The set of his shoulders was stiff inside his military uniform, the swell of his chest full of self-regard. This was a proud man, the man Sho might have become. Had he lived.

"This is Constance Hadley," Fitz announced in a flat voice.

Fitz, don't. Connie couldn't look at him.

"This is General Takehashi," he continued. "Father of Shohei Takehashi."

There was a pause, so slight it was barely perceptible, but Connie knew Fitz. It was the pause he made when he was angry.

"It is a great honor to me," he said, "that General Takehashi is my adoptive father, as Shohei Takehashi was my beloved adoptive brother."

A black pit opened up in front of Connie. She tumbled into it head first. *My beloved adoptive brother.* She had killed someone Fitz loved.

She gazed straight at him. "You knew," she said. "All the time you knew."

"Yes."

"Why didn't you tell me?"

He turned abruptly to General Takehashi and spoke to him in Japanese before addressing her again.

"The general wishes to know exactly what happened to his son."

Connie studied the features that were Shohei's, yet not Shohei's. She was still on her knees, and slowly she bowed forward until her forehead rested on the damp earth. At this moment her heart ached for the father she had robbed.

"A thousand apologies, General Takehashi," she said solemnly. "My heart is full because of the wrong I did to you and to your son, Shohei Takehashi." She raised her head a fraction. "I have suffered ten thousand regrets, but none of them can bring him back. Shohei's death was an accident—on my life, I tell you the truth." She touched her bound hands to her heart.

"What kind of accident?" Fitz demanded harshly.

"We had an argument and there was a struggle. I pushed Shohei away from me. Tragically, he fell on his knife."

The words tumbled out of her mouth, as heavy as stone, and a silence filled the air between them.

"I apologize humbly," she said.

404 · KATE FURNIVALL

Nothing more. But she knew she had signed her death warrant.

Fitz murmured in Japanese, and she heard the general growl a reply. There was a clink of porcelain and the scent of jasmine in the air. Minutes ticked past, and finally Connie rose once more, upright on her knees. Shohei's father was gazing sorrowfully into the bottom of his cup, the muscles of his cheeks bunched and hard, but Fitz was staring at her. For one fleeting moment she saw something in his eyes that stopped her heartbeat. It was a look of such despair that she longed to leap to her feet and run to him. To find the truth of him. But it vanished before she could draw breath to speak, and an expression of guarded disdain returned. *Did I imagine it? Does my mind no longer see straight?*

"Mr. Fitzpayne," she said softly.

"Yes, Mrs. Hadley?"

"Tell me how you know. I would like to be told that much." *Before I am shot. Before I forsake my son.*

The general leaned forward, both hands placed flat on the silk square, and he said in perfect English, "Tell the whore. Tell her how you smelled out her trail like a hound smells out a bitch."

Fitz looked down at his own hands. His chest expanded, drawing in air urgently as if there could never be enough air for him inside this khaki tent. Then he raised his eyes to hers.

"I once saved Shohei's life," he said in a voice that was quiet and unemotional. "It's not important how. What is important is that at the time I was drifting aimlessly around eastern Asia, and General Takehashi took me in. Adopted me. It was a great honor."

He faced his adoptive father and bowed low over his hands. Connie saw something pass between them, a flicker of affection, and for the first time the hard line of the general's mouth relaxed a fraction and he murmured something in Japanese, as he placed a caring hand on the knee of Fitz's damaged leg.

"Shohei and I became blood brothers," Fitz said simply. "When he traveled to Malaya—"

"Spying for Japan," Connie interrupted.

"He was serving his emperor," Fitz corrected sternly. He studied her face. "Is that what you quarreled about?"

"Yes. I found out."

He poured himself a tiny cup of tea but didn't sip it. "Shohei wrote a letter to his father every day. Did you know that?"

"No, I didn't."

"Telling him all that he saw and did."

Connie shuddered. *Not everything. Please, not everything.*

Fitz drew another long breath and continued, "He told his father about you, about your house and your husband's rubber estate." He stopped, as though the words had run dry.

General Takehashi waited, his fist clenched.

"Shohei described your hut beside the river," Fitz continued, his voice flat, "the love nest you used for your trysts. He wrote that he intended to bring you back to Tokyo to be his wife. He told us he was going to meet you that day, but we never heard from him again. He said that he intended to ask you . . ."

Connie shook her head. She remembered the silk square on the floor of the hut, the shock of Sho's request. The belated realization that he wanted so much more from her. How could she have been so blind? But in those days back in Palur, her eyes were half closed and her mind paralyzed by the loneliness of a loveless marriage.

". . . to marry him. Did he do that?"

"Yes."

General Takehashi spat on the dirt floor. "Why did my son want the whore? Look at her."

Connie felt the weight of their slow inspection of her. Her face was covered in bites and scratches, her hair was plastered to her head by filth and sweat, her clothes were in rags—and when she looked down at her body she was shocked to see how wretchedly thin it had become. The general was right. Why would anyone want her?

"She's not a whore," Fitz stated quietly. He sipped his tea.

"Did you say yes to my son?" General Takehashi demanded. "Did you agree to marry him?"

"No," she said, "I didn't. I was aware of the great honor he was paying me, but I couldn't leave Malaya because of my son."

"You have left it now."

"Of course. What do you expect, General? You have decided to take Malaya for yourselves."

"To liberate it from the tyranny of Western imperial domination."

She didn't argue. Not now, not with so much at stake. Instead she said courteously, "General Takehashi, your son was a good man. I would never have wished him harm."

"Too good for a whore like you."

She turned away. "How did you track me down?" she asked Fitz.

He stood up abruptly, ignoring his adoptive father's hiss of disapproval, and started to limp back and forth along the length of the tent on one of the crutches. He must have been in pain, but he gave no sign. "It wasn't exactly hard," he said. "I traveled to Malaya, made inquiries about the Hadleys, and on the train from KL had no trouble hitching up with Flight Lieutenant Johnnie Blake, whom I already knew was the Hadleys' dearest friend."

"I see."

"Do you?"

"Yes. You used us. Abused Nigel's hospitality." She spoke angrily, lashing out. "It was despicable."

"I went to the hut," he said coldly.

Shame flushed up into her cheeks.

"There was nothing there," he said.

"I burned everything."

From the pocket of his clean trousers, Fitz drew a cigarette case and flipped it open. A gasp escaped Connie's lips and he swung around. He followed the direction of her gaze to the silver case in his hand, as he lit his cigarette.

"You recognize it?" he asked.

"It's identical to the one that belonged to Sho," she whispered.

"Yes. Except for the initials. My father"—he gestured toward General Takehashi—"generously gave us a gift of a cigarette case each." After a moment's thought, he added, "Do you have it?"

"It's in Palur."

"Where?" The general leaned forward hungrily. A father wanting the last piece of his son. *Ask the monitor lizard. Ask the voracious ants.*

"Will it make any difference if I tell you?"

The general swatted her question aside the way a houseboy swats flies. "Where?" he asked again, as persistent as his son.

"It was in a drawer in my dressing room when I left. At Hadley House."

A smile, so like Sho's it sent a shiver through Connie, flashed across General Takehashi's face. "We will find it," he said to Fitz, his lips taut.

But Fitz's eyes were on Connie, and she could read the question in them. *Why did you keep it? Did it mean so much to you?*

No, it meant nothing, I swear. I only kept it to stop myself from wiping him from my memory, erasing him out of existence.

Abruptly the general barked an order to the guards, and she was yanked back onto her feet. She heard the breath escape from Fitz's lungs, as everything came at her, bright and clear and fast, her brain aware that this was the end. It clamored to fill its final moments.

"Fitz," she said urgently. "Were you the same as Sho, a spy for Japan? Is that what you were doing all the time? Was it all a pretense, while you betrayed your country?"

"I have no country."

His words struck chill. He spoke in low tones to the general, and although she couldn't understand what he was saying, it was clear he had cut himself off from her. No sign of love for her. She longed to speak to him again one last time, but she was frightened the wrong words would come out, as everything inside her started to hurt.

The older man was growing impatient, eager to be rid of her, and he waved a dismissive hand as a signal to the guards. She saw Fitz's mouth tighten but he said nothing, raised no objection to what was about to happen. He did not lift a hand to save her. As the guards marched her back to the doorway, her feet managed to move. She didn't know how they could walk her to her death when her life lay in this dark khaki tent.

"Constance Hadley."

It was Fitz's voice. When she turned, she saw tension in the flare of his nostrils and in the fingers that held his cigarette. The guards halted. Her eyes feasted on him whether she wanted them to or not.

"What is it?" she asked quietly.

"Did you love him?"

"Shohei?"

"Yes. Did you love my brother?"

Say *yes*. Say *yes*. Say you adored him so much you had decided to abandon your son for him. To desert your husband for him. To surrender your whole life to him. Say that you yearned to spend the rest of your years at his side in Japan, to grow old with him. Say that he was the sun and moon and stars to you.

Say it. Say it.

Then maybe his father will relent and grant you a life.

"No, Fitz, I never loved Shohei Takehashi."

In silence she walked from the tent.

∽·⅁

Why didn't they put a bullet in her?

She craved water. The walls of her tent prison were stifling.

Nothing made sense to her. Was General Takehashi set on playing with her mind? Was his intention to torment her the way he was tormented by the loss of his son? She blinked to bring her thoughts into focus once more.

An image hammered at her brain as she lay on her side tethered to the stake once more—it was the thread of smoke curling out of Fitz's mouth. It had brushed over the moist surface of his lips and swirled around his nostrils in a vain attempt to creep back in. She saw it over and over again—Fitz breathing out what he no longer wanted; expelling her as easily as he expelled the smoke. There was no question in her mind that it was he who had summoned Sho's father, and she realized now that it must have been his plan from the start.

She tried to work it out, but couldn't. Whenever she thought of Teddy, sickness rose in her stomach, but she willed Johnnie to take good care of him—the son General Takehashi was denying her in revenge for the loss of his own. Her dehydrated mind still struggled to understand why Fitz had not summoned the general before now. Once he had maneuvered her onto the island, why wait so long? Why all the pretense? Betrayal was betrayal in any language.

"Fitz," she whispered angrily. "Fitz, why did you entice me to love you?"

Abruptly something broke loose within her and erupted out of control, searing her insides. Everything she'd been holding tight tore out of her grasp and she began to shiver uncontrollably. She saw nothing but blackness in front of her.

ᎨᎬ

Hands touched her face. Water washed over her lips and trickled onto her tongue. The side of her head lay on something warm and solid, and she heard a gentle drumming in her ear.

"Connie!"

It wasn't over. Not yet.

"Connie, don't you dare give up on me now."

"Go away," she mumbled.

She didn't want illusions or fantasies, or whatever the hell this was. Because it was Fitz's voice, Fitz's touch, Fitz's heartbeat in her ear, and she knew none of that could be real. Lips brushed her forehead with a kiss so real that it made her suddenly aware of the foul smell of her own body. She opened her eyes.

She was cradled in Fitz's arms. The rope around her wrists had been removed and it was dark outside, the tent just a triangle of blackness around her. Only a thin brush of moonlight had sneaked in through the door flap and painted Fitz's thick hair silver. She smiled at him. She no longer cared whether the moment was a figment of her fevered imagination or not, because all that mattered was that he had come to her one last time.

"Stand up," he told her.

"So that your Japanese friends can shoot me? No, thank you. Tell them to come and do it here. Or"—she smiled sadly up at him—"are you going to be the one to finish the job yourself?"

He shook her. "Stand up, Connie. Be quick."

He put a bottle to her lips, and she drank the water greedily. It took a massive effort of will to make herself move out of his arms.

"What trick are you playing now, Mr. Fitzpayne?"

"Oh, my precious Connie, I can't blame you for not trusting me. But it was the only way I could think of to save your life when the soldiers seized you out at the promontory." Gently he lifted her to her feet. "We have to leave."

"What about the guard?"

"I have removed him."

"Where are we going?" she demanded.

"To find your son."

CHAPTER THIRTY-NINE

The darkness whispered to Connie. It teased her mind. She had to fight to find the line between what was real and what was shadow. Her heart was pounding enough to make her teeth rattle, but her steps were quick and silent on the dirt trail, and her arm fastened firmly around Fitz's waist. She didn't know if he was holding her up or if she was holding him up, any more than she knew whether her anger at him was deserved.

It was the only way I could think of to save your life.

What did he mean by that?

A fitful moon shimmered through the trees and the wind had risen in the night, stirring the jungle around them, so that every sound, every creak of a branch or rustle of a frond made her head turn, alert for danger.

"It's all right, Connie," Fitz whispered, "I know where the sentries are posted. We're safe."

She made herself believe it—but if it were true, why were they fleeing in stealthy silence? She took his weight when his bad leg made him stumble in the pitch dark and he cursed under his breath, but when they emerged from the jungle onto a narrow stretch of riverbank upstream from where the camp had been, she stood still. She placed her hands on each side of his face, holding him, pinning him down, conscious of the stubble on his jaw, and asked in a voice that was scrupulously devoid of any blame, "Where is my son?"

"On the *Burung Camar*."

"Still alive?"

"Yes."

Relief drained away her anger. "So how do we find the *Burung Camar* now? It was days ago that it left here."

"I have a boat for us. Hidden in the mangroves."

For a long moment she continued to hold his face in her hands, sensing he had more to say.

"I came for you, Connie."

"I know."

He took her hands in his and anchored them to his chest. "Don't ever do that to me again." His eyes were in darkness. "Don't ever," he said, no more than a murmur, "don't ever put me through such agony." He wrapped a strong arm around her neck and pulled her cheek against his. He held her there. Silent. Breathing hard. "To see you like that," he continued softly, "in front of General Takehashi was . . . unbearable."

"I saw the anger," she whispered, "inside you, but I didn't know it was on my behalf. I thought it was because . . ."

"Of course it was for you, my precious Connie." Abruptly he stood back from her to let his gaze scour her face. "Don't you know I love you? Don't you know I cannot let you die, even if it is the path you would choose?"

"I am not ready to die," she assured him fiercely.

"I know. You have a son."

"General Takehashi had two sons. Now he has none—because of me. He has good reason to want me dead. How did you persuade him not to have me shot?"

"I made a deal with him."

"Oh, Fitz. What kind of deal?"

He put a finger to her lips. "Trust me, Connie."

Why? When you betrayed me? The question lived for no more than one second in her head. She only had to listen to his words. Just as in that seedy bar in Palur, when she had asked him to skipper her yacht, she could trust him. She knew it then, and she knew it now.

ᏉᏣ

The boat was holed, its bottom smashed out. It was a flimsy rowboat that Fitz had concealed in the embrace of the mangrove roots, but some sharp-eyed Jap soldier had crawled in among the tangled branches and taken his rifle butt to it. Connie saw the despair on Fitz's face in the darkness.

"Not this," he moaned.

They were crouched down beside what was left of the rowboat, and only then did realization suddenly come to her, so that she rose to her feet, acid in her throat.

"What is it, Connie?" He reached out a hand.

She stepped back. "Tell me, Fitz, what deal did you make with your adoptive father?"

"What?"

"Tell me what you offered him in exchange for my life."

Slowly he struggled to his feet. "Don't, Connie."

"Tell me!"

"I promised him your son."

Connie staggered, as though punched, and forced herself away from him when he tried to hold her.

"No," she hissed. "No."

"It was the only way."

"To exchange me for my son?"

"Yes, you took his son. Now he wants yours."

His earlier words—*I cannot let you die, even if it is the path you would choose*—now they made terrible sense.

"You know I would die a thousand times before I would let anything happen to Teddy. You know that, you know that. How could you think I could live after—"

Fitz stepped forward and gripped her wrists like shackles. "I know, Connie," he said fiercely. "I knew I would lose you by making such a deal, but I couldn't let you die. I couldn't."

She tried to pull away from him, but he held her firm. "I told General

Takehashi that your son was on the *Burung Camar*—which he knows is my boat—but that I didn't know where it was now, as it was taken over by natives when the Japanese planes attacked."

She tried to listen. Tried to think straight. To decipher his words. But all that rampaged through her head was the fact that her son was in danger while she was stranded on this Jap-infested island.

"Listen, Connie." His face drew close, as if he could physically force his words into her brain. "Teddy is safe. Takehashi has no idea where the *Burung Camar* is."

"Neither do we."

"Of course we do. Nurul will be at the promontory tonight."

"All our hopes are pinned on Nurul? My son's life depends on that man?"

"Don't sound so scathing. Nurul will be there. Night after night until I come."

She shook her head violently. "He won't. He'll be long gone."

"Connie, I will not let Takehashi take your son, I swear to you."

He pulled her to his chest and wrapped his arms around her, pinning her there until her struggles ceased. "Without a boat, we'll have to walk. Tonight we won't make it across the island by dawn, which means we'll have to hide again during daylight hours tomorrow and look out for Nurul the following night." He rested his lips against her forehead. "We will make it, I promise you."

Connie's mind started to function. His voice, with its calm certainty, steadied her. There was a sudden sound in the forest, and he drew her deep into the mangroves as two sentries inspected the shoreline, cursory in the darkness. They were careless because they believed they had already flushed all the rats from the island.

"Fitz," Connie whispered in his ear, "I know where there is a boat."

꒤꒤

"Hardly a boat," Fitz remarked under his breath.

"It will do."

"It will probably drown us."

"I'll take that chance."

It did look precarious. It was a dugout canoe, the ancient one that Teddy and his friend had been sheltering under when she came to confront her son about taking payment for reading to the other children. It was well weathered and somewhat chewed around the edges, but it was still in one piece and looked watertight. Together they maneuvered it silently to the river's edge, and Fitz made Connie clamber in front while he slid himself in behind her with a grunt of pain. For paddles they made do with two pieces of split bamboo that had been blasted onto the shore by the bombs that fell.

Without a sound and carried by the current, they drifted downriver. They could see the bulky outline of the khaki tent onshore, but Connie turned her head away immediately. She made herself concentrate instead on keeping her makeshift paddle dipping in time with Fitz's smooth stroke. The hulks of burned-out boats loomed out of the darkness as their canoe dodged between them, but when the clouds closed in over their heads, Connie was grateful for the cloak of invisibility that the night now draped over them.

When they approached the mouth of the river and the water grew choppier, Connie felt the swarms of mosquitoes fall away, as intimidated as she was by the booming of the sea's breakers. The canoe seemed far too frail, far too shallow to survive the pounding ahead of it, but when a warm hand lay on her back, resting against her spine, it seemed to reassure her on a level far deeper than words. She leaned back against it, and for a brief moment the paddles paused. The sea stretched out in front of them, a vast black sheet in constant motion.

"We have to keep up our speed." Fitz shifted his weight forward. "It will help us ride the tops of the waves. Less danger of getting swamped," he told her. Again his hand lay on the center of her back, anchoring her.

"Now!" he said, and they spurted out of the mouth of the river.

Ͽ·Ԑ

Maya kept hearing a drum. *Boom-boom-boom.* But each time she twitched her head to find the noise, she realized the drum was inside her own ears.

Jo-nee had gone to talk to the man with the gun. "This can't go on," he'd said as he strode over to crazy Madoc. They argued, and crazy Madoc pointed the gun at him, as well as at Nurul. Maya had covered her eyes and tried to shut her ears to their words.

"Stop this idiocy, Madoc, at once," Jo-nee had said, but Maya could hear that his voice was all wrong. "You are committing a serious criminal offense—piracy and the kidnapping of British citizens. You must stop now, for God's sake, man, and hand over to Nurul. We won't report you to the authorities."

Crazy Madoc didn't like the voice and shouted bad words at Jo-nee, but his wife didn't join in. She looked as if she'd swallowed a snake by mistake, her face tight, her mouth pinched shut. The weapons of the crew had all been gathered in a pile and bound together into a spiky bundle of rifles and knives at Madoc's feet, while the single black eye of the gun in his hand stared unblinking at Nurul's chest.

"I have no charts for sailing to India," the pirate bleated.

"So navigate by the stars, damn you. There's the Southern Cross. Use that. It's due west to India. Simple."

But when Maya looked up at the black sky she could see no cross, just millions of eyes. The moon was sliding higher to watch crazy Madoc as well, and it sprinkled its light on the pale, upturned face of the little Hadley boy. He was standing in front of Madoc and begging him to turn the boat around, tears on his cheeks. It made the booming in Maya's head grow louder when she heard his voice. She scuttled to the long pointed nose of the boat, where Razak was doing something to one of the foresails. Maya wanted comfort from her brother, but he looked at her sadly and told her that this was the work of her mother's angry spirit.

Maya scowled at him. "It is *Mem* Hadley who has taken care of us," she told him. "Not our mother."

"Show respect, sister."

"The one who deserves respect is the white woman."

"Hush!" he hissed. "Lower your voice or our mother will hear."

"Stop it, Razak. Stop it." The booming was loud in Maya's ears, and the night wind felt like cold fingers on her cheeks. "Our mother is dead. *Mem* Hadley will be dead too if we do nothing."

For a moment he was silent, staring down at the rope looped in his hands. "Do you care so much?" he asked softly.

"Yes, Razak, I care. *Mem* saved my life. My spirit now walks step by step with hers. I cannot run from her, any more than I can run from you, my brother." She heard a shout of anger come from crazy Madoc's mouth somewhere in the darkness. "Help me, Razak," she whispered. *Boom-boom-boom.* She still heard it.

Without a word Razak lifted his tunic, revealing the black bulk of a gun tucked into his waistband. Maya reached out and touched it. It nudged her fingers, as though wanting to talk to her. She snatched it from him.

"No, Maya."

Yes, Maya. Yes, Maya. That was what the gun said. It was heavy.

She sneaked back through the darkness to where the crazy man—who was leaving *Mem* Hadley to die on the island—was standing, his back to the sea. He still held the big ugly pistol pointed at Nurul, and she could see his eyes darting all the time over the crew. But he didn't imagine that Razak had brought a gun from the island and he didn't take any notice of Maya because she was a no-notice mouse who scurried around in the dirt. *Well, crazy Madoc, you will notice me now.* She had seen men in Palur with guns before, and she knew about safety catches, so she crept behind him in the dark and pointed it at his crazy back. She shut her eyes, spoke silent words of farewell to her mother's spirit, and pulled the trigger.

The gun roared in her hand. The explosion knocked her to the deck and the gun leaped away from her as though it were finished with this no-notice mouse and wanted someone else. Teddy pounced on it and picked it up, waving it immediately at Kitty Madoc, who rushed forward with a roar of rage, but Maya didn't care because her own wicked hand was shaking so violently. She stared at her fingers as if they belonged to someone else and possessed a will quite separate from her own.

But when her eyes looked across at the body of Madoc lying on the deck in what looked like a pool of oil, she knew he was dead, crazy dead Madoc now. His wife had turned him over and was cradling his head on her fat thighs, leaning over him and dabbing with her hair at the black trickle of blood that had oozed from between his lips. As she kissed his eyelids and his sharp nose, she was making a strange, mind-numbing noise that pierced Maya's skull.

But still the drumming grew louder. *Boom-boom-boom* inside her ears.

৯·৫

Maya followed Jo-nee around the deck of the pirate's boat the way a cat follows a piece of string, trotting behind it, ears pricked. But every now and again she would pounce forward and lay her paws on him. She knew now that she was *astonishingly brave*. Jo-nee said so. So it must be true.

"Brave and bold," he had said.

The boat was not a nice boat, not like *The White Pearl*. Only fit for sea scum. It was lying offshore, muttering and grumbling to itself in the night wind, waiting for Fitzpayne and *Mem* Hadley to leap up out of the water like dolphins, but Maya was cross with Nurul. How would *mem* know that *Tuan* Teddy had sailed around to the other side of the island? *Mem* would be upset. Very upset.

"She's dead," Razak insisted. But he spoke behind his hand, so that the boy wouldn't hear.

"No," Maya scolded. "*Mem* and Iron-eyes will stick bayonets into the yellow-bellied soldiers."

Razak stared at her as if she had gone mad. "Did you see how many Japanese there are on the island? There's no hope for *mem*. This waiting is dangerous, as well as a waste of time when we could be sailing away from here."

"To where?"

"To India."

"Where is India?"

Razak waved a hand vaguely at the expanse of blackness behind him. "Over there somewhere."

Maya scowled. "I like white people."

"There are many white people in India."

"How do you know?"

"*Tuan* Hadley told me."

"Crazy Madoc wanted to go to India too."

At the mention of Madoc, Razak looked warily at his sister and gave her a cold little smile. "He isn't able to want anything any more."

The way he said it scared her. "Razak," she said desperately, "you are still my brother. I am your blood."

"Yes," he said thoughtfully, "you are my blood."

"Jo-nee says I am brave," she told him.

"My sister, if you had not put a bullet in Madoc, we would now be far away from here. Safe from this danger. How is it brave to throw us into the path of the Japanese soldiers? It is"—he hesitated, looked at her face, and swallowed the words that were on his tongue—"not wise," he finished more gently.

She was grateful. She did not want Razak to hate her because she had killed a man. Already the fat wife of crazy Madoc had poured bad words on her head, words that still buzzed like black flies in her brain. In the middle of the night Jo-nee had given the dead man *a decent burial at sea*—that was what he said—and had read out words from their holy book, but to Maya it seemed more like chucking his body overboard in the dark to feed the sharks. Kitty Madoc was trembling. But she didn't cry, not one single tear, as if the shame of what her husband had done blocked their path. Yet Maya saw the way her hands clenched and unclenched, mute shrieks of pain, and the way her body seemed to crumple inward.

Afterward, when Kitty Madoc poured the bad words on Maya, that was when Jo-nee told her she was astonishingly brave. But in her heart she didn't feel brave. She kept staring at the hand that had held the gun and wishing it belonged to someone else.

CHAPTER FORTY

The wind was fresh in Connie's face and the canoe rocked violently as she struggled to keep her rhythm. Salt from the sea spray had coated her lips and given her a raging thirst. The waves slammed against the bow, knocking it off course, and it was her job to bail quickly with cupped hands. They were rounding one of the island's rocky claws where the wind was at its strongest, but Fitz had promised her easier going on the lee side of the island. He was right. It was as though a curtain had dropped, as abruptly the sea became steadier and the paddling smoother.

They traveled fast now, and Connie's hopes rose. She even started to have faith in Nurul's constancy. The tumult inside her grew calmer along with the seas, and she was able to listen to the comments Fitz made behind her as he sought to keep her believing.

"Teddy will be relieved to see you again," he assured her.

And later: "We're making good time."

But once, when she turned, she caught him glancing to the east, keeping a sharp eye on it. They both knew that the moment the sun painted the horizon gold, the *Burung Camar* would hoist sail and leave.

꽁

Maya watched the moonlight dodge in and out of the waves and dance in the rigging. It made her nervous. Jo-nee said that the Japs would have scout planes patrolling the area at night, and even though the *Burung Camar* carried no lights, in the moonlight it was a sitting target. The thought of more bombs made Maya's knees loosen and her mouth taste of seaweed. She tucked herself in a ball behind the little hut at the back of the boat and listened hard.

Maya was good at listening. She collected words for Jo-nee. He was grateful when she informed him that she had heard the pirate with the pig's belly tell Nurul that they should wait no longer for Fitzpayne, so now she crouched in a squat black shadow and listened to Kitty Madoc and Nurul talking inside the hut. Kitty Madoc's voice sounded strange, as if her tongue weren't working right. It sounded broken, like Jo-nee's shoulder. It hurt Maya's ears to listen to the woman's voice, and after only a short while she slipped away and instead found Jo-nee with Razak. He liked speaking with her brother; she could tell by the way his handsome smile hovered around his lips, waiting to spread its wings. A tiny pain between her eyes jumped into life each time she saw it.

"Come here, Maya."

Jo-nee held out his hand to her, and when she took it, he drew her to stand in front of him on the deck. She was glad it was night-dark, so he didn't see her cheeks turn to fire.

"What has my little blackbird been up to now?"

"Listening."

Blackbird? Black and ugly. Pecking at crumbs.

He laughed. "What did you pick up this time?"

She saw the way Razak looked at Jo-nee, and the way that Jo-nee looked at Razak.

"Nurul think *Mem* Hadley is dead," she said cruelly, to see Jo-nee's face turn as white as milk in the moonlight. Yet when he stroked her hand, she wanted to snatch back her words. "But Kitty Madoc says *mem* too tough to die. She want to wait here long time for *mem*."

"Mrs. Madoc is a strong woman. Despite her grief, she has her head screwed on right."

Head screwed on?

"She say she sorry crazy Madoc use radio."

Jo-nee's grip tightened, and his blue eyes blazed at her as if she had hit him with his cricket bat.

"Radio?" he demanded. "What radio?"

"On boat."

"What? There's a shortwave radio on this boat?"

Maya nodded, pleased that he was squeezing her hand.

"Do you know where it is?" he asked.

"Yes."

Of course she knew. She had sniffed around the boat after Nurul.

"For heaven's sake, Maya, why didn't you tell me earlier? Take me to it at once."

"Crazy Madoc used it and Japs came. You no use it, Jo-nee. More Japs come."

He dropped her hand. "Good God, girl, don't be foolish. It's our only way out of this unholy mess."

୬·ૄ

The moon surprised them. It slipped away from the grip of the clouds and trickled a thin, luminous sheen across the waves. From the back of the canoe came Fitz's grunt of disapproval, but Connie welcomed it. The darkness had been jamming her thoughts in an unrelenting circle.

"Fitz," she asked suddenly, not breaking the rhythm of her stroke though her arms ached, "what did you think at first? When you came to my house. Did you hate me?"

She heard his breath stop. After a long moment, it started again.

"Yes, I hated the concept of Mrs. Constance Hadley, the woman I was certain had destroyed my brother. But"—his voice altered, softened—"I never hated you, Connie." He gave a strange low laugh. "God knows, I tried. I tried so damn hard to hate you that I nearly wrenched my guts out. But I didn't stand a chance. I tried staying away from you, and then I tried hanging around so much that I could discover all your weaknesses and dislike you."

"And did you?"

"Learn to dislike you?"

"Yes."

"No, I didn't. I grew to love you so much it nearly killed me. Seeing you with your husband each day was torture. Sometimes I even imagined that it was Shohei's punishment to me for not avenging his memory."

She swung around to face him, sending the canoe into a dance they both ignored. "Yet you betrayed me to General Takehashi. And you betrayed my son. How can that be love?"

He shipped his paddle in a jerky movement. "Connie, when the Japanese troops captured you, I could have stayed hidden, I could have waited for Nurul and sailed away that night. I didn't. Because a life without you would be no life."

She laid a hand on his as a wave splashed over the side, leaving their fingers fused together in the wet and the dark.

"The only way I could save you, Connie, was by summoning up the name of the great General Takehashi. It scared the pants off the local troops, and they sent a message to him in Okinawa. He flew down immediately. The rest you know."

The canoe was drifting, a dark speck on a faceless sea.

"And that scene in the tent?" Connie said. "Was that real?"

"Oh, Connie, my love, how can you ask?"

"It felt real."

He leaned close, blurring the lines between them. There was no longer an end of her or a beginning of him. Something important was changing.

"I never loved you more," he whispered, "than when you knelt before my adoptive father. Your courage was beautiful."

"You were cruel," she told him.

"I know."

"Why should I forgive you?" She meant her words to sound angry, but her smile crept into them as he drew her forward and kissed her salty lips.

The canoe rolled dangerously, and Fitz snatched up his paddle.

"Now," Connie said, "now find me my son."

⊃·⊂

Don't leave me. Maya shouted the words so loud in her head that she thought Jo-nee would hear her. *Don't leave me.*

He was arguing with Nurul. In the back end of the boat, Nurul kept pointing to the thin ribbon of gold on the eastern horizon and shaking his head. He wanted to leave. The wind was tugging sharply at the rigging, adding its voice to his, eager for the *Burung Camar* to be off. Nurul was angry that Jo-nee had used the radio. The native captain had smacked Maya for revealing it, but she didn't care because Jo-nee had kissed her cheek and told her she was *a godsend*.

"What would I do without you?" he had asked.

She was about to tell him that he didn't ever have to do without her, and that they must stay together to wait for *mem*, when he called out to Teddy on deck that an aircraft was coming to pick them up. Maya snorted out loud. An aircraft? Where could it land? But Teddy believed him.

"No," Teddy said, his face very stern and very sad. "I won't go. I won't leave here without my mother."

"Teddy, we've been here for four nights," Jo-nee explained gently. "I'm sorry, old chap, but the best we can hope for now is that she will turn up in one of the Jap prisoner-of-war camps."

Teddy looked sick.

"We need to be back home to find out news of her," Jo-nee urged.

"I have no home."

"There's always England, Teddy," Jo-nee reassured him, and put an arm around his shoulders. "England will always be your home."

Jo-nee is good man. But he didn't understand. The boy was right. They *must* stay for *Mem* Hadley. The white woman's voice seemed to murmur to her from the waves.

They all stared out across the sea at the island, hunched in the darkness, as the shifting moonlight made it look as though it were crawling closer.

"What kind of plane?" Teddy asked eventually. He couldn't resist it.

"We're lucky, there's a Short Sunderland on reconnaissance patrol on the lookout for Japanese submarines in this area. To drop depth charges on them. It should be here within half an hour—before the Japs can pinpoint my radio signal." Jo-nee hugged the young boy. "Then we'll be gone."

Gone. Gone. Gone.

Don't leave me.

Maya edged closer. "What is Short Sunderland?"

"It's a flying boat."

For one delicious moment she thought the whole thing was Jo-nee joking. He did that sometimes. "How can a boat fly?" She imagined *The White Pearl* with wings, and laughed.

Jo-nee frowned at her. "It's a plane designed to land and take off on water. The Sunderland is the military version of the C-type flying boat, which flies passengers long distances all over the world."

He didn't like her to laugh at his planes. He gazed up at the night sky, a blur of black clouds and stars. "Listen for it—as well as for Japanese aircraft," he warned, and went over to argue with Nurul, who was already preparing to hoist sail.

How could she listen for it when all she could hear was her heart crying?

꓀·ꓹ

"Fitz, will General Takehashi come after you when he knows you tricked him?"

"I have no doubt of it."

A noise had made them stop paddling. They listened intently in the darkness. There was the sound of an airplane somewhere in the distance.

"Connie, I didn't betray Teddy."

Fitz's words sounded sad.

"I always knew that I would reach your son first, that I could keep him safe from General Takehashi's vengeance. I swear to you."

The canoe shifted under them as Connie again turned to face him.

"I couldn't let him shoot you, Connie." He raised her chin so that he could look into her eyes. "You know that, don't you?"

"Yes, Fitz. I know that."

꓀·ꓹ

The noise of an aircraft approaching shattered the night's silence, stirring the waves so that the canoe rocked and rolled, eager to turn turtle. Fitz reached for Connie and drew her into the cradle of his arms.

"General Takehashi is here sooner than I thought," he whispered.

The moon had dodged behind a cloud once more, and in the complete darkness they couldn't see the plane or the island—or any sign of the *Burung Camar*. They paddled hard together, aware of how fragile this moment was, how it could be snatched from their grasp.

"Fitz, what will we do?"

"We find Nurul, Connie."

"I mean, what will we do when we get away from here? Where shall we go?"

The joyous sound of Fitz's laugh echoed through the night. "My precious Connie, I love you. More than you'll ever know."

Ə·Ɛ

It was a monster plane, big and fat like a whale, its body dark brown and green. The roar of its four engines was enough to wake up the world and it buzzed in Maya's brain, but she remained huddled in the *attap* hut, unable to bring herself to say good-bye. Jo-nee was excited; she could see him through the open end of the hut. Excited to be leaving her. The rowboat was lowered to carry them across the water to the monster flying boat-without-sails, and everything was rush-rush.

Kitty Madoc seized Jo-nee's arm to anchor him in one place, right next to the hut. "I'm not going with you," she said. Her voice was still as dead as her husband. "I've decided to remain on this boat instead. I'll take my chances here."

"Mrs. Madoc," Jo-nee said quickly, "we can't delay, but please reconsider. It's not safe in these waters. Come with us."

"No."

"Are you sure?"

"I'm sure. I would rather sail than fly."

"With Nurul?"

"Yes. With Nurul."

Nurul was shouting for them to be quick.

"Good-bye then, Mrs. Madoc," Jo-nee said kindly. "I wish you luck. I'm sorry our acquaintance was so brief."

"Good-bye, Flight Lieutenant," Kitty Madoc interrupted with her no-life voice. "Tell that filthy chit of a girl who shot my husband that I hope she drowns." Her footsteps marched away across the deck.

Jo-nee ducked his head into the hut, and Maya put her hands over her ears because she didn't want to hear him say she should drown. But instead he reached in and pulled her hands away with a big hello-smile.

"Coming, little blackbird? Are you ready to fly?"

ᗯ·ᙅ

Connie and Fitz heard the plane hit the water.

"A bomber down," Fitz muttered.

"Let it be one of theirs," Connie said with sudden anger, "not one of ours."

But as she spoke, a boisterous tidal wave surged from the impact, almost swamping the bow of the canoe. "Look!" Connie cried.

Moonlight had spilled over the sea, and not far away they could make out the huge bulk of an aircraft.

Fitz waved a paddle in the air. "It's not a Jap bomber that came down, Connie," he shouted. "It's a damn RAF flying boat."

Not far behind it, tugging at its anchor in the turbulent waves, bobbed the long-nosed silhouette of the *Burung Camar*. It was waiting for them.

ᗯ·ᙅ

They paddled hard, shouting with any spare breath, but the plane's engines drowned out their voices and the wind was against them. As they struggled to close the gap, throwing their weight into each stroke, cursing their flimsy paddles and willing both the boat and the aircraft to wait, their hopes died. They watched the mainsail being hoisted on the *pinisiq*, followed immediately by the mizzen and the foresails. Like a night bird, the native boat spread her wings and flew westward into the secretive banks of darkness where she could not be traced.

"They can't see us," Fitz groaned. "We're too low in the water."

Connie brandished her paddle and shouted but knew it was in vain.

They set off doggedly in pursuit of the plane instead, but as they did so Connie had to thrust away from her a sense of the curse of Sai-Ru Jumat that seemed to rise from the sea with the salt spray. She felt its cold fingers, its sharp teeth. She concentrated on dragging the paddle through the water, in and pull, in and pull, concentrate.

But it wasn't enough. It seemed that Sai-Ru Jumat had finally won. The engines of the flying boat developed more power, and again the moon vanished as if frightened by the noise, so that darkness descended on them. Connie let out a cry of anger as they both heard the plane start to taxi away from them, thundering across the water.

"Connie." Fitz's hand came to rest on the back of her neck, calming her. "Teddy will be on that plane. He will be safe. You needn't worry about him."

She tipped her head back against his knees. "And us?" she asked. "Should I worry about us?"

"Do you fancy canoeing all the way to Australia?"

"Just point me in the right direction," she said, and gave what could pass for a laugh.

"It's over there in . . ." He paused. "Listen!"

The plane's engines had changed their pitch.

"Connie, she's turning. She's changed direction to take off into the wind."

Connie sat up straight as she heard the plane charging across the water directly toward them. Without any of its lights showing, she still couldn't see it and knew there wasn't a hope in hell of it seeing them, yet her eyes strained to find it. To catch just a glimpse of the plane that was carrying her son. Swiftly Fitz tore off his shirt. Hunched in the bottom of the boat he pulled a box of matches from his pocket and, sheltering it from the wind behind the curve of the canoe, he struck a match. Nothing happened.

"Damp," he cursed.

"Try again." Connie's heart was hammering.

He struck them again and again until finally first one and then another flared into life, and Connie held the thin material of his shirt over them. It smoldered miserably for a second but then caught fire as the noise of the engines drew closer. Fitz raised his arm and waved the burning shirt back and forth in an arc through the cool night air, the wind sweeping the flames into a fireball, but they were acutely aware that the flames would attract attention on the island as well as on the plane; they both knew what they were risking.

Abruptly, the flying boat's engines lowered in pitch.

"It's slowing," Connie said, and snatched the burning shirt from Fitz's hand, throwing it on the front of the canoe to save his hands. "They've seen us."

Relief swept through her when a searchlight suddenly leaped from the plane. She could see it now, a vast lumbering angel with wings of metal.

"Connie, paddle like hell!"

Even as they started to paddle furiously toward the plane, they could hear somewhere behind them the engine of a Japanese gunboat in the distance. *Not now. Not when Teddy is so close. Not now, Sai-Ru Jumat. Let me go.*

The canoe was taking on water badly in the disturbance around the plane, but Connie didn't waste time bailing it out. She paddled harder until they skirted the floats and headed under the great slab of the wing to the tiny door that opened into the body of the flying boat. It lay directly under the raised cockpit, a rectangle of welcoming light, and the pilot's voice shouted down to them, "Don't take all day, chaps. I've got to get this crate up in the air or we'll be eating raw fish for breakfast."

Another voice inside the flying boat called out with good humor, "Get a move on, will you, skipper? Don't you know there's a bloody war on!"

Connie heard laughter. There was laughter on the plane.

CHAPTER FORTY-ONE

What worth can you put on life, when you thought you were dead? What value can you put on holding your son in your arms and feeling his hot tears on your cheek, when you thought you'd lost him forever?

What does it mean to sit shoulder to shoulder with the man you love, and see him smile at you?

Words don't even come close.

Connie sat inside the huge cavern of the flying boat, its metal spars arching over her like the ribs of a whale, and experienced the violent juddering of the plane as it hurtled across the sea in a mighty effort to rise into a planing altitude and come unstuck. The waves were reluctant to let go, pounding the hull as it raced past. Machine guns opened fire from the enemy gunboat and a wingtip was hit, but the lumbering plane shook it off and took to the air in a great rush of energy. Connie heard its sigh of joy. It loved its freedom as much as she did.

"So, Fitz"—she leaned her head back against the quivering metal skin—"where now?"

"Darwin." Fitz's face looked tight with pain, but his eyes were bright and expectant. "Darwin," he repeated.

"In Australia?"

"That's the one."

She hadn't expected that.

"I thought it would be New Guinea."

"No, too dangerous," he said. "We're heading for Darwin. It's a vital port for the Allied military campaign in the Pacific. Its position is so strategic that its naval harbor and airbase are crucial in maintaining attacks on the Japanese." He studied her reaction to the idea, as he added, "The Thirty-Third Pursuit Squadron is stationed there with its War-hawks, as well as the Hudson patrol planes. There will be all kinds of war work to be done there."

Connie felt a jolt of excitement at the prospect of becoming involved, of playing an active part in some way.

"But what about your boat?" she asked. "What about Nurul?"

"They can wait." He laughed softly. "But some things can't." He leaned forward and kissed her lips.

She slipped her hand into his, and his fingers closed around hers. The interior of the flying boat was laid out as a military plane: rough and ready, with few seats but a chart table for the navigator and an elaborate wireless set for the sparks. Two gunners with machine guns sat on platforms high up, keeping watch, but Connie's eyes were drawn to the flight deck ahead. The early-morning sun painted it golden, and she could see her son's brown curls gleaming like copper as he stood, enthralled between Johnnie Blake and Pilot Officer Reeves, who was explaining how to throttle back.

Teddy would recover; she knew he would. Her son was young and he was strong, but it would take time and love to heal the gashes in his heart. He had clung to her with tears and kisses at first but was already moving on; his natural curiosity and enthusiasm for flying were drawing him from her side.

What surprised her more was to find Maya and Razak onboard. Maya was lying flat on a bunk with a pillow over her head, mewing pitifully, but Connie was certain she would survive the journey remarkably well. Maya was an extraordinary young girl with astonishing resources. Dar-win didn't know what was coming its way.

"I'm pleased she's here," Connie told Fitz, "so that I can keep an eye on her and teach her things."

Fitz frowned. "Just be careful she doesn't teach you things," he grum-bled, which made her laugh.

Maya had rushed over to her earlier, wide-eyed with disbelief, and a huge smile had spread across her young face as she prodded a finger into Connie's shoulder, making certain she was flesh and blood.

"You real!" Maya said. "You here!"

"Yes, I'm real and I'm here. And no more treehouses for us!"

"I glad you here," Maya beamed, and held on tight to Connie's wrist. "I make sure you stay here."

Simple words. But they meant much to Connie, and she hugged Maya to her, until the plane gave a sudden lurch and the girl scuttled back to her bunk and her pillow. It was Razak who looked uneasy. He sat silent and nervous in a corner, uncertain what lay in store for him and his sister. Connie couldn't imagine how on earth Maya had managed to bully him away from his pirates and onto the flying boat, but their blood was thick, and it flowed between the twins as if through one network of veins. There was one other man in military uniform on the plane. At first Connie thought he was a member of the crew but quickly realized her mistake. He was sitting quietly now at the opposite end of the plane, but when they'd first arrived he had approached Fitz and offered him his hand.

"How are you, Fitzpayne?"

"Well enough."

"Good to see you out of that hole. Much trouble?"

"Nothing difficult."

"Fine."

That was it. They didn't speak again. But when she asked Fitz who he was, Fitz had closed the shutters a fraction and she had felt a part of him withdraw behind his well-constructed barriers.

"His name is Hodgkins. He's in Intelligence, I believe. That lot are always on the prowl."

She asked no more. Fitz had so many layers, it came as no surprise. This Hodgkins clearly knew Fitz. Had they worked together? Had Fitz been feeding information about Japanese movements in these waters to the British? Was his relationship with Japan just a sham?

There was so much she didn't know about him yet, but she had all the future ahead to discover more. She could sense the way his mind entwined with her own and was conscious of the sorrow she had caused him, as intimately as she felt the pain he had caused her. But they would heal. She loved him too much to try to cage him, and she knew there would one day be a place for them to be together when all this was over.

The old world was crumbling, the old order vanishing, yet she was confident that the Western world would roll up its sleeves and build a new one. A better one. A world in which countries were no longer obsessed with hurling themselves into wars that killed and crippled their young men. Teddy was growing up fast and had seen more than enough death to last him a lifetime. She looked out one of the tiny windows, but all she saw was an expanse of vivid blue water. Malaya was gone, but when it was safe, she promised herself, she would take Teddy back to see his father's home.

"Connie."

She turned to Fitz with concern. "Is your leg bad?"

He shook his head, dismissing it. "Connie, Hodgkins is a bit of a maverick who relishes a challenge in his work and has the courage to see it through." He raised one of his thick eyebrows. "Like someone else I know."

He laughed and she felt his laughter reach inside her.

"So?" she asked.

"So I could speak to him for you, if you'd like. He's always looking for good people."

Connie felt excitement quicken her pulse. "Darwin could be a good place to start a new life," she said, noncommittally. A new life with new opportunities, somewhere to make herself useful.

"I could visit often," he told her.

"In your boat?"

"Yes."

"Teddy would be safe there."

"And when this war is over, together we could . . ."

She put a finger to his lips. "One step at a time, Fitz." She felt the warm pressure of his arm on hers, and his long thigh firm against her own. The future rolled out before her, as enticing as new grass. "We'd be safe, because Japanese planes will never get to Darwin." She smiled at him, her decision made. "Will they?"